Wearing the Cape.

"This is such a solid book that I have difficulty believing it is Mr. Harmon's first novel. The story is polished, well edited, tightly plotted, and stocked with interesting characters. Like Peter Clines' debut novel, Ex-Humans, this sets the bar so high for follow-up work that I'm sure Mr. Harmon is feeling the pressure."

Michael of Dover, Delaware

Villains Inc.

"A riveting follow-up to Wearing the Cape, Harmon's sophomore novel continues to satisfy those of us who need a fix of well-written superhero fiction. Fans of the first book will not find its sequel lacking, and while it might be more of an adjustment to readers who haven't picked up the first book, it stands well enough on its own."

Avander Promontory

On the *Wearing the Cape* series.

"The Wearing the Cape *series is the gold standard that all other superhero novels should aspire to."*

Hero Sandwich

Young Sentinels reviewer.

The world of Wearing the Cape *just keeps getting more interesting with each passing book. The characters grow deeper and old plots resurface in new ways.*

Kindle Customer

Books by M.G.Harmon
Wearing the Cape
Villains Inc.
Bite Me: Big Easy Nights
Young Sentinels
Small Town Heroes

Short Stories by M.G.Harmon
Omega Night

Small Town Heroes

A *Wearing the Cape* Story

by

Marion G. Harmon

Copyright © 2014 Marion G. Harmon

Cover art by Jamal Campbell and Jessica Chang

All rights reserved.

ISBN-13: 978-1502598967
ISBN-10: 1502598965

DEDICATION

To all of my merciless proof-readers, but especially to Sister #2, without whom these stories would be a lot more...bumpy.

ACKNOWLEDGMENTS

Still not going to try and count everybody, but thought I should add Maxwell Alexander Drake, David Marshall, and Andrew M. Greeley to my list. Thank you.

"Do not act as if you were going to live ten thousand years. Death hangs over you. While you live, while it is in your power, be good."

Marcus Aurelius

Episode One

Chapter One

Bad things happen and people need help all over the world, but even when superheroes have the power we can't always help. Inside the US, we need to get permission from state governments or deal with FEMA. Internationally, sovereign nations can refuse to let you come in; when the Sentinels went abroad they went as volunteers for Heroes Without Borders, *the international organization founded to aid and protect civilian populations trapped in disaster and war zones.*

From the journal of Hope Corrigan.

We were doing everything we could, and Mother Nature was still kicking our butts. The high winds, blowing hard enough to weaponize the sleeting rain, kept rescue copters out of the sky unless aerokinetics like Tsuris and his dad Jetstream flew with them to carve out zones of still air. The Ohio River was doing its best to drown Cairo, Mound City, and Paducah, and trying to help the Mississippi laugh at the spillways and floodways to submerge Wickliffe and points south. Even Riptide couldn't stop that much water; the best he could do was protect rescue boats and find desperate swimmers.

Three weeks of heavy rains dumped into the Mississippi and Ohio watersheds, and we were dealing with more destruction than any supervillain had ever caused with the sole exception of Temblor.

"*Astra, is your load stable?*" Lei Zi asked through Dispatch. She knew it couldn't be the wind slowing me down.

"Yes — affirmative," I responded absently. The US Army engineers had done a good job on the hitches, and I'd turned the 10-ton concrete barrier so it sliced into the wind as I flew. I'd slowed because— There it was again. The pitch black night and nearly horizontal rain cut even my super-duper vision down to less than thirty feet, but a twinkling flash of red light teased the edge of my sight. No-one was supposed to be down there.

I slowed again and dropped lower, so tired I couldn't be sure of what I was seeing. The stacked-up storm fronts that had been soaking seven states had put the whole region on alert as aquifers filled and rivers rose. Three states had begun evacuating low ground last week and the flooded ground beneath me, north of Cairo, was supposed to be clear.

There. A sudden wind shift opened a hole in the rain curtain and brought me another red flash. It moved, flying below me and pulling away now that it had my attention. Lower, I could see the drowned fields where the Mississippi had thrown out a new ribbon across the lower ground, creating a temporary floodway. Someone would get to that, but right now we — the Young Sentinels — were trying to save Cairo.

"*Astra, Grendel is ready for the next levee section.*"

We'd been working on it since early this morning, me flying in the sections as Grendel prepared the foundation — mostly by hammering iron rods down into the collapsed earth levee to anchor the sections as they arrived. But the light below me was bobbing and weaving, trying to keep my attention like Lassie telling me Timmy had fallen down the well, and I couldn't just ignore it.

"I'm minutes out. Investigating signals north of town."

"... *Understood. Be quick.*" She didn't sound happy, but possible civilians in the evacuation zone took precedence over a town that had been completely evacuated two days ago.

Dropping till the wall section beneath me skimmed over the flooded fields, I followed the dancing red light. Could I see wings on it? It certainly moved like a bird working hard to fight through the wind. One minute, two, and I spotted the house. A solid building with no trimmings, it looked ready to shrug off tornadoes. Someone had circled it with a sandbag berm, but the sandbags were just a ring in the water now and the low-slung house sat half submerged.

And the roof was crowded, lit up to my infrared sight.

"You're kidding, right?" Shell popped in to float beside me, rain sleeting through her virtual projection onto my mind's eye. "They skipped evacuation to stay here with *kids*?"

Five adults, seven children, and, yes a dog and a cat in a carrier, huddled together under a tarp between storm lanterns.

I slowed, made sure of my load. "Who are they?"

Shell's abstraction lasted less than a second.

"Based on head count, property and tax records, and the AR-15s and military gear, I'm betting they're the Carletons and their neighbors down the road, the Stewarts. County sheriff's report says they were told to evacuate, but wouldn't believe the government if it told them Sunday was coming."

I sighed. "Paladins?"

"Nope, just part of a local citizen's militia."

That was something, anyway. Maybe I wouldn't get shot at. I brought us down, dropping the concrete barrier beside the edge of the roof, which caused a few screams. It must have looked like the piece of emergency levee had just flown out of the night to sit down by their house.

I landed on top of it, which put me at roof level. I was probably a more reassuring sight. Half the reason for the colorful costume was so that bystanders would recognize and trust you in any situation (the other half was marketing), and Andrew was experimenting with textured and reflective fabrics. I'd left my armor at home to try out the patterned blue and white one-piece unitard outfit he'd come up with, and even in the storm my star crest glowed like a traffic reflector in the light of the lamps. Of course none of them could see Shell, standing beside me completely unbothered by the storm. She saw no need to cater to reality, so the gusts didn't stir her hair and the drowning rain didn't so much as spot her green tank top—which read *If you can read this t-shirt you are freaking amazing*.

"Hi," I said.

Shell rolled her eyes. "Great heroic entrance. Way to make a memory."

"I'm not here to sign autographs, Shell," I whispered, raised my voice. "Does anyone need a lift? And who does the dragon belong to?"

The shining red "bird" I'd followed turned out to be a fist-sized ruby dragon. It had stopped fighting the storm to perch on a tow-headed boy's shoulder, and he couldn't take his eyes off it even to look at me.

"It's —" Shell started.

"Shhh."

One of the moms stepped up, pushing back her hood. She was soaked from boots to waist, and even with the heavy jacket her teeth were chattering.

"It just appeared. Circled the kids and then went away."

To do its Lassie thing, obviously. I nodded.

"It came and found me. I'm headed to Cairo. It's evacuated but still dry, and we're raising the levees to keep it that way. I can give you a ride." I threw the offer out there, doing my best not to give off any suspicious *I'm From the Government And I'm Here To Help You* vibes.

They decided fast: Mom One simply told her husband she was taking the kids before they died of hypothermia, and Mom Two seconded her. The men, however paranoid they might have been, caved. Fortunately they had plenty of rope — they'd planned on tying everybody together and escaping on inflatable river rafts if the water covered the roof. I distributed them on top of the barrier and they tied themselves to the hitches. A moment to balance the load, and I got us out of there. The tiny jeweled dragon flapped around anxiously until we lifted off, circled me twice, then disappeared into the night.

Headed for Cairo.

I focused on bringing us around till Shell's own glowing virtual targeting caret pointed ahead of us again. Straddling the levee section beneath me, my passengers looked too cold and tired to be terrified — or maybe straddling a concrete barrier two feet wide at the top and steady as a flying mountain was reassuring.

"Shell?" I whispered. "Dragon?"

"Actually it's a drake." She sounded distracted.

"Drake— Shell!"

"Okay, okay. It's got to be one of Kindrake's pets. And if she's in Cairo…"

I still wasn't getting it, but aside from some Army engineers, weren't we the only ones in town?

Apparently not. Sometime during my last flight out someone else (it had to be an Atlas-type or transport-level telekinetic or teleporter) had dropped a passenger frame in the middle of Cairo. Not much more than a steel storage container with seats inside, it had been dropped off in the school bus parking lot kitty-corner to the brick First Presbyterian Church and across the street from the newer City of God In Christ chapel. Guard and Army Corps of Engineers were using the chapel as a relief base, and before heading for the levee I landed the barrier in front and unloaded my shivering passengers so they could run inside. Then I got it where it needed to be.

"Glad you could make it," Grendel said when I finally set my load down beside him. The water swirled less than a foot below our exposed and sunken stretch of earth wall. This was the last section needed for the collapsed earth levee, then we could sandbag the cracks and call it a night — or at least a few hours.

Grendel didn't look any fresher than I felt; he'd been shoring up sections as I flew, laying whole pallets of sandbags, generally putting it all together under the guidance of the engineers. He'd stripped down to shorts and bulked up for raw strength, and looked like a gray and hunchbacked Mr. Universe with fangs. His obsessively styled dreadlocks dripped rainwater down knotted shoulders and arms and off his huge pecs. He could lift more than I could in this configuration, but if he wasn't careful his feet sank into the waterlogged earth.

As tired as *he* was, he didn't sound unhappy, just curious.

"I followed a dragon. Were you okay?"

A stoic shrug. "Just wondering if I should grow gills." He could, too. I perched on the barrier for a breather and watched as he pounded ten-foot pylons into the earth behind it.

FEMA had moved fast when the flood warnings got serious. The Federal Emergency Management Agency had streamlined its response system after the California quake a year ago last January, tying participating Crisis Aid and Intervention teams across the country into a fast-response network and organizing CAI capes with emergency-appropriate powers into specialized teams. What had been a mad scramble after the quake had turned into a much smoother mobilization this time around.

For all the good it did. The problem with floodwater is it has to go *somewhere*, and obviously staying in the riverbed God and the Army Corps of Engineers had made for it was just boring. One whole stretch of our "new" levee was a line of day old hundred-year oaks anchoring waterlogged earth (Ozma had stolen a page from the Green Man's playbook). Beyond the levee I couldn't see the river, just an expanse of water that rolled away into the night.

Shell popped back in beside me, looking disgusted. "It really is Powerteam."

"Who?"

"Powerteam."

"Oh. That's…"

"Not good? You *think*?"

"Every hand helps, Shell."

Her smirk gave her opinion of that, and I couldn't say she was wrong. I really should have remembered. Kindrake had been big just a few years ago. A super-celebrity not much older than Shell and me, she had gained her child star fame when her breakthrough manifested her obsession with the Rainbow Drakes, the cute little spectrum-colored flying lizards of the kid's cartoon. The producers of the show had rolled with it, given Kindrake her own live-action series showcasing her adorable pets, but that was years ago and Kindrake and her drakes weren't so cute anymore. And she was running with Powerteam?

A sigh escaped before I could catch it.

"I know, right?" Shell snickered. "Kindrake brought them and their film crew in on that passenger frame."

"How—? Never mind."

Grendel finished pounding the brace in and I pushed myself to my feet. Rising I felt heavy, dense, not the leaf on the wind I usually was when I flew. We locked grips, my hold barely halfway round his wrists while his huge hands swallowed my forearms, and I flew us back into town. We'd practiced the move in the months since the Green Man Attack, had it down till a tiny squeeze from me and he'd let go so I could throw him at the target of my choice—three hundred plus pounds of incoming Grendel was a great opening to any fight. Tonight we just both wanted to get out of the rain.

We weren't the only ones; Crash and Tsuris had come inside now that the town was out of immediate danger. They huddled talking with FEMA engineers by the coffeepot, away from Powerteam. Crash gulped down energy bars while he listened, and he looked completely wiped; subjectively, he'd been doing this a couple of days longer than the rest of us. The Carletons and the Stewarts had camped on the other side of the recreation hall, wrapped in blankets. The parents stood between their kids and the capes while Ozma talked to them and the kids kept trying to see past the grownups to what was happening on the other side of the room.

Because there was a show. The production crew Powerteam had brought inside with them was big enough that each member had his own camera-jockey, and they were earning their paychecks filming the drama.

"Shell?" I whispered. The reality show's team lineup changed fast and wasn't something I'd ever followed—Kindrake was the only one I recognized, and I only recognized her because of her rainbow swarm of drakes; the raven black hair with rainbow highlights, deep shadowed eyes, and purple and black goth-cape outfit was totally new to me.

"Spinner." Shell pointed at the skinny blond boy yelling the loudest. "Team leader. He generates and controls strands of indestructible silver threads, can spin them into entangling traps, barriers, cocoons, armor, really anything until they melt like yesterday's promises. According to the tabloids, he makes a lot of those, too."

Her virtual finger targeted a shorter boy, standing quiet and arms folded but smirking. "Boomer. He's a B Class Ajax-type with the added boost of explosive punches." A finger-twitch, to the worried-looking kid by Boomer. "Spaz. Low-level teleporter. He 'blinks' in a fight, in and out, likes to use stunners, flash-bangs, whatever will take someone down." She dropped her hand. "The looming lady Ajax-type backing up Kindrake is Slamazon."

Looming was right; "Slamazon" had to be at least seven feet tall, and she was what Mom would describe as Junoesque and Tsuris would cheerfully call *stacked*.

"B or A-Class, all of them except Spaz," Shell finished. "The show doesn't stint."

Grendel had ignored my distraction to head for the coffee. Even if the only one besides me who could see Shell's virtual presence was Ozma—and that was only when she wore her Seeing Specs—the team all knew the voices in my head were real. Ozma watched me now with arched eyebrow, obviously wondering what I was going to do about the drama.

"—they were *our* rescue!" Spinner shouted in Kindrake's face.

Kindrake wasn't backing down. "Flame went for the closest help! They were freezing!" Behind her, Slamazon folded her arms and scowled, and my super-duper hearing picked up a low but rising hum from Boomer. What was going on?

Grendel looked over at the blanket-wrapped rescuees, and changed course to position himself between them and Powerteam. They *couldn't* be...

They could. Slamazon easily reached over Kindrake to shove Spinner back.

Oh *crap*.

I put a smile on and crossed the room fast. "Hi! When did you guys arrive?"

People facing off usually have to work themselves up to a fight, with lots of posturing and escalating verbal confrontation until both sides know nobody is backing down and it's time to commence. If I was lucky I could short-circuit that.

Spinner whipped around, focusing his lip-curling sneer on me. "And here's the Girl Scout. Come to tell us to move on?"

What?

Shell talked fast. "They didn't get FEMA clearance to join the effort until tonight. They're certified, but not so much mission-specific powers so they got sent down here."

Where they couldn't do much to mess things up. Great.

I kept the smile on. "Everyone's welcome to help, and the town isn't safe yet. We should—"

"What? Pitch sandbags? We didn't come all this way to do grunt-work, and now you're dogging our saves."

"That's not—" Kindrake tried to interject as Boomer moved up behind Spinner.

"Shut up! You're in this, too! Miss Kiddie-Show Star, coming on like you can teach us all about cape-work." The background hum rose in pitch.

I put out my hands. "I think we all need to—" Boomer swung and the concussive power released from his fist lit up my world.

"Hope! Get *up*!"

When you're clocked *hard* you don't feel it, or what happens in the next few seconds, really—your shaken brain-stem isn't letting any information into your head until it clears. Hearing Shell yelling at me wasn't unwelcome, and after months of fight-club style training with Watchman and Grendel I bounced back to full wakefulness pretty quick. And tasted rain. I was back outside.

Boomer had blasted me through the wall.

We'd just wrecked a *church*.

"Hope!" Shell gasped when I sat up. "Get back in there! It's *on*!"

Instead they joined me, Boomer first. He widened the hole on the way out, arriving in a rain of bricks. Whoever had ejected him had practically aimed him at me and I took full advantage, catching him as he skidded on his knees to kick him behind the ear. Ajax-type or not, he dropped without a sound. Watchman would be proud.

Grendel followed him out in a charge that carried Slamazon with him and I breathed a sigh of relief; not that he was needed out here, but if he'd gone on the offense that meant that the civilians were safe—probably evacuated by Crash.

"Shell?" I asked. She'd be getting everyone's dispatch-cam feeds.

"Ozma used her scepter and magic belt to grow a forest from the wood of the rec room floor and Crash and Spaz are evacuating the bystanders behind it," she reported. "Tsuris is fighting Spinner, burying the creep under his own weave, and—"

The final bit got cut off by the huge beast that dropped out of the night. *That* I hadn't seen before, but it *had* to be Kindrake's. The thing's landing shook the street, its rainbow-colored body making elephants look small as its wings covered us.

Wow.

"Is it a fusion?" I asked needlessly; the rainbow-patched hide was a big hint that all Kindrake's flying friends had joined up to become greater than the sum of their parts. *Well, now I know how she flew the passenger frame here.* "Where's Kindrake?" I spotted her before Shell replied, standing in the hole in the wall and pointing at Grendel and Slamazon. She shouted over the storm, and my heart sank as I lunged forward. The dragon's head darted down, lizard-quick, and Grendel disappeared into its jaws.

"Brian!"

"Now that's something you don't see every day," Shell said, wide-eyed. I smacked into the beast's side and it was like hitting a leather sack full of sand; it bellowed, slammed back against the passenger frame, and I hit it again before Slamazon hard-blocked me. Not braced, I flew backwards. Kindrake's projection or not, the thing had a sense of self-preservation; it took to the air, the sweep of its wings adding to my tumble. Then the wind hit in a blasting roar. *Tsuris*.

The column of air wouldn't have pushed *me* if I was braced for it, but I didn't have a hundred foot wingspan for it to grab onto, and it caught the escaping beast—Great Drake?—like a helpless leaf, throwing it back down to crush through the parked FEMA vehicles and roll away into the night. It roared its frustration, getting some height only to get smacked down again, this time right into— *No no no...*

"Oh, *shit!*" Shell swore.

It hit the nearest wall of raised levee like a ton of—like *tons* of dragon. Then it exploded into rainbow confetti as Grendel ripped his way out of its stomach. Kindrake screamed in pain and collapsed behind me, caught by Ozma as she stepped through the holed wall wearing a new green fedora.

"Ozma!" I yelled. "If you're wearing Spinner, I need him *now!*"

Spinner was too shaken by his experience as a fashion accessory to stay pissy at being ordered around (Ozma's victims tended to find their memory of contentedly snuggling her head *disturbing*), and I let all of them know that, as the senior officer of the Illinois State Militia in an Emergency Zone, I could arrest them just for being complete idiots (officially I'm a 1st lieutenant and nobody finds that funnier than me).

An hour later we'd patched the hole in the levee. It took all of the FEMA team's reserve sandbags and countless yards of de-hatted Spinner's threads, but we were able to use the temporary patch to buy time for me to fly more levee sections in and Cairo didn't get more than a couple of inches of Mississippi floodwater before we finished. Six inches, tops.

By then we were all bone-tired—even I could feel my thoughts drowning in cold black fatigue. Powerteam's crew manager explained that Kindrake's feedback-trauma would be fine by morning and that she'd be able to reconstruct Terraflore (nice name for a big rainbow-lizard) and fly the battered passenger-frame out of Cairo. Job done, I ordered everyone to bed.

Half of Powerteam thought that would be a good idea, so Spinner backed down. He even slapped a patch on the hole we'd made in the church. Ozma couldn't turn the wall of trees she'd made back into the smooth wood floor it had been, but there was enough open space left that we could set up cots and dividers so everyone, capes, evacuees, crews, and engineers, could get some sleep.

The warm grass felt like the memory of a summer day and the stars shown as bright as they only could without air or light pollution to dim their glory. The snow of petals from the blooming cherry tree danced across the hill in the warm night breeze, and the silver fox beside me sighed contentedly as I stroked its ears. Together we watched the town below us burn and vanish.

I opened my eyes and stared at the ceiling, still smelling smoke and cherry blossoms.

Nuts. Not *again*.

Chapter Two

You'd think I could have a "normal" superhero career. After all, I might be strong but my powers are as common as dirt. But no, apparently I'm a Chosen One. Like the Teatime Anarchist hung a glowing neon sign on me for all inscrutable meddlers to see. It makes life way too exciting.

From the journal of Hope Corrigan.

Everybody dreams, unless something has happened to leave them with damaged parietal lobes. Some people never remember their dreams, and others are natural lucid dreamers, oneironauts. I'm a vivid dreamer with high recall, which sometimes creates more awkwardness than I need. But once upon a time, no matter how weird or embarrassingly blushworthy my dream life occasionally got, I could at least say it was All In My Head. Not anymore.

I hadn't experienced a *Kitsune* dream since the end of the Villains Inc. mess, but last night's had the same *un*dreamlike quality, as crystal-clear as any waking memory. That made it Important, but the fox had snuck into my dreams just before morning light and I had stuff to do. I found a notebook and quickly wrote out everything I could remember, details like the eagle-in-a star design on the burning town's water tower. After two minutes of tapping my pen and blanking on more details, I gulped down a couple of energy bars from my go-bag, washed them down with bottled water, and got moving.

The latest storm front had moved on, which made a morning flyover of my search grid easier. Not that I expected to find any more holdouts after this many days of flooding, but I hadn't expected to meet the Carletons and Stewarts last night, either. With the rain past, the predawn gloom actually made it easier for my infrared sight to pick up on the glowing lights of body heat but the only people I spotted in my area of responsibility were emergency crews who were supposed to be there. I waved.

"*Good morning, Astra,*" Blackstone greeted me through Dispatch. His power-set wasn't really useful for this kind of emergency, so he'd remained at the Dome. "*Shell tells me that Powerteam has decamped from Cairo. How do things look to you this fine day?*"

I smiled but kept the laugh out of my voice as I reported in. *Decamped* was a polite way of putting it; I imagined that they got yanked out of Cairo so fast that they left a vacuum behind them. Last night I hadn't been interested in speaking with Spinner beyond stuff like "Do it *here*" so I still had no idea why FEMA had even let them into the operation zone, and now my day was brighter just knowing I wouldn't have to deal with them again.

"*Can you give me a report of last night?*" Blackstone asked when I finished.

Frowning, I looked for a place to land. Sure I could talk and fly at the same time (Shell would have gotten me killed long ago if I couldn't) but I was supposed to be flying a patrol and if I had to think then I might miss something. An abandoned and half-drowned farmhouse offered a convenient roof for me to touch down on, and I absently tucked my cape under me to sit.

"Sir? Is there a reason it can't wait for the after-action report?" Something was obviously going on; team regs didn't require a report until we'd stood down from the current emergency. His pause wasn't reassuring.

"Humor an old man, my dear."

Okay... I started with spotting the tiny glowing drake and kept the commentary out; Blackstone liked facts first, then impressions. He was silent when I finished and I watched the sun rise to throw a bar of gold across the water. Then he said the *last* thing I could have expected.

"Thank you, Astra. And now please return to Cairo. The Young Sentinels are being recalled."

"That's just bullshit!" Tsuris' response was typical. Crash's easygoing shrug was, too. Blackstone had left the announcement to me, but Ozma didn't seem too surprised. Grendel simply nodded—he didn't talk much, but didn't miss much either. Shell had stayed remarkably silent and out of sight.

I sighed.

"Blackstone didn't say why, but with the levees secure FEMA can handle things with a quick drop-by from another assigned CAI team. Since over half our senior team strength is down here, too, it's a good idea for us to go home anyway. *Regardless,*" I shut down Tsuris with a glare, "our ride is on its way so we need to be lifting in fifteen."

Blackstone hadn't explained, just let me know our pickup was coming, and I didn't ask Shell. Months of weekly packing drill meant that we had our kits and go-bags closed up and stowed on our field pallet before our ride had time to arrive and circle Cairo more than once. Crash, Grendel, and Ozma climbed on and clipped themselves down, and I attached myself to the lift harness and took us up and away. We climbed smoothly, and with Tsuris flying alongside to stabilize the pallet, even the cargo plane's turbulence didn't rock us as we slid into the open bay. The loadmaster guided us in and I dropped us inside the painted yellow lines with barely a bump. Crash unclipped and locked the pallet down in a blur the instant the bay doors closed. The load-light went green, and we were safely in.

Touching down, I unhitched with another sigh.

"Kick back, everybody," I said needlessly. We had nothing to do until we reached Chicago, then we'd reverse the drill and be home in the Dome. Heading forward to the passenger section, I took a seat and relaxed. Shell popped in to virtually take the seat beside me. She wasn't smiling, and the levity of last night was gone.

"Do you want to hear what's going on?"

Yes. "Can I do anything about it?"

"Not really."

"Then nope. Could you do something else?" My notebook was back in my go-bag, but if I gave her permission then she could access and replay the Teatime Anarchist' implanted sensory-net "download" of me writing in it. I did and her eyes widened as she processed it.

"No freaking way! Kitsune's back?"

"I don't know." I closed my eyes and leaned back. "It *might* have been just a dream. I really, really hope it was, but I'm going to ask Chakra to check me out."

Shell went quiet for a minute.

"No agencies admit to catching up to him, at least the files I have legit access to don't have a whisper. Do you think I should…" She made the offer tentatively, and I opened my eyes with a smile. The fact that she even *asked* approval to perform cyber hackery was serious progress.

"No. If he *is* back, then it's up to Blackstone to tell us if there's anything we need to know. But thanks."

"So what do we do now?"

"Can you find the town? If it's a real place, looking for that water tower might help you find it."

"Did it look at all like a military base?"

I gave it serious consideration, shook my head. "But Midwest, maybe? The kind of place with one stoplight you find in the middle of hundreds of miles of cornfield? Not that I saw any corn, but it's spring."

"Maybe, if the town burning—and disappearing—is happening *now*." She laced the qualifying statement with doubt.

"Yeah…" I closed my eyes again. Last year's Kitsune dreams—all two of them—had never been literal, but nothing as mundane as buildings had shown up in them, either. I wanted to shrug it off, but as different as it had been from the others, it still had that same realer-than-real clarity. And although I'd felt no sense of alarm *while* I'd been in the dream, a weight was growing, cold and heavy in my chest. Not quite panic but close, a growing gut-certainty of looming awfulness. What I'd seen was real.

With no more from me to go on, Shell faded out (she'd added a nice whispery sound effect and a feel like a puff of cool mist on my skin). Off to play the Ghost in the Machine, she'd shake the data-built foundations of cyberspace. If an image even remotely matching what I'd seen existed she'd find it.

Why did I feel like that wouldn't be a good thing?

We could have landed at the airport, but doing a loaded drop was always good practice and the pallet had to come home anyway for repacking. We bailed out high over Chicago. The storms had hit us here, too, but the major cells passed to the south and east.

Looking down at Grant Park, I almost couldn't have said that the Green Man had ever been there. After a lot of debate, the business-owners on Michigan Avenue had won and most of the dense thickets of trees left over from his last attack had been removed. Ozma had "walked" a bunch of them into orderly rows along the avenues and a couple of groves were preserved. The Atlas Memorial and Buckingham Fountain had been restored.

With the load blocking my line of sight, Tsuris guided me down for a perfect insertion through the Dome's bay doors, where Shell welcomed us wearing her new Shellbot shell.

"Off the clock, everybody," I said as Crash, Ozma, and Grendel unclipped. "Don't leave the Dome. Five hours, then we inventory and repack the pallet and go-bags." Some CAI teams let their staff pack their kits but not ours, especially since Lei Zi had taken over as field leader; when we went away from Chicago we had to *know* that we had everything we needed.

Crash saluted and everybody else just nodded; we all knew the system. I stayed to watch the bay doors close above us, and Shell and I headed downstairs. She didn't say anything in the elevator or the hallway, waiting for my apartment door to close behind us before she opened her mouth.

"Tired?"

"You think?" I stripped off my mask and wig, running fingers through my much shorter, bobbed hair, and kept stripping. The new costume bodysuit covered me from neck to toes in layered Vulcan-created fabric styled by Andrew. The new stuff wasn't just enormously damage-resistant, it wick'd sweat and oils away from my skin into its layers and shed dirt and field stains away like nobody's business, but I *still* wanted a shower so bad I could taste it. Especially since I'd been in a fight and even been knocked out for a second. Dr. Beth was going to want to poke at me.

Shell sat on my bed and watched, wincing at the bruises that came into sight. The twist of sympathy in her lips looked totally natural—Vulcan had done a great job again.

"How's the new Shell-shell?" I asked before she could open her mouth.

She wiggled her new eyebrows, stuck out her tongue and curled it. "Feels real, and there's no signal loss as long as I stay close to the Dome. The Galatea shell can go farther since it doesn't require as much signal load to drive. I still couldn't have gone with you guys."

"Shell…"

"I know, I'm useful riding along through Dispatch. It's not like I'll be *risking* myself with the Galatea shell."

Shell didn't remember the months when she'd completely downloaded herself into the last Galatea, or almost dying in the last Green Man attack, but she'd learned from her downloaded self's experiences anyway; she wasn't going to expose herself to direct harm again. Not that I'd *let* her—she'd only won my approval the last time by lying to me, letting me believe that she'd been uploading a running backup of herself into memory. The future quantum-tech to Verne-tech interface hadn't worked that way, and the first I'd known about that was when I'd almost lost her.

I *had* lost her in a way; the Shelly who'd downloaded herself and spent months as Shelly-Galatea, gotten close to Crash, fought beside me, was flesh-and-blood now and living with her mother in Springfield. The Shelly sitting cross-legged on my bed was Shelly 3.0 and she knew it. She insisted we all call her 'Shell', not just as a nickname anymore, and now she'd styled her hair as short as my own shoulder-length bob and colored it black as Artemis' raven locks. She'd also "aged" herself a bit, and looked like her chronological age of 20 instead of the 16 years she'd experienced.

Shell and Shelly, one a quantum-ghost and wingman and the other a high school freshman who texted and video-chatted a lot. Neither talked about the other much. Shelly still hadn't used the bio-seed she'd taken with her to establish a neural link with Shell and I didn't know why.

Shell read my look and stuck out her tongue again, an attitude display instead of a demonstration of Vulcan's craftsmanship. She hopped up and followed me into the bathroom.

"So, do you want to hear about Powerteam now?"

I turned on the water and stepped in, yelling over the heavenly waterfall-spray of five showerheads. "How are they even *real*?"

I could hear her snickering.

"Their reality show format is built on tryouts and training. Crisis Aid and Intervention Certification is the official reward for those who make the team, but it's really an excuse for vicious competition in the selection phase and soap opera drama in their headquarters-slash-communal residence. They're a parody of a real team, but they don't have to answer to a city or county that pays their bills so they can get away with it."

I lathered my hair, trying to wrap my mind around what that had to be like; just thinking about the awful social dynamics made me slightly queasy. It had to be like getting out of bed and jumping into a ripe cesspool every day.

"Okay, so how did they end up *here*? In Cairo I mean."

"They have to do something besides train and scripted bickering. Usually they pursue specifically vetted General Warrants, but they also handle emergency relief. They're not bad at it. Last night…"

She trailed off, but I knew that tone.

"Shell? Who did you hack?"

"Just their studio files after the fight. They were hardly protected at all."

I bent my head to rinse so I wouldn't have to say anything.

"Spinner's been team leader for two years and they're forcing him to move on," she said through the spray. "The studio broadly scripted an argument built on whatever excuse the team could find, and he was supposed to get in a fight with Slamazon and maybe Kindrake. It would be a 'character turning' inflexion point for him, he'd realize he was out of control, resign, go off to China to gaze at his navel and discover himself, maybe come back in a year or two to join a real CAI team or an older reality team. He didn't want to go, but the producers are ready to just terminate his contract if he doesn't follow the script."

"The fight was *planned*?"

"Improvised with guidelines."

"That's just—" I couldn't think of a word bad enough, at least not one I could say. I finished up fast and grabbed the towel Shell handed to me. Blackstone's decision to pull us out this morning, fuzzy before, now made horrible sense.

"What's the rush?" Shell asked as I toweled my hair hard, looking for clothes.

"Does Blackstone know what you know about the script?"

"No…"

"Tell him. Tell him *now*."

Chapter Three

Rules of Engagement in a Civilian Environment: avoid an encounter-with-force if at all possible, use only powers that can be applied without collateral damage, use all *powers that can be applied without collateral damage, do not escalate, stop any escalation, and neutralize civilian risks as quickly as possible.*

Chicago Sentinels Training Manual.

I finally settled on a fresh costume minus the mask, pulling the bodysuit on over damp skin. Boots, gloves… Somewhere along the line I'd started treating my costume (whatever my Andrew-imposed style this month) like a uniform; going anywhere "official" in the Dome without it was unthinkably improper even if the mask wasn't necessary anymore.

Shell watched me scramble, more and more worried. "Okay, he knows now. What's the big deal?"

Hopping on one foot, I realized my stupidity and floated to pull my boots on like an astronaut.

"Oh I don't know, Shell! If they staged it and it went bad, do you think they're waiting for us to call them on it? Don't you think they've got to be—drat!" I popped the seams of my supposedly indestructible left boot like most girls rip a stocking and tossed it for a replacement. "—spinning it already?" Boots on, I grabbed up my gloves and ran.

Laconic Bob—Mal's name for him and it had stuck—nodded in passing as we blew through the downstairs lobby. Shell had probably told Blackstone I was coming when she dumped the news on him; he didn't seem at all surprised to see me when I came through his open office door. Legal Eagle looked up smiling, and my heart sank.

Not that I didn't like Tommy Brannigan, Esquire. He was cute, funny, and he'd kept me out of court over the infamous Paulina Street Noodle Incident (which had *not* been my fault). His breakthrough story had inspired Shelly to jump to her death five years ago, but I'd never held that against him and he would never, *ever*, know.

But I only ever saw him when legal badness loomed.

"Hello Astra," Blackstone greeted me, acting for all the world as if our breathless entrance were a social call. Seeing Shell behind me, Legal Eagle blinked. He knew who she was now, but she bizarrely refused to wear a costume (her Galatea shells didn't count) and today her lace trimmed sleeveless black t-shirt said *Life: 3* in bold white.

He shook his head. "Hey girls. Is there a fire?"

"Don't be a dumbass," Shell huffed, making me wince as she dropped into a chair. I sat down with my usual cape-tuck. Blackstone looked... calm and I unpanicked a little; maybe it wasn't as bad as I thought.

"Thank you for having Shell pass along that piece of information, my dear," he said, eyes twinkling as he watched Shell glare at Tommy. "It adds one piece to the puzzle, and forewarned is always forearmed."

"But it's not why you pulled us out this morning." At least it looked like there was no fire. I could live with that.

"How could it be? No, for that you can thank Powerteam's early morning web release of the teaser for their next episode. Quin's excellent staff caught it this morning."

"Their what, now?"

Shell rolled her eyes and Blackstone chuckled at my bewildered look. Turning his desk screen around for my benefit, he tapped a key to play the Viewtube file displayed there. Clips of the flood and Cairo, all of us in the church rec-room, the argument between Spinner and Kindrake, my entrance…

"I *started* it?" The camera angle and editing made it look like I'd started arguing with Spinner, put up my hands aggressively, and Boomer had stepped in to defend his idiot leader. Punched first in self-defense? The rest of the cut footage showed our guys leaping in before the rest of Powerteam could move. How could they *possibly*…

"I did *not*—" I closed my mouth. The look on my face must have been priceless; Legal Eagle wheezed behind his hand as he tried not to laugh.

Blackstone didn't laugh. "Of course not, my dear. I never would have thought it, and your mask-cam footage shows very clearly what happened up till that point. However." He frowned, pinching the bridge of his nose. "This hastily released preview cut isn't provably fraudulent, only misleading. It is obviously intended to shape the story by getting out there first. And as you can see, it is succeeding."

The counter below the final frozen image registered over a million hits.

"What are we doing?"

"Following Tommy's advice, we have spoken to Superintendent Redmond. He has agreed to launch an immediate investigation and a pair of Internal Affairs agents will arrive within the hour to interview each of you, take statements, and receive copies of all Dispatch footage from the time in question."

"That's *helping* us?"

Legal Eagle cleared his throat.

"By launching a full investigation, the CPD is able to immediately subpoena all relevant recordings and testimony—and that includes all the video footage taken by Powerteam's camera crew, too. Jurisdictionally it's iffy, but Cairo's bench is cooperating by issuing a mirror warrant."

"Oh. *Oh.*" The complete video record would absolutely exonerate us, and Powerteam's producers couldn't withhold the video—it was material evidence.

"But won't a full IA investigation just strengthen the impression they're trying to make?"

"Only short term. I've asked Quin to issue an immediate public statement that the Sentinels are fully and immediately indemnifying the God In Christ church for all damages, and suing Powerteam's production studio to recover all repair costs. The lawsuit will force them to settle or attempt to prove they are not at fault, and we will not let them off the hook with a private settlement."

Blackstone nodded agreement. Even Shell looked approving, and Legal Eagle wasn't her favorite person (he kept telling her what she *couldn't* do). I finally relaxed, let myself smile even though it all left me more confused. I was missing something. *C'mon, Hope. Just because you're blonde doesn't mean you have to be one.*

"So the faster IA clears us, the faster Powerteam's spin spins out. That can't be all there is to it."

"No." Blackstone's smile faded and he leaned back as my stomach clenched again. "Public image be damned, this may turn into a fight over certification."

"Wait, what?"

"That's—" Tsuris stopped short of racking up another point in one of my and Shell's private point games (each predictable *That's (fill-in-the-blank)!* protest scored a point).

The team meeting wasn't going real well, but this was the junior team's first exposure to a Certification Review—and they weren't even fully certified yet.

I wanted to put my head down on the table and not look up until...well until everything was normal again. Powerteam's viral teaser had inspired *WTF?* texts from the Bees (and snarkier comments from Megan). *Mom* had texted—the teaser had been picked up by her favorite Chicago morning show. Her only comment had been *LUV-U*, but if she'd seen it, Dad had seen it, and they worried.

And the thing that made me want to laugh *and* cry was that the teaser wasn't the problem. It wasn't even close.

"Your sentiments are shared," Blackstone agreed with Tsuris. The Internal Affairs agents had come, done their job, and gone, and with everyone's testimony given we could finally meet to talk about it. Sitting beside him, Chakra looked as serene as always, but The Harlequin looked ready to say something stronger. The three of them faced us across the Assembly Room table, and the only one not in costume was Shell.

"So, I don't get it." Crash sounded more curious than bugged, but he obviously spoke for pretty much everyone else.

"Astra?" Blackstone raised an eyebrow at me, smiling.

I sighed and paraphrased. "The rules of engagement in a civilian environment are: avoid a fight if possible, don't do lots of indiscriminate damage if you can avoid it, don't escalate, and get the civilians out of the way or if you can't do that then shut down the fight as quickly as possible. How many of those boxes did we check off last night?"

"They started it!" Tsuris, of course, but Grendel's deep grunt was practically a growl. Ozma smiled, but she always smiled and sometimes that was scarier.

"And we escalated instead of attempting to talk," I pointed out without looking at anybody. Fortunately, Shell assured me the Dispatch recordings showed us shielding and removing the bystanders first. "We also caused some unnecessary damage." Destroying a section of built-up levee had let some river into Cairo, even if it wasn't nearly as bad as it would have been without our work before the fight.

"And we ended it." Grendel smiled, showing fangs. According to Dr. Beth, getting swallowed whole by a dragon hadn't hurt him a bit.

"Of course we did," I agreed, wishing I could return the smile.

Powerteam was fully certified while we were only provisionally, but we trained *hard* and the fight hadn't even been close. And it wasn't that Grendel didn't get it; he just didn't care. *Not our fault, so not our problem*. I wished. I turned to Shell.

"Shell? Since the Event, how many times have CAI-certified teams fought each other?"

"Outside of training? Zero."

"Seriously?" Megaton started to protest, but thought about it.

"Yep," Shell said. "Certified and licensed teams? Never."

Blackstone cleared his throat. "And there are two reasons for this. First, all professional capes are very much aware of the public relations side of their role. Public confidence and trust is everything. Superheroes fight each other all the time in the comics and movies; in real life, it is as unthinkable as seeing local police and the FBI shoot it out over the jurisdiction of an arrest. We're all on the same side.

"The second reason is that capes who pick fights with other capes get dropped from team rosters very quickly. It's a question of certification and, of all things, insurance." He smiled drily. "No municipality will hire a cape they can't purchase liability insurance for, and no insurance company will cover a superhero who is not certified by a reputable association. No certification, no insurer. No insurance, no license to wear the cape as a professional."

That sank in. We'd won our fight, but a panel of strangers might decide we shouldn't have fought it. I kept my hands folded on the table, my back straight, my face boardroom-blank.

"So, what happens now?" Megaton asked. He hadn't been there but the Young Sentinels was his chance to redeem himself. Or at least that was how he looked at it.

This time I answered, trying to project optimism.

"We certify through the American Superhero Association, the same association that certifies Guardians and Knights teams. After Internal Affairs publishes its findings, the ASA will rule on what, if anything, needs to be done about individual or team certification. Until IA is finished we're off of field duty, even those of us certified for non-combat activities. After that, the ASA may decide to place us on probationary status, or completely clear us of fault."

Or they could completely decertify us. I kept smiling. "Hopefully the latter."

"Any questions?" Blackstone asked, pulling the focus back to him. Of course there were. That took up nearly another half-hour, and wasn't fun at all. Tsuris stayed pissed and even Jamal looked worried. *Megaton* was worried and he wasn't even subject to possible censure. Ozma remained her usual serene self and Grendel stayed quiet, but that didn't tell me anything about what either really thought.

The meeting ended with Quin's admonition to not respond to queries, personal or otherwise, about the investigation. The public spin? "Superintendent Redmond has moved quickly so that the city's confidence in the Young Sentinels can be speedily affirmed." No mention of the ASA or certification.

We'd beat the *Green Man*, and we might get taken down by a review board. How unsuperheroic was that?

Chapter Four

Today marks the third cycle of open elections in the US Territory of Byzantium since Congress ratified the Byzantium Convention's territorial constitution. Across the Bosporus in East Istanbul, large demonstrations marked Voting Day as thousands of Turks marched to protest the US seizure of West Istanbul as "Constantinople," the capital of the territory taken from Turkey in the peace settlement ending the Caliphate War. In Constantinople, territory troops stood ready with the city's ten CAI teams to respond to Caliphate attacks, but the day ended peacefully; this year at least, the Islamic-nationalist terrorist organization has failed to make any public attempts.

AP Archives: Byzantium Elections.

Grendel hit me so hard my breastplate rang and I bounced hard off the impact-wall before I could recover. But I didn't drop Malleus and I used the bounce to come back harder. The physics were simple; wearing my armor and swinging my short-handled titanium battle maul, I massed more than twice what I did standing in my underwear and that meant twice the imparted force from the same hit. Grendel managed to move with my swing, but it still hammered him off his feet.

But he'd expected it and tried to turn his fall into a grapple. Claws denser than steel carved my armor and *almost* got a purchase before my backswing caught his shoulder and pushed his fall harder. The impact-wall boomed again, third point for me.

"Match!" Shell blew her whistle. Grendel couldn't see her and the short referee uniform t-shirt, black kickin' booty shorts, and baseball cap she was wearing, but he could hear her through his earbug Dispatch link.

He climbed to his feet while I waited and watched him change, floating so my toes barely brushed the floor. With anybody else I'd have rushed to give him a hand up, but sparring with me always put Grendel in full fight-mode (the reason I wore the armor). He braced against the wall while his hunched posture straightened, his subcutaneous armor plates melted away, his skin smoothed out, and his claws and fangs receded.

His eyes changed, too, from pure black to human irises circling shrinking pupils. Night-black with silver flecks. I liked his eyes.

"Three to two," I gasped, breathing hard. "Good match."

He breathed, held it, let it out—a tantric breathing technique Chakra had taught him—and pushed his dreads out of his face. They'd come out of their tail somewhere in the match.

"Good one," he agreed, voice steady and grin mostly fang-free. He pointed at my gouged breastplate. "You okay?"

I fingered the deep slanting grooves and shrugged. "Vulcan won't be happy, but it did its job." Touching down, I joined him at the wall. When I slid down to sit, he joined me on the floor. Shell obligingly faded out; she was getting good at knowing when I wanted some one-on-one time.

Resting Malleus beside me and leaning back, I pulled off my mask and wig to wipe at the sweat. I still felt a little light-headed; sparring all-out with Grendel was always... hard on the hindbrain. Buffed up and ready for battle, his loominess and claws and fangs always made the ancestral monkey in my head want to run screaming and throw fruit and nuts at him from a safe tree branch.

He turned his head to look at me. In his stripped-down mode I could see traces of the Brian Lucas I'd seen in his confidential files, the upper-class black kid from St. Louis who'd rebelled with his dreads and danced like a man burning to move every moment of every day.

Not that I'd ever met that kid, which was the problem; now the boy was a freaking *wall*, tougher than the one we rested against. After half a year, I didn't know Grendel much better than I did from his Hillwood file. I didn't know *Brian* at all.

"What are you thinking about?" the wall asked.

Huh? I blinked, realized I'd been staring at him. At least I didn't blush. *Smooth, Hope, reeeeal smooth.*

"You did good," he said. Rumbled, really. "Down in Cairo."

"You think?" I let my head fall back against the wall. "I let Boomer completely blindside me. Atlas would *so* have called me on it. One of the first things he taught me was not to step into a hot superhuman fight, even if it's just verbal. 'If you get that close, you should be swinging first.'"

"Mmm." Just the rumble, no words. Like the world's biggest lion. "What was he like?"

"Really?" I drew my legs up, clasped my hands around my knees. "Amazing. Hard. Not— Not perfect, but...what he had to be, I guess." Almost a year and a half after the Whittier Base Attack I could actually think about him and smile, but Grendel's question surprised me anyway. Most everyone I knew didn't ask me about Atlas. "You didn't do so bad, yourself. How are you doing? After everything?"

Grendel shrugged. He *hadn't* done bad; in fact he'd done the best of anybody in last night's disaster. His first shot—knocking Boomer through the wall right after me for me to finish—had gotten the most potentially destructive opponent away from the civilians. Then he'd grappled Slamazon and taken her outside, too. Grendel had come off better than anyone else; Tsuris wasn't going to score any points with the IA investigators—his wind attack on Spinner had been effective, but there in the church rec room it had almost sucked in Ozma, Rush, and the civilians.

No, Grendel had been great. But then he'd been *eaten*. Doctor Beth had cleared him, but who wouldn't be seriously bugged by being swallowed whole by a rainbow-colored flying lizard?

I watched him out of the corner of my eye. Half the time his psychomorphic body was as good as a mood ring—bulking up, shrinking, claws and fangs growing depending on how easygoing or aggressive he felt at any moment—but he practically *defined* stoic. And recently he'd been getting a handle on the unthinking changes, too, so those visual cues were starting to go away.

So I still didn't have any idea what went on in his head, and that was the problem. I was strong, Watchman was strong, and people thought we were pretty awesome; *Shell* thought Grendel was awesome with a side of awesome sauce, and had the numbers to prove it. Morphing into his strongest configuration he was already the strongest Ajax-type known, and he was getting *stronger*. According to the future-file he was *never* going to see it had taken three US supersoldier squads to take him down in the end—and the after-action report had concluded that the only reason they'd won was *he let them*.

Go into a berserk rage and slaughter a village full of innocent civilians along with the bad guys, and you might not be as motivated to fight back as you could be.

But that was a future that hopefully would never happen. Here and now he just gave me a shrug. A huge and yes, *awesome* shrug, but that was it. *Sigh*. Moving on, then.

"So." I kept my gaze innocent. "Going out today?"

There was an upside to being "out of the field"; after inventory and packing we were all set to enjoy some R&R and Ozma's Anonymity Specs let Grendel go out with the rest of us without causing a panic or fan-frenzy. I thought I'd seen everything until I watched Grendel swallow three monster burgers in the middle of a crowd of students at the Artist's Café. Nobody noticed the looming gray beast in the room because he was *wearing glasses*.

Magic is *weird*.

Now he actually grinned. "Navy Pier's arcade has a Dance Dance Revolution machine that can take me, and I'm two up on

Crash so it's on." The rat was laughing before he finished, toothy grin widening as my brain shut down at the mental image.

"That's…good…" *Don't laugh don't laugh don't laugh don't laugh*. I dissolved into helpless giggles.

"So, did you get him to talk about his feeeeelings?" Shell mocked me.

"No." Out of my armor, I started stripping again. My day could involve a lot of changes.

Shell sat on my bed and watched as I chose civies for the night, a sea green party dress. Above the knee but flowy, it had been Julie Approved—part of her inspiration-collection and her campaign to create a Look for me that fit with the level of fashion the Bees intended to work with when they launched their first boutique.

The one real upside to being grounded *now* was Shell and I weren't going to miss Annabeth's wedding-date celebration, which was great because I'd gotten us reservations at Fancies before the flooding began. Shell was already dressed to go out, in a black party dress that matched her hair. All dressed up, her Shell-shell looked older than I did, which hardly seemed fair.

"Told you so. He's a *guy*. You're a *gurrrrl*. He could be completely weirded out from starring in his own production of Jonah and the Whale, St. George and the Dragon, whatever, and he's not going to tell you about it." She dropped her voice as far as it would naturally go. "Hey, man, it's cool. I'm just going to go crush Jamal on Dance Dance Revolution. Because I *can*."

I smiled in spite of myself. "Think he'll talk to Jamal?"

"Probably. In the two word sentences boys use to communicate. Wear the silver pumps."

I snagged them, started working on makeup. We had time, and Julie had been specific about what the night required. "Anything on the water tower search?"

Shell groaned theatrically. "No," she mirrored me. "And I even went international *and* into the Big Book of Contingent Prophecy."

That was *not* what I expected to hear, and I stopped, tube of lipstick in my hand. "Really? That's—" That wasn't right. The dream had seemed so *real*. And what possible use was an allegorical water tower? But everything had a picture somewhere in the interconnected world of the internet cloud, and if I'd seen a real place Shell should have been able to find it. And it was *important*; remembering it brought back that cold sense of certain doom. I stared at my lipstick.

"Shell? Could you search for this?" Reaching up, I drew an outline of the six-pointed star I remembered on the vanity mirror, a less exact squiggle of the eagle in the middle. *No...* I grabbed a wipe, rubbing out the eagle and drawing it bigger, overlapping with the star's edges. Shell sat up and scowled at it for a moment, then filled it in virtually using our neural link. She added a ring around it with words, and a familiar symbol defaced the mirror.

"It's the US Marshals symbol," she said needlessly.

I stared at the star, thought of the dream. She'd nailed it; I'd forgotten about the ring until now, hadn't tried to read the words in my dream. *Justice, Integrity, Service*.

Finishing my face on autopilot (years of Mom's foundation meetings made it easy), I thought hard. This was going to involve *government*. How?

"Call Blackstone?" Shell guessed when I didn't say anything.

"No... Call Jacky. We've got time. Secure me?" New Orleans was in our time zone and it wasn't sunset yet there, either, but she liked to be awake and outside for it. I grabbed my cell, punched Jacky's icon. Shell gave me two thumbs up as it rang—the line was secure as only a twenty-second century cyber ghost could make it.

It rang twice. "*Hi, Sunshine.*" Just hearing her voice, deep, confident, take-no-prisoners, made me feel better.

"Hey, you. Can I take advantage of my favorite fiend of the night?"

"*Tell me*." Keeping it light hadn't fooled her, and her voice tightened. I told her about Kitsune and the dream. She was quiet after I described the Marshals symbol.

"Jacky?"

"*Give me a moment.*"

Shell rolled her eyes. "Well, this is reassuring. Not"

"Hush."

"*What?*"

"Not you."

"*Have Shell send me the details and don't talk to* anybody. *I'm flying up tonight.*" She hung up, leaving me staring at my cell.

"Okay, *I'm* freaked now," Shell quipped. "Sent and done, so let's go—we're going to be late."

Shell and I found New Tom waiting for us when we came out the Dome's "back door."

"Ladies," he greeted us, tapping his chauffer's hat. New Tom's black suit hid body armor and at least two guns that I knew of, but his passengers weren't always as tough as me or Shell. Holding the passenger door of one of the team's tinted-window town cars for us, he climbed into the driver's seat once we were settled.

"You can relax, ladies," he assured us as we settled and he got us moving. "Traffic is clear, and certain sources assure me that there is zero chance of paparazzi tailing us tonight." That let me breathe easier, but I suddenly wished I'd thought to borrow a pair of Anonymity Specs, anyway. Professional paparazzi might not be the only problem.

Dane and Annabeth had officially set a date for next spring, and tonight was supposed to be both a girlfriends' celebration and the meeting when Julie handed us all our responsibilities. Annabeth's mom was long-divorced from her dad and not in the picture, and Annabeth changed her own mind as often as she changed everything else but Dane so she'd thankfully surrendered to Julie's usurpation.

And it all might not be as *private* as we wanted.

Of all the complications I'd dreaded from being outed as Astra last year, having fans put my *friends'* lives under a microscope hadn't been one of them. Facebook pages, Twitter accounts, the fact that every phone was a camera, meant that anyone could know almost as much about you as your closest friends—and be loudly judgy about it.

It wasn't all one-sided and the Bees were using the exposure to develop an amazing platform from which to launch their fashion business once they graduated. But complete strangers now knew Megan was gay and got to comment on it. Not that she'd kept it in the closet, but she didn't exactly fly her gay flag or join the campus clubs or demonstrations—she voted Republican, although *that* might be from a desire to shock. And so she got criticized for not being *proud* enough or showing solidarity.

Ugh, and so bizarre.

And even Dane and *Annabeth* got unfair criticism; they were marrying too *young*, making Big Decisions before they were even old enough to drink. Did it matter that they'd been Danabeth for nearly five years, Dane had a promising soccer career, and neither of them was hurting for money to start a family with? *No.* Annabeth even got grief for never having dated anyone else, for announcing she wanted babies and soon, for planning to change cities if Dane didn't get picked up by our local Chicago Fire.

Double Ugh.

All of that was a big reason for choosing Fancies; special occasion aside, the establishment catered to a lot of rich and celebrity patrons so we could count on privacy.

New Tom pulled us up under Fancies' front canopy and a valet attendant opened our door. The Bees waited for us in the lobby, just as glittering as Shell and me, and we stopped for hugs all around. They embraced Shell with the same enthusiasm (they already knew about her new look), but I frowned. Julie was always determined that Megan's current romantic partner be included in our circle, but I didn't see Clare anywhere.

I looked at Julie. She hovered behind Megan but wasn't giving off any *Megan's fragile right now so don't ask* vibes, so I relaxed.

Since Julie, Annabeth, and Megan lived in Palevsky Commons, we mostly hung out in the Pizza Cellar or Calvert House or one of the just-off-campus coffee shops or burger joints, but all of us came from money and were "poor college students" only in theory. Still, Fancies was upscale even for us; our hostess seated us in one of the smaller dining rooms, and since we were underage, the sommelier recommended a variety of spring and sparkling waters with fruit slices for each course.

And there were a *lot* of courses. Fancies boasted a tasting menu, which meant a parade of dishes; my favorites were a chilled crab starter with roe and fragrant herbs, a cold milk soup with scallops and nasturtium, Wagyu beef ribeye with mustard seeds, the basil waffle fancy bread, and a dessert of rich custard garnished with coconut. There were lots of others, some very strange (can you say *molecular gastronomy*?). Some were definitely an acquired taste, like the oyster with huckleberries and lavender or broth garnished with edible flowers. And of course there were desserts, desserts, desserts.

All through the courses, Julie kept up a running monologue of wedding notes and plans, happily seconded by an Annabeth who only really cared about her wedding dress—provide Dane and the dress of her dreams and she'd be happy to be married by an Elvis in Las Vegas.

But it was off. Julie wasn't as *intense* about her plans as she should have been. She kept looking at Megan, and Annabeth kept watching *me*. Shell didn't pick up on anything, but she hadn't had my three school years with the Bees. *What is going on*?

I finally put my fork down and asked just that.

"Guys?"

Julie dropped her spoon, looking caught. "Um. What?" Annabeth sighed, giving Megan a look that practically shouted *Tell her*. I tried not to panic.

Megan sipped her soup. "Julie and I are together now. We picked tonight to tell you." They shifted, obviously clasping hands under the table, while I opened and closed my mouth. My fingers tingled and my face felt cold.

Megan and Julie were together. Megan and Julie were together *and they hadn't told me*. They were staring at me, I wanted to cry, and it was the most selfish reaction in the world. I almost blurted

How long? but my social brain ruthlessly crushed it. *But Julie's straight!* didn't make it to my mouth either. When my inner editor gave up I did the only thing I could think of; I stood up, dashed around the table, and *hugged* them. As long as I was holding onto them, my inability to form a coherent sentence wouldn't be taken horribly horribly wrong.

Julie cried, Megan laughed, Annabeth just smiled, happily misty, and we were good. My brain finally unlocked enough for me to manage a clichéd "How wonderful!" And I meant it, really. The rest of party went much more smoothly; obviously the wedding-date celebration had been an excuse in case Julie and Megan got cold feet—it had been a case of Annabeth's riding them to "Tell Hope!" I managed to make all the right noises while feeling completely detached. The perfect cap on the night came as we were leaving, when a bottom-feeding paparazzi jumped out of the bushes and snapped shots of us outside, shouting questions about why I was partying when people's homes were underwater.

New Tom almost shot him before he realized he wasn't a threat. Annabeth punched him and then burst into tears. I was so numb I didn't even think of asking Shell to wipe his camera's memory.

Back at the Dome, Shell made herself scarce and I changed into workout clothes. Aches from my sparring match with Brian still lingered, but I had to punch something hard—and maybe scream where it could be mistaken for power-punching.

Screaming and punching is therapeutic, but it narrows your situational awareness; I didn't hear Jacky until she said my name. My final scream wasn't a power-punch.

"Sweet—! Jacky, are you *trying* to kill me?"

"What, no 'great to see you'?" She stood there in full Artemis costume, hood back and black mask dangling from her hand.

"How did you— You got a ride, didn't you?"

"Argonaut. That Jamaican boy knows how to fly and owes me a favor or two. I didn't want my trip showing up on the DSA's radar yet."

So she'd recruited New Orleans' resident Atlas-type to give her a lift. I nodded, shaking out my stinging fists.

She cocked an eyebrow. "No questions? Okay then, mind telling me what's got your panties in a twist? It can't be what Shell thinks it is."

I grabbed my towel and wiped my forehead. "And what does Shell think it is?"

"Shell thinks you're upset that Julie has discovered Megan is the love of her life—which makes no sense to her, either."

"*No*." I threw the towel at the wall. "If I've never had a problem with Megan's orientation, why would I have one with Julie? I'm upset because I didn't *know*. I *missed* it! And they weren't sure I'd be *happy* for them. Dammit!" I wiped my eyes. Maybe they weren't any more sure of my feelings than Shell. Well, they would be.

Jacky nodded like she followed all that. "Right. More information?"

"Julie was Megan's first crush, way back in middle-school. But Julie was straight, right? She picked out a boyfriend each year, just one, even if he didn't last till spring. I'm pretty sure she traded in her 'V' senior year."

But she hadn't had any college boyfriends. Um.

"And?"

I blinked and refocused. "Megan didn't have *any* romantic partners till our first year at U of C. She cycled through a bunch of them, then, but this year it's just been Clare. I actually managed to meet Clare a couple of times, but she dropped out of the picture over winter break, at least that's what Annabeth said."

"So, you're upset because you didn't know Julie was bi?"

"*No*. Yes. *Nobody* knew in high school, not even Julie." I laughed, not happily. "Megan—"

Had it been rooming together that did it? Or seeing Megan have a serious girlfriend for the first time? I scrubbed my face. Julie had the most solid sense of self-identity of anyone I knew—going from *I'm straight*, to *I'm in love with my BF*, must have been terrifying, and I was being horribly selfish making it about *me*.

Taking a deep breath, I let it out with a sigh.

"They might have needed me, they might— We were supposed to be roomies, and I was *here*. I'm upset because they didn't share, and I'm upset because I'm upset, and I'm upset because I can't *change* it. I *can't* be there, and that won't change any time soon. *Damn* it!"

I retrieved the towel, dropped it in its bin.

It always came around to this, and I was tired of it. I knew it would get better; Ajax had managed to balance wearing the cape with family and a successful academic career. U of C had just named the new Superhuman Studies department for him, unveiled his statue on the campus quad. *Hero, Scholar, Teacher*: not a bad memorial, not a bad life. The tradeoffs still sucked, but I was done thinking about it.

"Let's just—let's just go."

"Good." Jacky could see I'd moved on, and approved. She fell into step beside me. "Because I've been to the town you dreamed about, and if your dream was prophetic then we're in deep shit."

"Oh. Joy."

Chapter Five

"A historical fact: In FDR's last speech, the one he never gave because he died the day before he was scheduled to give it, he concluded 'Today we have learned in the agony of war that great power involves great responsibility'. It's a ringing statement of an unoriginal declaration. A famous fictional superhero's uncle said it more recently. Voltaire said it, and Jesus Christ long before him: 'To whom much is given, much is expected.' Clichés become clichés because they state human truths; the power to act is the responsibility to act, or not to act, but most of all to act wisely. If there is no God to hold us accountable, we do the job ourselves."

Prof. Charles Gibbons (Ajax), Class Lectures.

Having something else to think about actually improved my mood, not that it could have gotten much worse.

Jacky took us down to her rooms. She still used them; last fall when she'd come back to Chicago to help find me during my accidental "abduction," she'd stayed a couple of weeks to do a little cleanup in her old neighborhood. Goons, minions, local street-gangs, they'd all had to be retaught that engaging in business or recreation in *Artemis'* territory was a bad idea. Now she came back for random nights every week or three.

How did she sow that much terror with a short drop-by? Nobody died, and more than that I didn't want to know. Cowardly? Yes, but I *liked* Jacky, a lot. I didn't want to know anything that might make me have to judge.

And she'd moved her coffee shrine to her rooms—she didn't trust the newbies with it—so I got to sit and watch her work. It was almost like watching a formal tea ceremony; she measured and prepared ingredients with ritual precision. Ozma said Jacky would make an excellent witch if she'd had a spark of magic, and the air filled with the brain-melting aroma of roasted and ground coffee bean fine enough to make the most exacting gourmand cry.

"Irish Ka'u," she said, setting my cup down. "Hawaiian Ka'u bean, one jigger of Irish cream and Irish whisky, a little chocolate and nutmeg. One cup would knock out someone as light as you if you weren't, you know, the Iron Maid."

That got a tired giggle; the first time she'd called me that in range of my dad's—*Iron Jack's*—hearing had been a treat. I cautiously sipped—not a fan of liquor—and sighed. Perfect. Before she settled down with her own cup, Jacky put a ring-sized jewelry box on the dining nook table. Flipping it open, she touched the elegant pearl-cluster ring inside and nodded. I ignored the weird procedure, even when the pearls started glowing.

"A gift from Shell." Sipping her drink, she watched the pearls. "I use it when I talk to her from home. Twenty-second century tech from the Teatime Anarchist's box of tricks, absolutely unbreakable anti-bugging countermeasure."

"Oh. *Oh.*" I couldn't help looking around. If Jacky didn't think that even the *Dome* was secure...

Jacky shrugged. "She didn't recognize the water-tower. That tells me it's a secret that managed to even stay out of the Anarchist's future-files. I don't know if that's good or not, but before we talk to anybody else about this, *you* need to decide whether or not opening this door is a good idea."

"A good—what— Jacky!"

"What if I told you to just leave this door closed? No more questions? I don't know what game that freaky ghost-fox is running, but… You get enough scrutiny from Certain People because of Shell. This is a secret that might take it to another level. Serious Need-To-Know stuff."

"What would they do if they decided I don't need to know?"

"Probably send someone like me to make it so that you *don't*."

And that opened a whole different can of worms; I didn't ask if she used her vampiric mind-powers on people, and she didn't tell. I touched my neck, jerked my hand down when I realized what I was doing.

If I say the wrong thing, will I remember this conversation?

Her mouth twisted as she followed the thoughts I couldn't keep out of my face, but she didn't instantly reassure me. She looked suddenly dark and dangerous, watching me over the rim of her cup, and I shivered. Being her friend made it too easy for me to forget she wasn't *safe*, and I waited till I could keep my voice steady. Not that she'd ever hurt me, just…

"Do I get to know what you might make me forget?"

Her face didn't change, but the *danger* drained away and I wondered if she'd been mentally pushing me already, testing. Why?

"Have you ever heard of Guantánamo Bay?"

I blinked. "No… Is it in Mexico? It sounds Spanish."

She snickered. "Good guess—the Spanish held it until we took it from them in the Battle of Guantánamo Bay. The Spanish-American War? It's the war nobody ever remembers, and anyway Guantánamo Bay is on the south end of Cuba, which means it's the ass-end of nowhere as far as the public is concerned. It's ours under a perpetual lease. We don't trust the new Tyrant of the Most Serene Republic of Cuba any more than we did Castro, but we're willing to leave His Tyrannical Excellence alone as long as he leaves Guantánamo Bay alone."

"*Why?*"

I couldn't help but shiver again, for a different reason. Last year Shell and I had helped intercept and knock out a missile launched by an insane Verne-type supervillain—a missile what would have triggered a high-orbit EMP attack and killed millions in the power-crash. The Overlord had been hiding on the tiny island of Celubra and it had been our Caribbean Fleet that had taken him out. The after-action intelligence had given it a good bet that he'd been funded or at least tolerated by the mysterious superhuman master of Cuba.

"Because we can't afford to lose the place. It's where we tucked Camp Necessity."

"And Camp Necessity is…"

"My home away from home. Since the Event, DARPA has used the naval base as an isolated and totally hush-hush superhuman research facility. They're the people who accidentally created Camp Necessity. The US Marshals Service uses the camp as a sanctuary for Witness Protection subjects, but it's bigger than that. It's a place that isn't there—which is why we have to keep it."

I tried to see the joke, but she wasn't laughing and I put my cup down with a sigh. "Too much has happened today, Jacky, so keep it short or I'm going to shake you so bad—"

"Okay, it's where the DSA sent me for testing when they thought I might be 'contagious'. They moved the labs *into* Camp Necessity because it's really not there. It's a place that one of DARPA's less stable Verne-types accidentally created because Cuba's too hot in the summer. We can't move it so we have to keep the bay, and besides the Witness Protection residents it hosts maybe half of DARPA's Verne-Type scientists with their projects. It's more Top Secret than anywhere else that *I* know about, and it's bad that you saw it at all. If you saw it being *destroyed*…

In the end I agreed not to say anything to anyone else without her go-ahead. Not that I really thought she'd try and stop me if I wanted to. Jacky wasn't a government agent; she acted as a "civilian contractor" to the DSA and in return they looked the other way so she could take care of her dietary needs without creating fang-addicted blood donors.

(It said a lot about Jacky's world that she considered it more moral to assault random strangers, steal their blood, and then wipe their memories of the attack than to get their consent and let them remember the mind-blowing rush it gave. It said more that I *understood* that decision. From *experience*.)

So if Jacky thought I was in danger of attracting the wrong kind of attention from the Powers That Be, I wasn't going to ignore her. Besides, the Irish Ka-something tasted great, but I was yawning and ready for bed and Jacky was absently staring at my neck. I left so she could change for her evening out, but didn't get halfway to my own door before Virtual Shell popped up.

"You have a caller…"

"Who?"

"Just Superintendent of Police Big 'The Fixer' Red."

I closed my eyes and groaned, then opened them and looked down at myself. My workout shirt had dried, but I felt *sticky* and was sure to shine on the image-feed. "Phone?" I asked hopelessly.

"Nope. He's being nice with full video."

"Swell. Could you—"

"I'll make it so you're in uniform, no worries."

"Thanks." I stepped inside and closed the door, smile ready. Shell switched on the flatscreen TV in my living room, camera-rigged like every other screen in the Dome. Superintendent Sean Redmond appeared and I barely kept the smile on. The unhappy line of *his* mouth put deep creases in his cheeks. As late as it was he still wore a three-piece suit, perfectly knotted tie and shiny lapel pin, making me feel even grungier.

"Superintendent. To what do I owe the pleasure?"

"To Eric Litner. I apologize for the lateness of the call, Astra. How are you holding up?"

"Okay. As Atlas would say, it's not my first rodeo." A small exaggeration; After-Action reviews were routine, IA reviews not so much.

"No, it's not," he agreed. His grimace deepened, working his mustache. "However, that's not why I called."

"Eric Litner?"

"The gentleman of the press you met this evening. From what they tell me a real piece of work. However, he has filed an assault complaint against you."

That killed my smile. "Wait, what?"

"What indeed. According to his statement, your friend— Annabeth?— hit him and then you pushed him down. Hard enough to inflict injuries."

"That's, that's…"

"Yes. Of course any time there is a complaint against one of the city's contracted superhumans, there is an investigation. Did you touch him?"

"He fell against me and tripped. I helped him up."

"And broke his camera?"

"I—" I didn't *think* so.

He nodded unhappily.

"Of course it would be highly improper of the Superintendent of Police to speak to a CAI cape under investigation. I don't know yet if the investigating officer—who is not Inspector Fisher—will find enough to warrant formal charges. However, I wanted you to know…"

He stopped, pursed his lips like he tasted something sour. "My predecessor had a problem with 'superheroes', and that affected the relationship between the CPD and our city's CAI teams. I do not hold his prejudices, and I hope that you know that. But this is a matter of politics and media optics, Astra. Your high-profile image…"

I nodded, stomach sinking. Even with everything that had happened since Atlas' death, some people just couldn't let our "scandalous" romance go; I'd become a scandal-generator and they latched onto every little thing that might smell of favoritism or super-celebrity entitlement. *Other* people talked about me like songbirds should be following me around, and I honestly didn't know which was more embarrassing. I had yet to acquire my own feathered chorus, although I *had* seriously freaked more than a few innocently migrating flocks in passing.

"I understand, sir. And I appreciate the courtesy. Naturally the CPD has to take the allegations seriously. Is there anything I can do?"

At last he smiled. A little, showing dimples deeper than his scowl lines. "For the investigation? No. Just be forthcoming. Personally? I would *like* it if you let your mother know that she need not speak sharply to me the next time we meet over catered chicken, but of course this conversation never took place."

"Of course."

"Well then. Good night, Astra. And thank you." He didn't say for what, and I didn't ask.

"Aaah!"

I lurched upright in bed, every muscle quivering and my heartbeat loud in my ears. It took long breaths for me to realize I wasn't still dreaming, and then I had to gulp air to keep from bursting into tears.

It had been a dream. *The* dream, again, but this time part of me had been desperately trying to *move*, to get off the freaking grass and fly to the burning town. Forget detachment; every rational thought had drowned in rising certainty that horrible things were going to happen if I couldn't break out of my stasis and act.

I lay back, working on breathing normally. My sleep-top was drenched in sweat, and a distant part of me was surprised I hadn't woke up bumping the ceiling. *Only a dream*.

I didn't sleep again until night officially became morning, and then the Dispatch alert threw me out of bed.

Chapter Six

Can there be anything more clichéd than a supervillain robbing a bank? Aftershock tried it and fought Atlas in the first 'superhero vs. supervillain' fight a day after the Event. He lost. But it still happens, and just about the only time the bad guys win is if they get out before the capes arrive. And only the best or dumbest of them try it in Chicago.

Terry Reinhold, *Citywatch.*

"Blackstone wants you in Dispatch *right now*." Virtual Shell's face was the first thing my blinking eyes could track. "There's a bank robbery going down." For the second time in two days I fast-dressed in the air, more and more thankful for Andrew's latest—and easiest—design. This time I didn't destroy a boot.

"Stand down, Astra," Blackstone said. Not the words I expected to hear upon arriving in Dispatch. "Your feet aren't on the floor."

The room hummed, all stations live while Blackstone watched the big screen. Beside me, David swallowed a laugh while he tracked CAI movement at his station.

I forced my feet to get familiar with the carpet. "Sir? What's happening?"

"Somebody has decided to take advantage of the fact that almost all of our heavies are away south to rob Chicago National." Blackstone sipped his coffee—coffee!—eyes roaming the icons bordering the screen.

"And why aren't I— I'm grounded, aren't I?"

"Indeed, my dear. Until the investigation and review is complete, we aren't fielding you unless there is nobody else and loss of life is imminent. SaFire has just gone in to perform a forceful recon."

SaFire's icon showed the source of the mask-cam view we were seeing. Sound brought us the shriek of the bank's emergency system, and it looked like nobody was chasing the bank employees exiting the bank around her. This early in the morning there weren't many of them. We could see one guard, down but no blood.

"David?" Blackstone didn't look away from the screen. "Teams?"

"West Side Guardians are closest, but SaFire's the only really robust West-Sider available now. The rest are south."

The screen lit up with a flash and boom, throwing paper from bank desks. SaFire didn't stop.

"They're busy," Blackstone observed. "Why aren't they keeping anybody from leaving? No hostages?"

"Professional crew?" David suggested.

Blackstone nodded. "I think you're right. In which case... Instruct the police to maintain a withdrawn perimeter. This will probably be over by the time they finish—"

A second bang and flash and I almost leapt into the air again as an orange and green fireball filled the screen. The view spun, came to rest pointed at the ceiling.

"So it's the Repo Men."

"Yep," David looked up, checked boxes on one of his touch-screens and I watched profiles come up.

"Who? Shouldn't I be out there?"

Blackstone looked my way and actually *smiled*. "The Repo Men is the name the media has given this particular team. They're a four-man heist crew, and the flash you just saw is the signature power of one of the four. It operates like a high-powered stun grenade. Improbably enough, it is effective against Atlas-types at closer range without turning normal victims into trauma-center cases. The good news is that if it is the Repo Men then it should be a zero fatality heist."

He studied the main screen again, a shadow of a thought wrinkling his brow. Leaning in, he spoke more softly.

"It really is good news, but the FBI's local anti-terrorist unit has already contacted us with a problem. They've been sitting on this bank for months—their sweep of Doctor Pellegrini's holdings last year turned up a box here under a different name. They won't tell me what's in it, but they've been hoping to catch a member of the Ascendancy coming back for it. So…"

"So why aren't the Wreckers here?"

"Exactly. The perfect window opens for the Wreckers to be in and out, and instead we get a hired heist crew. Interesting."

Interesting? Six months after learning the identity of the superhuman terrorist who styled himself The Ascendant we were no closer to learning his ultimate goals. We knew he wanted to encourage more breakthroughs and strengthen manifested breakthroughs. We knew he believed that breakthroughs were a new and superior humanity. We *didn't* know why he engineered the Detroit prison-break, or why he'd mainly freed younger breakthroughs incarcerated there. And we didn't know where The Ascendant or any of his followers, known as the Ascendancy, *were*.

Blackstone sipped his coffee like it was no big deal, but I just wound tighter. David seemed to buy his "everyone be cool" pose, but I could hear his teeth grinding together. Was everybody insane?

"So we just *watch*?"

"We just watch. You can be there in less than half a minute if it goes bad, but you'd be the only A Class. So we—"

"Here it comes." David toggled something on his station and the big screen's image changed to an exterior shot of the bank. It hadn't opened for business yet, and it looked like all the employees had gotten out and away from the building—a good thing when the wall exploded.

"What is *that*?" I was floating again, and I realized I'd crossed myself.

A construct of brick, stone, metal, pieces of floor and walls and even desks, lurched through the hole and straightened up. Vaguely human-shaped, it had to be at least fifteen feet tall.

"Dr. Beth calls it a construct projection. Much like the Tin Man's creations last year, except they make it by crushing together whatever is handy. The media call them wreck-golems."

It looked like it had bits of bank vault attached, and it lumbered into the street.

"Bystanders?" Blackstone asked.

"Evacuation count has everyone who was supposed to be there out of the bank. Outside…" David flipped through video feeds. It looked like the street had emptied in true Chicago fashion, only cops and capes showing their heads. I spotted K-Strike and Red Robin, other West Side Guardians. The wreck-golem thumped towards the police cordon and Chicago's finest opened up on it. Pieces began to come off the thing—at least half the police cars had to have racked heavy arms in their trunks, a couple of small shoulder launchers—but it didn't slow down.

"Blackstone…"

SaFire hit the thing in the back, shooting from the hole in the bank to flatten it. *Yes!* A couple of dispatchers were unprofessional enough to applaud even as a second wreck-golem pulled itself through the hole.

The dragon diving out of the Sun landed on it.

"*Hey what?*" Shell shrieked in my ear. My mouth stayed open.

"Astra, go! Get Kindrake out of there!" Blackstone pointed at the exit hatch in case I'd gone deaf, started yelling into his headset. I was up and out in a rush, my heart in my throat, almost clipping the side of the shaft in my haste.

"*Get Kindrake off her ride and out of the combat zone.*" Blackstone clarified as I flew. "*Terraflore is tough, but she most definitely is not.*"

"On it," I manage before my parabola ended with the much-too-crowded street. I dropped under the first golem's reach to spring sideways and sweep Kindrake off her beasty's back.

"Hey!"

"Did you come to Chicago to die?" I dropped the Goth-girl behind the police line. "Stay here!"

SaFire and Terraflore had the second golem down, and I hammered into the first before it could grab at SaFire. It broke in half and I punched its head off for good measure—it's not like it had brains, but the psychological rules that governed breakthroughs and went into stuff like this usually meant taking off its head would finish it.

So naturally the pieces *merged*.

"Just keep yours away from everyone, Astra," Blackstone instructed. *"Terraflore and SaFire are keeping the first one pinned."*

"What. If. There's. More?" The thing kept mindlessly trying to twist past me, but hitting it focused its attention.

"Then we'll handle it. Fight your own and stay away from the bank—you saw this crew's area-denial power and I don't want you trying them alone."

Pounding the construct to pieces that stayed pieces took work, and I saved my breath for doing the job. Action happened out of the corner of my eye, and once green and orange "flame" washed over everybody close to the bank, and then the thing gave up. It stopped trying to reform, and a few punches scattered it across the street in a cloud of concrete dust.

When Dispatch gave the "stand down" I resisted the urge to drop to the street and just breathe. Media had to be taping—probably broadcasting live—and yes, a Chicago News drone hovered just up the street. I didn't look at it.

"Deliveries?" I gasped.

"Not this time, my dear. Amongst yourselves, you kept everything contained and there are no injuries to move. Say hello to Captain Verres, and come—"

"*Astra, ignore that last direction,*" The Harlequin broke in. "*Do not leave the area without congratulating Kindrake. If you can, get her to come to the Dome. Understood?*"

I pushed dust-caked hair off my mask, hands still shaking a little from the adrenaline spike and the sick fear when I'd seen Kindrake drop into the fight. "Understood."

Optics. Spin. Never mind that Kindrake had dropped into the middle of an action without authorization or coordination, or that she'd risked getting smeared into something Chicago News would have to pixelate out of its broadcast footage—the two of us had mixed it up less than forty eight hours ago in a mess that was sure to become the most watched hero-on-hero fight of the year if not ever. My mother's daughter, I understood perfectly; media perception was everything.

I went to find Kindrake.

"*Hollywood heroes. Just when you think that all the clichés and stereotypes can't be true, you realize 'Yup—they are'.*"

"Be nice, Shell. Seven isn't like that."

"*Seven is Seven. Why is she* here*, and what's she doing out without her handlers*?"

Shell had me there—I had no clue, and I was pretty sure that when her people found out she was in Chicago her lawyer's head would explode. Lawyers plural, a whole firm's worth. A not-so-nice part of me wanted to be there to watch.

Kindrake knew how to "not notice" the cameras as well as I did, but the smile she showed the police and newsies disappeared when she saw me headed for her. Maybe her scowl was habitual, it certainly went well with her brooding Goth look, but she couldn't do dark. Knowing Artemis, I knew dark from dramatic posing and the rainbow streaks in Kindrake's raven hair didn't help. But she had to coordinate with her flying lizard accessories somehow, I supposed.

The cameras got shots of my smile and her scowl when we shook hands, spinning the game into my court. I leaned in before she could open her mouth.

"Hello again, Kindrake, and welcome to Chicago. Blackstone sends his compliments and extends the hospitality of the Dome." I nodded to Captain Verres. "Captain. Sorry I can't stay."

He knew what to do and played the moment with an easy shrug. "We'll take it from here. Thanks for coming, Astra."

"Hey—" Kindrake managed, but I'd already released her hand and floated upward. A last nod and lazy salute so the newsies could see I wasn't ignoring her, and I sped away.

"*Good job,*" Quin said. "*Now straight home. She might not follow, but she'll look pretty lame standing there and this keeps a potentially explosive conversation away from the listening media.*" It said something about how much awkward media experiences I'd survived that she didn't have to tell me that. Talking with Kindrake in front of the newsies would have been risky as poking a Siberian tiger (well, risky for anyone else, *I* thought the big kitties were cuddly), but publicly ignoring her would have been unthinkable.

"*She's following,*" Shell observed. "*Terraflore makes a hell of a downdraft taking off.*"

"Okay." I didn't look back. "So, what happened there at the end?"

"*There was a third wreck-golem still in the bank, kept all of the other Guardians' tougher guys from poking their heads too far in. Sprints made a fast run in afterward—that last "flame" blast covered the crew's blowing an exit into the sewers and they were able to break contact and get gone. Same MO as in Florida except they pick a different departure route each time.*"

"Any idea what was— Never mind, I'm sure Fisher will tell us later. Is Kindrake close behind me?" I'd flown a lot slower than usual, but had no idea how fast a dragon moved along.

"*Right behind you,*" Shell chirped as I descended on the Dome. The bay doors rumbled wider, but there was no way the beasty was going to fit through. Dropping to the floor of the bay, I looked up to see what Kindrake's solution would be.

"*Wow. Now* that *is cool.*"

Terraflore burst into a rainbow explosion of light, dumping Kindrake from her perch, and reformed into a flight of *much* smaller jewel-bright drakes that grabbed onto various parts of her before she had a chance to fall more than a few feet. The whole bright cloud drifted down, wings beating like hummingbirds.

"Cool," I echoed, debating her mass and their relative wing-size. "And breaking so many laws of physics."

"*Says the floaty girl.*"

I touched back down—yes I'd started up to catch her.

"Hey!" Kindrake started as soon as her feet hit the bay floor. "I came out here to talk to you!"

And just like that, I'd had enough.

"Really? *Really*? And you decided to announce yourself by dropping into the middle of an action without coordinating with anybody? You—" I gulped a breath, tried for less than a scream. "Who *trained* you? What made it a good idea to put yourself into the middle of a fight with *concrete puppets*? Do you know how close you came to—I nearly had to call your parents to explain that their daughter flew to Chicago and ended up a *messy smear on her dragon's back*!"

"That would have been my job," Blackstone said from the doorway. Ignoring Kindrake's agitated friends, he stepped into the bay and let the door close behind him. His tux and hat trumped Kindrake's Gothy black without even trying; it wasn't a costume or pose, it was *him*.

"Stand down, Astra." He doffed his hat, vanishing it with a twirl. Okay, maybe a *little* of it was pose—he did like the stage. "However, I too find myself considering the question of your training, young lady. Indeed, Astra nailed the *concrete points* on the head. Surely you can do better in the absence of a director?" He tapped his cane absently and metronomically.

Kindrake winced, the first real expression I'd seen that wasn't angry or sullen.

"I came to *apologize*."

"I would think that, of those involved in the events the other night, you are the one who has the least to apologize for."

"Terraflore *ate* your teammate!"

"Ah. Of course there is that. You wish to apologize to Grendel? Astra can take you to him."

"It's not just—" The girl visibly deflated. "My agent pushed me at Powerteam. Said it would be a good transition into my adult career…"

"Say no more, certainly not while our lawyers are still dueling each other. And you have my sympathies. However." He tapped the cane once, emphatically. "I must tell you that, should you pull another stunt such as today's in Chicago, I will ensure that you cannot even fly over this town without being fined enough to put a dent in your generous syndication residuals. Am I clear?"

With a nod for me and a smile Kindrake could interpret any number of ways, he disappeared in an understated sparkle of light.

"*Tah-daaaah!*" Shell supplied. I opened my mouth but had nothing.

I stripped off my mask. "Okay, let's go see Grendel."

We found Grendel in Ozma's lab, and nobody could have been more surprised to see Kindrake than he was. Nix instantly hated her, and the sight of Nix and Kindrake's ruby-red drake glaring at each other from their shoulder-perches had even unflappable Ozma covering her mouth.

I left them to it, confident that Ozma could handle any ego-driven stupidity, and *finally* went to deal with my own issues.

Only to find that Jacky was already asleep. She didn't sleep like the dead anymore, but being a living breathing daywalker only meant she didn't burst into flame on contact with sunlight and could enjoy a solid meal—she preferred to work at night when she was most powerful, and *I* wasn't going to risk waking her. Besides, she'd left a note in my rooms. She'd written it down so I could swallow it or even reduce it to plasma in Vulcan's lab if I was paranoid enough. According to Jacky, I was *never* paranoid enough.

It read *"I'm getting stonewalled by my handler. Contact says some kind of big conference. Wait."*

"Drat." I sighed.

"You have *got* to do better than that. Someone's going to take away your Adult Card." Today Virtual Shell's t-shirt just read *Boo!* She tended to descend to ghost-girl humor when Jacky was around.

I tried to scowl but my smile won. "Don't you have something to do?"

"Doing it, but Jamal's cheating so he's probably going to win our Halo game. What are we going to do?"

Wait until evening? Let Jacky try again? That was the smart thing to do, but the echoes of last night's nightmare twisted my stomach every time I remembered. It hadn't felt like the other Kitsune dreams. Had it come out of my own subconscious fears or had Kitsune amped up the warning? Whichever, now the thought of waiting even a few hours made me queasily sick. Why did I always have everything but time?

I sighed again. *Jacky's going to kill me.*

"I'm going to make another call."

Chapter Seven

I'm the leader of a team of heroes. I'm the <u>leader</u> of a team of <u>heroes</u>. I'm still wrapping my head around what that means.

From the journal of Hope Corrigan.

Jacky once told me that if you wanted to get an intelligence agent's attention, you should tell him something that you're not supposed to know. It might not be the kind of attention you wanted, but it would be undivided.

Technically, Veritas wasn't a spook and the DSA wasn't an intelligence agency, but it still engaged in spooky activities and kept its own secrets; from what few things Artemis was willing to share, I had a pretty good idea that labels like "black ops" and even "wet-work" could be applied to some of its activities. The DSA monitored Persons of Interest, and after everything with the Teatime Anarchist I was that already. The benefit was that I knew people and they knew me; Veritas' number sat on my speed-dial and I'd been the focus of his attention before.

"*Veritas here,*" he answered after two rings.

"Something bad is going to happen at Camp Necessity."

"*Is it?*"

"Yes. Kitsune warned me."

That got several beats of silence. I wasn't sure how far up the chain of authority Veritas hung out, but he was certainly somewhere on the other side of the stone wall Jacky had run into. His cosmically creepy breakthrough power to sense all lies—over the phone, recorded, or even *written down*—meant he had to have access to people who made hard decisions fast.

They were probably careful talking to him, too.

"*You have spoken to him?*" Of course he knew the name; after last year Kitsune was a Person of Interest to the DSA. And to the CIA, Interpol, and Naichō (he *was* a Japanese national, after all).

"No. Just a message his usual way."

"*Why?*"

"I don't know. He probably wants to put me in the middle of it."

"*What do you need?*"

It was my turn to think hard. "—I think I need to get in the middle of it."

"*I see. Thank you, Astra. We will be in touch.*" He hung up.

I inhaled. I'd stopped breathing in and out sometime in the conversation.

Shell had been watching my cellphone like it was a bomb. "Could he *be* more sinister? 'We will be in touch.'"

"The base is a DSA-US Marshals operation, Shell."

"And you need to be in the *middle* of it? What is *that* about?"

I laughed helplessly. "He asked."

I hadn't even thought about it until he did. If a warning was enough, would Kitsune have reached out to me? *Why* me? And I had to remember that Kitsune wasn't a Good Guy. Last year he'd plotted to take down some very bad people, and he had, but his motive had been personal and he'd started an organized crime war that left innocent people dead, even helped it along. He was a thief, a criminal, a vigilante at best. In at least one possible future he had gotten Blackstone killed.

So you're on the mental speed-dial of a supervillain. Yay, Hope.

At least we didn't need to worry about DSA attention the way we had when Shell had been living inside Galatea last year—if the government got paranoid now, the worst they could do was bar her access to the Dome's computer system. Probably.

I wiped my face. Yuck. First a shower and a change—concrete dust got everywhere—and then things to do. There was always something.

The therapeutic shower seriously improved my outlook, and finally being able to answer the flurry of texts from the Bees—normal after any public cape-action—helped even more. They always knew I was fine since Shell had promised to tell them if I wasn't, but one text from Julie simply read *Talk soon? Please*. That one got a *Tonight. Love U*. Come hell or high water (an Atlasism too appropriate to the past week), I'd see Julie tonight.

The after-action report of the morning was easy enough to write; Dispatch always attached relevant audio and video files, which meant I could get away with a bare "went there, did that, see video log" when my actions didn't need special explanation.

Reviewing Detective Fisher's preliminary case report wasn't much fun; Max confirmed Blackstone's assessment that the heist crew was almost certainly the team the media had dubbed The Repo Men. But that meant they hadn't cracked the vault for the usual fungibles: cash, bonds, family jewels. And it did look like they'd ignored all of that and gone for a specific box—a queasy-making echo of the bank heist that had started our desperate fight with Villains Inc. last year.

But the resemblance ended there; they'd taken out the vault cameras, and the bank was playing Switzerland. Max was waiting for a warrant to get the records showing who the deposit box belonged to—he believed that if the Repo Men stayed true to form, they'd "repossessed" something on behalf of someone else.

And Blackstone couldn't tell Max what we knew; the FBI had confirmed it to be The Box, the one they'd been watching. And that meant...what? Pellegrini had known the feds had been using the box as a trap, so he'd had it "picked up." But why hire someone when the Wreckers had shown they were as capable of in-smash-out as anyone? It wasn't like the feds would think the heist had been ordered by someone *else*.

It was Blackstone's job to ask what it all meant—Jacky's, too, if she ever took him up on his standing offer to come back for good—but even if there was no discernable connection between the bank job and my dream the knot in my stomach wouldn't go away. The Sentinels go out of town, and suddenly old business was back. *All* my old business.

You're being paranoid, Hope. I ignored Jacky's past observations on the subject of paranoia.

Paperwork done, I found the rest of the team hanging out in the Clubhouse—Jamal's name for the Young Sentinels' common room.

Everyone says that girls are more emotionally evolved than boys, but sometimes I wonder. Brian sat talking to Kindrake like her dragon hadn't eaten him less than two days ago. *I* held an unworthy grudge, and I hadn't even been the victim. Typically, Reese was trying to edge into their conversation; buried in Goth makeup or not, Kindrake was reasonably cute and the self-evident fact that she just didn't seem to be into *him* made her that much more irresistible.

Jamal and Shell—physically present in her prosthetic body—were still playing Halo. His fingers moved too fast for natural reflexes, which meant he had to be speeding but... I laughed and shook my head when everyone looked at me. From the speed of the enemy on the screen, Shell was ticking up the clock-time in the game to match Jamal.

"Boss?" Mal asked. *He* was typically studying, although he'd already been accepted to the University of Chicago.

"At ease, everybody." I'd left my cape, mask, and gloves in my rooms—in an emergency I could always grab a set on the way out. I chose a couch opposite the chatty trio, slouching down next to Ozma. She sat quietly, knitting lace. I didn't ask.

"And don't call me boss." *Because it completely freaks me out.* "Fearless leader if you really must. Anyway, we're still all grounded—they let me out to play this morning because I'm the only A Class flying brick in town today and something came up."

Kindrake had the grace to look guilty, and I tried to think nicer thoughts.

"She seems to like our Brian," Ozma observed quietly, tucking her legs up to give me room. So much for nicer thoughts. And that wasn't right; whatever stupid choices she'd made before, Kindrake was here and apologizing to the right person—taking it any other way was just wrong. I looked away and caught Ozma's smile, the one that said she was aware of my problem.

I *liked* Brian. It was as simple and as stupid as that. After my false-positive alarm with Seven, I'd wondered if I was still able to "fall in love," or at least the heart-pounding, attention focusing, love euphoria that Shell blamed on oxytocin and dopamine. It turned out I still could, and I wasn't happy about it.

Shell's theory was that I'd imprinted on Brian when he'd rescued me, and it had certainly been a high-stress moment, but this time I flatly refused to play. I wasn't the kind of girl Brian went in for, and that was okay, really. And in retrospect, I knew I hadn't fallen for Seven because if I really *had* then I would have been too scared to risk it. The way I felt about Brian… if I got crushed again I wouldn't be able to stay. Or he wouldn't, and he had to; in a weird way, Ozma—and Nox and Nix—had become his family.

So I'd have to go join Heroes Without Borders or the Hollywood Knights or something, and that wasn't going to happen either. It was what it was, and I'd get over it. I'd grown up that much, at least.

"One little drop of Love's Measure would clear that right up," Ozma murmured without looking up from her needles.

I barely kept from rolling my eyes. Using magic to play with people's minds wasn't exactly verboten in her rulebook; she'd turn you into a contented hat and then use crystalized Water of Oblivion to wipe your memory of it afterward if she didn't feel you deserved to keep the experience as a lesson (a favor she hadn't done for Spinner), but I'd been relieved to find we drew the same line at anything that shaded into brainwashing. So her offer was a dig and a test, and not a nice one. Which was totally Ozma; she was royal, she was courteous, she was Good, but she wasn't *nice*.

Nice hadn't ruled a small empire for a hundred years, and nice wouldn't liberate Oz.

She made a final twist with her needles and neatly bit off the threads, spreading it out so I could see it: a short ribbon of delicate snowflake lace, so white it seemed to glow.

"Moonmoth silk."

"Okay…"

Instead of explaining, she took my hand and wound it round my ring-finger, tying it into a neat little bow so that it made a tiny lace ring. "Don't take it off until you have to." she whispered and leaned in to kiss my cheek, soft as the brush of a falling petal. A bloom of warmth pulsed where she touched my skin, echoed in my finger where the lace hugged it tight.

I rubbed my cheek. Amazingly nobody else even blinked. Only Grendel seemed to be looking our way at all.

"Well, thank you? I didn't get you anything?"

She laughed quietly, an innocently inscrutable sweet-sixteen centenarian. "You will. Remember, do not take it off too soon. The Question Box said you will be traveling a long way today. Alone."

I froze, breath caught. "Then what—"

"*Astra*," Blackstone spoke in my earbug. "*I need you to get your go-bag and go now. You are meeting your ride over Ohio.*"

Sometimes I really do hate magic.

I ran. "How long will I be gone? Where am I going?"

"*Classified. This comes through DSA channels.*"

I stumbled and stopped. The DSA. Now I knew where I was going and wasn't sure I wanted to go there. Alone?

"*Astra?*"

I got going. "I'm here. I— What's happening?"

"*I don't know, my dear. The call came from Director Kayle's office. Your help is requested and required, and you've been called up through your Illinois State Militia officer's commission.*"

That almost stopped me again. Our state commissions were partly intended to *protect* capes like us from getting drafted by Washington—which meant the DSA had had to get hold of the *governor* and get his permission to activate me while I'd been showering and doing paperwork. Telling myself that this had to be a good thing didn't stop the churning in my stomach. What was going *on*?

The elevator doors didn't close fast enough for me, and I spent the seconds before they opened on the bay spinning in my head. Every question I wanted to ask would just have led back to "classified," so I didn't. "Understood, sir. The review? The team?"

"*Will be taken care of. Your testimony is recorded and if there are further questions then they can wait. Good luck, Astra.*"

The doors opened and it took just seconds for me to pull the rest of my uniform off my designated rack. Sliding my gloves on, I was careful of Ozma's gift. Go-bag over my shoulder, I launched up and out of the still opening hatch. "Shell?"

"Right here!" Shell floated beside me. "What the hell is going on?"

"Like I know? Shell…" I swallowed the thickening lump in my throat. Sunday was two days away, but… "I need you to tell Mom and Dad I probably won't be to Mass and dinner Sunday, that I'm away for a while and they won't be hearing from me. Tell them everything's okay."

"No worries, I'll cancel for us."

"No! You should go. And—" I'd forgotten about Julie. The lump got worse. "I need you to keep my promise with Julie tonight. Please."

"Huh? What would I *say*?"

"Tell her everything's alright with us. Tell her I'll be back and we'll talk for just hours. Tell her I love her?"

"Okay…" Nobody could sound more dubious, and I had to laugh despite my twisting gut.

"Love you too, Shell. Point me?"

She nodded and faded out. A virtual targeting icon appeared in my sight, red glow laying out my course. I turned and poured on the speed, trying to shut out the useless questions filling my head. It was barely lunchtime, hours till sunset, but I couldn't keep one thought away.

Jacky is so going to kill me.

Chapter Eight

"As a cape, probably the hardest things for me to get used to were the concepts of authority *and* legal jurisdiction. *In the comic books and movies, superheroes see a problem and they help because they can, any way they can. But national, state, and city governments are authorized and empowered to keep their citizens safe and do justice, and capes work with the system and the laws or they're outlaws by definition. Vigilantes. And Vigilantes are public challengers of the rule of law; they undermine what we try and accomplish and get a lot more attention than simple lawbreakers from every government agency. As a cape, if you want to do any good and have it last, you've got to have the backing of those empowered to let you do it."*

Astra, from her speech at the 20th Midwestern Crisis Intervention and Aid Conference.

I love flying, and even with everything happening Ohio was beautiful from three thousand feet.

I could have spent the time making personal calls, but I'd learned from experience that doing that at the beginning of a mission didn't help *anybody*. While they sound great in dramas "I might not make it so I just wanted to tell you…" conversations are never good. I could have asked Shell to try and find out what was happening, but Blackstone had told me everything he could without violating security; encouraging her to hack her way into government files to see what wasn't supposed to be seen qualified as a Bad Idea. So since I hadn't had time to stop in the chapel and light a few candles, I directed a few prayers to Mary of the Pagans and enjoyed my high-speed flyover while I could.

All too soon I saw my ride. A business jet, I'd have blown right past it with a wave except that Shell's targeting icon settled right on it.

"Shell?"

"That's it. And your costume sensors say they just lit you up with military lidar. Smile, I'm talking to them."

I tried to look unthreatening—not that hard for me—while wondering where the plane's hidden metal-storm gun might pop out from if they didn't like what they heard; laser targeted metal-storm machine guns that could empty their hundred-thousand round barrel magazines in seconds were the military's preferred defense against ground-to-air missiles and hostile fliers these days.

"You're cleared, and Dispatch is handing you off. See you!" Coming from her, the cheerful handoff was a coded promise; she'd still be with me through our neural link, a silent ghost.

Closing with the unmarked plane, I spotted its non-standard hatch—a sliding hatch instead of hinged. Etiquette dictated I match course and drift forward to where the pilot could see me, but the hatch opened first in obvious invitation. I accepted.

Pulling myself into the snug "airlock", a tight fit for me and my bag, I closed and dogged the outer hatch. The inner hatch, this one hinged, opened before I could undog it.

"Hello, Astra." Veritas held the door, greeting me in his usual uninflected near-monotone even as our ride banked into a hard left. Even on a plane he wore his ubiquitous shades, and I never had figured out if they were Verne-tech or fashion statement. "Glad you could join us."

"Us?"

Stepping by him, I lowered my go-bag to the floor with a heavy clank. That elicited a raised eyebrow (like he thought I'd leave my armor and maul at home?). He dogged the hatch and stood back, and he hadn't changed a bit in the time since I'd last seen him; hands on hips and halfway into his pockets, head cocked, he looked at me like I was something very interesting but probably inconvenient.

"Us. Right this way." He pointed us down the short hall leading away from the hatch and cockpit. The oak-paneled door at the end stood open, and he ushered me through ahead of him. I nearly backed right back out.

The executive's cabin was crowded, half the space taken up by five helmeted US Marshals in full blue and gray body armor. The guns they cradled had to be Verne-tech; obviously designed to be able to put a dent in me if they needed to, I'd never seen anything remotely like them outside a blockbuster sci-fi movie. If they missed, they'd probably blow big holes in the jet; if they didn't miss, *I'd* probably put a big hole in the jet. The guns pointed down, but that wasn't very reassuring because the man sitting across from them could order them used with one word.

I was sharing my ride with Director Kayle, head of the Department of Superhuman Affairs. And he didn't look happy.

"Hello, Ms. Corrigan. Won't you sit down?"

And just like that I felt like a fraud in a stupid costume. It had been awhile since I'd last felt awkward wearing my superhero outfit—especially since I'd gotten Andrew to redesign it without the wedgy-inducing thong butt—but here everyone was in a suit or a battlesuit and I was just the girl in primary colors.

But the Director didn't *look* like a man who made conspiracy theorists salivate like Pavlov's Dog in a cathedral bell choir. He could have disappeared into any crowd. Thin face, high receding hairline, he looked like a fussy corporate suit except that he watched me with eyes that weren't vague at all.

And they wouldn't be. As President, the man had successfully led the country for six years, through the aftermath of the Event and everything that went with it plus two short wars; he was *sharp*.

"Please," he said, pointing to the seat across from him. Next to it, a steel bucket filled with ice offered bottled water and sodas. I sat, tucking my cape back.

He watched me settle, smiling at something. Reaching over, he selected a bottle of spring water and opened it for me.

"When was the last time you were called to the principal's office?"

"What?" came out before I could stop it, and I flushed hotly.

He opened a bottle for himself, took a sip.

"I have a daughter not much older than you, and she didn't have your sterling school record. She was summoned to the principal's office a number of times, and I imagine she wore a face much like yours—wondering which of her crimes she'd been caught at and sent up for.

He gave me what he probably supposed was a reassuring smile. "You haven't been 'sent up'."

"Oh. Okay," was all I could think to say.

"Not that there aren't some consequences of your being here. Have you heard from your friend since you boarded the plane?"

"My— Shell? How do you know—? Shell!" She should have been in my ear with a whispered *Great googly moogly!* the instant she saw the Director through my eyes. "Shell?" Complete and thought-numbing silence.

The Director waited for me to un-panic and I took deep breaths, remembered I was holding a bottle, and gulped down cold water. I focused hard on not destroying the bottle. Was this the day they came for Shell and I became a supervillain?

He seemed to read my mind.

"Perhaps I should also tell you that your friend is not being called to the principal's office, either. We are aware of many people whose actions are not always strictly legal, who nonetheless are useful to us or to people useful to us. Your other friend Jacky, for example. So long as they follow some form of Hippocrates' dictum 'Do no harm' and do not publicly flout the law, we are mostly content to leave them to their own devises. Even my department's resources are not bottomless, after all."

"So Shell is safe?" I asked, not believing it.

"As long as she does not do anything which would make it necessary to commit resources to find her, yes. And as long as you are somewhere in the picture, I do not think that is likely to happen. Apparently, you are a moderating influence."

Okay. Okay. I could live with that. They knew. They knew and they had countermeasures, but if they'd always known then we were alright, right? I took another breath, made myself relax. "But she can't be here? She— she'll be going crazy not knowing what's happening to me."

"A good opportunity to see how she behaves without you to check her. Considering what we believe her to be capable of, that in itself pays for this trip. But no, she can't be here because she won't be able to be there, either. And while we are aware that your link and her access to your memories makes it impossible for you to keep any of this from her afterwards, you will not share any classified details of your trip with anyone else. In fact… Veritas?"

Veritas had taken a seat beside the bodyguards, and now he produced a leather-bound file for his boss. The Director handed it to me.

"Sign it."

I opened the file. It held a stapled set of pages spelling out that Camp Necessity and all operations associated with it came under the heading of "secrets vital to national security." By signing I acknowledged that any further unauthorized disclosure of what I now knew or might learn regarding said base would be considered an act of espionage and quite possibly treason.

I signed.

"Thank you." He handed the file to Veritas and sat back. "Now tell me about your recent communication from Kitsune, in every detail."

It didn't take long, even with my good dream recall. When I finished, he sat silently tapping his chin for what seemed like forever, and I almost hiccupped on a sudden thought. I never *did* get Chakra to check my head. Now didn't seem the time to say that.

Finally, he sighed. "I won't ask how you got from a dream of a burning town to knowing about Camp Necessity." He ignored my wince. "But I do need to ask why you feel that you need to become more involved in this. Surely your previous communications from this Kitsune were also merely informational? Do you think that he expects you to act directly on this one, seeing that it is rather distant and in no way affects you or anyone you know personally?"

I was so used to having Shell pop up with a snarky comeback at a moment like this that my thoughts spun, completely unbalanced.

"Camp Necessity is a town, right?" I asked, feeling my way.

He nodded. "Certainly a special town, but yes."

"Then there are civilians there. Bystanders. If… if whatever might happen happens, someone should be there for them. Not to protect projects or secrets. Someone needs to be there for them."

He tapped his chin some more (I wondered if he knew he was doing it or if it was his "tell") then gave a quick smile. This time it looked more natural.

"That will do." Reaching into his suit jacket, he pulled out a silver disk and dropped it in my hand. "Veritas will brief you on your way there." He rose and buttoned his jacket, nodded to his bodyguards, and they all vanished in an eye-twisting motion that seemed to yank them beyond the horizon without leaving the room.

I turned the disk over, and almost dropped it.

It was a deputy's badge.

Episode Two

Chapter Nine

"Expertise is only good for what you know. The problem is that experts think they know more than they do about stuff that they just don't."

   From the journal of Hope Corrigan

As Iron Jack, Dad had been a deputized US Marshal for the first months after the Event. Then-President Kayle had federally deputized *all* the early capes as an end run around uncooperative state governments, but the temporary measure lapsed as things got organized and the Crisis Aid and Intervention team system made it unnecessary. And this wasn't a marshal's badge; it was a deputy sheriff's badge for some place called Littleton.

   Turning the badge over and over in my hands, I realized that its back had been designed to clip to my left shoulder where my cape joined my suit. They'd made it for me.

"Where you're going, your CAI certification and militia commission are irrelevant," Veritas guessed my thoughts. "You'll need it for as long as you stay, which could be awhile."

"What is going *on*?" My voice sounded as small as I felt, and I cleared my throat. He shrugged.

"How much do you know about the Most Serene Republic of Cuba?"

"That it's an island? That the Tyrant is a mysterious superhuman nobody knows anything about? Only what's available in public news sources; Cuba hasn't come up in Blackstone's threat assessments."

"No, it wouldn't." Veritas made himself comfortable where his boss had sat. "The US government has never changed Cuba's 'rogue state' status, but the Serene Republic's new government doesn't vocally threaten us or, so far as we have been able to determine, sponsor international terrorism aimed at America. But it does refuse to allow extradition, and it harbors international fugitives and their money and gives material support to superhuman revolutionaries as long as they're not targeting the US."

"Why?"

Veritas shrugged. "No idea. The Tyrant has pretty much transformed Cuba in the short time he's ruled it. He's liberalized its command economy to something approaching American capitalism. He released all of the old regime's political prisoners, he allows freedom of the press, he's made local government completely elective, and he's opened Cuba's borders for international observers, tourists, free trade. He even allows Cubans who want to, to emigrate. But he *is* a superhuman autocrat and dictator."

He actually smiled, a stunning first for him even if it wasn't a nice smile.

"At least he's honest about that—he did name himself 'The Tyrant' after all. He's just not a totalitarian tyrant; so long as you don't break the stripped-down law code he's imposed, you have nothing to worry about. Stay inside the lines he's painted, and it's almost libertarian. But break any serious criminal laws, or convince the Tyrant that you're a threat, and you may find yourself visited by the Upright Men. If that happens you *will* disappear, and you may never be seen again. There is no legal due process and no appeal."

He opened a bottle of his own, a fruity soda I never would have guessed for his preference, and took a sip, lounging back.

"So the Serene Republic prospers. It's been less than two years since the Second Revolution brought capitalism and 'democracy' back in, and the average Cuban's income has increased more than five hundred percent. Now they're just poor instead of desperately poor, but unless something changes they'll catch up with the rest of the developed world in a decade or two. Naturally, most Cubans fanatically support the Tyrant."

"Then—I don't understand. If his government is popular, and he's not threatening us, why are we worried about him?"

"It's simple, really. Camp Necessity is vital to our security, and it's on Cuban soil. Its mere existence is an affront to Cuba's sovereignty. The Tyrant has refused to recognize the Perpetual Lease, and we have no idea what he, or his Upright Men, are capable of if he decides to try and seize it."

He took a long drink, stretched out his legs. "In my opinion, the Tyrant's playing a long game—he knows if he tried to take Camp Necessity then he'd be at war with us, but so long as we don't know if he could actually take it then we'll leave him alone so that he's not encouraged to try. But he's not the only threat, especially with the conference coming up, and he would benefit from any event that closed it. So here you are."

"So here we are," I echoed, determined not to ask about this *conference*. "I need to speak to Blackstone."

"There's a phone that can call out in front. Satellite uplink."

"Thank you." Standing and making my way forward, past the hatch we'd come in through, I found a tiny room with a desk and screen. It had no instructions, just a pad, so I dialed Blackstone's cell. One ring.

"Astra, good. Just one moment." A second later the screen lit as he forwarded the connection to his desk. "And how are you?" His smile fought with the deep lines on his brow, but I couldn't read any anxiety there.

"I've been deputized, sir, and might be gone awhile." We were certainly being recorded, and I took a moment to match his calm. "Will that be possible, given everything?"

He scowled thoughtfully, nodded. "The Sentinels are staying south for a few more days, but given your performance this morning I think that as long as we don't allow you to disappear from Chicago we should be able to keep the public reassured."

"But I *am* gone."

"And *I* am a magician, my dear. Trust me on this." He smoothed his beard, considering. "Public calm aside, I don't think we need worry unduly about a few days." He looked through the screen at me for a long moment. "Yes, we can cover your responsibilities here for the days you need. So, go with my blessing. And be careful. Hope? I would miss you should anything happen."

I nodded, swallowing around a suddenly tight throat. "Yes, sir. I'll be careful."

"Until later, then. God bless."

He hung up, and I sat for a minute before making my way back to the lounge room. Veritas sat reading an epad, and he set it aside to show me the rest of the jet's amenities, especially the freshly stocked pantry—but he wasn't interested in speculation and wouldn't tell me more about the camp. I made a roast beef and provolone sandwich and managed to eat most of it, but I spent most of the flight playing with my new badge.

I felt the damp air the instant they undogged the hatch, both inside and outside hatches this time since we'd landed. And the heat; Chicago was warming, but it was obviously sweaty shirt-sleeve weather in Cuba. Two Navy sailors boarded the plane and one opened a cabinet to heft what had to be Veritas' luggage. The other—

"Don't—" I said too late to stop him and he fell over my go-bag when it didn't come *up*. I helped him up, picked it up and slung it over my shoulder. "Sorry! Do you need to take it through security?"

"No ma'am. You're clear." He shook himself, watching my bag like it might *do something*. I smiled apologetically and he shook his head again. "Right this way."

The Caribbean sun beat down on the runway as we climbed in the jeep that pulled up beside our ride. I half expected Shell to pop up once we pulled away from the jet, but she didn't. How good *was* the government's anti quantum-signaling tech, really? Back at the beginning of everything, the Teatime Anarchist had told me that he'd been carefully "seeding" the present with future-tech to speed scientific progress. Or maybe the government had actually managed to recover something from the Dark Anarchist's secret lair in Nevada—or had they broken his network and found other bases? Of course it could always be Verne-tech at work, and probably was.

And the silence in my head seriously bothered me; even when she'd *been* Galatea instead of just piloting her, Shell always been able to link with me through my earbug and mask-cam. Doctor Mendel would probably have something to say about my dependence when I got home.

I expected them to take us to the big naval base I'd seen as we landed but instead they drove us towards the hills, in the opposite direction. Five minutes on a well-paved road took us past three checkpoints with nothing to see beyond them but fencing, pill-box barracks, and the next checkpoint. Passing the last dropped us into a valley with one long garage bunker at its near edge.

We pulled into the open end, through doors big enough to pass loaded semi-trucks, and they passed us off to armed and armored marshals looking like the ones that had guarded Director Kayle on the jet. Our new escorts brought out pallets for our bags and whisked them away, then led us down a hallway with suspiciously heat-active walls. My super-duper vision picked out weird and changing infrared patterns along the entire hall and I snuck a glance at Veritas, but he kept his shades on even in here. The doors at the end opened before we got to them, letting us out into another bay, and I blinked. The marshals had loaded our stuff into the back of a dusty red... pickup truck? What?

They'd parked the truck on top of a steel grid that sat flat on the concrete but was framed so that it could be raised if they needed to get at whatever sat underneath it. A matching grid hung suspended over the truck, holding up a machine that looked vaguely like a generator. Veritas accepted the keys from a marshal and waved me in.

"Say cheese," he said as soon as I closed the door.

"What—" *Flash!* "Hey! What was *that*?" I blinked automatically, realized that the flash that had whited out the world hadn't left any after-images burned into my eyes.

But the bay we'd sat in was *gone*. The truck sat in the middle of a dusty road, and the only thing in sight was a big wood gate with a wood sign painted in big white letters that said "Welcome to Littleton."

I read the sign twice, looked around.

"Gee, it's kind of small. And unpopulated."

"Smartass." Veritas actually laughed—one short "ha!" but I was too busy looking around to score a victory point. The air was *dry*, no hint of coastal humidity or smells, and almost as cool as Chicago's. Beyond the gate the road wound over a low hill, and I firmly sat on the impulse to scramble out of the truck and launch myself to get a better view—somehow I knew I wouldn't see the blue Caribbean, but I had no idea what I'd see and it was unnerving. Veritas climbed out and opened the gate, then got back in and started the truck. He pulled far enough forward to close the gate behind us then drove us over the hill, and now I was well and truly freaked.

Well, there's the water tower.

Big and white and proudly painted with the US Marshals seal, it stood over a town that could have been lifted out of the Iowa heartland. A grid of tree-lined streets with shops and community buildings surrounding a town square in the center, it looked like the kind of small but close-packed township laid out before cars came along and replaced feet for urban transit.

"Population five thousand, give or take," Veritas supplied.

I nodded. "Uhuh." It was like staring at a Thomas Kinkade painting. Or a Christmas town in a snow globe, minus the snow. "Does it have seasons?"

"Yes. Midwestern and like clockwork. You can set your calendar by them." Downshifting with a grind of gears, he drove us down the hill and into town.

Up close it didn't feel any less surreal. Evening shadows angled across sleepy streets, and even Main Street wasn't busy enough to merit a stoplight. People we passed *waved*. I waved back; it was so completely and utterly *Mayberry* that I was hearing the whistled Andy Griffith theme music in my ears.

No, I was actually *hearing* something; a high, thin percussion barely on the edge of my super-duper hearing's aural range. So soft that birdsong drowned it out, it came from everywhere—or from the odd looking lampposts, white globes on top of white poles under wide white metal bonnets. Besides the cars, they were the only things that didn't look like they belonged in the 1930s.

Right, officially weird now.

"You can take off the mask," Veritas said. "The US Marshals Department contracted with a big Merlin-type for an added layer of security. Photographs or video files that might identify Littleton or anyone in it just turn into gray screen or fogged shots when taken out of here—you won't be spreading images of your naked face around."

"I'll think about it." I looked out at the sleepy streets. "What am I doing here?"

He gave me his usual bland look, but his lip twitched. "What do you mean?"

"If this was a Sentinels operation, I'd have had a mission briefing by now! Not 'Here's a deputy's badge, Astra'. What am I supposed to be *doing* here?"

"You invited yourself, remember? Director Kayle just thought you should have something to do while you're here. Idle hands and all that."

"Yes, but—" I shut my mouth. The man was laughing behind his poker face and what *had* I expected? To be shown right to a situation room, read in on Camp Necessity's security measures, handed a role in their threat-response plans? Littleton had to have the best security and best security people available to the government and I was just an independently contracted cape with less than two years' experience. And I'd had a *dream*, one really short on details; what could I offer beyond "I think something's coming?"

I was lucky they'd even let me *in*.

We turned a corner and drove down a street that ended in open gates, brick pillars topped by an ironwork arch. The plaque declared the redbrick and white trim buildings beyond to be the Harper Institute. The main building we parked in front of wasn't that big, only three stories, but with more buildings behind it. It looked like a tiny but very elite university.

We got out and reached I back for my bag.

"Leave it." Veritas squinted at the building in the late afternoon sun.

"Unofficially? You're the gun in the nightstand, the fire extinguisher in the car trunk. Officially? You're here to consult with the Oroboros Research Group."

"The what now?"

"The Oroboros Research Group. Your Teatime Anarchist adventures exposed you to future knowledge, which means you're aware of their field of research. Besides, you know another member of the group already. C'mon, let's get you introduced."

I stumbled and almost took a chunk out of the curb with my foot. *What?*

Chapter Ten

"I have a vampire for a friend and another who's a computer AI and her twin. I've talked to time-travelers and been to space. Now I've been to a town that isn't there. How strange can the world get? Oh let me count the ways."

From the journal of Hope Corrigan.

The inside didn't match the outside, but the chrome and smart-screen glass entry hall was the least interesting thing about it; the most interesting thing was the lady who greeted me. She was a cat.

Well, not a *cat*, not even a smiling Cheshire Cat, more an anime cat-girl except that the Japanese fashion for anthromorphs was big-eyed and cutesy. This lady was what would happen if you took one of the performers from Andrew Lloyd Webber's most successful musical and put her in a business suit: a corporate Jellicle Cat.

"Good morning, Astra." She shook my hand without hesitation. "I'm Director Althea Shaw. Call me Ali." Her slightly inhuman features made it hard to tell if she was happy to see me, but despite her welcome her voice sounded flat. Opening the folder in her other hand, she handed me a gold security pass to hang around my neck.

Veritas abandoned me to her care with a parting "Astra." I blinked, watching him walk away until Ali cleared her throat. She led me to the elevator bay, a row of glass-sided tubes next to an open well in the center of the entry hall. We rode the elevator cab down three floors; through the glass I could see that each floor opened to the well with hallways branching off in a starburst pattern.

"We stacked the complex deep instead of high to preserve the small town feel outside," she explained when I looked down and tried to count the levels below us. "Twelve stories deep, most of the facility is underground."

"How long has it been here?"

"Seven years. It started with the labs, but expanded for data storage and then for the think-tanks and research groups. We almost held the Omega Operation briefings here—we did design and build the Gungnir Platform in-house."

That got my attention. "Was that *safe*?" The anti-missile Gungnirs I'd helped deliver to target in last year's attempted Electro-Magnetic-Pulse attack—a near save the public still knew nothing about—had been *nuclear-bomb pumped* gamma lasers. Small nukes, but still nukes.

"Safe enough; we tested them elsewhere. Right this way." She took me down a wide glass-walled hall. Everyone we passed gave her a nod and me a look but left us alone. Stretches of the walls were frosted, but others were clear and looked into conference rooms and offices.

"While you're here you will be working with a select research team," she explained as we walked. "You have a great deal in common and I think you'll like them; they have a secret handshake and you even get to spit."

Turning us down a smaller side hall, she ushered me into a conference room with an island of standing desks surrounded by large smart-glass screens. The room wasn't small, but the five people already in it filled it nicely—one of them the *last* person I'd have expected to see here.

Standing together as a group when we came through the door, they'd obviously been told I was coming. Ali introduced them as the Oroboros Research Group: the dark, uniformed man with handlebar mustaches was General Arun Rajabhushan, the thin, bearded European man wearing a scholar's jacket with padded elbows was Doctor Leiman Hall, the large blonde woman in the blue suit was Doctor Vivian Ash, and the deeply black and completely bald man in the sport coat and sweater was Doctor Kelly Humphries.

General Rajabhushan gave me a warm smile. The rest of their responses to our introduction were mixed, but I paid barely enough attention not to be rude; the *fifth* team-member couldn't possibly be here and it was all I could do to keep from screaming, from grabbing onto her and flying us out of here, up the open well, through the entry hall's skylight, and *out*.

The fifth Oroboros was Shelly.

"She's all yours," Director Shaw informed everyone. "Send her back to me when you're done." She turned and walked out. *Huh?*

Behind everyone else's back, Shelly grinned wide enough to break her face. I had to tear my eyes away from her to focus on the general, and I couldn't have formed a coherent statement to save my life but Mom's social training saved me.

"It's a pleasure to meet all of you." Okay, not exactly a clever response, but better than babbling. The old general's eyes crinkled, like he saw right through me and knew just how badly I was boggled.

"The pleasure is mutual. I understand that you are not certain how long your stay will be?"

Pull it together, Hope. "No, I'm sorry, but I don't."

He nodded. "Of course. You are far too valuable out in the world. Then we shall treat you as a new adjunct, and take as much advantage of your experience as time permits. We should start, I think, with an explanation of our purpose. Doctor Hall?"

The scholar cleared his throat, dropping into lecture mode.

"Long before the Event, physicists considered time travel to be possible in theory while offering no solution to the problem of causality—the principle that causes must precede effects. How can 'after', which depends upon 'before', have any effect upon 'before'?

He watched me for objections or confusion, went on. "The problem of causality is not limited to time travel; visions of the future, precognitive awareness, prophecy, all violate causality. If a psychic foresees a disaster, and that disaster is then prevented, since it did not happen what did the psychic see?

"Although of course the scientific community still takes an interest in the question, the Event rendered the whole argument moot. The apparent paradox of future-knowledge is beside the point; breakthrough psychics and mystics have made future-knowledge very real."

Dr. Hall's pedantic drone reminded me of every tenured University of Chicago professor, but everyone kept quiet for it. Having pronounced the reality of foreknowledge, he even stopped to give me a moment to raise my hand. I didn't.

"The Defense Advanced Research Projects Agency quietly set up the Oroboros Research Group the year of the Event, under the direction of the Department of Defense. DARPA brought together a team of scientists, statisticians, behavioral psychologists, economists, historians, and a collection of the first confirmed precognitive 'psychics.' Their emphasis was national security but their first question was simply, 'Can a foreseen future event be changed?' Or is future-knowledge itself causative? Are we doomed by our foreknowledge, as in the Greek tale of King Oedipus?

"The answer to that question was a resounding No. Foreseen futures can be changed and psychic and mystic visions are warnings, not unalterable prophecies which fulfill themselves.

"The second question the team asked was, 'Can we learn enough about foreseen events to guide policy?' The answer is 'sometimes'. The Kayle Administration's international policy benefited tremendously from Oroboros Research Group projection papers. Oroboros' prediction of the collapse of China based on extrapolations from three precognitive episodes led to President Kayle's Pacific Initiative and the creation of the alliance system that became the League of Democratic States."

He paused again for any questions from the class. Inside I was...not panicking, exactly, but working hard not to wig out. This was one of the Big Secrets. Maybe the biggest.

I hadn't followed politics much, before my breakthrough. *Now* I knew that a lot of people had wondered how President Kayle—before the Event a political party player with zero interest in international politics—had managed to guide not just *us* but pretty much the western world and half of Asia through the blowup and mess that followed the Event. Half the nations that came through it intact owed it to the alliance web he'd seemed to spin up out of nothing but pure will, an uncanny sense of timing, and the ability to always seem to guess right. President Infallible.

Most of the conspiracy theorists out there believed that Director Kayle was a secret breakthrough. Instead he'd had the Oroboros.

"Who knows?"

"Excuse me?" Obviously not the question he'd been expecting from me.

"Who knows about the Oroboros and what you do?"

"The leaders of the nations making up the League," General Rajabhushan answered for him. "The US President, the prime ministers of India, Australia, Japan, Great Britain, and the other parliamentary states. They agree to have their memories of the group's true nature removed when they leave office. The same deal applies to members of the group itself, with a few exceptions. In Littleton, only the Institute Director knows what we really do."

He chuckled, eyes crinkling in wry amusement.

"Wheels within wheels. Even here, to everyone outside the inner circle the Oroboros Research Group is just a think-tank of historians, economists, analysts, and political scientists dedicated to organizing intelligence data and pooling their expertise to write projection papers for the League's leadership. We have our own segregated system and security measures."

"So you keep your...precognitives?...here in Littleton?"

"No. Our psychic resources are scattered. Some are publicly known psis, but most aren't. *Here* we keep something much more valuable."

And this was it. I could tell by the way the others inhaled almost in unison. Even Shelly had an odd look on her face.

"Ms. Corrigan, do you believe in the possibility of time travel?"

...

Really? I mean, *really*? The big secret of the secret-handshake-and-spit Oroboros Research Group was the *Future Files*? If it wasn't for Shelly begging me with her eyes not to say anything, I'd have asked if I was being *punked*.

Mom would have been proud; I managed to keep all of that off my face—Social Face was good for *so* much more than just hiding boredom at society parties. My "Wow, really?" response to the next revelation, that the Teatime Anarchist (publicly America's most wanted terrorist before his confirmed death), had been a time traveler was a piece of art. I held it together while Doctor Hall rambled through an explanation of the massive file of multiple-choice future histories the Anarchist had left behind and told me all about the reconfiguring of the Littleton Cell of Oroboros to analyze and data-mine it.

It wasn't even the same Big Book of Contingent Prophecy that the Anarchist had entrusted to Shelly and me—it couldn't be, since they'd been working with it for over a year, before Shelly and I had finally turned it over to Blackstone to pass on. Which was a no brainer that made me want to face-palm; *of course* the Anarchist wouldn't have entrusted something so valuable just to two teenage girls.

I managed to keep it together and not melt with relief when the general passed me over to Shelly for "task orientation." Shelly solemnly ushered me out of the conference room and into a tiny office—her office, judging from the pictures. I was in half of them.

She closed the door, took two skipping steps, and threw her arms around me.

"Eeeee! This is fantastic! They told me you were coming! Where are you staying? Isn't this the best? *So* good!"

I managed to return the hug, mind spinning.

"Shelly, *how*?"

She pulled away, still almost dancing. "They waited till I'd spent two months going crazy in Springfield before they recruited me. So? What do you think?" She posed. Hair as close to my shade as it was possible to naturally get and pulled back in a tail, dressed in office pants and suit—even sensible slip-on shoes—she looked like a peppy teen intern.

"But *why*?" And when would I be able to manage more than two words?

She stopped bouncing, tapped her head. "The Future Files, duh. That, and my other post-death brain mods. Hope? You okay? Do you want to sit down?"

I nodded and dropped onto a little half-couch that crowded the wall under all the pictures.

"What are you *doing* here?"

"I said. They recruited me."

"But you were out of it!" I fought to keep my rising voice down. "You were back with your *mom*, back in school! Why would you... Shelly, you promised me no more tall buildings."

Her smile dimmed.

"That's not—that's not fair. It's not like I'm in the field, this is probably the safest place on the planet. And Mom's here. David, too. They always need good administrators."

They'd even brought in Mr. Hardt? I shook my head. "What about high school? Couldn't you—"

"Finish? Hang around for three years sitting in class learning stuff I already know? *You* liked school. I always thought it was a waste of a perfectly good day. Besides, they've got one here; I get three hours a day, art, PE, and lunch. Math? Science? I'm pre-loaded for biochem and biophysics degrees—I could *teach* the high school stuff. In my *sleep*."

"And you like it here?" She'd complained about *Springfield*—I couldn't imagine her happy in Littleton, population five thousand. And in a lab?

She shrugged defiantly.

"So it's a little quiet. But I'm *useful*, more useful than I would have been back in the Dome—they *need* me here." She scowled, looking at the screens that ringed her desk. "Fighting the future is tougher than I'd ever thought." Her eyes slid back to me. "And the attraction for Mom is we live in one of the safest places there *is*. That and I'm away from the internet. And now you're in, too. So sit and spill. How the hell did they pry you out of Chicago?"

"I volunteered?"

That took some explaining and she joined me on the couch while I went on about how I'd found out about the place— especially since I hadn't been looking for *her*. Nobody was; she'd spent the last few months pretending in all her texts and emails that she'd still been going to the private school they'd enrolled her in in Springfield. Because of course not only couldn't she tell me what she'd been *doing*, any references to Littleton had been redacted so cleverly I'd never notice any holes in her texts.

She pulled her feet up to rest her chin on her knees while I explained about the Kitsune-dream, Jacky's revelations, everything. I didn't have the heart to tell her that the pose didn't go with the clothes (and that was just the Mrs. Lori in my head, who Shelly had never listened to anyway).

When I finished she stared into space, absently rubbing her nose. Then she reached up and squeezed an earring I hadn't noticed, an elegant little pearl-in-silver piece. It *really* looked like the one Jacky had used just yesterday.

"Do you know why they brought you down here?"

"I asked—"

"I know why *you* came, but do you know why they let you come? Really? Are you going to help them mousetrap Kitsune?" My expression answered her question and she shook her head. "Geez, Hope. Jacky shouldn't have let you out of her sight."

"What are you *talking* about?"

She groaned, throwing up her hands.

"Hope! *You* wonder how Kitsune even knows about this place? Well, *they* have to be dropping bricks over it. The best security in the world, and I should know, and that sneaky little fox has *gotten in*. He has to have, because if he hasn't then... Forget it, Occam's Razor says he's here or at least popped in sometime so he knows what the place looks like. But if he's here now, how did he send you a dream? We're in a separate freaking universe—*telepaths* can't call out of here. So he really is 'magical', not that there was a whole lot of doubt there.

"And if he's here, why is he here? He's an *international criminal*, so the answer to that question can't be good. And why contact you? It makes no sense, but one thing our sneaky spy-guys have to be saying is that if he wanted to bring you here, and he's *still* here, he might try and touch you. So dangling you and watching very, very carefully may be the best chance they have to catch a magical shapeshifter who's already inside their security perimeter."

"Now that's just..."

She rolled her eyes. "Paranoid? We're talking about the DSA here. And the US Marshals Service. And the Office of Naval Intelligence. *Professional* paranoiacs. They're probably all hoping that Kitsune's running some kind of con, throwing up smoke to cover a steal, because then the only threat is him and not some 'other' that he knows about but they don't. But they won't be betting on it—they can't afford to."

I *so* wanted to disagree, but... "Veritas came with me."

"See? See? He's *got* to be running checks on everybody, beating the bushes to see if a fox jumps out. Even Kitsune can't hide from his truth-power if the guy asks him straight out. Easy question: 'What is your date of birth?' The boy or girl who lies is a four-legged varmint."

She flashed her old grin, eyes bright.

"But you know what this means, right? Kitsune has *challenged* you—to stop him or to help him. So let *them* try and find him—*we* are going to figure out if he's playing it straight and who he's warning us is coming to light up the town."

I wasn't quite as certain of our plan of action as Shelly, but it seemed like it would be a better use of our time than playing Nancy Drew and trying to find Kitsune ourselves. And *I* was beginning to wonder just how long I was here for; until Kitsune showed his hand or someone really tried to light the town on fire? What about everything else? I'd left a lot in the air in Chicago. The Bees. School. A media-crisis. At the very least, I needed to find a way to phone home.

Shelly had to go over an intelligence package before she headed home. She didn't threaten to drag me home with her, which would have made me suspicious if I'd had any brain left to think about it with; since the Oroboros didn't expect anything from me on my first day here she synced our phones and called a guide, a tiny Frisbee-shaped drone to escort me to the Director's office. The drone led me up to the third floor aboveground, taking us through three automatic security checks along the way and past Director Shaw's receptionist.

Ali welcomed me into her office with the same coolness as before, and I wondered if she was just one of those people who didn't accept capes. Which wasn't the same thing as not accepting breakthroughs, a good thing since she had to be one of the most exotic breakthroughs I'd ever seen; she was a calico cat-girl— predominantly white and orange but with black spots, one on the side of her nose that made her face oddly lopsided. She was also barely taller than me but much better endowed, which made her a *sexy* cat-girl even in the office suit, and she seemed comfortable enough with herself.

She pointed me to a chair. "So, are the two of you caught up?"

"Um, yes? I hadn't known we *needed* to catch up."

"Security protocol. Nobody living here is allowed to let anyone know they're living here. We all have covers, usually residency in a small town in the wilds of South Dakota."

"And how do you—" I shook my head. "What will I be doing here?"

"Other than working with the Oroboros and Sheriff Deitz?"

I didn't recognize the name. "If you already have the files, why do you need me? Or Shelly?" She didn't blink or ask what I was talking about.

"Shelly should be obvious."

"But she's not— She's not a computer anymore. She's just Shelly."

"So she's not useful?" Ali considered me, absently rubbing the black spot on her nose. "She's still got the highest IQ I've ever seen. You didn't know?"

"She never said!" *That* had to be obvious from my face.

"She scores above one-sixty on the Wechsler Adult Intelligence Scale. She also has true eidetic memory, she's effortlessly multilingual, and even her motor-learning levels are off the charts; she learned how to play the violin to a concert-worthy standard at the school here in only two months. She can multitask without loss of speed or reliability to the order of three parallel tasks, and that's something brain researchers have proven impossible. Her mind is unique."

I'd have sat if I wasn't already sitting. *Shelly, why didn't you tell me?*

Tilting her head, Ali made an odd little humming sound. "Shelly calls you her Blue Fairy? She says that she became a 'real girl' because of you?"

I laughed weakly. "I made a wish…"

"Then I would guess that your wish was for the Shelly you knew—who happened to be a hyper-intelligent AI—to be a living and breathing human being again. The result is a Shelly with as smart a meat-brain as it is possible to have. Magic tends towards the literal, but there are limits when outcomes conflict."

She said it nicely, for her anyway, not implying that I should have thought of all this. It didn't help; I'd made the mistake of thinking that human Shelly meant the same Shelly who'd impulsively jumped to her death at the age if fifteen, just with some memories added. *Stupid, stupid, stupid, Hope!* Then I'd cheered at the idea of her going just back to school, like she wasn't any different and the last two years hadn't happened. Why hadn't Shelly laughed in my face?

Obviously deciding she'd given me enough time, Ali stood up.

"The plan while you're here is to plug you into Shelly's own intern role while you are not working with the sheriff's office. Shelly has been focused on data-mining for patterns behind events recorded in what she likes to call the Big Book. I don't know how useful you will be, but while you are here you have been given to the Oroboros to offer…field perspective. And I would appreciate it if you could keep Shelly happy and not distract her."

She actually smiled, with the possibility of real warmth this time, and shook my hand again while I fumbled for the right answer to her underwhelming expectations. "The girl really is one of the best minds in the building."

Ali led me back down to the lobby, where Veritas mysteriously reappeared. He kindly ignored my befuddlement; if my head hadn't been still trying to wrap itself around how badly I'd misunderstood my BF and what she needed, I'd have started to feel like a package the way they handed me off.

This time he drove us less than three blocks, back onto what passed for their main street, pulling into a diagonal parking space while I was still thinking over everything that had just happened.

"This is your last stop," he said cheerfully. "Then I'll take you to settle in."

"Where—"

He pointed at the bronze plaque on the single-story brick building in front of us. *Littleton Sheriff's Office.*

He pulled out his cellphone. "Sheriff Deitz will orient you while I make some calls."

Okay... I got out, looking up and down the quiet street. Nobody nearby looked at all alarmed or even curious to see a cape get out of a truck. Squaring my shoulders, I pushed through the door.

And blinked. It really was a sheriff's office—in fact it reminded me of the one in Grand Beach: it was all wood paneling, with a big open space with three desks and extra chairs for people there on business. A huge photographic map showing everything from the X marking the Garage's entry-point in the south to the lake bordering the north side of town covered one wall. A wood rail divided the visitor's area with more chairs from the business side. It even had the cells in one corner, keeping everybody together in one big public room that was empty now except for Sheriff Deitz. *Deitz*, and I should have recognized the name.

"Astra." He looked up from his desk when I came through the door, then stood up and came around it, hand out. I pushed through the gate at the rail and we shook. "Glad that you made it. Did Veritas drop you? I can get your bags."

"No you can't. Well you probably could, but you'd sprain something and anyway he's outside—" I stopped talking. Same long-jawed, earnest face, same "How can I help you, ma'am?" attitude. Same small-town sheriff, except that he should have been in *Grand Beach*. I was meeting far too many people I knew today, and I took a breath. "Hi, Sheriff. It's good to see you again." *When I'm not under arrest, and what are you doing here?*

"You know, you can take off the—"

"I know." I took another breath and finally pulled off the mask and wig. Shaking out my bob I tried a smile.

He returned it. "That wasn't so hard, right? Sweet is out right now, but she'll be happy to see you."

"Angel is here, too?"

"It's a small world. When your little fight in Grand Beach last year put a media spotlight on the place, they rotated us both in here." He waved to a chair. "I never got a chance to tell you, good work with Villains Inc. Glad it turned out well; I see they gave you the badge."

"Yes. Why?"

"Really? They didn't tell you anything?"

I shook my head and he sighed. Leaning back, he propped his feet up on his desk.

"That figures. Let's start at the top. What do you know about Littleton?"

"Population five thousand, give or take? You use it for Witness Protection? Really, what *is* this place?"

"Brigadoon."

"What?"

"Sorry." His easy smile showed dimples. "Bad joke. About eight years ago, one of the crazier Verne-types working out of the Navy base labs got tired of the heat and decided to create himself a little home away from home. He was from Wisconsin. It took a while for the Navy guys to figure out where he was disappearing to and coming back from with lake fish you don't find in Cuba. Littleton is an extra-reality pocket."

Extra-reality: the first time I heard the term I'd thought it applied to virtual reality, but it was meant like extra*terrestrial* – something outside of our reality. Like Hypertime, or the Teatime Anarchist's potential futures. Or where Ozma said she came from. Brigadoon. *Now* I got the reference, and it didn't make me happy. Shelly had said—

"We're in another *reality*?"

"The Littleton Pocket. That flash you saw back in the Garage? That tuned you to Littleton's 'frequency', whatever that really means."

I tried to control my breathing, almost floated out of my chair. "How big is it? How do you get *out*?"

"All *you've* got to do is fly high enough, you'll pop right out of the bubble and be hanging over Cuba. Of course you might have a problem with the anti-air defense system locking onto you with Stinger missiles. If you need to fly out, hugging the ground and getting over the hills to the west takes you away from the bay. Walking or driving out is okay. We stick to the entry-point at the Garage for obvious reasons. All you've got to do is step across the boundary—it's not really sealed from the *inside*."

"That…that's good to know."

He frowned and leaned forward.

"Are you okay? It takes a lot of people that way, when they first realize they're 'somewhere else'. The point is, Littleton's an easy place to leave, but not an easy place to get to. You could know right where it is, but unless you're translated through the Garage it might as well be on Mars."

I made an effort to pull myself together. *Like you haven't seen lots weirder things than a town that isn't there.* "I can see where that would be attractive to Witness Protection, hiding out in another *reality*."

"Complete signals blackout, too. People, and the stuff we brought in with us, are the only things that can 'fall back' into the world. Nothing on the electromagnetic spectrum crosses over either way except through the Garage's translator system."

"So, everybody here is a researcher or a protected witness?"

"More or less. Plus political refugees, Witness Protection guests, Institute staff, teachers for the school, the kinds of service and civic people every town needs to run smooth. And us."

"And us. Me?" I reached up and touched the deputy's badge.

"And you. Somebody thought it would be a good idea to take advantage of you while you're here. And you might like something to do. You can get cats out of trees."

I found myself grinning. "Yeah, I can do that."

Sheriff Deitz, Paul, showed me "my" desk and issued me a special deputy phone. He also told me I could *text* out or send files, the exchange linked to the naval base and from there to the world through a repeater system, but to phone home I'd have to go back to the Garage, the secure building Veritas and I came in through.

Angel hadn't gotten back yet, but he didn't expect anything else tonight. Which was good; Littleton might be its own little world, but it was a world synced with Eastern Standard Time so they were an hour ahead of me and the whole day was starting to hit me hard anyway. He followed me out the door and watched as I climbed back in the truck, giving Veritas a nod as my handler shifted into reverse and backed us out.

"So are you square?" he asked as we drove down the street and around a corner.

"Gun in the nightstand. Got it."

"Good girl. And here we are."

I looked around; we'd barely come two blocks, and he pulled us up in front of a yard with low hedges fronting a gabled house of an architectural style at least a century old (with Dad's restoration hobby, I would know). The big tree in the front yard looked just as old as the architecture, which told me they'd either built around whatever the extrareality pocket's Verne-Type had created or they'd brought in a pretty powerful florakinetic or a versatile sorceress to "age" the town's trees.

And obviously I was done for the day if my mind was wandering away thinking about the age of local trees.

"Holybrook Rest," Veritas waved at the house; all that the place needed was snow to look like a holiday Hallmark card. "Best bed-and-breakfast in town. The two of them will take care of you."

I climbed out and got my bag. He didn't.

"The two of them? Aren't you—"

"Miles to go before I sleep, and it won't be here. See you around town." He shifted to first and drove away with a wave, leaving me once again to watch him go. I was beginning to think the man *liked* being mysterious. Or maybe he just liked doing it to me.

I hooked my go-bag over my shoulder. The walk up to the door had been planted with spring flowers, and the curlicue letters on the glass spelling out Holybrook Rest shouted taste and class. A bell over my head tinkled cheerfully when I pushed through the door into the cozy lobby.

"Welcome, Ms. Corrigan!" my host greeted me, and I stopped short before recovering. He didn't fit the postcard picture. Dark skinned, bearded, accent something Middle-Eastern—Iranian?—with diction that screamed "fancy English school," he instantly made me think of the evil vizier from Disney's *Aladdin*.

Which just *had* to be wrong; after all, Littleton was the safest place not on Earth, right? I still almost checked his shoulder for a smirking parrot.

"May I take your bag?"

"No— I'm sorry, I'm not being rude. It weighs more than two hundred pounds."

"I see. Well then, come right this way." He led me up the stairs, asking in friendly fashion how my flight had been. "Of course the Institute let us know you were coming," he supplied before I asked. The room he showed me was small but warmly welcoming, with a west-facing window that captured the evening sunlight. It had its own bathroom with a claw footed tub and everything was spotless and shiny, nothing worn. "Will this be acceptable?"

He sounded perfectly ready to order in carpenters and interior decorators if it wasn't, and I nodded automatically. His smile deepened.

"Very good then, I will leave you to your rest. Breakfast is served in the dining room at seven, and if you desire breakfast earlier or later cereal and fruit are always available. Good night."

He handed me the key and closed the door behind him with perfect silence, and I stared at it for a moment. Although the room was still warm and comfortable, part of the easy peace that had wrapped itself around me went with him and now I just felt tired.

A small table by the door held an old-fashioned house phone, and I picked up the card beside it. Under a boldly printed phone number it read *Holybrook Rest, Ibrahim Darvish, proprietor*.

I put the card down and unpacked.

The wardrobe didn't exactly have a place to hang my armor and maul, so I lined them up beside the bed where they looked ridiculously out of place with the patterned wallpaper and wainscoting. The rest went into the wardrobe and dresser: one spare field uniform, one set of casual civvies, one carefully packed "formal" costume (because you never knew), basic field gear, toiletries, several changes of underwear, and…glasses? Opening the little case, I discovered that someone—probably Nix—had slipped me a pair of Ozma's Anonymity Specs. I sat on the bed and just looked at them.

Why? For the first time since flying out of the Dome, I remembered her other gift and pulled off my glove.

The snug lace ring—moonmoth silk?—still hugged my finger. My glove hadn't smooshed it at all, and the tiny bow glowed almost impossibly white in the last beams of sunlight. Touching it brought a ghost of the petal kiss back to my cheek. She'd said not to take it off until I had to. She'd told me *twice*.

And now the specs. Like I'd need to be anonymous *here*.

Outside, the weird streetlamps were coming on as dusk settled on the town. What was going *on*? And really, what was I doing here?

Chapter Eleven

"According to the Littleton Almanac, today will be sunny with light breezes and occasional clouds, with a light rain after midnight when no-one is out to look at the stars. Tomorrow will give us a light rain at ten in the morning, but you real rain-lovers will have to wait two weeks from Saturday for the first big storm of the season. It will feature thunder and a great lightning show around six in the evening."

Littleton Radio weather report.

I stretched deliciously, opened my eyes, and the little girl sitting at the foot of my bed smiled shyly.

"Good morning!" she chirped. Long dark hair, warm brown skin, deep black eyes, arms folded around a much-loved teddy bear, she waited to see what I would do next.

"Save me from the cuteness." I covered my eyes, peeked between two fingers. "Nope. Still here."

She laughed, bouncing. "Silly! It's time for breakfast!"

"And you're my adorable little alarm clock?"

"Yes!" She nodded the way only little kids can, like their necks are made of rubber. I looked at the clock on the nightstand. Fifteen minutes till breakfast.

I kicked my feet up and down under the covers, bouncing her and making her giggle. "Then go tell your dad I'll be down to eat. Shoo. Go brighten his morning."

She scrambled off the bed and out the door, and I skinned out of my sleep shirt and shorts, wrapped a waterproof bandage from my field kit around Ozma's lace ring to protect it, and showered fast. Then I spent a long moment looking at my costume. If I wasn't *officially* functioning as Astra, girl-superhero, it just felt too weird to walk around in uniform. Fortunately I did have civies, even if only white shorts and a blue athletic shirt, matching sneakers. I pulled everything on in a moment, clipped the deputy's badge to a belt-loop, tidied up and went downstairs.

"Astra," General Rajabhushan greeted me at the breakfast table. Doctor Hall sat across from him, both in their soldier and scholar uniforms. My little alarm clock wasn't there, which was too bad—I'd been looking forward to a side of giggles with my eggs. Was she the number two of the *two* who would take care of me?

A cozy-wrapped coffee pot flanked by cream and sugar sat in the center of the table, and the general courteously poured for me. It wasn't *quite* up to Jacky's standards but definitely four-star hotel quality, and before I'd done more than properly appreciate it our host appeared with a menu card to bid me good morning and ask what I would like to try—which was anything and everything.

Breakfast talk covered the weather (and like in the musical *Camelot*, in Littleton it never rained till after sundown), the spring blossoms (beautiful and once again on schedule), and the breakfast (fantastic). I told everyone about my alarm clock, which won indulgent chuckles around the table. The general showed me pictures of his children while Dr. Hall focused on his food. Breakfast done, the general asked if I was joining them at the Institute. I shook my head.

"I am sorry, but no. I need to phone home, first."

"Of course." He nodded. "I am sure you have other duties here as well. Come when you can."

Stepping outside, I looked back at the B&B. Above the trees the sky looked like a Maxfield Parish painting, stacked landscapes of white cotton clouds against a pale blue heaven. Only the weird white streetlamps broke the illusion of perfect mundane, normalcy. Part of me wanted to go back inside, find a comfortable window-seat, and settle in with a good book or maybe with the princess of the house.

Instead I lifted off.

Late in the night it had become obvious to me that the DSA had planned for my indefinite stay; I was here until the town burned or they caught Kitsune or otherwise managed to neutralize the threat. It only made sense, but while I couldn't regret my impulsive decision to help I'd been telling the general the truth—I desperately needed to phone home.

Yeah, way to be grown up.

A quick call to Sheriff Deitz expanded what he told me yesterday; the Garage kept a phone service for anyone who wanted more than relayed texting or emailing and my phone had an app that I could use to reserve a booth. I accessed the app and learned that weekday mornings were low-traffic –I'd find a booth waiting for me.

After nearly two years of being careful, flying in public out of costume felt *weird* but got me there faster than a car.

Exiting Littleton meant just crossing the boundary but it made sense that the Garage was the only *official* entry and exit point, so leaving meant flying back up the road I came in on, over the hill, and past the gate. On the other side, to the left of where Veritas and I had appeared, I found the lane marked by white chalk. Its open end faced the town, and I dropped to the lane at the gate and started walking.

Thirty feet down the road, past the point we'd come in, the world blinked and I was standing in another bay of the Garage in a yellow and black painted square. I turned around to stare at the wall behind me. In yellow on white it said *Warning: Exit the square immediately*.

"Ma'am? If you could move along please?" The orange-suited Navy sailor beside the square waved me on. "We know there's nobody coming behind you, but anybody standing in that space makes us nervous."

I scooted out of the square. "Is it dangerous? If you exit the pocket into space that's occupied?"

"It can be, ma'am. Not fatal, but if something comes in on top of you then you get displaced pretty hard. You're here to use the phone? Right through those doors."

I thanked him and went. Another sailor—Warrant Officer Clark according to her insignia and patch—waited at the door and I guessed the US Marshals only dealt with incoming security. She greeted me with a "Right this way," and led me down a wide windowless hall. Despite the air conditioning, the humidity and the seacoast smell they couldn't completely scrub out told me I was definitely back in Cuba.

"Security already has your biometric information, ma'am." She stopped in front of a heavy door and palmed the lock. "You'll be able to use any booth phone and computer. All calls are monitored. Anything you choose to upload will be scanned, as will anything you download. You can take cleared files back with you on the provided flash drives."

"Is this really the only way to call out?"

"For texting and email we have the repeater service between the pocket and the world. Scanned for content of course, but you barely notice the lag even if you know about it. Here you go, ma'am."

The room she'd led me into was one long bay with another door at the other end. Booths ran along each wall, twenty to a side. Sliding doors gave privacy to anyone in a booth, with a light over the frame telling you which were occupied. Only six were in use now.

Clark palmed the terminal in the closest empty booth and closed the door on me with a polite "Use the door at the far end when you're finished." I listened to the sound of her retreating footsteps, barely more audible than the murmurs of the other callers. Without my super-duper hearing I wouldn't have heard them at all.

Okay then.

The Dome dispatcher who answered recognized my voice and code and forwarded me instantly. One ring…

"Hope! Where *are* you?"

"Brigadoon."

"What? Oh. Oh that's bad." Shell's mom hadn't been into all things Broadway and Hollywood Musical like my mom was, but she'd probably looked it up on Wikipedia and read the whole entry between her "What?" and her "Oh."

"Sorry." It really was a bad joke, but I couldn't keep the giggle in as the knot of anxiety in my gut loosened. "I'm staying a few streets over from the water tower. You're here, too. It's all classified."

"Shut the front door!"

But she didn't sound *shocked*. "Shell…"

"Okay, I knew about her government job and that she was 'out of range'. She made me swear not to pry and we worked up five unbreakable texting codes to make sure the DSA wasn't just using the job as bait to lock her up somewhere and empty her head or examine her side of our neural link—we were *careful*."

"So you're linked now?" And here I'd been worried that Shelly wasn't joining us through Shell in our cyber-neural link because the two of them had issues. Instead she was good to go, just blocked by her *secretly living in another universe*.

No, I wasn't upset about being left in the dark at all.

Shell didn't give me time to brood. "Like psychic twins whenever she's not 'covered'—I just hadn't known she was where *we* were looking for, what are the odds? So what's going on out there? I haven't been able to reach you since the plane—which, considering you're with Shelly is, well, duh."

"It looks like I'm here until the fire starts or we stop the threat. Tell everybody I'm sorry? I'm sure Blackstone already knows, but… What's *happening*? Should I be here? I wish—" I wished Jacky was here. Or Blackstone. Nobody else was as good at the twisty kind of thinking that the situation screamed for—although it looked like *Shelly* might be learning it.

"Everything's happening." I could hear the laugh in her voice. "And nothing you could do about it even if you were here."

"Powerteam?"

"Uhuh. Legal Eagle got a court order against them and they've taken down the edited preview video, but it's still all over the net. Pirated. You know."

Unfortunately I did. Hardcore cape-watchers everywhere would have copied the files. They would enjoy eternal life in personal computers and on international servers beyond the reach of any court orders.

"So we've gone ahead and cut our own little home movie from the Dispatch footage." Her voice cranked up to gleeful. "The download demand almost crashed our server."

"Oh. Oh boy." I covered my eyes, not sure whether to laugh or cry.

"Yup. Can't say that it makes you look, you know, on *top* of things, but it definitely shows who started it!"

"That's..." That was alright, actually. I could live with looking stupid if it helped get the team off the hook. "Right. So okay, maybe it's best I'm not there."

"*De*finitely. And the whole assault thing with Litner? The sleaze got some great shots of us looking shocked and pissed off, and yeah the tabloids are running with it. But!" she kept going over my groan, "Between the Bee's testimony and the valet attendant that saw it all, you're solid. And do you think he's going to go after *Annabeth* for assault? Yeah, right."

Right indeed. All she'd have to do was sit in the witness stand and cry and any jury would spontaneously award her a million dollars. And probably rush out of the jury box to lynch Litner—there wouldn't be anything left for Dane to finish. And was it wrong that just thinking about that made me feel better?

"And what about the Bees? How are they?" *How is Julie?*

"Yeah... Julie's..." I knew that tone.

"What did you say to her?"

"Hey, I went and saw her like you asked! Okay, I *might* have told her how pissed you were that they'd kept you out of the loop. Hope?"

Banging my head against the side of the booth didn't help at all.

"Really? What part of that is 'Tell her everything's alright?' Okay— That's...that'll do. I'll text later. I've got to go, okay?"

"Okay. Give me my best. Love you."

"Always. Take care of everybody."

We hung up and I sat for a moment to catch my breath, proud that I'd managed to keep from asking how Brian was doing with Kindrake. It really was all good news. Really. And the Navy would be able to get the dent out of the booth wall. Five breaths later I dialed again. One ring, two...

"Yes?"

"Hello, Mom?"

"Ma'am? If you could come with me?"

Stepping out of the booth, I hadn't expected to find Warrant Officer Clark waiting for me.

"Is there a problem?" My talk with Mom had been...fun. Like always, she had been bravely supportive of what I was doing, and like always I was left feeling wrung out, an awful, awful person for risking myself and making my parents worry. I couldn't handle any more problems right now.

"No ma'am, but the station CO would like to talk to you."

She took me through the far door, but instead of following the green line labeled "Littleton" she led me through guarded doors down a side hall and up a secure elevator. An armored receptionist waved us through an armored door, into what had to be the Garage's security center. The far wall was floor-to-ceiling glass, looking over the bay Veritas and I had departed from yesterday. Three stations of screens monitored the Garage and its traffic. Clark brought me to two white-uniformed naval officers standing behind an elevated desk by the windows, and saluted.

"Sir. Hope Corrigan, sir."

"Thank you, Warrant," the officer wearing commander's bars returned the salute. "Dismissed."

She spun around and marched off, leaving her CO to look me over. He did, and the way his mouth tightened screamed that he didn't like what he saw. "Ms. Corrigan. Thank you for coming upstairs." He offered me his hand and we shook. "Commander Steven Rosack, station CO. I guard the door."

That explained the patch with the three-headed hound on his shoulder. Of course Cerberus guarded the door.

"What can I do for you, commander?"

"We'll see. This is Captain Lauer." The second officer stood too far away to shake hands, but he nodded. His sharp, weathered face was deeply creased didn't look as old as his white hair. I guessed he spent as much time as he could outdoors.

"Ma'am." His gravelly voice sounded as wind-worn as he looked. "The Navy would like to ask a favor." And he wasn't happy about that, not at all. He waved me over to a screen.

"Do you recognize this man?"

The picture showed a big man, beefy, bald, scars on his face. His beaten, irregular features said he'd fought hard more than once and not had bones reset when he healed. None of it went with the Hawaiian shirt.

"No… Should I?"

"He's Ernest Winman. You might know him better as 'Brick.'"

A bolt of icy shock ran through me, shaking me from head to toe. "Oh. I didn't recognize him." I never would without the gargoyle leer on his face the night he'd almost gotten me. Burned into my brain, it was the only way I'd ever remember him. "He's in Detroit Supermax." *Please* let him be in Detroit.

Captain Lauer's expression told me he wasn't.

"He's in Guantánamo City," he said, eyes still measuring me. "And he's our problem now."

"*Why* isn't he in Detroit? Sorry." I closed my own eyes, breathed, opened them. Lauer obviously didn't like my reaction, neither of them did; I knew the look—they didn't want me here, didn't want to have to be talking to me, and the part of me not focused on Brick wondered why. Was it because I was a cape, because I looked so young, or because I was a civilian?

Lauer started to say something, stopped, continued with a sigh.

"The Whittier Base Attack cost us too many heavies, and left us—especially the Army—scrambling to provide supersoldiers for all of our areas of responsibility. Winman was one of many superhuman convicts offered commutation in return for military service. The Army gave him a new name and put him on a first-in squad."

He rubbed his jaw, frowning hard. "The file Army Intelligence sent over shows he served ten months in China helping to punch out local warlords, and then his squad got hammered hard on an operation so screwed up by bad intel that there were only two survivors. The Army thought Winman was dead but unrecoverable. Since Guantánamo City isn't Hell, they were obviously wrong."

"Obviously," I echoed, but my heart wasn't in it. I kept looking back at the screen. "What do you need me to do?"

The captain's jaw actually clenched, grinding on words he didn't want to say.

"We need you to help recover him, ma'am. We have a consulate in Guantánamo City, and a few minutes ago they got a phone call from the provincial governor's office telling us Winman is there. The picture you see is the attached CIA station minder's confirmation. The Cuban government wants Winman *off* of Cuban soil, and they want him off now. They are willing to give us time to extract him, but not much time. If they have to do it themselves, they'll make the arrest and deportation public. That won't look good."

Despite the situation I almost laughed at the understatement. I'd been around Blackstone and The Harlequin long enough to know what the headlines would look like: *American Invasion? Cuba captures US military criminal!*

"It will look even worse if Winman doesn't go down easy and creates civilian casualties," Lauer continued. "And we don't have a supersoldier unit that can get here in the window they've given us."

"What assets do you have?" I tried to sound like Watchman—a Sentinel now but still the supersoldier's soldier.

He looked at Commander Rosack.

"We have three armored infantry squads on base, ma'am," the commander said. "Two light, one heavy, with one always buttoned up and ready to go. Our heavy would ordinarily be enough to take Winman out, but not without civilian casualties in an urban engagement."

Just the thought made me wince; a straight-up firefight with even a B Class Ajax Type in the middle of a populated area would be…bad.

"So you'd like me to get him out of the city?" *You can take him, Hope. You've done it before.*

Captain Lauer nodded unwillingly. "We can send the squad for support. If you can get him clear of civilian involvement, they can finish the job."

He didn't exactly stress the *if*, but it was implied and more than anything else shouted how much he didn't like the situation. He didn't want me in this, and he was looking at a potential disaster because his bosses weren't giving him time, forcing him to work with an asset he didn't trust. Lei Zi called these kinds of situations "unforced risks," strategy driven by politics, and hated them.

I exhaled. "Okay. I can do that. I'll need to change—"

"Not for this mission." Lauer shrugged. "I'm sorry, but having an identifiable American cape engage on foreign soil without even being in the country officially would be…almost as bad."

I looked down at my civvies. No armor?

"I understand." I *preferred* to bring my full kit to a fight but I trained to fight with less. Tough as he was Brick was a mid-A Class, but I'd beat him twice before and I would have backup. *How hard can it be?*

Chapter Twelve

"We're not soldiers, at least we shouldn't be. I've got nothing against soldiers, fine men and women. But they're trained first and foremost to break things and kill people, follow orders that tell them when to do that. Superheroes are all about protecting and helping people, though we can kill people and break things when the need arises. Different priorities, which doesn't mean we don't work together sometimes."

Atlas, *Chicago News interview about the China War.*

It had to be the first time I'd ever been *driven* to a mission. The only thing I asked for before they loaded me with their team was a strip of carbon-fiber tape—I doubled it over and turned it into a damage-resistant bandage cover for Ozma's lace ring. The truck they loaded us into looked like a beat up vintage produce truck; the recent change to free market capitalism hadn't yet replaced Cuba's decades-old fleet of work vehicles and anything newer than the 60s or 70s would at least be noticed.

The truck didn't match its contents; I'd never ridden with more dangerous looking cargo. The heavy marine "tin-man" squad looked ready for anything and I wouldn't want to be downrange from them for *anything*. Their bulky suits—fully articulated ceramic battle armor—looked capable of stopping anything less than heavy artillery and had to weigh at least 500 pounds without the weapon mounts racked onto them; which meant they had to be supported by powered exoskeletons although I couldn't hear the servo-motors.

Their Cerberus Watch decal patches, cartoony three-headed grinning and slobbering Scooby Doos, didn't match *them*; with their helmets off, their heads looked ridiculously small peeking out of their armor shells but they also looked totally comfortable wearing all that metal and potential death.

And they kept calling me "ma'am," even the lieutenant who outranked my state militia commission.

"You ever danced with a team like ours, ma'am?" Lance Corporal Balini asked. Beside him, Lance Corporal Tsen leaned in to hear over the engine and road. They both looked young enough to need fake IDs to drink.

"I've worked with a US Marshals fireteam?" Of course the *team* had all been duplicate Platoons, Bobs in cutting-edge SWAT armor.

He shook his head. "Then you haven't danced, ma'am. Don't worry—we know the steps." Our ride bumped over a particularly deep pothole, shaking us about, and started to slow. "When Charlie dances, we bring the foxtrot! We—"

"Button it, people," Lieutenant Corbin interrupted.

Lieutenant Corbin looked like a computer geek who'd bought a tennis club membership and gone crazy; thin-faced but seriously tanned, short blond hair bleached by the sun, most of the time he focused on data streaming across his glasscam shades. Beside him his second, Corporal Stein, focused on everything in the zone of engagement, not talking, eyes moving as if he could see through the sides of our ride.

The truck stopped and we listened to our driver talking in Spanish. None of the team as much as twitched when two Cuban soldiers came around the back of the truck to look at us. One of them shot a question at Lieutenant Corbin, who answered fluently. Papers were passed, including an ID with my face on it and an official-looking stamped page. The soldiers read carefully and snapped pics of everything with their smartphones, and the one doing the talking pointed at me and asked another question. Whatever the lieutenant said, I didn't hear "Astra" or "Hope Corrigan."

And whatever the soldiers thought of the tiny blonde girl and her hulking tin-men escorts, they returned our papers and waved us on. Our ride rumbled into gear and we drove through the checkpoint, the yellow gate dropping behind us.

"Welcome to Cuba," Balini quipped. "The weather today will be hot and dry. And tomorrow. And the day after that. Did you bring your sunscreen?"

"No," I laughed. He wasn't joking about dry. Out the back of the truck, I could see *cactuses*—not really what I expected for Cuba. "Where are the palm trees?"

"Guantánamo Province is surrounded by mountains and mostly in a rain shadow. North coast? Rainforests. Down here? Not so much. These days Hollywood uses it for desert location shots for low-budget cowboy movies."

 "Done playing tour guide, Ball?" Lieutenant Corbin puffed a flavored e-cig, blowing a cloud of nicotine and mint. "Or do you want to tell her about the pretty birds?"

"All done, sir."

"Wonderful. Ma'am, here's the mission. Our eyes have Winman enjoying the view in the middle of town. We want him out of town where there's room to bring it to him without blowing shit up. Civilian casualties are not an option in a fight we're picking ourselves, so we need you to move him."

"How? I mean, how should I approach him?"

"Don't you CAI capes drill for that? Assume he will be completely freaking hostile to any approach and take any opening move you want that gets him from Point A to Point B without giving him time to argue about it."

"So grab him, get him out of town, then subdue him?"

"Yes ma'am. Bringing him in alive is optional but preferred. He is a deserter, armed, and extremely dangerous and technically invading another country, but base will want intel from him. Like why the hell he's in Guantánamo."

I wanted that, too. Part of me was burning up with curiosity—Captain Lauer had sidestepped that question in his too-brief briefing. I made positive noises while wiping my palms on my shorts and measuring my breath; not nerves, really, just my usual physiological reactions to an anticipated fight. I doubted I'd ever get over them and, looking around, I realized they were shared. Corbin puffed his e-cig methodically. Stein focused over my head. Balini and Tsen checked their armsracks. The truck stopped again.

"This is the team stop," Corbin said, handing me an earbug and watching me adjust it. "We'll set up away from the road. When your piece tells us you're moving towards us, we'll light up a flare. Good luck." They locked down their helmets and dropped out the back of the truck bed, the camo-layers of their suits going live to blend them into the brush as they trooped away. I climbed forward into the front passenger's seat.

The lance corporal behind the wheel looked at me, tapped a screen between the seats. The image showed an aerial shot of the road with four green icons moving away from it and the centered icon of the truck. Ahead of us, a red icon blinked warningly in the center of town. I nodded and divided my attention between the screen and the road as she drove.

Guantánamo City wasn't what I'd been expecting, but then I wasn't sure *what* I'd been expecting, really. The Serene Republic was less than two years old, but it was changing fast.

Maybe I'd pictured a worn and run down Central American slum town. This wasn't it. Only a handful of buildings were higher than two stories, and the style was old—with their vertical fronts and balconies they reminded me of New Orleans' French Quarter homes and businesses—but the roofing was solid and most buildings were well patched and brightened by fresh coats of paint in bold palettes. Flowers were everywhere, in boxes and hanging pots. And it wasn't just dressing up old stuff for show; we passed a ring of new construction on the way in. The narrow streets were a bit rough but getting resurfaced. At least half of the pedestrians strolling the streets or lounging under shading café awnings in the afternoon heat looked American or European.

"Tourists, developers, studio people," my driver, Lance Corporal Stevens, answered my unasked question. "Visitors from the base."

"Okay." I decided not to worry about seeing a familiar face—other than Brick's of course. If things went smooth, I'd be out of here fast enough it wouldn't be a problem.

Stevens pulled half up on the low curb and stopped, engine idling. "Here." She handed me a broad brimmed hat, suitable for casual window-shopping under the Cuban sun. Wide shades came with it, and didn't clash too badly with my shorts and shirt. Nice. Maybe I'd look like an incognito movie star. When I put them on, she pointed up the street.

"He's two streets up, outside the Café Cubano. The only Hawaiian shirt in sight. Ready?"

"Seriously? I never am." I hoped my smile said I didn't mean it, and I slid out of the truck before she could say anything else. She drove away, grinding old gears. I stood still until the exhaust cloud faded into the heated air, then started walking. Casual now…

"Don't react," Shell whispered, a disembodied voice beside my ear. I yelled and almost tripped. She faded in like Marley's ghost, rolling her eyes as I recovered from my stumble.

"C'mon, really?" she groused. "Should I use a ring-tone? You popped out from the quantum-signaling shield you've been hiding under a few miles back. FYI, Jacky has disappeared from the Dome. Just thought you should know."

I whipped out my cellphone and pretended to answer it. "Don't *do* that. Anything else you need to tell me?"

"Fisher finally got the warrant and got the bank to cough up its records, so he knows that the broken-into deposit box belonged to our good friend Doctor Pellegrini? The *Ascendant*? The secret and now really *really* wanted cult leader of the Ascendancy, the guy whose crimes *he* investigated last year?"

I closed my eyes. "And how mad is he at the FBI—never mind." I liked Fisher, and the way Shell was going on he had to be seriously pissed. "Shell, I'm a little busy. How much did you see out here? Forget it, just access everything after our phone conversation."

My usual sense-memory download had to have updated the moment distance from the Navy base's shielding let our quantum-link reestablish; she reviewed it in a second and her eyes got wide. "Brick? Crap on a cracker, Hope. What is *he* doing here? And all you've got for backup is four tin-men a couple of miles down the road?"

"How hard can it be? Whatever training they gave him in the Army, he's still a B Class." I started walking again.

"Okay…what can I do?"

"Be my wingman? Please?"

"You've got it—now go kick his ass. I'll save pictures."

I couldn't help laughing, suddenly feeling loose and ready. "Right. Bye." She actually mimed hanging up, fading back out as I crossed to the next corner.

I could see my target and I focused on walking towards him without *looking*. He sat at a sidewalk table, not sweating at all while fellow drinkers fanned themselves; anyone who knew what to look for would have wondered if he was a breakthrough just by how the heat wasn't touching him. He leered at the waitress refreshing his drink, grabbing her butt as she twisted out of his reach, and now I recognized him from memory.

He laughed as she scooted away, shrugged and chugged his drink, and then he was checking *me* over, the kind of look that made me want to put on more clothes. I looked down and kept walking, angling to pass between his table and the curb.

And he grabbed *me*. For a heartbeat I froze, unable to believe it as he wrapped his fingers around my wrist and tugged with a "Hey little girl, have a drink with me." Then I spun around, facing and behind him to grab *his* wrist. My twisting motion pulled his arm back and forced him to let go, and I *launched*.

"Shit!" was all he got out as he flailed and we climbed. I angled us back the way I'd come, flying south and praying he was too drunk to— He pulled himself up one-handed and I flinched and let go to keep him from grabbing me again. And realized what I'd done.

When I dove for him he battered me aside, *laughing*, and I only succeeded in pushing him to smack down in the street instead of into a house.

Which didn't slow him down at all. He took the fall with a roll and bounced to his feet, laughing harder.

"And who are *you*, little girl?"

We were still in *town* and I couldn't have screwed up worse—my plan to come back at him from behind and lift him in an underarm headlock had disappeared the instant he'd grabbed me and now people were going to get hurt unless I finished it *quick*.

I forced myself to touch down. "I'm Astra."

"Well f—" His grin widened and the leer was back. "I've imagined this for*ever*. Happy birthday to me." He clapped his hands and *exploded*.

Blinding light, thunder, a wave of overpressure that shattered windows, and as I blinked to clear my eyes Shell was yelling in my ear.

"Hope! He's got dragon armor! Up!"

I leaped skyward reflexively. "He's got *what*?"

"Dragon armor! A Verne-tech and sorcery fusion made in freaking China!"

My watering eyes cleared. Brick stood inside a scorched ring, dressed in what looked like ancient Chinese armor with horribly modern weapon frames attached.

I wiped my eyes. "This can*not* be happening!"

"Yeah? Do you think if you tell him that, he'll go away?"

Guantánamo City wasn't Chicago and had no civilian-response system for superhuman fights, but obviously its citizens knew what to do; the people out braving the afternoon sun scattered—one or two stopping only long enough to grab kids not yet smart enough to run instead of stand and watch.

And that was a *good idea*. "Shell, can dragon armor fly?"

"Short distances! It—"

That was all I needed. I took off, dropping lower and *not* opening up my speed. If he'd just follow…

"Incoming!" Shell screamed before I realized what the roaring blast behind me meant. I couldn't even count the flashes and tumbled from the sky in blind, deaf, spinning vertigo.

"Flash-bangs!" I heard Shell over the ringing in my ears only because she was in my *head*.

"Really?" I'd been flashed before but those had been police grade flash-bangs; *this*... my eyes weren't clearing, the ringing tinnitus in my ears deafened me, and the vertigo-triggered nausea made me want to vomit. This was military grade dialed up to *eleven*. "Where is Brick I can't see him!"

"And I can? I'm using your eyes! I'm calling in your escorts!"

I could at least feel the shattered concrete under me, managed to roll over and get up off my elbows. I found out where Brick was when he kicked me in the groin, lifting me off the ground to land in a helpless sprawl.

"Hope!"

When Brick kicked me over onto my back I rolled with it and launched for the sky I could finally see. *Now* I heard him, his laugh punching through the tinnitus.

"Leaving? The party's just started!" The little rocket that caught me this time was a straight-up explosive—the first mistake he'd made. It threw me sideways but hurt less than his kicks.

"Shell, the team! Which way?"

She obligingly flared a virtual targeting icon in my still-spotty eyes and I twisted around to get distance between us and everybody else.

"Fly faster!"

"When I can see!"

"What's to see? Fly *up*! What was *that*?" A ripping sound signaled the arrival of Lieutenant Corbin and his team, a stream of metalstorm rounds leading the way. I heard Brick shout behind me as the rounds punched into him, and the crash turned me around. I almost laughed in relief. The nearest building was at least two hundred yards away; our engagement zone had moved out of town.

"*Stay down*!" Lieutenant Corbin shouted in my earbug as he bounded by me. He ate thirty feet with each leaping step, the others right behind. My tearing eyes worked well enough again and I watched as his team fanned out to each side, laying down fire. Corbin fired his own arm-mounted chain gun in controlled bursts, the tracer-marked sabotted rounds flashing away to explode off Brick's fancy armor.

"*Medical status?*"

"I can still fight! What can Brick do?"

"*I saw that dragon armor crap in China—it's like putting a bull in battle armor and giving it an infinite supply of ammunition. Not high-tech, but it doesn't have to be. Shit!*"

Brick lit up explosively and snaking flame trails from multiple launches reached out to Corporal Stein's hulking form.

"*Screen and move!*" All four of them ejected canisters throwing up clouds of smoke, kept firing.

"Wow," Shell said, fading in beside me.

"Uh-huh," I agreed weakly. My super-duper vision meant I could still see them as shining heat sources, moving like a choreographed dance with the partners a hundred yards apart. Under the light wind the smoke stretched into bands, spreading to cover the zone. Then Brick moved, a single superhuman leap that came down on Lance Corporal Tsen.

I screamed. The shooting stopped as Shell yelled "Go go go!" and I did too late. Brick hit Tsen hard enough to crumple his chest armor and throw him fifty feet to crash into the brush. *He's dead he's dead he's dead.* I smashed into Brick without slowing, off-center and spinning him. He didn't fall.

He recovered laughing, leering at me under his open-faced helmet.

"Having fun Astra? Ready for a good time? They can watch!" He dodged my lunge and kicked me in the gut just below my breastplate, his armored boot driving the air out of me and freezing my diaphragm. This time I rode the shock, doubling around his foot and grabbing it, pulling it as I spun us away on the force of his kick.

Brick roared as my spin flipped him, boots up to slam him head down. *Now* my superior strength paid off—locking his leg, I twisted for leverage and stomped on his closest arm just above the elbow. It snapped with a sickening *crack* and he screamed.

"Are you still having *fun*?" I twisted his leg down, pushing like I was trying to drill him into the ground, brought my knee down on the pit of his opposite shoulder and felt the pop and rip of tendons as the ball and socket of his shoulder joint separated. He screamed again.

A final flip planted him on his face and I dropped on his back, fists together for a hammer. And froze, breathing like a winded sprinter. Brick screamed with each twitch, boots kicking the ground, and I wanted to hit him again and again and *again*.

"I trained with Atlas and Ajax you *idiot*," I panted. "I can take a beating from *Watchman* and you think you can play with me?"

A pair of armored legs stepped into my sight and I looked up. Lieutenant Corbin stood by Brick's head.

"Ma'am, if you have issues to work out, we can always leave and come back."

"No. I'm good." Really not; rising nausea was replacing fading adrenaline. My breathing hitched. "Corporal—Corporal Tsen?"

"*Feeling no pain*," the dead corporal laughed in my earbug. "Good *drugs*."

"You're not going to believe it, Hope!" Virtual Shell stood laughing over Tsen's crumpled form. "They're all Ajax-types! C Class, but strong enough to pack a couple of tons of armor and gear around and tough enough to take a hit and not squish inside their cans."

"Oh. That's—that's good. Brick's your prisoner, Lieutenant. Excuse me?"

I managed to get off of him and stagger a few yards before I threw up. Repeatedly.

Chapter Thirteen

"Hate is the worst emotion. When you hate someone, you can't think rationally about them. You can't forget about them. They burn in your soul like acid thorns."

Hope Corrigan (Attributed)

The lingering flash-bang vertigo, the kicks I felt only now, the memory of Brick's bones snapping under my feet kept me doubled over and heaving while the team closed in to take care of Brick and Tsen. I wondered how much penance Father Nolan was going to assign for the sin of wrath when I made my next confession. Maybe he'd consider my wanting to keep vomiting till my soul felt clean to be penance served.

Shell gave me a minute, staying respectful of my condition until I sat back on my heels.

"Hope? Are you thinking what I'm thinking?"

"I hope not. Shell? If I *ever* say something as stupid as 'How hard can it be?' again I want you to slap me with the biggest brick you can find."

"Okeydokey!"

"So, what *are* you thinking?"

"I see London, I see France, I see Astra's underpants?"

I looked down at myself and started laughing. Brick's second missile had pretty much shredded and burned off my kicky summer outfit; the only thing saving my modesty was the virtually indestructible underwear Vulcan made for me out of his polymorphic molecule goo. He'd spun the stuff into a weave as strong as carbon fiber, fireproof and soft as cotton, and Shell called them my Unmentionable Indestructibles. Which still left me in my underwear, but my white and blue sports briefs and bra—complete with white Astra star crest—covered enough to be worn in the gym. Yes, my life was interesting enough that I wore indestructible underwear. If I was ever caught dead, I'd at least be a modest corpse.

Finished giggling, I spit and wiped my mouth and went to help.

Stevens had arrived, driving off the road to get to us, and Stein and Balini had kits out. Balini used a tool to crack Tsen's chest armor and Stein unhitched his helmet while Tsen swore at them. Lieutenant Corbin looked up from where he worked on Brick.

"Three minutes to lift, can you give me a hand?"

I nodded shakily and he handed me a brace. Brick's armor had disappeared sometime while I'd been heaving, and Corbin had put titanium hobbles on him. Now he showed me how to slide the brace on. Brick screamed again when Corbin planted his foot and *pulled* to set his shoulder for the brace, managed to keep it in when we set his broken arm and put the field sleeve on it. My hands shook and I was dizzy again before we were through.

"Good job," Corbin said encouragingly. "You going to be okay?"

"Eventually?" Dirt and bits of brush swirled under the beat of arriving extraction helicopters, giving me an excuse to wipe my eyes.

"Then let's load everyone up and go get a drink."

The extraction teams got us off the ground in less than a minute after landing, moving like we were in a hot zone about to receive fire. Only Corporal Stevens stayed to drive the truck back to base, and they left her one copter as an escort. I didn't even try to fly, just squeezed in beside Balini. I rode out, I could ride back in.

They flew us to the naval base, passing over the Garage and the empty valley it sat in. By the time we landed I was steady again, even brushing off the remains of my outfit. A medic had dabbed a few bleeding scratches but I'd been only lightly scorched. Sore from my ribs down, tender in places I didn't want to think about, I'd still gotten off lucky. When our rides touched down with the softest of bumps, we reversed the process and Tsen and Brick disappeared, whisked away.

"Tsen's going to be fine, ma'am," Corbin said as we watched them go. "Cracked sternum, ribs, he'll be getting loving attention from a nurse he's been hot on for a week."

"I'm going home."

"Ma'am—"

"Home to Littleton, I mean. I'm not Navy, I'm not a Marine, I'm going to go shower and put some clothes on and play with a little girl. Tell whoever that I'll write up an after-action report tonight."

He nodded—and then he *saluted*. Stein and Balini too as I stood there mouth open. I finally returned it, feeling stupid standing there saluting in what amounted to a modest bikini, and flew away.

The marshals at the Garage passed me through to Littleton without any delay, and the town looked so normal I almost cried. Mr. Darvish met me at the door of Holybrook Rest, looking far more concerned than a sinister grand vizier had a right to. He didn't so much as blink at my returning dressed for beach volleyball.

"Miss? The Garage sent a message to expect you. Are you well?"

"Yes, thank you." I was focused like a laser on the shower upstairs, but my mouth moved on autopilot. He stood aside.

"I will make tea. Please come down when you are ready."

I nodded and went up the stairs, thankful no one else was home. Everyone kept asking how I was.

Turning the water up until billows of steam turned the bathroom into a sauna, I sat in the tub under the shower stream, legs pulled up and head on my knees, and let it all go. Eventually I stopped shivering and remembered to take off the top and briefs. Dropping them to lie in a sodden pile on the tiles beside the tub, I turned my face up and into the direct shower stream and stayed there until the water started to run cool.

With my civvies gone I dressed in my formal costume, the one that looked like a figure-skater's skirted outfit. Leaving off the accessories, I brushed out my hair and went downstairs. Mr. Darvish met me at the foot of the stairs with a tray and English tea set and directed me into the B&B's little study. I sat in one of the Queen Ann chairs and looked at the shelves of old, leather-bound books while he set up and poured. The aroma of Earl Grey teased my nose, relaxing me more, and I gratefully accepted the saucer and cup he offered me.

"Milk? Sugar?" He slid the tray closer to my end of the table. I shook my head, took a sip.

"Thank you. This is perfect." And it was, the citrusy tang of the bergamot orange adding just the right edge to the heavy black tea.

"The biscuits are fresh."

"Thank you." We sat in silence while he prepared and enjoyed his own.

"I'm sorry," I blurted, remembering my manners.

"You are?"

"You're from the Middle East. I should have covered up more." Suddenly my legs felt naked, and I blushed remembering what I'd shown walking through the front door.

His smile was broad and genuine.

"It is refreshing to meet a young person who is culturally sensitive. My compliments to your parents. However I have lived in Littleton for a year now, England for five years before that. You are modestly attired." He set his cup down. "And how are you?"

I found myself spilling the story of my fight with Brick, ending with the way I almost kept hitting him until he would never hurt me or anyone else again. He took the news that I'd been ready to beat a man to death so calmly I almost thought he wasn't listening, and he let me finish before speaking again.

"You have killed before," he observed quietly.

"Yes, but not…"

"Not in judgment? Not as the angel of righteous vengeance?"

"No." I tried to figure out why thinking about it wasn't sending me into another sick spin.

"I could say that it is in your nature as it is within every man's. Islam knows the fallen nature of man as well as does Christianity."

"Have *you* ever—I mean…"

"Oh, yes. When a bomb killed Atifa's parents, I would have cheerfully and instantly consigned every last jihadi to Gehenna had I the power." He pointed to a picture over the fireplace, the happy child I'd met this morning, with a smiling man and woman. "But part of my anger was guilt. The bomb had been meant for me."

"She's not yours?"

"She is now my responsibility and my delight. Certainly a gift from God."

I still didn't feel anything except sadness and curiosity. "Why did they try to kill you?"

"Because I am a heretic, a Sufi imam who preaches many condemned errors, the worst being that the call to jihad has been misunderstood, that Islam properly understood is truly a religion of peace. Most condemnable is that I am also a confirmed awliya, which makes other Muslims listen to my words."

"An awli—"

"An awliya. A holy man blessed with *keramat*, miraculous gifts of power. You have felt the Peace?"

The question seemed a total non sequitur, but I instantly knew what he meant. The way I'd felt the moment we met, the way I felt just sitting here now. The reason I completely and unreasonably trusted him.

"You're a breakthrough?"

"Just so. The Peace of God is irresistible, and it came to me when I needed it most, when I needed it for others. No one feeling even a small part of it can hate, or act on that hatred." Now he frowned. "This does not stop a man who is not in my presence from acting, however. So, a bomb, or poison, or a sniper can end my life."

He stirred his tea.

"The fatwa pronounced against me drove me first to England and then into hiding, for the safety of those around me. I would ask you not to share this, of course. I merely felt that, having known the dark edge of Islamic fanaticism, you should know the light."

Of course he knew all about the Whittier Base Attack and our losses there. I nodded.

"So, be at peace." He said it like a blessing. "Know your heart is human, and it brings you great merit in Heaven that you did not act on your anger. And now I recommend rest, and tonight quiet dreams, both of which you will find here."

I spent the rest of the evening reading dispatches from Shell and writing up my promised after-action report. Shell thoughtfully emailed Detective Fisher's investigation reports, something she really shouldn't have even *had*. Finally working together with the feds, Fisher had gotten them to hire an expensive psychometric esper to do a "reading" of the vault before time faded the psychic impressions of the heist too much to be useful. The reader had brought a sketch-artist with her and psychically read the events, providing images of the thieves (not that that helped a whole lot since they'd been masked) and what was in the box; which turned out to be nothing but a flash-drive. What?

Regardless, at least they were all on the same page now, and I was obsessing about it to avoid thinking of other things. I included a note in my report about my panicked reaction that dropped Brick back into Guantánamo City's streets; thinking about how many ways that could have ended badly still made me shiver a little, and I wondered how much of my rage had been from knowing my mistake had almost precipitated a tragedy.

And what was Brick *doing* in Guantánamo? Could it really be coincidence? I dreamed that Littleton was threatened, and a mercenary supervillain armed to the teeth by Chinese sorcery shows up? What were the odds?

I fell asleep obsessing about *that*, but Mr. Darvish was right; my sleep was mostly dreamless and what dreams I had were of stars, the Milky Way shining in all its misty glory over Littleton. No sneaky fox entered to disturb them. He probably couldn't, as long as I slept at Holybrook Rest.

So naturally the next morning pitched me right back into the mess.

Chapter Fourteen

"Whatever you would make habitual, practice it; and if you would not make a thing habitual, do not practice it, but habituate yourself to something else."

Epictetus *(First Century AD)*

My adorable alarm clock woke me again and this time I chased her laughing out of the room with expertly thrown pillows. Then I looked at the text on my flashing cellphone. *Garage 0800 hours action review.*

I fell back and scrubbed my face, ran fingers through my hair.

Suck it up, Hope. The Sentinels had always done action reviews, and they'd gotten a lot more detailed and formal since Lei Zi and Watchman—both ex-military—had joined; *of course* the Marines had them. The whiny Hope in me argued for just blowing them off. *You're not in the local chain of command. You're not even in waving distance.*

I quashed whiny Hope, called Shelly to tell her where I'd be, and looked at my second text. It turned out to be a relayed text and two attached video-files from Shell.

"Guantánamo City fight caught on digi-cams, claimed as official Cuban-USA joint operation. Blackstone covering for you in Chicago, so good luck with that."

The first video file (time-stamped yesterday!) showed me flying over Chicago. Since Shell said Blackstone was involved I had to guess that he was conjuring an illusion over another flyer—maybe Safire. The second video was shaky hand-cam cuts, some distant, some zoomed in close, of our fight with Brick. I had lost my hat and shades early on, and was easily recognizable to anyone who knew me.

I took a moment to scream into my spare pillow.

Quin was so going to *freak*. Blackstone would make cutting comments about "low profiles." *Shelly* thought it was awesome and had added her own text expressing her amusement, because naturally Shell had to share the news with her "older sister" and now that Shell knew about Littleton they were texting and chatting without any need-to-know restraints.

I texted back an *Ignoring U all* and got in the shower. If I hurried I could enjoy a waffle.

Warrant Officer Clark saluted when I translated into the Garage. Did military protocol include saluting capes in "uniform?" I had come in my field costume complete with armor and maul, partly for psychological support and partly to make a point; should I salute back? I'd never saluted anyone in my life except half-seriously and I settled for a nod, which seemed okay. Clark took me downstairs this time, to what had to be the Garage's armory, and I relaxed when other enlisted we passed didn't come to unnerving attention or repeat her salute.

Optional, got it.

She stopped at a security door. It had just a number on it, but over the door frame hung a big wood plank with *The Dog House* carved and painted in black and red.

"Ma'am." She swiped her pass, stepped aside with another salute.

"Thank you...Warrant?"

She smiled. "That's correct, ma'am. Good luck." On that note, she left me to my fate.

Okay... I stepped inside, letting the door close behind me. The heavy latch closed with a *thunk* and the light over the second door turned green. Going through that one, I found the Dog House.

It looked like a locker room, equipment shop, and recreational hall. Four tin-men sat playing cards, helmets racked beside them. Their suits weren't as massive as my Scoobies' had been, and they carried lighter mounted ordnance. Tin-man suits for non-breakthroughs? Despite good AC and a big ceiling hatch that probably opened into the bays above us, to my supersensitive nose everything smelled of polish, gun-oil, and sweat.

Beyond them I saw my guys, gathered in a space fitted with screens and a display board and the kind of comfortable chair-and-desk setup I knew from college lecture rooms. Even Corporal Tsen was there, leaning stiffly against a desk.

"Astra!" Balini shouted, seeing me. The card game stopped as everybody looked at me, even the third group working out with weights and playing video games on the other side of the room.

I apologized and squeezed my way between the card game and weapon racks to a quiet chorus of "ma'am"s. At the desks, Lieutenant Corbin gave me a nod. "Astra. How old are you?"

"I—what? Nineteen?"

He extended his hand, and when we shook he passed me something flat and hard.

"You know what that means?" he asked the room.

"First challenge in two years!" at least half the room shouted back. The rest stomped their feet and cheered.

I looked at the disk in my hand. It was a burnished steel medal, at least twice the weight of a silver dollar, but with no hole for the ribbon. One side showed the Scooby-Cerberus on the team's armor patches, this one howling, growling, and chomping into what looked like a zombie—it had three heads, it could do it all. The other side showed the stylized symbol of *Ajax's* old Greek-style helmet, over a Latin motto. *Quis exire canes?*

"Um, 'Who let the dogs out'?"

"Our team challenge coin, ma'am. Corporal Stein, what are the rules of a challenge?"

"Sir, when a challenger presents his coin then all other team members must also present their coins! Any team member who does not present his coin must buy drinks for the rest of the team! If all other team members present their coins, then the challenger must buy drinks for the rest of the team, sir!"

"Thank you, Stein. And being Ajaxes, ma'am, *we* drink from kegs. We're honored to have a Sentinel who knew our namesake hold our coin." He grinned. "Even if you won't be legal to challenge for two years unless we do it off-base, and they won't let us go bar crawling in Guantánamo for some reason."

Looking at the coin, tracing Ajax's crest, I swallowed and had to blink suddenly wet eyes. Corbin understood; his grin faded, but stayed a smile. "He was a Heroes Without Borders cape abroad, ma'am, and not a soldier, but he lived and died a warrior."

"Attention!"

The shout came from the door and Captain Lauer's aide, and everybody but me snapped to attention until the captain waved them back down.

"Take it easy, gentlemen. I am only here to observe. Lieutenant Corbin?"

"Sir." The rest of the team settled into chairs facing their lieutenant. I followed their lead, slipping my new coin into the hidden pocket in my armor and setting Malleus on the floor beside me. Captain Lauer took a chair behind us.

Corbin grabbed a remote and clicked it, bringing the big center screen to life. It showed a split-screen view, on the left four boxes showing the view from their helmet cameras and a fifth blank box, on the right a drones-eye view with green icons showing our positions relative to the road and city streets. A second later all the faintly visible bystanders in camera range lit up with their own red icons. Brick's icon flashed in yellow.

"Settle down guys, questions and comments later. Enjoy the show."

A digital clock on the bottom started up as the images unfroze and the chatter began. *The team piling out of the truck and taking positions to cover a zone. My ride into town seen from overhead, my half of my conversation with Shell. The approach, the grab, the too-short flight dropping us still in town. Brick exploding into his dragon armor. Panicked chatter from the team, Corbin shouting "Go go go!" My short flight, shoot-down and brutal kicking*—I didn't *remember Brick kicking me so many times—my second flight and the second hit shredding my civvies.*

I tore my eyes from *my* box—the fifth screen had lit up with what had to be an insane civilian cameraman's footage of my kicking from Brick— to watch the overhead icons of the team closing, spreading and shifting to make sure their fire lines didn't reach into town. The fifth camera filmed my reversing course. When we all met on Brick's position my box went mostly dark again—the cameraman trying to get footage while ducking behind a fuzzy shape that might have been a low wall. My gut clenched seeing Brick punch into Tsen, winced at *my* final grapple with Brick even though from a distance it didn't look nearly so bad as it had been.

The video ran another couple of minutes, covering their restraining Brick and our getting him and Corporal Tsen loaded, then it was done and I realized that my heart was pounding in my chest. I closed my eyes and tried deep-breathing.

Lieutenant Corbin led a round of comments and observations, focusing on fire-lines, response time, and commended Balini and Stein for *not* shooting me when I jumped Brick (reviewing the video, I'd come breathtakingly close to taking friendly fire). The lieutenant offered to run some drills with me if I was here long enough.

"Any other comments?" he finished.

I raised my hand and he nodded.

"I dropped the ball, yesterday." *Nobody* had mentioned my dropping Brick short of their chosen engagement zone.

"What happened?"

"I intended to get a headlock from behind where he couldn't get any leverage, but he… He grabbed me first and scared me." I flushed hotly. "So I caught his wrist and lifted him by it instead and I didn't have control. He pulled himself up to grab me and— I panicked and dropped him. Sorry."

He nodded again.

"Thank you for that. I would say 'No harm no foul,' but it got pretty close there—much closer than it should have. We don't do sorry here—we suck it up and fix it. We can add some grappling practice to the drills. Anything else?"

There wasn't, and the review broke up. I looked around; usually if I didn't have a task this was the point where I headed to the chapel to light a candle or two and thank Mary of the Pagans or go to my rooms for homework. Sometimes it was really homework; most of the time it was mental breathing space to burn off my nerves and rebalance. I *really* needed to rebalance.

"Astra?" Captain Lauer stood behind me.

"Sir?"

His lips thinned and then he smiled. "Good job. Is there anything we can do for you?"

"I'd really like to know why Brick was here," I said without thinking. "And I'd like to see him."

The captain's eyebrows rose. "We have him at the base. I don't know how much, if anything, we'll be able to share, but I'll see about visiting. Anything else?"

Maybe he'll talk to me. But it wasn't likely they'd accept that. "No, I'm good. I should get back to Littleton."

He looked at me, but I didn't know what else he was waiting for and he finally stood aside.

"Well then, you'd best be about it. Good day, Astra."

Warrant Officer Clark got me back to the bay where I flashed back to Littleton, still wondering what that had been about.

Chapter Fifteen

"I have the best friend in the whole world, even if she is stupid sometimes. Okay, a lot of the time, but mostly about herself. And she's too serious, thinks she's responsible for the world, and is always getting into trouble. But that's what friends are for."

Shelly Boyar-Hardt, *Confessions of a Former Ghost.*

Apparently nobody at the Institute did anything besides stream the news from Powers TV. Half the people I passed in the lobby and halls either carefully *didn't* look at me or gave me smiles, winks, or "Good job!" in passing. It was like I'd suddenly developed an adult Team Astra! fan club, and the few scowls I got—because not everyone's a fan of superheroes—were actually *refreshing*. I decided that before I "came to work" tomorrow I was going to get a new civilian wardrobe.

"Hail the conquering hero!" Shelly greeted me when I stepped into the Oroboros' not-so-secret lair. General Rajabhushan gave me the nod and no comment as we passed through to Shelly's office, but he and Doctor Hall had been at the breakfast table when I'd come down and inhaled my waffle and coffee; they already knew about yesterday and how I felt about it.

Shelly waited until we were in her office to poke me in the ribs.

"Hey! Ticklish!"

"All one piece? Nothing broken, ribs okay this time?"

"Yes!" Stiff, sore, tender, and if not for my ability to *heal*, probably unable to move without whimpering (how did I not remember Brick kicking me at least *five times*?), but okay.

"Great! So, business!" She passed me a display epad, threw herself into her chair. "Since you didn't come around yesterday, I did a lot of organizing, research, boring analyst-type stuff."

My lips twitched helplessly as she grabbed her own pad. "So let's go over the likely suspects for the Great Littleton Fire!"

"Terrorists?"

"That's what I thought first, but there are problems. Look."

She fiddled with her pad and mine brightened with a list, a couple dozen terrorist organizations. I recognized Deep Green and the Ring, and they were the only two in bold.

"Most terrorist organizations are regional; they survive because of their imbedded networks, and it is virtually impossible for them to project attacks against 'hard targets' outside of their regions."

I nodded. I'd been doing a *lot* of catching up on politics, conflicts, international *everything* since the Whittier Base Attack showed me how naïve I was about the world. Terrorism 101 was invisibility—if you lost that, if you couldn't blend into your host population, you were finished unless you were somewhere your enemies couldn't get to you with their superior firepower.

"And that is really the reason for the Ring; it's a coalition of terrorist groups that work together to support operations outside their regions. It was my number one suspect, but look."

She opened a file and a list of names scrolled down. Dozens of names, but a majority of them either in red or green.

"The green names belong to superhuman Ring terrorists who have been captured. The red names are Ring terrorists who have been killed. Not all of the ones we know about were captured or killed in the Whittier Base Attack, but they lost practically *all* of their known heavy hitters there and haven't engaged in significant joint operations since."

"So what about their parts?"

"Their parts are rebuilding, but still regional. Here." Three names popped up: the Undying Caliphate, One Land, and Free Mexico.

"Free Mexico's territory is closest, and it's still awash in money from the drug cartels. Mexico's northern provinces are almost completely under cartel control, at least outside of strategic towns controlled by the Federales. The Reform Government in Mexico City has actually managed to purge itself of most of its corrupt officials, initiate liberal reforms, and hold three rounds of safe and fair elections; but there's enough bad blood with the north that Free Mexico is still popular there.

"CIA analysts believe Free Mexico is actually avoiding conflict with the US; they're downplaying their Aztlan rhetoric—their claims to the territory we took from Mexico ages ago—and playing up the Mexican Government's older civil-rights abuses. The CIA thinks that Free Mexico has changed tactics and is trying to build international pressure for Mexico to recognize the secessionist provinces as a new state. So they're acting as little like a terrorist organization as possible, *especially* abroad."

"Would they be a viable state?"

"*No.* More like an elective kleptocracy. Every real northern leader left is owned by the cartels. A lot of them are bought off, but the cartels also fund elections and buy votes to replace uncooperative officeholders with their own people. They're also perfectly happy to kill a politician's whole family if he won't play ball and he's too popular to replace electively. It's like the Chicago Mob during the Prohibition, but *lots* worse."

She frowned unhappily. "We're staying out of it, too. Other than helping Mexico strengthen its military and closing the border to weapons smuggling, there isn't anything we can really do without invading northern Mexico ourselves. Like *that* will happen."

Neither of us mentioned the more militant outcomes for the US in the Future Files—where that *would* happen.

"Okay, so what about the other two?"

"The Undying Caliphate is a bit more likely, but they lost as many heavies at Whittier Base as the others. Losing Seif-al-Din—

again–was a huge blow. Of the three they're the only ones ideologically dedicated to our destruction, but they have *much* closer targets of opportunity. Turkey. Egypt. Israel. Byzantium."

"Oh."

"Uhuh."

That one I understood: Byzantium—the formerly-Turkish territory on the west side of the Bosporus with the renamed Constaninople as its capital—was always in the news, the best and smartest thing America had done in decades or our worst act of imperialism *ever*, depending on your politics. Just its existence under the boot heel of Crusader Occupiers was a huge propaganda and recruiting tool for the Islamic-nationalist terrorist organization, but they still couldn't *do* much about it. And if they didn't do something soon, then the influx of persecuted Christians and Muslim "heretics" like Mr. Darvish' Sufis immigrating from all over the Middle East meant Byzantium would be lost to them forever.

So the UC had a strong reason to focus on Constantinople, to "liberate it" or destroy it; the Whittier Base Attack had been an attempt to weaken us enough to let them do just that. It had cost us a *lot* but it had cost them a lot more, and Shelly was right—a repeat visit to US assets over here just wasn't that likely in the near future. It still cost us too much.

Shelly gave me time to process that, scowling ferociously at her notes.

I refocused on my pad. "What about One Land? Brick went missing in action in China, and the Dragon Armor—"

She was shaking her head.

"Yesterday has put One Land at the top of my list from the Big Three, but…" She shrugged. "One Land may not be a problem much longer. It's bankrolled by Beijing and used as a means of asymmetrical warfare against the new Chinese states and our US and League troops there—the Whittier Base attack has been its *only* operation outside of Asia. And it's looking like the Kyoto Talks are moving in the right direction; most of the key Chinese states are ready to sign on for a new confederacy with its own unified government." She chewed her lip.

"Beijing is internationally isolated and almost as bad off as North Korea used to be before Unification. The oracles who judge this kind of thing predict the dissolution of Beijing's ruling communist party within a year and the new government signing on with the other states."

Which the Big Book of Contingent Prophesy predicted with high confidence. I sighed. "It's good to see some things are still on track."

"Yup, and that will mean One Land wins, just not quite the way they wanted. With a few holdouts like Hong Kong and Manchuria, the Chinese will have a unified nation-state again. But right now One Land is focused on local warlords, hoping to bring as much neighboring non-state territory as it can under its control before reunification. They haven't even focused on US and League targets in *China* much in the last year; they're just not interested in us right now."

"But who's left?"

"Not Deep Green. Much as I'd like them to be the Bad Guys here, this just isn't their kind of gig. Sure they inspired the Green Man last year, but something with the potential for mass civilian casualties? That's not really how they roll."

"Who else *is* there?"

"In the super-terrorist business? Potentially it's still anybody. Realistically? Nobody who isn't so far out in left field we'll never see them coming by watching the horizon. We've been thinking about it wrong."

I huffed. "Okay, so enlighten me."

"What if burning down Littleton isn't the *point*? What if it's collateral damage from a different mission? Littleton is a safe haven for lots of people wanted by very bad people out in the world. The Institute is home to lots of top-secret projects. So, what if a person or secret is the target?"

The sinking feeling in my stomach was horribly familiar.

"If that's true, how will we figure out who?"

"We might not be able to. But your dream gives us a clue about *how*. If it's the truth, of course." She dropped her pad on her desk. "C'mon—you have to see something."

Shelly took me back upstairs to the chrome and glass entry hall. Leading me around the other side of the open well, she pulled me behind a smart-screen array to an unobtrusive guard station.

"Hi Bob! Can I show Astra the rings?"

The *very* familiar guard gave her a nod and she stepped up beside a chrome plated pillar next to his station to pop a bio-lock sealed hatch, whispering unnecessarily all the while.

"First thing when I got here, they had me review the Institute's security system—next best thing to having Shell do it. I still run checks, so I have access. Look."

Behind the hatch was a glass panel, clear but so thick its clarity meant it couldn't be glass. Behind *that* was...

"What *is* that?"

The pillar was hollow, an armored shell around... something. It *looked* like someone had suspended three rotating steel rings in a magnetic field. They twisted around inside each other without touching the bottom or sides of the chamber, nothing visibly holding them up. The rings, shiny and slick-looking as liquid mercury, nested in each other and spun around a common center—but didn't. As they rotated around their center, my eyes kept insisting they couldn't be *doing* that.

"They're Borromean rings," Shelly explained, like giving them a name made them any less weird. "The smallest spins inside the radius of the middle ring but outside the radius of the largest ring. Each is larger than the ring that spins outside it, smaller than the ring that spins inside it."

"How is that even possible?" Staring at them too long did funny things to my brain. When I looked away every perpendicular line around me became something else, twisting to a vanishing point that was *close* without changing anything at all.

"It's not. And it's the source of the extrareality pocket that is Littleton."

I blinked and everything settled. The transient weirdness reminded me of the inside-out way the world had looked last year when Shelly and I had watched Doctor Cornelius accidentally conjure a thing so *wrong* it still gave me the willies to think about it.

"Magic?"

"Nope, but definitely Clarke's Law stuff; superscience so super that you can't tell it from magic without drippy candles and a pentagram."

I was grateful when Shelly closed the hatch. *Nothing* should do that.

"If that's what creates the pocket... What happens if someone stops them? Or cuts power to the magnetic field?"

She grinned. "And that's the zillion dollar question. DARPA scientists say that the pocket will collapse and everyone and everything brought into the pocket will just drop out of it, merge back into the real world. Like you do when you cross the pocket's boundary."

"That's not so bad."

"Nope, but they *don't* know what will happen when you start it up again. Will the pocket our mad-boy Verne created to go fishing in come back, or will we get something else? Can we restart it at all? That's why they didn't just shut it down and move it onto American soil when they found it. It's too valuable to risk."

"Can't they move it while it's on?"

"Tried. The thing is the center of its little universe, so nothing in its universe can move it—just like you can't pick yourself up by your own feet. Well, why *I* can't. That's why they built the Institute around it instead of burying it at the bottom of the lake. They'd have shielded it more if they could."

The leftover wooginess turned into an icy weight in my stomach. "Because anyone who wants to attack Littleton just has to get someone inside to shut this down," I managed. At least I could be master of the obvious.

"Yup. You saw the town burning and *vanishing*—exactly what it would do if the pocket collapsed. Littleton would find itself sitting naked beside Guantánamo Bay. Hope?"

I couldn't believe it.

"Hope?"

I couldn't believe it. *To End World, Break Glass. Littleton might be a small world, but still! They might as well have a switch! Or a big red button. Oh wait, they* do *have a switch, unless there's a backup power source inside there with the rings!*

"Hope! So, are you all done freaking out?"

I shook my head. "Yes?"

"Good, 'cause you know when you pull your hair like that you look, like, twelve. Here." Shelly took my new cell phone and dialed a number on it, hit star, handed it back. "It's tied into Institute Security now. If anything happens here, you'll get the memo the same time as yummy Sheriff Deitz does. I got approval from Ali and set up the other end of the link last night."

She grinned like an urchin.

"She probably just said 'yes' so she could explain it to the sheriff over dinner at Jemmy's—but who cares why, right?"

"Deitz!"

"What about him?"

"I need to go. Cats. Trees."

"You're making no sense, but whatever. I'm going to bug Ali for whatever projects she can tell me about—maybe I can narrow down the target list. Mom says you're coming to dinner."

"Right!" I almost hugged her, remembered the guard. Turning away, I stood frozen. I needed to go, but the pillar mocked me. It was Red Base, the goal. *Why* hadn't they surrounded it with more reinforced concrete and built a bunker on top? I had the worst, mind-clenching feeling that if I took my eyes off it for a moment then my Kitsune-dream would come true. I left at a fast walk.

Chapter Sixteen

"Today's flash-mob will be catered to by Best Wishes, as thanks to their many, many customers, and will move around town viewing performances at currently unknown locations. Be sure to find it on The Littleton Eye, which of course sees everything. Everything. So stop that."

Littleton Radio, The Daily Hour.

It wasn't like Sheriff Deitz was *expecting* me; he'd been really nice about it, but basically he had told me he'd call if there was a cat in a tree. But he and Deputy Sweet had to be Littleton's first line of defense if anyone got past the Scoobies in the Garage, even if the big gun I remembered Angel carrying that night in Grand Beach didn't seem like much beside the three tin-man teams guarding the door.

But I trusted Sheriff Deitz to keep me more in the loop than Veritas, who I hadn't even seen since he'd dropped me at the B&B, which meant telling him why I was here. He hadn't *asked*—probably used to people doing classified things on a need-to-know basis. But it was his town and I should have.

Walking down the street, I realized how off-balance I still was. The Thomas Kinkade America look of the town, the weird streetlamps and the high, percussive hum I kept forgetting I was hearing—the perfect Midwest weather in *Cuba*. And the Institute? If this was the movies, I'd find out that The Institute kept a secret cryogenic prison for storing uncontainable lethal breakthroughs on ice and the Bad Guys wanted to unleash all that Evil In A Can. *None* of it was normal, which didn't help my growing feeling that its artificial perfection was under siege. Little Atifa and her...godfather?...were in danger and I didn't know *why*. And, and...

"*What* is that humming sound I'm always hearing?" Not what I'd been planning to say when I walked through the door. Sheriff Deitz looked up.

"The echo-mapping system? It's built into the street lamps. Full aural surface mapping of the entire town, AI-monitored in realtime. Atlas-types always hear it."

"Really?"

"Oh yeah. That plus the mics, cameras, and the infrared imaging pretty much means we know when a sparrow falls and can positively ID the cat that took it down."

"That's..."

Deputy Sweet snickered from where she sat stripping and cleaning a gun at her desk. "Creepy? You think? But it's what 'high-security environment' means these days. We've got dozens of Witness Protection subjects to keep track of, scientists to protect, spies to spy on..." She laughed at my look. "Nah, that part is handled by Navint—Naval Intelligence."

"Hi Angel. Sorry about not saying hello."

"That's alright. Should we be worried that you're loaded for bear?"

"What? Oh." I'd forgotten I was still in armor and carrying one hundred pounds of titanium maul. "No—I've been to the Garage."

Deitz kicked a seat away from his desk. "Sit. Talk to us. Coffee?"

Angel went to pour us some, her attention staying on me. In contrast to Deitz's easy way, she always reminded me of a dark-eyed hawk. Even her smile was assessing.

"So, what's going on?" Deitz asked after I'd stripped my mask off and taken an obligatory sip. I kept my eyes on my cup.

"How much did the DSA tell you about why I'm here?"

"Just that you're an asset the DSA wants to exploit for a while." He grinned at my look. "And I mean that in a nice way. Consensual. Probably mutual."

"And why they gave me the badge?"

"Well, that just makes sense while you're here...but there's more to it than that, isn't there?"

I looked over at Angel. Her smile was gone.

"I'm here because of a dream." And I told them. I was getting pretty good at it by now. They didn't interrupt, and I finished before my coffee got cold.

Deitz sat back when I finished, absently rubbing his long nose.

"Well, that explains just bunches of things. So, just so I have this straight, right now you've got a public-relations nightmare playing out in Chicago..."

I sighed glumly, realized I was fiddling with my hair and stopped. "Unmitigated. Without mitigating circumstances. *No* upside."

"And in the middle of that, you have a dream—which you are pretty sure is a warning—that a town you've never heard of is going to be lit on fire, and your response is 'I want some of that'."

"Um, pretty much?"

He chuckled, leaning way back. "What a totally cape thing to do."

"What would you do?"

"What *will* we do. We're going to prepare the town, *deputy*."

Preparation didn't involve a lot of the steps I would have recognized.

"Look," Deitz said after I'd spent five minutes trying to absorb what the big screen on the wall was telling me. "The security situation in Littleton is a bit...different. Think of it like being tucked away in the world's most impregnable fortress. *Nobody* is coming at us over the walls. They can only come in through the gate, and the drawbridge is *up*."

I nodded, watching him flip through grid maps on the screen that had looked like an innocent white-board. He was right; someone trying to fight their way in wouldn't just have to capture the Garage, they would have to gain control of the "translation" equipment that flashed us into Littleton.

He followed my thought. "Yeah, anybody who wants in has to already have access. You can bet that in a frontal assault the Navy will let us know what's happening outside and then blow the crap out of the bridge. We've got enough stored food for months if they have to rebuild the whole Garage, but I'll bet my last paycheck that they have a backup system stored far far away that they can fly in and rig up once they beat back an attack."

"No bet." Sweet finished assembling her gun, holstered it.

"And we're not looking at a stealthy insertion over the wall, either. Littleton is its own little extrareality world, and we can count the known breakthroughs capable of any kind of extrareality travel on one hand." Deitz stayed focused on the board. "Since they're not getting in through the door, if they *can* get in then it's the same as a teleport drop. Anybody popping in from outside will set off every alarm we've got when echo-location maps something that just wasn't there a second ago."

Now the Orwellian Panopticon security system made sense. "What about inside buildings? Doesn't surface-mapping stop at the walls?"

"Air pressure sensors. Any sudden arrivals displace several cubic feet of air..."

I nodded. We had those at the Dome; any teleporter popping in would find himself painted and isolated in less than a second. Then Shell would taunt him until we swept him up—she might clean up personally using a Galatea.

"So what are you looking for?" He hadn't taken his eyes off the board.

"Just running a grid check. We want everything green before we start drills—it's been long enough since the last ones."

"Drills?"

"The Institute is responsible for its own security. We have the rest of the town."

Behind me, a voice I knew said "And what are you going to do with the rest of the town?"

I spun in my seat, almost fell out of it. *Jacky* stood just inside the rail separating the "office" from the visitor's area—and how she'd managed to enter without the street door making a sound was one of life's mysteries.

"Jacky!" I couldn't keep the huge grin from spreading across my face.

Her smile showed fang. "What part of 'don't say anything to anyone' wasn't clear?"

"There wasn't *time*."

"There never is."

"Ma'am, can we help you?" Sheriff Deitz didn't sound at all put out, but Jacky kept her eyes on Deputy Sweet—who had her service pistol out and pointed at my friend. It took me a moment to realize what that meant.

"You *snuck in*? Into *Littleton*?"

"And into this office. I got in last night and you have conveniently accessible storage space, Sheriff."

I closed my eyes. At least Jacky wasn't in uniform; showing up as *Artemis*, all black leather and guns, would probably have had Angel shooting already. Not that my pale dark fiend of the night didn't look scary enough in shorts and a beach top—she'd probably look scary in nothing but folded arms and a stare.

Deitz still hadn't moved from in front of the board but his hand fell to his belt, inches from his own gun. "So trespassing goes without saying, which on US Navy property is espionage. Are you turning yourself in? Just asking." My super-duper hearing picked up the clicks and latches as doors and windows sealed themselves. "And how did you get in?"

He wasn't asking about the office, but *I* knew. Not the little details but the biggest one, and I almost laughed. "Your mist form!

The transition to solid isn't instantaneous, so it didn't trigger the alarms."

"Smart girl." Her smile got thinner. "Smarter than the government—and they've hosted vampires here a couple of times. I hitched a ride with some grocery pallets, Sheriff. It was easy. But I've been here before, I know the territory."

He nodded. "I can see that. Angel."

Deputy Sweet holstered her gun.

"So you're not an in-house test?" He smiled wryly. "I ask only because it will be easier to fix if somebody gave you permission to make a run at us."

"Sorry." She didn't sound it. "I've got the security clearance but not the permission slip."

"Then we'll sort it out later. And you're here because..."

"Because of Princess Sunshine here."

"Hey!"

She ignored me. "She thinks someone is going to light up this town and I want to be here for the festivities."

The sheriff coughed, trying real hard not to laugh. "Well, not that that's not...admirable, but this sort of thing usually requires an invitation."

"Like I ever wait for those." Now she just sounded bored. "Check with the DSA and tell me if I need to move my things into one of your cells."

Jacky got more than one appreciative look walking down Main Street; her Evil Snow White, sunlight-never-touches-my skin goth look was a hit, and somehow Shell had gotten her to pack one of her printed tops or slipped it into her bag: *Bite Me*, red on black.

"Jacky, how could you! They could have—"

She smirked. "The DSA thinks I'm a valuable asset in the vamp community, the only blood-sucker not delusional enough to believe she's really a vampire. Worst case they'll tell me to get out of town, but they won't. The department is full of cowboys. They'll make *bets*."

I couldn't think of a thing to say to that, but we were almost back to Holybrook Rest. Sheriff Deitz had given us homework, procedures to get to know while he got approvals for us, and sent us on our way for the day. Now Jacky stopped and looked at the cute B&B, too picturesque for words in the afternoon shade of a dappled oak, then glared at me.

I smiled innocently. "What, you never stayed here?"

"Are there any talking animals?"

"No, but my alarm clock giggles. C'mon, they have great coffee."

Episode Three

Chapter Seventeen

"Success is not final, failure is not fatal: it is the courage to continue that counts."

Winston Churchill

"If you stop before you're dead, you aren't trying."

Atlas

I almost held my breath, watching Jacky's reaction to Mr. Darvish's saintly Be At Peace field. Jacky had once described her own vampiric own powers of psychic influence as *pushing*, and her eyes widened as she recognized the effect from experience. Then she…relaxed and my breath caught.

I'd known Jacky for nearly two years and thought I'd seen her in all moods, from homicidally angry to happy and mellow. I'd been wrong. Under Mr. Darvish's influence she softened, lines of tension and alertness in her face smoothing away, her whole body unstringing from the graceful and tight predator's lines I'd thought were natural to her existence. Maybe they were, but here they flowed away and for the first time I could see what she must have been like before her psychotic "master" killed her family and made her what she was. I had to blink wet eyes and swallow before I could introduce her to our host.

Jacky's unexpected arrival meant Mr. Darvish didn't have a room available, but taking us up to my room he flipped up the bed skirts to reveal a trundle bed for her to sleep on, and he got bath items and an extra robe hung before she finished putting away the bag of things that she'd brought with her. It wasn't much more than her costume and gear—we both needed to shop, especially since *we* were going to dinner. Shelly had texted the invite for Jacky the second I'd texted that she was here.

As a species, vampires *love* shopping; I think their obsession with The Beautiful is part of their psyche. But Jacky *hated* it—all you had to do was mention accessorizing to make her eyes glaze, and I was pretty sure she had her own professional dresser in New Orleans. Fortunately for her, a dash down to the town square turned up only two boutiques with party dresses and we found everything we needed at Stuff and Things.

In the spirit of being prepared, I kept my *special* phone with me. Jacky brought her guns and a belt of clips in a bag. The shopkeeper at Stuff and Things found me a cute thigh-length dress with a high waist you could draw tight under your breasts with a ribbon. For Jacky she found a colorful flared skirt and matching vest to go with a white peasant blouse. I grabbed some new shorts and shirts for myself, Jacky reluctantly chose a pair of sandals with me, and we were good. I got Jacky out of the place before her glares upset anyone.

I'd come to think of shopping with Jacky as combat-shopping, and since pulling it off without the Bees was a stunning accomplishment—possibly due to lingering effects of Mr. Darvish's aura—I insisted we celebrate at the ice cream shop next door. Where she turned out to be a French vanilla and red velvet girl, and the sidewalk tables under the street awning turned out to be the perfect place to relax and indulge.

From where we sat, I could see the top of the Institute building over the trees and I watched it as I licked my cone. "So...we're sitting outside the most top-secret labs in the world. Eating ice cream."

"The most dangerous labs are outside in the naval base and a lot of people know it's here—they just don't know what goes on inside."

"They tested you here?"

"Yes." That was it, no details. The only thing she'd ever said about it was that it had been unpleasant and that I didn't want to know. Once in a while I'd wonder how you tested to make sure a vampire couldn't reliably sire progeny and kick off a vampire apocalypse—and my mind would scream at me to think about something else. Bunnies. Rainbows. Ice cream.

Jacky read my face. Or my mind—it was hard to tell, with vampires. "This isn't a black-research lab dressed up in Pleasantville. Nobody needs saving here."

"I know. Or I think I do. I've met good people, they wouldn't—"

"Anybody will do anything if they have to. But if our side keeps that kind of place it isn't here. Trust me, I'd know."

I nodded and focused on my cone.

She shrugged, careful of drippage. "Anyway, the Institute isn't our problem, the town is. Do you really think something's coming? That it's not all a con? A diversion, maybe?"

"'By the pricking of my thumbs,'" I quoted, "'something wicked this way comes.'" I really did think it was real, but a feeling wasn't enough, was it? "How long do you think they'll let us stay here?" My appetite for the fudge-and-chocolate goodness of Extreme Moosetracks was gone. "How long can I ignore— How long can I stay away from Chicago?" *And where is Kitsune?*

Then I saw the naked man.

Jacky forgot about her cone. "That's something you don't see every day."

I fumbled for my phone, hit *one* for Shelly. She got it on two rings. *"How's shopping? Jacky threaten anyone yet?"*

"No… Shelly, is Littleton clothing-optional?" I tried looking everywhere else but at the black-haired man ambling towards us down the street and nodding to other pedestrians.

"Arion is out again? Wait and tell me who gets him!"

"Arion— Who gets— Shelly!"

"He's the Server of Ganymede, you know, an 'extraterrestrial visitor' here on Earth with a message of peace and universal beinghood." I could hear the bracketing quotes that signaled *extraterrestrial visitor* meant *delusional breakthrough*.

"And part of his message is 'no pants'?"

"No, but if he decides he's in the mood for some loving he goes for a walk without them and waits for somebody to bring him a coat and take him home."

"And they do?"

"There's a betting pool."

"And they *do*? I mean—"

"I know, and yeah they do. All they'll say about it is it's unique. Mom says even she has no idea what they mean."

"I—" I stopped because Angel had pulled up in the sheriff's jeep, lights flashing. She got out with a coat.

"Bet's off. Angel just arrived."

"Really? Cause Mom picked her for the pool."

I closed my eyes, something I should have done a couple of minutes ago. "Too much information." Hanging up, I glared at Jacky; I had to be red—the day had gotten hot and she was laughing. "This town is *weird*." Sinking down in my chair I focused on my cone. It had taken advantage of my distraction to drip all over my hand.

My cellphone chimed and I jumped. Jacky smiled and kicked her bag.

"Maybe that's them telling us this is it. We could get a good workout and be flying home tomorrow."

I fumbled again, handed her my cone. The cell wasn't screaming or flashing red, but my heart raced anyway until I read the text. "It's from the base. The naval base. They approved my request to see Brick, and want me to go there now."

"Really? Then I need to change."

I hadn't expected them to say yes, and now my brain raced in circles asking *why*? Either Jacky was much more Zen, or better at hiding confusion. We took our loot back to Holybrook Rest where she stripped and skinned into her Artemis outfit complete with hooded half-mask and all four guns—her real ones, not the stunners she used in Chicago. I flew her to the Garage and from there to the base, touching down on the same pad we'd landed on yesterday. Lance Corporal Balini met us there, in full Scoobie armor but minus the ordnance mounts, and took us inside.

"Who's your friend? Kidding—I know. Great to meet the infamous Artemis." He turned all his charm on her. "Listen, I know this great place in Guantánamo that serves—"

"No."

"We could get drunk and make bad decisions."

"You just did."

I smiled since he couldn't see it, and didn't look at Jacky. The part of the base we were walking through looked and smelled new, newer than the Garage, and I couldn't smell the tinge of water's-edge rot that was part of every seacoast not too cold for it. That meant a sealed environment and an air-scrubbing AC system. Proof against Jacky's mist-form? Probably, making it even more secure than the Garage.

Balini took us through three doors, two with guards that I could see. Past the third one, my ears told me we were under echo-location surveillance. Surface-mapping would be a good way to make sure that a visitor wasn't covered by a visual or mental illusion, so the Invisible Man wasn't getting in here either. The walls and doors were solid enough that no noise got through to tell me *anything* was on the other side, and each layer of security I spotted wound me tighter. There was no traffic, no bustle like I'd seen at the Institute. This wasn't a research facility, at least not this part; it was a holding facility for superhumans.

"Who do you keep here besides B Class Ajax-Types, Corporal?"

He looked back at me. "You're quick! Relax, Winman's not going anywhere and he's an easy guest. There's a few we have to be lots more careful for—guys *you* couldn't handle. Here we are."

Instead of a door, the hall ended in a framed wall of silver liquid—like someone had managed to paint a layer of mercury to the wall and make it stick. I could see the three of us in its not-quite-solid surface, me standing small beside Jacky's supermodel-height and Balini's hulking shape. My eyes looked huge in my mask and caught the reflected light. Then the wall flowed away, receding into the frame around it, and I realized it was some kind of force field.

The room on the other side was a big hexagonal space. Each wall held an open-framed cell and force fields filled the open frames, translucent instead of reflective. Half the cells were occupied, and three guards in sealed armor watched the prisoners from a recessed station under an inverted quicksilver ceiling dome in the middle of the room.

"The fields are one-way mirrors," Balini said, but I could see that none of the prisoners had reacted to our arrival. The guards had no excuse, but they didn't look up either. I turned around. The field had reformed behind us, translucent on this side; the guards hadn't needed cameras to see us coming down the hall.

"Is the dome a weapon mount?" Jacky asked.

"Good call. Its field can pulse to allow the synchronized guns to fire out but not let anything in. Very nice."

I nodded absently, sure there were lots of other weapons and security measures we couldn't see. This was the kind of superhuman-containment stuff that Atlas and Blackstone and the other founding Sentinels had refused to allow the government to build into the Dome.

Balini steered us to a room to the left of our entryway—a small lounge where we found Veritas waiting, as well as Lieutenant Corbin and Captain Lauer. Fatigue lines I hadn't noticed at the action review had deepened, and I guessed that he hasn't slept much last night and hadn't napped today.

"Astra, Artemis," Veritas greeted us, back to his deadpan public manner. "Glad you could make it."

Jacky just smiled, one of the few people I knew who could out-cool him.

"Astra." Captain Lauer nodded.

"Sir. Thank you for letting us come over."

"We've already got everything he'll say without amnesty, which is nothing, and we're sending for a telepath who will be here tomorrow. Will you be alright doing it alone?"

"Yes." *Not* what I'd been expecting at all, and I felt Jacky shift beside me. "Is there anything you don't want me to say?"

"No. At this point I don't believe anything you might say will make him less cooperative."

"Okay." I took a breath. "Where is he?"

Where turned out to be in the next room. Brick waited for me past one more force field gate, manacled to an anchored table with shackles that weighed more than I did fully loaded. At Captain Lauer' signal they cut the field, and the bite of harsh soap and chemicals in my nose told me they'd thoroughly deloused him. One step, and the silver field went back up behind me.

"Heeey!" Brick's battered face broke into a smile wide enough to show chipped and uneven teeth. He shifted and winced; his orange prison suit had been cut to accommodate a brace on his left elbow. A sling-brace immobilized his whole right arm. "I was hoping to see you again!"

I forced myself to step forward again, set down my maul, and take the seat opposite him. And sat. Now that I was here, I had no idea how to start. My eyes went to his manacled wrists where they rested on the table, and I saw red skin above them.

"What happened there?"

He looked down, pulled on his shackles. "Those? They used a laser to remove my dragon tattoos. No tats, no more instant armor and toys. No problem—the Army will fix me up again."

"They will?"

"Sure! Haven't killed anybody since going AWOL, and they need rough guys like me." He shifted, winced again. "They'll just stick a tracker in my gut next time, maybe a bomb, maybe get a brain-twister to plant an order in my head—but hey, I cooperate and I'm back out of stockade."

I reached out without thinking, touched the angry red flesh and flinched back. He was already healing the way Ajax-Types did—on a normal person they'd be at least a week old—but even with soft bandages between cuffs and skin it still had to hurt to be manacled.

"I'm sorry," I said.

"Huh? Girl, you think *that* hurt?"

"No— I mean, sorry about the shoulder. I didn't need to do that after I got you down and broke your arm."

His forehead creased into a network of wrinkles, then he barked a laugh. "Hey, it was a good fight! You win, you get your licks in. You've gotten better since Chicago, so have I, maybe next time I'll last longer."

"But—" I stopped. The distance across the table was an entire world. I licked dry lips. "Why do you do it?"

"What, fight? I'm good at it. It's my good time. Girl like you, you'd never understand. Doesn't mean I won't enjoy the next time."

What did I say to that? See you then? All the other questions I wanted to ask, who, why, had already been asked and not answered. My social brain took over.

"It was…" *too weird for words*. "Good to speak to you, Brick." I collected Malleus and stood. "I hope you're wrists are better soon." *And I never see you again.* I turned to signal the captain.

"Hey!" I turned back. Brick sat thinking, brow wrinkled, and then a grin stretched his face. He shrugged again, ignoring the pain.

"Call me Ernest. And you might want to go back to that bar tomorrow night and look for a guy with a white hat and a blue flower on him. He was going to give me a job, but hey, it could be fun for you."

Chapter Eighteen

"There are three types of supersoldiers: soldiers who achieved their breakthroughs under the rigors of basic training or tailored stress-programs; civilian superhumans who couldn't pass up the huge recruiting bonus, excellent pay, and lifelong benefits; and the parolees. The military recruits from federal and state prisons, because it can't get enough of the first two types. Parolees' benefits are different, as are their missions and often their rules of engagement. Some of them finish their parole tours and move into the regular ranks, others return to civilian life. Many of them don't survive to finish their tours."

US Senate Military Briefing Extract.

"Well that was interesting." Veritas came as close to a real smile as he ever did. The captain's eyebrows were still halfway to his hairline. "And it wasn't a joke. He really thinks a drink at the bar would be interesting." He looked at me and his eyes sparkled. "If you're game I can arrange it."

"No, you can't." The captain wasn't protesting, he just said it like it was so. He looked around the lounge at the rest of us, back at me. "Astra, thank you for that. Now would you care to speak with me in my office?"

Jacky snorted and I almost saluted; I knew an order when I heard one. She pulled out her cell. "You guys do that, I need to make a call."

"Corporal Balini, show her a room. Astra?"

I left with the captain. Five minutes and three security checkpoints later he ushered me into his office, closing the door behind us.

"Well that was interesting. Not an original thought, but true. Water?"

"Thank you. Captain Lauer—"

"Call me Frank." He took off his uniform hat to sit and stretch out in the visitor's chair across from me. His office didn't have a single picture or knickknack. Seeing me look around, he nodded. "I'm here on assignment, too. Your assignment, actually."

"*My* assignment?"

"The one you made for yourself, anyway. To stop bad things from happening. The difference is, *my* focus is on the Institute and the base. *Yours* is on the town." He held up a hand. "And I understand. You get intel that it's going to be a hot time in the old town tonight, you come. You're a goddam hero. Well, I've seen towns burn before, and I'll see more. I'm tasked with assessing and responding to the threat to our research facilities, here and in Littleton, and our base holding facility which just happens to hold some of the most dangerous enemies the civilized world has ever seen. We lose control of them, or we lose our projects, we might just lose the long war.

"And of course there's the conference—Washington has tasked me with giving the go or no-go on it. If our most secure facility isn't as secure as we thought, the conference will need to be scrapped and we have less than three days to decide."

He took a sip of water and leaned forward, not in my face but close and not looking away.

"*But*. The only intel we have on a threat is you. *Your* warning. If I say 'go', half the projects will shut down and fly away, and we'll lose months, years, not to mention losing a meeting a year in the planning. So I have to believe that there is a credible threat first, but

Veritas has been shaking the trees and beating the grass at the Institute for two days and he's got nothing. An army of accountants and computer specialists have crawled through every resident's bank-account, travel history, sex life, checked every firewall and security system. They've got nothing, and I'm coming up with bupkis on the military side, in a place where the only way in is for someone inside the walls to open the gate to the enemy."

He sat back.

"So, go or no-go? Based on a dream sent by an international criminal known for complicated games, the kind where other people take the hits?" Fixed on me, his eyes glinted in the overhead lights. "I don't know, I really don't. But then comes 'Brick.'"

He put his bottle down.

"It's interesting that you have a history with him, but the superhuman world isn't so big it's unbelievable. But is he a probe? A decoy? A Trojan Horse? Or a coincidence? Guantánamo City's airport is a gateway to the Gulf and the Caribbean. And then there's you."

"Me?" My throat had gone dry.

"You. My first instinct after getting the background was to send you right back to Chicago just to remove a piece from the board that this Kitsune put there."

"You can't." My mouth was dry.

"I could have. I still can. The US Navy holds seniority in the base and town. Kayle would have to go to the Chief of Naval Operations to trump my authority, and Ricky would tell him to pound sand."

"But you didn't."

"Doesn't mean I won't. I sent you out with the Garage team when Brick popped up, and I wasn't too impressed. You made a rookie mistake for your opening move, pulled it out in the end by luck. I don't like luck. And there's the discrepancy between your report and the video record. You don't remember half your fight."

"Why—" I hadn't come here expecting to get attacked, and he gave me a moment to think. Finally remembering I held a water bottle, I took a sip too extend the moment and wet my throat.

"So you think I'm unreliable?"

"I wondered." He kept his eyes on me. "I understand you do full-contact fight training?"

I nodded.

"Then you've been trained to 'play through the pain.' You were utterly focused on the next thing you could do, so the hits you took first weren't important enough for your brain to file away."

He played with his own bottle. "Combat-amnesia is actually pretty common. In extreme cases whole sequences of events are blocked, and not just traumatic ones. You've probably experienced it before—actions in combat that took longer than they seemed to, or happened more quickly than you remember. It's simply that you've never had as big a contradiction between memory and reality caught on camera. Do you remember anything else that didn't look the same when you watched in the review?"

"I... Yes! Lance Corporal Tsen..."

"Go on."

"When Brick hit him— I remember his breastplate just, just completely caving in, right through his chest. It would have killed him, wouldn't it? Ajax-type or not."

"Very likely. You've seen that kind of hit before? It's what you feared most when you saw him take the hit, and your mind manufactured a completely illusory memory. You've heard the cliché, 'Who are you going to believe? Me or your lying eyes?'" His mouth creased in a humorless smile. "In the stress of combat our eyes do often lie—or at least our minds play tricks with what our eyes tell us. At this point, even a telepath walking through the memory with you couldn't tell us the story the video showed."

"So, it's normal? I'm okay?"

"Probably. That's why I brought you out to watch you with Brick. If it was deeper, if he was a source of trauma for you, you'd have showed it in there and I could send you home." He took another sip, laughed. "Did *not* expect to get more intel from it."

"What are you going to do now?"

He smiled crookedly. "Keep my own assets in position. Do *you* want to go have fun?"

"No, we're not. Not until dark." Jacky stated it as a simple fact. She'd still been on her call when the sailor escorting me showed me into the empty conference room they'd given her, and she barely heard me out before stepping on my plan to go *now*. "We'll have to rain-check dinner."

"But—"

"Don't worry, we'll still get to dress up."

"*Are you two always like this?*" The voice on the other end of her cellphone dripped warm Nola honey, all masculine amusement at our girl-talk.

"No." Her glare should have melted her cell.

"*Jacky, are you sure? And who's that? Do I get to meet him?*"

"Yes." She scanned the walls of the conference room we'd been given for privacy, and I could just *see* her thinking. The Navy had to be listening, if not on the line then to the room—but whatever she didn't say now, she wasn't going to keep them in the dark for long.

She decided, and relaxed. "That's Darren. He confirmed your White Hat and you'll meet him tonight. I thought we might need backup so I stopped in New Orleans on the way and brought some friends. You'll meet them, too."

Oooh, I practically hallucinated Shell's—or Shelly's—response to that tidbit. I opened my mouth, closed it because even if the Navy knew she'd still be uncomfortable confirming that she'd brought vampire backup—the only thing it could be if we had to wait till *night*.

"*Got it.*" Darren said. "*So what do you need, sweetheart?*"

"Hope and I are going to go change and get our party stuff together," she said, ignoring me as I mouthed *sweetheart?* "We'll meet you at the hotel where all of you can get your curiosity out of your system, then we'll *all* go dancing. And don't worry, we have a ride."

She cut the connection before he could say anything else, glared at me. "What?"

"Are you sure about missing dinner? 'Cause Mrs. B— Mrs. H makes a great pot roast. To die for, not that you want to do *that* again. Hey, you could bring Darren…" Yes I was being evil, but it was too much fun and I needed a little.

"Are you finished?"

"I suppose. Wait— Yes. Shelly is going to yell at you, though."

"I can live with that." She barely gave me time to grab Malleus before she was out the door. I flew us back to the Garage and Littleton, getting us back just in time to hear the wailing sirens.

Chapter Nineteen

"The important thing to remember in a crisis is not to panic. But since you're going to panic anyway, the most *important thing is to have a menu of responses you know so well that you can take the immediate steps while your brain isn't giving you 100%. If you picked the wrong response, at least you're moving and that makes you harder to hit."*

Astra

Now? My heart raced, skipping a beat when my *special* cellphone shrilled and buzzed. Jacky put a hand on my shoulder, ready to grab on as I flew.

"Astra!" It was Sheriff Deitz. "*Drop Artemis at the B&B and get high. I want eyes, and you're safe under three hundred feet. Move!*" I launched from our entry point, flying *low* over the hill and under the tree line into town and through the streets. Jacky dropped off my back outside Holybrook Rest and I spared one thought for Mr. Darvish and the cherub before going vertical.

I didn't have Shell to give me a virtual-marker reading of feet-above-ground, but I'd gotten pretty good at eyeballing distance and I stopped to hover at maybe two hundred and fifty feet. Every hooded streetlamp in town wailed below me, the light-domes that topped them flashing red or green. In the streets marked by green-strobing lampposts, people raced out of buildings and houses. Some jogged away down the streets, others jumped into cars.

I spun in a slow one-eighty, looking for the danger, spun again. I couldn't *see* anything, but at least nobody was panicking; on some streets the cars moved along slowly, picking up pedestrians as they went. Parents guided children—at the school they wound from the building to the buses in a tight two-by-two chain. In other streets the cars didn't stop but I saw the runners were aiming for marked shelters. At the ends of the town not blocked by the lake, I could see that everybody was headed for a couple of gated bus parks; obviously they'd load and drive across the bubble's boundary line when full-up or told to scram.

"I've got nothing up here!" I yelled into my cell. "What am I looking for?"

"*If you don't see threats, move over the red zones.*" Angel this time. "*If it goes green, move on. If you see any threats or someone takes a shot at you, report. Any threatened residents, use your discretion.*"

"Got it." I stayed high, moving directly over the largest red zone then curving outward from there when my super-duper vision failed to spot anybody moving in a way that screamed threat. Threats failed to arrive from above as well, but I made a mental grid and stuck to it.

Scan, turn, scan, move on. Nobody tried to shoot at me, nothing moved outside of a few residents caught in the open and scrambling for shelters. One by one the red zones went green, marked by eruptions of residents exiting buildings and joining the orderly exodus. Maybe five minutes after the alarms sounded, the last zone went green with no threats in sight.

The sirens cut off, the green lights went steady.

"*Stand down, Astra,*" Angel said. "*Drill's over.*"

"That was a *drill*?"

"Yup." Deitz watched the replay on his big board, symbols in the grid scrolling numbers I didn't understand. "Pretty good one, too. We haven't done a full-town drill in a while."

"And you're not going to do one again!" Director Althea Shaw was practically hissing, glaring at Deitz from the side of the board set for video-conference. Stepping past the rail brought me into her field of vision and she turned her attention to me.

"I trusted you not to distract Miss Hardt! Her reports to the team are down fifty percent after just two days and now you've got Paul—Sheriff Deitz conducting drills that are shutting down research! Just what do you think is going to happen?"

I sucked in my breath at the sudden attack, and then my mouth took over.

"Do I look like I *know*?" I swallowed rising bile but the words poured out. "If I knew *what*, I'd know *who*! If I knew who, then Blackstone, the DSA, Director *Kayle* and probably the freaking Joint Chiefs of Staff would know! Holy hell would be raining down on *somebody* right now!"

She opened her mouth, looking stunned. I rolled right over her.

"But I don't even know *when*! So I'm stuck here while everything goes to crap back home because something is coming and I have to be here!"

I heard clapping, turned as Jacky came in the door behind me.

"Ali." Deitz finished reading the board. "It was my call, and we needed to include the Institute. Also, your people's response time stinks; barely half of them bothered to check their cells for instructions."

"Because the alarm wasn't internal!"

"I'm still summoning everyone who didn't check in for a mandatory meeting. If they don't come, I'm evicting them. That's my call, too."

Ali's short face-fur hid her cheeks, but I was pretty sure she'd gone apoplectic-red underneath it. Her whiskers stood out stiff and her ears laid back in classic fight-mode, but she didn't actually spit. I watched her count breaths, and it obviously worked for her, too; her ears and whiskers relaxed though her eye still shot sparks.

"*Fine. Fine. I'll be there, and I'm calling this upstairs.*"

"Looking forward to it. We still on for dinner?"

She blanked her screen.

"That went well." He gave me a lopsided smile. "Can you promise at least a small fire in town? Soon? If it's before Sunday night then I think she'll forgive me."

Angel snorted and I couldn't repress a shaky laugh. My own crisis-adrenaline high fading, I felt queasily sick. *Did I really just have a shouting match with Shelly's boss?*

"I'll try?" I took a deep breath of my own, sighed. "And what kind of apology does she like?"

"Oh no, you don't." His smile disappeared. "You're my deputy and you had nothing to do with this. If anything it should go the other way, and it will when she's had a chance to calm down." He rubbed his brow, looked at the blanked screen. "She's been off since her trip to Washington. Probably the upcoming conference. So, let's review the drill."

"Well, that was interesting." It seemed to be a day for saying that.

Jacky laughed, and not for the first time I decided it wasn't fair. When *Jacky* laughed it was a deep contralto, with undertones; *I* sounded like a giggly schoolgirl. I'd never heard her sing, but she probably had a beautiful smoky singing voice and mine could charitably be called "thin." Pedestrians returning from the drill waved as we proceeded along, me nursing dark thoughts to keep from thinking about yelling at Director Shaw, Jacky thinking about who-knew-what.

"Do you feel better about the town, now?" she asked.

"I suppose. No, I really do. I thought Chicago was pretty well organized, but Littleton could teach us a few things."

"You'd feel even better if you'd seen the inside of the shelters. They're not just fully loaded emergency response centers—bio, radiation, wrath of God, take your pick—they're arsenals. And from the way the locals were loading up I'd say one in four of them is a proud member of the Littleton Militia."

I stopped in my tracks. "Really?"

"That, or all adults who aren't researchers or refugees are retired military. Or not so retired."

I started walking again. "So, the alarms go off, and the shelters open to unlock the armories?"

"Something like that. Let's just say that I don't think anybody is going to be robbing the municipal bank. Aaand now you're wondering if you really should be here at all."

"Wouldn't you? I'm not sure this place needs Awesome Girl."

"Like that'll make you go away. We're here, and we have an interesting evening ahead. You can reconsider everything in the morning."

As much as I wanted to stay unreasonable, she had a point; we had a job Brick thought might be *fun*. Knowing Jacky, she would probably agree with him. Or call it therapy, which much as I wished it wasn't so was totally normal for her. I shook it off and hooked her arm in mine as we turned down the street to the B&B.

"How are you going to hide all your guns under that skirt? Think we can find a *really* big purse?"

She snickered. "And how are you going to keep from getting recognized by half the Americans in town? They'll be watching for you after yesterday. With cameras."

"Easy. I'm going to cheat."

Chapter Twenty

"There are three basic reactions to mortal combat, all very human: revulsion, acceptance, and pleasure. The first is most common—most people are profoundly shaken by physical conflict and a majority of police officers or superheroes who kill someone in the line of duty resign or ensure they are not in a position to do it again. The second reaction is less common but many people take no lasting trauma from fighting or even killing if they believe it is necessary. The third reaction to mortal combat, intense pleasure, is fortunately comparatively rare. But a higher percentage of breakthroughs in the third category are dangerous breakthroughs indeed.

Dr. Alice Mendel, *Breakthroughs and the Crisis of Being*

Jacky's eyebrows climbed into her hairline when I pulled the Anonymity Specs out of their box. If they would let Grendel eat in peace in the middle of a crowded restaurant, they'd keep me below the radar of a town full of would-be filmmakers. At least as long as nothing serious started to make them pay attention.

"So did Ozma loan you any more of her toys?"

"Just this." I held up my hand, showing her the still-pristine lace ring. "And no, I have no idea what it is—just that I'm not supposed to take it off till I have to. Whatever *that* means."

Told that we had to rain-check dinner, Shelly had come over to help us dress. She turned my hand to look at the ring, wrinkled her brow. "Couldn't she have been any clearer? I hate magic. Every variety out there has its own set of rules."

"And Verne-tech is any different?" Jacky tossed a hair scrunchy at her. "A Hand of Glory is the same as a somnolence field."

I grabbed an Alice band for my hair. "A hand of what? Do I want to know?"

"No!" Shelly threw the scrunchy back. "It's disgusting."

Shelly had brought a couple boxes of accessories with her, and the three of us made a crowd in the little bedroom with wide-eyed Atifa and her bear sitting cross-legged on the bed as a happy audience. Which officially made this the weirdest mission-prep I'd ever experienced.

And one of the most frustrating; we couldn't figure out a way to hide Jacky's guns.

Then I spotted the brilliant rainbow-colored beret. Dropping the Alice band, I set the jaunty cap on my head, rifled through Shelly's biggest box for the wide shades I'd seen. They matched perfectly.

"Here." I handed Jacky the Anonymity Specs. "We can put you in full costume, body armor, all your guns, nobody will notice a thing until you start shooting." I frowned. "They might not fit over your mask."

Jacky's scowl went away. I wasn't sure which made her happier: being able to strap on her full arsenal, or getting out of dress-up. That left me for Shelly to focus on while Jacky changed back, and by the time she was through I looked like a teen Hollywood star trying to go incognito. Thinking about the possible festivities ahead, the short, light skirt didn't make me happy but if it did come to a serious and wardrobe-destroying fight at least I had my modest indestructibles.

Shelly changed her mind on my necklace three times, finally choosing a cheap but sparkly crystal. "So you won't feel bad if it gets, you know, scratched." Her smile wavered, and suddenly I understood what was bothering her. I was going into battle and she wasn't going with me, not even in my head.

"Hey, Shell will be there when I get to Guantánamo City," I said, and winced. That wasn't the point, and I fumbled for a distraction. "Not that she's been too 'present' today, not even texting, really. What's going on back home? What's everybody doing?"

That got a smile, a weak one but I'd take it. "They're ignoring everything and training. They went to the open range outside of town the last two days, and Tsuris is practicing making water-spouts out on Lake Michigan—you know, small tornadoes over water. Shell says he's the only one the newsies are getting any sight of at all."

"Well, tell Shell to keep you in the loop tonight. In case."

She bit her cheek and nodded, looking around. We were done, out of excuses.

Jacky and I left Shelly with Atifa and I flew Jacky to the Garage, where the enlisted on watch set off alarms and locked down the bay until Jacky took the glasses off so he could see that we were both the arrivals he'd been told to expect. A perfect, if heart-stopping, field test. Corporal Balini—who volunteered—waited for us in the exit bay with a not new but well-kept sedan, smile wide and dressed in civvies appropriate for a hookup-hunting bar crawl. A cheerful chauffer, he drove us to the checkpoint that marked the border between US and Cuban sovereignty, talking all the way about how good it was to get out of the tin can.

And there we got a surprise.

The American and Cuban soldiers at the gate both checked the papers the Garage had given us, and then gave way to a Man in Black.

Really.

"Young ladies, I am Mister Black. I will be joining you this evening." He touched his black Panama hat.

He spoke with a thick accent but perfect diction and, looking up at him, my eyes slid away from his face with no memory of a feature I could name. Magic? Mental powers? Corporal Balini's return salute shut down my objection. "He's an Upright Man," Jacky whispered. "Go with it." The strange man slid into the passenger's seat beside Balini.

"It is a beautiful evening, ladies," he addressed us over his shoulder as the corporal drove. "Since you are guests, it is my task tonight to ensure that your night in Guantánamo involves only those whom you have come for, and is not an unfortunate night for anyone else."

"It's very nice to meet you," I replied without thinking. "What, exactly, can you do?"

"What I need to do. So long as I do not need to, I wish you the best of luck tonight."

Okay... This just got weirder and weirder. Did Veritas know any more about the Upright Men than what he'd told me? Or didn't our own people know? Could our babysitter really "vanish" us if we stepped over the line he *wasn't* drawing very clearly?

It *was* a beautiful evening, shading into night as we drove into Guantánamo City. The main street, renewed and colorful during the day, turned festive as the light died. Lit colored lamps outside cafés and coffee shops dressed the street for a party. Music, electroacoustic guitar and piano mixed with drums and even steel drums in bright Creole fusion. When Jacky started to give Corporal Balini directions to a hotel, I stopped her.

"Darren told you White Hat was camped out at the Café Cubano? Let me borrow the specs—if I eyeball him then Shell might be able to tell us more than we know already." Which was exactly nothing in the few hours we'd had since Brick let us know about them. "Can you tell me anything, Mister Black?"

"I am sorry, but no. You understand, our own intelligence agencies do not receive much international cooperation even now. We only know they are men of power up to no good."

I blinked. "They?"

Mr. Black looked improbably innocent. "Your own sources didn't tell you? There are three of them together."

That didn't help my Zen, and I almost turned us around on instinct; Blackstone's first response would have been to put everything on hold and Get More Information. But there was really only one way to get it.

"Right. Okay then. Stop here and wait. I shouldn't be long."

Jacky passed me the specs and Mr. Black actually jumped—suddenly noticing so much more about my friend. It made me feel better somehow. Trading her my shades, I slipped the specs on and got out of the car.

The music and laughter from bright-lit establishments enticed, floating out to mingle in the street as I made my way up the sidewalk through the growing crowds. Yesterday the street had been empty by comparison in the heat of the day.

"Shell?" I whispered.

"About time! I've been listening since the guard post."

"Shelly caught you up?"

"Oh yeah. And while waiting I learned a bit about *Darren*. You're going to love him…"

Her voice carried the unmistakable note of wicked glee familiar to anyone who knew the many voices of Shell, and I barely resisted the urge to ask. Jacky hadn't said much of anything about Darren and the backup she'd left in Guantánamo City when she came into town to get me, and I was beginning to feel set up.

Priorities, Hope—you're not fifteen. "Well now it looks like there are three of them. I'm legal drinking age in Cuba, I'm going to go in, look around, order a drink at the bar and take it out to the sidewalk tables. Tell me when I get a good enough look for you?"

"Right! Let's see these guys!"

I made it down the street and to the open doors of the Café Cubano with minimal jostling, only to get slammed with barely time to instinctively brace by a happy drunk exiting with his friends. He bounced off me and sat shaking his head while they laughed and I cringed and tried not to look around for our targets. They *had* to have seen that.

I let out my breath when nobody moved in the sudden, purposeful way that signaled *threat*. Even the traveling drinking party forgot about me, helping their friend up without a second glance.

"It's official," I whispered.

"What?"

"I love Ozma's glasses. I'm going to *marry* them."

"Cool. Could you move to the middle of the bar?"

Good choice. The bar stretched along one long wall and gave an open view of nearly all the tables around the small dance floor. My height was a serious problem, but with the sun just down the place wasn't so crowded yet that I'd be staring at a wall of people. I made my way to the best open spot I could find—no chairs, you either stood at the bar or took a table. The American bartender gave me his attention with a once-over and a wink.

"He thinks you're way too young…" Shell teased as I watched him mix drinks. Seriously tall and skinny, with short curly hair, he reached and tossed with easy hands. Of course he didn't think I met Cuba's lower drinking age, but when he finished with the patron in front of him and came over he didn't card me.

"What can I get for you?" he asked. I blanked.

"Cuba Libre," Shell supplied.

"A Cuba Libre, please?"

"One rum and coke, coming up." He mixed the coke and white rum with two shakes, poured it over ice in a tall, thin glass, and added a squeezed lime. He traded it for my folded bill, but stopped with his hand over mine on the bar and looked me in the eyes. "Pace yourself. Yell if you need help, I can call a cab for your hotel."

"I— Sure."

"Awww," Shell teased some more as I turned away. "A Galahad. So sweet." Which was totally unfair now that I couldn't answer back.

I took a sip, tried not to wrinkle my nose at the rum and the clouds of cigar smoke, and looked around. If someone penetrated the Anonymity Specs, hopefully they'd just see a silly American girl drinking because it was legal and looking for a Cuban adventure.

"Nothing…nothing…nothing…there!" Shell flashed a virtual targeting icon on a white man, American or European, sitting in the corner with two compatriots. No hat, but he wore a blue carnation and his balding head glistened with sweat under the slow-turning ceiling fans; it looked like he'd taken the hat off. White Hatless sat reading a newspaper. The other two at his table, a beefy guy and a skinny one (I labeled them Big and Tall), just sat. I'd have had a hard time getting a look at their faces in the already crowded club, but all three sat so that they faced into the room with wide sight-lines. Professional paranoids; I let my eyes rest on them for only a second, focused on the table full of young and loud movie techies beside them while I thought about what I carefully wasn't looking at.

"Hope," Shell whispered needlessly. "Turn around now. Don't look again, finish your drink, ask Galahad for that cab, and get out of there. Now."

I managed not to freeze, turned back to the bar but stood stumped. "Now" and "Finish your drink," didn't go together. Shell made a rude noise and my cellphone chimed.

"*This is your excuse calling...*" She chanted in my ear when I answered. "*Hang up and get. Out. Of. There!*"

Yes, that would work. I took a deep gulp of my drink—my hand didn't quite shake, but my racing blood would burn it faster than it could possibly work its way with me. Holding up my cell for Galahad to see, I mouthed "Cab?" He nodded and reached under the bar for a phone.

I kept sipping while watching the door, and maybe two minutes later a man with a cap and vest that screamed "driver" walked through the doors and looked for my bartender. I slipped another bill under my nearly finished glass, waved, and walked out fast. On the street I let the cabby drive me two blocks, pretended to see someone, and got out with a "Sorry!" and a nice tip.

I pulled out my phone again to have an excuse to talk. "Okay, what *was* that?" Shell appeared by my elbow, making me jump.

"*That* was you walking very carefully out of a room filled with Canned Atrocity Wanting to Happen. Look." She pointed at a wall between shop windows, used it as a virtual screen while I pretended to read the flyers posted on it.

She painted the bald man. "Eastern European. C Class Ajax-type, but *fast*. Not Rush fast, but fast enough that you probably can't touch him. They call him Red; he likes to toss grenades around—and by "toss" I mean step into a crowd and drop them on the floor around him. He also likes knives, tearing digits off, anything that throws blood around, and he laughs while he does it."

Erasing him, she brought up Big. A brawler with a buzz-cut, small and close-set eyes in a battered face that reminded me of Brick, I'd have bet anything he had antisocial tattoos where we couldn't see them.

"Flashpoint. American, B Class pyrokinetic—a psychotic fire-starter who loves big fireball explosions. He can 'cook off' the ammunition in a gun or the fuel in a gas tank. If he can't do that, he'll light your hair or clothes on fire.

"And last," she brought up Tall, "*Brainworm*. He's the most dangerous of the three. He can project a neural scrambling field that affects anything with a central nervous system unlucky enough to be in range. The symptoms start with disorientation, escalate to hallucinations and loss of mental control. Victims run screaming, curl up into catatonic balls, attack whoever's closest to them… "

She erased the horror-show. "The three horsemen of the freaking Apocalypse. Four if they were supposed to join Brick. They all started as international mercenaries, all three are wanted by Interpol, and until tonight they've only been spotted in war torn hellholes or rogue states. "

"Have they ever worked together?" I asked weakly.

"Yes. Libya and Indonesia. So the other two must have some way of shaking off Brainworm."

"Really? Maybe we could *ask* them for it." I put my cell back in my purse, started walking. I could see the car a street away, and had never wanted sane and *not horrible* company more. Even Mr. Black was looking good to me now.

Chapter Twenty One

"Some smart guy said no plan survives contact with the enemy. Remember that cuts both ways and be the one who makes the contact happen. That way you get to rethink your plan first.*"*

Atlas

"You can close your mouth now." Shell laughed, a mischievous ghost beside me. "Really. Any time."

The good news was that I could focus on something other than impending insanity, death, and destruction. The bad news was that made me just too shallow for words. I'd hate myself later, when I could think about it.

Getting back in the car, I'd swapped glasses with Jacky again and she'd directed us to the Hotél Washington where her people were waiting. *Adonis* had answered the door, and since I was in the lead of our little party I blocked the hallway. He smiled at me and then the rest of our party as if four strangers knocking, one an obvious Upright Man, wasn't at all alarming.

And I was going to strangle Jacky—she was alive again so I could.

She had mentioned Adonis—*Darren*—to me once before, *once*, only to say she knew a fella in New Orleans who could give Baldur of the Hollywood Knights competition for the Most Beautiful Man in The World trophy. I'd thought she'd been joking, but she hadn't been: sandy blond sun-lightened hair, sparkling sky blue eyes with silver flecks, dimpled chin and high cheekbones, generous smiling mouth (even perfect teeth!), he made *Seven* look average. Looking below the neck revealed more tightly sculpted perfection, and when Shell started snickering I snapped my gaze back to his face, blushing so hot I had to be steaming.

 His smile widened. "Yes? Can I help you?"

Smooth and rumbly, it was the voice full of Nola honey from our teleconference at the Navy base, and I was in love. *I am so, so shallow.* Behind me Jacky cleared her throat and Darren broke brain-melting eye contact to look over my shoulder.

She stepped around me and removed the specs. "Darren, stop smiling at Hope and get out of the doorway."

Adonis'—*Darren's*—eyes widened; I was beginning to get just how upsetting finally seeing a hooded Jacky in black leather and body armor and carrying four guns had to be when she was standing right in front of you *and you hadn't noticed*. He backed into the room.

I only barely kept from smacking the doorframe on the way in, which just made ghost-Shell laugh more. The room was a suite, an open pair of rooms occupied by a large bed and a visiting area, a small couch, three chairs, and a coffee table. It all looked brand new—I could even smell the paint—and two more people waited for us inside; a tall and narrow, aesthetic looking vampire with black tousled hair that would have looked dreamy without Darren there to suck up all the female appreciation, and a vampire big and muscular enough to remind me of Grendel. The lean and looming vampire stood by the balcony door, but the big one sat, hands folded on the head of a thick silver-headed cane, watching us with steel grey eyes.

"Hope," Jacky said, ignoring our ride and our Upright Man, "meet Marc Léroy—" the tall one in basic business black nodded "—and Jacob Lichter." She rolled her eyes. "The Master of Ceremonies."

"A pleasure to finally make your acquaintance, Miss Corrigan." The big vampire bowed his head. Despite his name his deep voice didn't carry even a hint of an accent, not even southern, and the word for him was *regal*. Knowing nothing about him, my Mom-honed social instincts told me he had held and used power all of his life—certainly long before his breakthrough—and part of me filed that away to ask Shell about later.

"Likewise. And this is Corporal Balini and Mister Black. Mister Black is our watchdog this evening."

A thick eyebrow rose. "Indeed. And will he dance in our gavotte tonight?"

I looked at Mr Black and he shook his head, keeping his eyes—which I still couldn't describe—on Mr. Lichter.

Mister Lichter. I couldn't even think his name without tripping verbally in my head, and what was the master of New Orleans' vampires doing here? I knew Jacky called him MC, to his *face*, but I couldn't do that. And the fact that I was obsessing over his inconvenient name showed just how happy I was to think of anything other than the "gavotte" waiting for us.

"Shall we get on with it?" Léroy straightened from his guard post, Darren fading back to stand beside him. "I would prefer to be away from here before day."

"Indeed," MC repeated. "Darren has told us you need our help?"

I looked at the two vampires, felt Jacky at my back. Balini and Mr. Black faded into spectators.

"Yes, we do." I told them all about the Three Horsemen.

Jacky and I stepped out onto the balcony. The night was cooling, and I put my elbows on the rail to watch the street—which had gotten even louder and busier than it had been when we'd arrived at the hotel.

Shell had downloaded Interpol files for our three walking disasters to everyone's pads or cells so everyone could look them over. I'd explained the situation at the Café Cubano. Mr. Black had confirmed that we had tonight to collect our three, but if we kicked off a tragedy we would be held accountable.

This point didn't add a thing to my own issues with the op—of *course* we'd be held accountable; we always were.

The briefing complete, I unilaterally declared a break while everyone considered and discussed options and tactics, and went outside with Jacky. There was something else we needed to discuss, just us Sentinels.

Leaning against the railing, I listened to the music and laughter drifting up from the street. "Shell, tell us about the Upright Men."

She faded in beside us while Jacky inserted her earbug so she could join in. "Now? It's not like they're our mission tonight."

"Please?"

She sighed theatrically, blew virtual hair out of her eyes. "Fine. They serve the Tyrant. They're absolutely loyal and incorruptible—*maybe*. Nobody knows who they are, and the only time they show up is on official business. Ditto for their powers; nobody knows. The biggest Upright Man incident happened just after the Second Revolution; a supervillain-run drug cartel in Havana tried to intimidate the new regime, brought in lots of villain muscle. The Tyrant let them muscle up and show Havana's police how tough they were, then the Upright Men showed up en-masse for the chief and his bodyguards. Right in the center of their compound, and they just 'took them away'. Witnesses all agreed that no weapons or powers were effective against them. The Upright Men just appeared, took the ones they wanted, left."

"And the rest of the cartel?"

"Picked up one by one, a few each night and no matter how they tried to hide, till the last of the survivors managed to get out of Cuba. None of the ones taken ever showed up again."

"That's...wow."

"Oh yeah, and you can see why the Tyrant doesn't worry about superhuman guests other countries might have trouble with. It all makes Cuba a favorite destination for superhumans who have to leave home but aren't fond of the US. But really, mostly the Upright Men terrorize the Cuban government."

I straightened up. "*What?* They're terrorists?"

"Nope. They're part of the legal order, a *scary* part of it. The Serene Republic of Cuba really is an elective democracy, but if you abuse your office an Upright Man will show up for you, doesn't matter if you're the Prime Minister or a small-town mayor. If anyone sees you again you won't remember what happened—but you won't be the same, either. The new government of Cuba is less than two years old, and political corruption is statistically zero."

"Wow again."

"I know, right? Who are they? Forget about them, who's the *Tyrant*? They're why we don't trust the new Cuba—nobody knows what they want, other than to keep the Serene Republic serene. Blackstone thinks they're the first really successful superhuman oligarchy."

"And they're not in the Big Book of Contingent Prophecy."

"Nope. Never appeared before the California Quake and the Whittier Base Attack completely derailed the future right off the history books."

"Future Incognita." I rubbed my forehead. A huge question mark of an island state, and we got to play here. "*Why* are they letting us play here? They're big about non-extradition, so why did they let us collect Brick? Why did they let us come back tonight? If these guys are dangerous to them, why not come and collect, themselves, just tell us to go pound sand?"

"Pound sand? That's a new one, I like it. And *that's* what's bugging you? Would knowing the answer change our job?"

"It might. Here's the thing, Shell. *I* think that Brick came to do a job aimed at the naval base—maybe be part of the job that burns the town. Which means the Three Horsemen are the rest of the team. Why else take the chance of meeting here, in Guantánamo City? Yes, Guantánamo Airport is a gateway for smaller charters to the Caribbean and the Gulf, but so's Florida and the Bahamas."

I kept reviewing the map in my head, and it kept pointing back to *us*.

"The only way into the naval base is by land or by sea—you're not getting into it by air—and Guantánamo's port is too close to the base and too watched to safely come in by boat from somewhere else. And that's just one thing. The other is, from an underworld contractor's point of view, if you're linking up somewhere to do a job, why risk using a country with no due process laws and mystery-lawmen who freak *me* out as your jumping-off point, unless your target is *in* the country?"

"You learn well, my fine young padawan." Jacky had kept quiet so far, just listening to me rant. Now she smiled wide, showing fang. "Soon you will join me on the dark side and we will rule the world together."

"If it's all the same I'd rather not. Trying to think like you or Blackstone makes my head hurt."

"You're supposed to shout 'I will never join your circle of evil!'" Shell quipped. "And cry and look all pouty."

"Casper," Jacky shot back.

"Morticia."

I swallowed the giggles, but it was oh so hard.

"So we really are their most likely target," I went on. "But what we should be doing is waiting for *their* move. We keep eyes on them, and sooner or later they'll blow town to either head to the airport and out of here, or head for the navy base if losing Brick doesn't kill the job. Then we come down on them with everything we and the base can throw, *away* from civilians."

"But the Upright Men won't let us wait," Jacky gently reminded me.

"No, they won't. But if letting them collect the Three Horsemen themselves means not risking civilians..." I hugged myself. "I don't know. Even if we lose the intelligence these guys have."

"So you'd be okay with never finding out who hired these three?" Shelly asked. "I doubt the Cubans will tell us if we leave it to them."

Jacky looked out at the night. "I don't think you're thinking ruthlessly enough yet. I think the Cubans think that these guys are our problem. Our three are here for the *American* base, a base the

Tyrant doesn't even want on Cuban soil. So they're willing to let them get at us but they're covering themselves, too. By letting us know what they know, giving us freedom to act on their soil even if not as much room as we'd like, they're cooperating enough that if it does all hit the fan we can't blame them."

"And if we screw up tonight and innocents get hurt?"

"Then they've got a great diplomatic club to beat our country with. So come up with a plan where nobody who doesn't deserve it gets hurt."

I closed my eyes and breathed deep, remembering my vision of the burning town. Either way I chose, people who had never asked for what was going to happen were at risk.

But tonight we can control the risk.

I opened my eyes. "Jacky? If we bring them in, how likely is it we'll be able to find out what they know?"

Her smile turned evil enough to make every horror-flick director *ever* just give up and cry. "Leave them with me and I'll tell you every sin that stains their black little souls."

I presented my plan, asked for comments and suggestions. The scenario was really pretty straightforward; the whole thing felt like the kind of tactical problem Lei Zi or Blackstone liked to give me as homework, and depended on the depth of the retrieval kit the Navy had sent with Balini. I should have checked in advance; if it was a test, Lei Zi would have flunked me just for that.

Fortunately, when I asked the corporal what he'd brought he went downstairs and came back with a Swiss army knife of a kit; Blacklock restraints for super-strong types, sandman packs for anyone who could just slip through physical restraints, even a somnolence field cap for the drug-resistant.

Now MC simply looked amused. "Are you certain you're a superhero?"

"Yes, sir. If we do this right, nobody gets hurt and we get what we need."

"But it's hardly sporting. And if we fail… Perhaps it would be best to just kill them? Every one of them is wanted for war crimes somewhere or other."

"That would be inadvisable," Mr. Black interjected. "The Serene Republic's neutrality in these sorts of matters is being stretched enough as it is tonight."

"But you can do your part?" I asked. I *really* didn't want to rethink the whole plan.

"My instructions are to be a watcher tonight. However, where I do the watching is up to me."

"Then this will work." It was classic Lei Zi—she'd say it was a combination of Stratagem Six and Stratagem Thirteen; *Feint to the east while attacking in the west*, and *Beat the grass to startle the snake*. With a good dose of *Don't make it complicated*.

My projected confidence carried the day, or maybe they had all just decided to watch the kid and see how she did. Silent Léroy seemed content so long as his boss agreed, and Balini was only put out because he didn't have a hands-on role.

MC nodded. "Very well, then. And we will all hope that things do not get too interesting."

Chapter Twenty Two

"I meet the nicest people. And the bravest people, too. It's easy for capes to be brave and heroic when it all gets nasty, we're trained for it. But bystanders, with no powers to help them, will surprise you every time."

Hope Corrigan, *Notes From a Life*.

Galahad was surprised to see me, and not happy about it. I had the Anonymity Specs back on, but I had before and he "recognized" me as the too-young American girl in the cute dress. Café Cubano had only gotten busier since I'd retreated, without a single space left at the bar, and I began to think that the plan might be sunk just because we couldn't get a table until a small party sitting next to our targets got up en-masse.

"There!" I pointed imperiously and Darren laughed, tucking me under his arm to push us both through the crowd. Nobody beat us to the table, and the reason was our targets; their glares pushed away anyone less apparently oblivious than us. Darren ignored them to focus on getting me into my chair, and I focused on acting innocent and drunk enough not to notice Darren's laughable open leering. Ignoring the three behind me, I watched the dance floor.

Darren got a waiter's attention and ordered, and when our drinks arrived I took one sip and knew Galahad had mixed it; my "Cuba Libre" was all coke and no rum, which made me feel worse about what was going to happen next.

"So do you come here often?" Darren leaned over, partly to compensate for the music, obviously to look down my dress as if there was anything substantial to see. I almost choked on my drink, worked *hard* not to laugh.

"No! First night in town! I heard the drinks are good! But they're kinda thin!"

"Would you like me to order something stronger?" I could *feel* our target's eyes boring into our backs, but heard no scrape of chairs. We were in, and actually started drawing appreciative female attention from the surrounding tables. I imagined half of the women present deciding they'd ditch their escorts if only they could figure out a way to pry Darren away from the naïve toy he'd found to play with. If things didn't move along we'd have company at our table soon.

"Phase two," Shell whispered in my ear so I wouldn't go tense when Jacky made her debut.

Jacky had purely hated losing the specs and her guns, but if it turned into a mess the last thing we wanted was to give the crazy pyrokinetic villain stuff he could make go bang. She'd also ditched her hood and body armor and now she just looked like a dominatrix out clubbing. The two men with her made contrasting bookends, and when MC looked at their chosen table and made its occupants aware that they were in the way they cleared out without even a protest.

The table to our left, next-closest to our friends.

Now I heard our targets shift behind me, and I imagined Red and MC sizing each other up, two big alpha-males with too little space between them. Red was probably imagining fun scenarios, but the puff of impatient breath was one of the other two telling him *not here*. After all, they were in Upright Men territory.

So Jacky and her boys ordered drinks in peace. And they got to work.

Vampires aren't *obvious* unless you know what you're looking at, at least not to anybody who doesn't have nifty vision that sees into the infrared spectrum where the living look like walking lightbulbs. *I* could see that MC and Léroy were the temperature of the outside air, but living and daywalking Jacky was the temperature of every other "breather" in the room and none of them showed fang unless they smiled really wide. In the dim café lighting, even Jacky's pale shade and the boys' almost complete lack of pallor wasn't that easy to see.

But they didn't have to hiss theatrically to start emptying a room. Not when they could *push*.

Darren stopped leering at me and shivered, and he'd been braced for it. The noise-level from the tables around us actually dropped as patrons became increasingly uncomfortable. Three vampires extending their mental influence, whispering *there are predators here* to the monkey-brain, started clearing tables. More to the point, they focused our target's attention on themselves beautifully. *They* weren't leaving.

"Shit," Darren muttered next to me, tearing his eyes away from their table and leaning closer. Instinctively protecting me? Wasn't he *used* to this stuff? Then I figured it out—I'd made a mistake; now *we* looked out of place, not clearing away as the people around us shifted, tried to restart conversations, and decided that the party had gone flat here and it was time to move on. Even the girls decided Darren wasn't that interesting anymore.

I almost stood myself, trusting Darren to follow my lead, when Shell whispered "Stage three," and Mr. Black walked in.

He'd come to watch. It was his job.

Now it became a lot easier to tell the locals, who came in all shades after all, from the tourists who didn't know what an Upright Man was. Galahad knew; I could see him now through the thinning crowd and he'd backed away from the bar. Then he reached below it, looking at me, and my breath hitched. He thought the Upright Man was here for the obvious Bad Guys in the room and they were sitting at the table next to *me*. He was actually going to come to my rescue if things went really bad.

The tide became an exodus, and I stood because anything else would look too wrong.

Mr. Black stepped away from the door, calmly letting the more panicked patrons lead the rush. He ignored Galahad to turn his complete attention to the table full of fiends of the night. Now I could look at them—it would be out of character *not* to. They stood one by one, the Master of Ceremonies first and looking as masterly as it was possible for any human being to. He unbuttoned his suit jacket, clasped his cane.

And they attacked.

Straight at our targets, who had totally been expecting them to go the *other* way and probably wondering if they could get out quietly while the Upright Man took care of his obvious targets.

MC and Jacky went straight for Red, lunging into mist to clear the tables and chairs in their way. Léroy went for Brainworm, armed with a sandman pack. *I* went for Flashpoint while Darren hit the floor behind me.

Thinking later, I had to admire their training; Flashpoint zeroed on me before I hit him and my cute dress went up like a cotton ball held over a match. Then I had his shirt in my fist.

I flipped him around and onto his knees, wrapped my right arm around his neck, bicep against one side, forearm against the other, braced his head with my left hand to point his face at the floor, and carefully *squeezed*. He struggled, not moving me at all, and the table in front of us caught fire.

Ignoring the action behind me I held him till he slumped, out of it. Releasing my sleeper hold, I made sure he was breathing and then looked to see what everyone else was doing. Léroy had Brainworm on his face on the floor, shoulder of his shirt ripped away and sandman pack pressed against his pinned shoulder. MC and Jacky had Red in a double lock and Jacky was... I looked away.

Lowering Flashpoint to the floor, I signaled for Darren to bring the SF cap in my purse. When he knelt beside me with the cap, I unfolded and opened it, checking the red light. Fitting the cap, I closed the straps and flipped it on. The green light by Flashpoint's ear said it was working and I exhaled. *Easy.* Crossing myself, I promised God and Mary a few prayers later.

Darren watched our slumbering villain. "Why didn't you use that first?"

"I didn't want to risk him seeing it and frying its circuits," I said softly. "Caps aren't exactly robust."

"Gotcha." He looked behind me at the fang-action I wasn't listening to, smiled. "Does that bother you?"

"Are you a…"

"A donor? A fang-fan? No. I make a good beard, though—everyone assumes Marcus and I are a couple." His playful smile was back, this time without the over-acted theatrics, and my knees went a bit weak. "He's in a long-term commitment, but if you ever come to the Big Easy…"

I knew I had a goofy smile on my face, but I shook my head anyway. Shell ghosted into sight behind him, mouthing "What are you *thinking*?" and when I rolled my eyes Darren was smart enough not to ask.

He sighed, giving up. "You do know you're still on fire, right?"

I groaned and stripped the smoldering remains of the dress away, patting out the flames against the floor; Flashpoint was lucky I hadn't caught *him* on fire while clinching. The booming roar of a fire extinguisher signaled Galahad's arrival to put out the merrily burning table.

After that it was my turn to step out. The other employees had fled with the customers, and I supposed they were all locals. Standing in the café's doorway with Galahad and Mr. Black, I finally realized why Guantánamo City's police weren't arriving with screaming sirens: Mr. Black. Galahad—his name was Tim—had shown impressive presence of mind so far; he'd found me a coat left behind by a patron to cover my blue and white beach-volleyball uniform.

"Shouldn't I know you?" He looked down at me from his occupationally useful bartender's height again, and this time I did giggle. My sports-bra top had my *star* on it.

"You should. Don't worry, it's the glasses."

"Okay." He shrugged. "How long are your friends going to be in there? I really need to clean up the mess."

"They shouldn't be long." I tried to ignore the sounds from inside. "And they won't leave a mess." The sucking sounds had been bad enough; one of our prisoners was *crying*. Never mess with a vampire—if he's feeling nice, all he'll do is put you in a completely suggestible state and then ask you what your mother would think of what you've been doing.

"I meant the table. I can drag the torched one into the backroom, and as soon as you guys are gone I'll be pouring drinks and telling stories all night. *Serious* tips."

That got a chopped laugh out of me, and I made a mental note to tell Blackstone about him, see if he could recruit him onto the Dome staff.

Mr. Black turned to look at him. "You will say nothing about the three vampires. You will simply say that they were very strong."

"Um, okay."

I patted his arm. "Thank you, I appreciate it, too. And thank you for earlier."

His smile came back. "You're welcome."

The noises stopped. Hearing sighs, I assumed that they had just administered the remaining sandman packs. Jacky appeared at my elbow.

"They were paid to do a fast strike on the Navy base's armory."

I frowned. "Then they're still missing team. They don't have a driver, someone to help them get out fast."

"They haven't met their employer yet—he was supposed to show up tonight."

I looked at Mr. Black, but he didn't have the grace to look embarrassed. He gave us a nod that was almost a bow.

"If we find him, we will let you know. In any case, may I say it has been a pleasure and an education? Good work, ladies, and good night." He tipped his hat and was gone, leaving me pretty sure he hadn't just *teleported* away but not able to remember how he'd left.

Jacky looked up and down the street. "Nice trick. Our new friends won't remember anything from when we jumped them till they wake up in Navy custody. We should stop by their hotel rooms on the way and collect their gear."

Balini brought the car up in back, followed by a van sent by the base, and we loaded our sleeping prisoners before anyone out in the street decided to see if Mr. Black was really gone. We drove slowly through the streets like they were enemy territory, back to the Hotél Washington where our three were coincidentally staying, and Jacky and her boys retrieved everything including their own things; they weren't staying. From there it was a drive straight up Main Street and out of Guantánamo City. Leaving its outskirts, I breathed a sigh of relief.

Not a deep one. We had the Three Horsemen. We'd learned their mission. We'd *won*. But... "Good work," Mr. Black had said. Why did it feel like I'd been complimented by the Devil?

Episode Four

Chapter Twenty Three

"Dear Mom and Dad; —— isn't summer camp, but it's hard on my wardrobe and Shelly's here so it feels really familiar."

A recovered redacted email, preserved in the Hope Corrigan Library.

Captain Lauer took custody of the Three Horsemen at the base, and everyone was happy except Corporal Balini who was still grumbling about being left out of the action. The captain offered MC and Léroy secure beds for the coming day and a flight home tomorrow night, which they accepted. I was just beginning to realize how big a deal it was that they'd come out here with Jacky; for a vampire, the idea of spending a day sleeping in a hotel room that just about anybody could get into, with big windows and only curtains separating them from a good day's sleep and fiery death…

Jacky had explained on the drive back that they brought tailored mummy-bags (the sleeping bag variety, not ancient Egyptian wraps), and Darren pretty much stuck to the room from sunup to sundown. Naturally they'd chartered a private plane, checked in under assumed names, done everything to make sure insane vampire-hunters couldn't find them, but still!

"He is *so* into her," Shell whispered as we watched Jacky say goodnight to MC (she'd cut her link to Jacky's earbug again). "Or wants to be."

"Shell!" I choked, turning it into a red-faced cough when everyone looked. They went back to ignoring me.

MC tapped his cane. "Jacky."

"Lichter."

"Will you be coming home soon?"

"We'll see. Thank you for looking after Acacia for me."

"See? *See*?"

I rolled my eyes, wishing I could *think* a response to my obviously delusional BFF, and then almost busted up when Darren decided he wasn't having any of that.

"Who're we kidding? C'mere, you!" He stepped up and wrapped Jacky in a big-brother hug, winked at me over her shoulder. "And don't you be a stranger, y'hear?"

Okay, I went a little weak again, which was just wrong. I was a *big* girl, darn it. At least I couldn't get redder.

Then we were out of there with a promise to Captain Lauer to file a report tomorrow—which would promptly be lost since obviously the US Navy had had nothing to do with tonight's little action. And Balini and the other corporal had just gone out for evening drives. And returned with internationally wanted war-criminals…

Sometimes I think all government organizations are functionally insane.

"And what about *that*?" Shell squeed, bouncing beside me as we exited the base while Jacky projected Nothing to See Here vibes. "That was a *proxy* hug! He is so, so hot for you, her Majesty Oblivious the First, Queen of Oblivia, defender of cluelessness and ruler of all she refuses to see. *Tell* me you've never seen that before!"

I choked on my laugh. "I can honestly say that I haven't."

Jacky looked at me sideways, shook her head. "Shell?"

"Acting twelve."
"Hey!"

Shelly texted as soon as the Garage flashed us back into Littleton; switching between Shell and Shelly was getting disorienting, and when I went to text back I found that Shell had slipped a share file into my phone, an edited video-file recording and translation of her feed through my neural link; everything from the moment we left Littleton to the moment we got back. The file dumped before I could figure out how to stop it, leaving me groaning at a smiley-face screen with an animated wink. *Great, now Shelly's going to bug me about Darren, too.*

Our flight back to the B&B was as uneventful as a sleeping town could make it, which was great because I was *done*. We pulled out the trundle bed for Jacky and she gave me the first turn with the shower. She was gone when I got out, leaving a note that read *Gone to find the nightlife. Don't wait up.*

I stared at it for a long minute, and then texted Sheriff Deitz. *Maybe* he didn't know about Jacky's dietary requirements or chosen means of tapping a vein, but if Jacky ran afoul of the town's Orwellian security I hoped he'd call me first. Changing into a fresh set of indestructibles, I crawled into bed and dove into slumberland the moment my head hit the sinfully fluffy pillow.

I lay on the grass, warm wind tickling my skin, and watched the great wheel of the Milky Way turn above us as bright as it only ever looked from the very edge of space. The silver fox lying on my chest sat up and pricked his ears.

"What is it?"

He yawned. "Be still and listen, child," he advised me.

Closing my eyes, hands clasped under my head, I listened. Wind in the grass. The soft rustle of cherry blossoms clinging to branches, ready to fly. Crackling. Fire.

"Hope?"
"Mmm?"
"How do you turn off the alarm?"
"Throw a pillow at her."

Missing breakfast should have meant that all we got was fruit and cereal, but Mr. Darvish knew how much I adored his waffles and he made us a fresh stack. My waffle was a perfect warm puff, the butter rich, the maple syrup the real deal, the fresh orange juice and strawberries pure bliss. I took my uniform gloves off to keep syrup off of them, but halfway through my little slice of heaven the dream came back to hit me between the eyes. I dropped my fork and it rattled on the plate, spattering melted butter and syrup about.

How could I forget that? It had *never* happened before with a Kitsune dream, which it absolutely had been. Maybe the fox had a hard time pushing the dream through Mr. Darvish's bubble of peace? Which I didn't feel now; the B&B's proprietor must have stepped out after serving us and *why was I even wondering about that*?

"Hope? Are you okay?"

I must have looked as pale as Jacky as she watched me over her own piece of waffle. She'd woken fresh and as late as me (I vaguely remembered something about an alarm clock), which meant she'd had a good drink last night and didn't need as much sleep.

"We're not finished. It's not over." How could it not be over? We'd found the firestarter— Oh. "Their target was the *navy base*."

"What?"

"Their target was the base! They have nothing to do with my dreams!" I put my face in my hands.

"Shit," Jacky said. She thought for a minute. "Those dreams are never literal, are they?"

"No, but their allegories are pretty specific." I groaned. "I wouldn't have seen the town burning if it wasn't the *town*. Probably."

"Are you sure?"

"No. But he snuck into my dreams again last night. It's still on and we're not going anywhere yet."

She cut another slice of waffle. "Well, okay then."

After breakfast Sheriff Deitz took my prediction just as unflappably. I wondered if he should, but I was beginning to feel like the Oracle of Delphi—my dreams were certainly vague as riddles or oracular pronouncements. *The town will burn.* Why? When? Who? *Hot-line psychics* did better.

"Relax," he said, leaning back in his chair. "First, all your dreams have put the fires at night, so you don't have to be on full alert 24/7. Second, Navy Intelligence, the CIA, the FBI, they're all pulling on the strings this is attached to; sooner or later they'll find the right string, follow it back, and all will be right with the world. Well, as right as it ever is but you'll be able to go home. Third, the guys you brought in last night are a huge help, first confirmation this is serious. Resources were retasked while you slept."

"Resources?"

"Oh yeah. The details are above my pay grade, but I've been told that in a couple of days we'll have reinforcements. They'll be settled in with plenty of time before the conference. Till then, Captain Lauer has pulled the two light armored squads out of the Garage to reinforce the base—that's where the projects most vital to national security are, *and* the holding facility. We've still got Corbin's heavy-armor team guarding the door."

Jacky's response was making more sense, now. Shelly's, too; I was due at the Institute after seeing Deitz, but Shelly wasn't freaking over the new dream, either. In fact, she'd hinted at *lunch* later.

"So keep your phone with you," Deitz finished. "We're going to do at least one more drill before the conference, but we're going to prove that your guy's not a prophet."

That was my cue, and I left on it with a wave to Angel. Jacky had disappeared after breakfast so I went to the Institute alone. And walked into the Oroboros' den to a round of standing applause.

The Oroboros common office's main screen displayed mug shots of the Three Horsemen, with big red 'X's painted over them. Below each was a set of categories: soldiers and civilians. Each category had a number—for Flashpoint and Brainworm the numbers were triple digits.

"Congratulations, Astra." General Rajabhushan stepped forward, a truly wide smile spreading wrinkles across his face.

"What is this?"

"Your scoreboard. The most optimistic future-accounting, extracted from the potential futures left to us, yielded a count exceeding one thousand more deaths directly attributed to these three before they were brought down by enemy action. We cannot begin to list the thousands more second-order deaths attributable to their actions as well."

Doctor Hall lifted a fizzing Champaign flute, saluting me. "Really. Congratulations. Will all who they would have killed, live now? Perhaps not—they sold their services to whatever war would have them. But this is certainly a victory for the forces of order."

"And the intelligence the US may get from them could prove just as life-saving," Doctor Ash added less exuberantly. The rest seconded her sentiment, and only Shelly didn't have a glass in her hand.

The general lifted his own drink. "Truly, this is what the Oroboros are for and you have done us wonderful service. And now!" He put down his glass, clapped his hands once. "Let us to work! If we can find the route by which they came, we can learn of their recent work! We may be able to tag them to potential future operations which yet remain a reality!"

The group scattered, still chattering, all except for Shelly. I watched them go.

"Um, what just happened?"

"You scored." Shedding the serious demeanor she tried to project here, Shelly grinned from ear to ear.

"We do it every time one of our 'intelligence assessments' bags an operation or person responsible for Bad Things in the Future Files. It's happening less and less as we get further and further from the last potential future the Teatime Anarchist saw and divergence marches on, but big wins are still out there. You got one we weren't even looking for. So, c'mon. You can write up your after-action report, and I can get some work done, and then we are going to go eat."

She said *eat* with a sparkle in her eye that said she knew something that I didn't, but led me back to her office without clarifying. We spent the next little while in silence while she did her thing through the Oroboros databases and I worked on my report. It felt weirdly like our study-nights, back before everything.

And then she dragged me to lunch. At the *beach*.

Chapter Twenty Four

"We are reliably told that a couple of our guests returned to Littleton after a night out, one of them wearing less than she left with. So was it a hot night on the town? A drinking game gone wrong? Has the truth been redacted? Cal is opening a new betting pool. 'We'll never know' is not an option, but perhaps someone will find the courage to ask them when they see them at the lake."

Littleton Radio Morning Hour

"Now that's just..."

"I *know*, right?"

George Peppas, the crazy Verne-type responsible for Littleton's crazy pocket reality where it only rained after sunset and the seasons clicked over every three months like clockwork, had been all about the lake and it showed; Lake Peppas was the cleanest lake in the world, or out of it, literally.

The water was so clear in the midday sun that I could see the bottom with optical clarity. *Anybody* could—my super-duper vision didn't cut out distortion and obscuring particles, but there weren't any; the fish seemed to be almost hanging in air above the bottom where they weren't hidden by water grass and plants. One long strip was a sandy beach, but a wood pier sat further down, and beyond it the ground rose into a tree topped hill with a carved out cliff for diving.

"So? Let's party!" Shelly dragged me laughing across the sand towards a row of old-fashioned seaside changing booths. "Change! Jacky raided your bag!" Beyond them a party waited. I recognized the Hardts, with Atifa and—oh my gosh—*Jacky* in shades and a black one-piece bathing suit, then Shelly pushed me into the nearest booth.

Jacky had indeed raided my bag, and had laid out one of my backup pairs of indestructibles. I stared at them for a long moment and finally decided they were modest enough for the beach. Besides, Jacky had unbent her whole fiend-of-the-night thing enough to hit the beach in a *suit*; that was practically a dare. I changed quickly, barely beating Shelly out of the booths; she'd skinned into a green one-piece.

Ours wasn't the only party at the lake, and families had staked out spots up and down the beach. Kids ran from one group to the next, and after a squealing hug for me Atifa disappeared with a little gang of munchkins and a minder who assured us all would be well. I wasn't sure, but Shelly's mom gave her approval.

Mrs. H had a hug for me, too, one that went on awhile and I held on right back.

Stroking my hair, she let me go with a soft "Thank you." I didn't ask for what and with that lunch got underway, an elaborate sandwich buffet spread out on beach blankets. Mrs. H joked about eating first, *just in case*, and passed around the side dishes.

I stacked a huge sandwich and accepted a plate of her rich potato salad, talked to Mr. Hardt about his administration work, and tried to get dirt on how Shelly was behaving. Jacky talked mostly to Shelly and Mrs. H, and we all took a pass on two invitations to play volleyball with a group of boys more daring than smart. Jacky, a born Sports Illustrated swimsuit model if the magazine ever went Goth, was their obvious target.

Sandwich eaten and drinks drunk, Jacky decided to share a beach umbrella with me while Mr. Hardt napped and Mrs. H and Shelly ran the water's edge with a returned Atifa.

Jacky watched them with an odd smile on her face. "They did it, didn't they?"

"Did what?"

"Found normal again. It really is amazing."

She didn't sound sad, but my hand crept over and settled on hers. "It's all just family. Which you've got." I didn't say how long it had been since *I'd* seen a beach; we'd have to work on it, too. "You know, this would be a great place for team breaks."

"Club Cape?" Her laugh wasn't ironic or edgy, just nice. "Yes, it would."

"Hey!" Shelly yelled from the water. "You think you're going to melt? Get *wet*!"

Jacky and I got Atifa back to her godfather. The little girl talked fast all the way and called us Aunt Hope and Aunt Jacky, sometimes skipping along, sometimes swinging between the two of us and screaming with delight when we easily swung her to shoulder height. Jacky carried her piggy-back the last few streets after she drooped into a sun-worn and sleepy ragdoll, and Mr. Darvish gently took the boneless girl off Jacky's back with quiet thanks and carried her away. Jacky and I climbed the stairs to our room to change again, and I reluctantly skinned back into my uniform. Checking my messages, I found one waiting for me from Captain Lauer. Full video.

"*Good morning, Astra.*" The lines on Captain Lauer's face had sunk deeper, and his red eyes testified to more lost sleep.

"*First, thank you for handing me such interesting confirmation of your story. The conference is in two days, and given that you swept up what had to be a good-sized piece of whatever assets were being set up to operate against us here, I've given the go-ahead. At the same time we are moving things around out here. We have moved our two light squads to the base, but don't worry, the heavy squad should be more than enough to hold the gate against any direct assault. Before the conference opens we will also have* two supersoldier squads, one parked in the Garage and one in Littleton to reassure our guests. You'll know them—they're from S Corp and you met in California."

He sat back, rubbed his eyes.

"Thank you, Astra. You may very well have short-stopped an attack on a conference that, had it succeeded, would have destroyed the trust of our allies. Something we desperately need. In two days you'll be able to go home, job well done."

"We're going to see Watchman's army buddies?" Jacky had been watching over my shoulder. "Think they'll be willing to dish dirt on him? Or at least brag?"

I put down the cell. "Maybe. Think we'll ever learn what the conference is about?"

"Doubt it. They're holding it in the one place in the world they maintain full signals control and you can't take any pictures that survive departure, and that's all I care to know."

"And we'll just fly away?"

She snorted impatiently. "When they change the guard this place will be better protected than it is now. C'mon, Hope. Some missions, you just stand around and then go home. You know that."

I did. Back in Chicago, Detective Fisher would call a quiet watch something to be grateful for; loose ends didn't bother him so long as they didn't suddenly tighten up. Besides, did I *want* a fight? Here?

I spent most of the rest of the day catching up on correspondence from home. Shell had put together a bundle of files, stuff she trusted other people, government people, to see before I did. Some of it was news items. There was a flame-war being waged on the Powerline forums as to whether I was in Chicago or, for some inexplicable reason, in Cuba. The Sentinels would be getting back home tomorrow, turning their zone of responsibility over to other FEMA-supported groups. The Young Sentinels were still drilling and training, working on preparedness and emergency response times.

Shelly sent me an encrypted file detailing the Future File careers of the Three Horsemen that we'd cut short. I read it and erased it, but it did leave me feeling we'd done something really good here. Looking at the notes she'd attached to it listing the probable effects of taking them out of the picture, I also realized that Shelly would be alright, too. She'd found a place for herself, and was probably doing more to fight for the Good Future than I was.

"What are you smiling about?" Jacky had spent the time quietly stripping and cleaning her guns.

"Me? Not a thing." Watching her go back to oiling something that needed to be oiled, I decided I needed to formally introduce her to Angel; they could compare personal armories.

My special cell screamed at me and it took two seconds for me to wake up enough to fumble for it. The bright red screen shredded the clinging veils of sleep in a flood of adrenaline.

"Astra?" Sheriff Deitz sounded much more awake than I been until one second ago.

"Yes? What's happening?" I looked around. Jacky wasn't here. Jacky wasn't *here*. I pushed my hair out of my eyes.

"I don't know. It may be nothing. We've lost contact with the Garage."

"Sheriff's office?"

"Yeah. C'mon down."

Scrambling into costume, I thought for two seconds before adding the armor and grabbing Malleus and my go-bag. Softly stepping out into the dark hall, mindful of the squeak-potential of the hardwood paneled floors, I stopped and almost laughed. Lifting my feet, I drifted down the hall and down the stairs.

"Miss Corrigan?" Mr. Darvish stood in Holybrook Rest's brightly-lit entryway in a robe. "Something is happening?"

"I don't know."

He nodded, stepping out of my way. "Go with God."

"Thank you. You, too. Take care of—" I shook my head and gave him a reassuring smile, opened the front door and launched. I didn't fly straight to the office; first I popped up, careful not to fly too high, and spun in place to get a good look at the town.

Littleton's hooded streetlamps traced a grid of bright points through a shadowed town beneath a moonlit sky. The Moon hadn't been in my dream, but I still shivered. Below me nothing moved that didn't look like it should be there.

"What took you so long?" Angel looked up from her desk screen when I came through the door.

"I popped up to look around. Sorry."

Deitz kept his eyes on the board. "Don't be. Did you see anything?"

"No but I wouldn't see anything your panopticon system didn't, would I?"

He chuckled. "If you trust the system; I still prefer the Mark One Human Eyeball—or in your case the Mark 10 Superhuman Eyeball."

"Do you know where Jacky is?"

"She checked out through the Garage just after sunset, and hasn't returned. The Garage stopped sending its relayed signals packets five minutes ago, which has never happened before."

"Any alerts?"

Angel punched keys in frustration. "Nothing. None of the packet logs up to the blackout show anything at all."

I realized I was still holding my go-bag and put it down. "What happens if somebody attacks the Garage?"

"The translation system—which includes the signals transmitter—goes into lockdown. From there it can only be brought back up from the navy base."

"So from here it would look like this?"

"Not quite. The system is supposed to send an alert announcing interruption and flashing over the details."

I tried to channel Blackstone's Dispatch face. "Would a translation system failure look like this?"

"It would have to be catastrophic and instantaneous, but yeah, it would." He pinched the bridge of his nose, stretched and shook out his shoulders. "Normally I'd wait for confirmation, but..."

"I can go look."

"No. There's no reason not to trust our own system, and if someone is coming through then you popping up is just going to... What is that?"

I'd reached into my go-bag and pulled out Vulcan's chameleon-weave polycloth suit. I unsnapped my cape, started pulling it on.

"A gift Vulcan made for me back when I was hiding my identity." Floating, I got my legs in, careful of the footies. "Mal— that's Megaton—calls it my Plus Ten Cloak of Invisibility."

Angel got up to get a closer look. "I can see why," she approved. "I'd build it into my *suit*."

"I did have a chameleon-weave layer once, but the stuff is fragile and takes forever to fabricate even for Vulcan. Besides, it doesn't work with the armor on top." I tugged the gloves on over my costume gloves, pulled up the hood and closed it. Only my eyes peeked out, and Angel whistled.

"Get something behind you and even I couldn't paint you. How is it in the open?"

"Good enough that I used to use it to fly out of my parents' back yard. Sheriff? Can I go?"

He looked me over, nodded once. I pulled the hood back and inserted my earbug, linked the cell to its signal. "It's okay, Sheriff. I'll yell if I see anything."

"Don't. Not unless you think you can't make it back to report."

"Why— Okay." Like Jacky always said, I wasn't paranoid *enough*. I got out the door and in the air before he had time to re-think it, but stayed low to the streets. Littleton was the kind of town that, as Dad liked to say, might as well roll up the streets after dark; I flew over only a couple of cars that were going anywhere, one a truck. People were probably out in the town's very small club district—three little clubs, all on the same street—but everyone else was at home in their beds or watching movies on the couch. The ever-present thrumming on the edge of my hearing told me that the town's security system was awake at least, and the annoying sound was suddenly *very* reassuring.

Passing the last home on the edge of town, I dropped low enough to touch the road with an outstretched hand as I flew. Did I need to, with my cloak of invisibility? Probably not, but I was trying to think like Jacky and she didn't even like flying high and open as *mist*.

The road turned and went up the hill and I followed, eyes ahead. Nearing the crest of the hill I slowed to almost creeping speed. Over the crest and looking down at the gate and marked-out space that translated into the Garage's in-bound bay, I dropped and hugged the grass. I counted seven people standing where they had no right to be, clustered around two vans, and I recognized three of them by their armor and signature accessories; Balz, Twist, and Dozer—aka Gantry, Eric Ludlow. I was looking at the Wreckers.

The Ascendancy had come to Littleton.

Chapter Twenty Five

"Johnny's called the dance and it's a barn burner. Let's make ourselves troublesome."

Atlas, at the Whittier Base Attack.

"You're sure?"

"I'm sure." I'd stayed and watched for heart-pounding minutes to observe details, but they hadn't done anything except stand around the vans they'd obviously commandeered in the Garage. One of them worked away on what looked like an obsolete laptop sitting on the hood, and I guessed that one was Phreak. Balz had a swarm of his spheres out as a perimeter, but they stayed lower than the crest of the hill.

"Okay then." Deitz tapped a code on his pad, and through the windows I watched the streetlamp emergency lights begin flashing green. No sirens. The town grid on the main board changed, points that had to be the shelters lighting up. Four of them blinked gold.

"What's happening?"

"We've opened the shelters. The blinking ones are the armories—just about one in ten of our citizens are military or retired and a bunch like to keep their hands in. Your friends are about to get a welcome from close to two hundred veterans."

"The battle-hardened kind." Angel had opened a closet and pulled out the big tri-barreled dinosaur gun I'd first seen her with, and stood snapping on a heavy set of blue body armor; for the first time I wondered if she might be an Ajax-type. The touch of a button brought the familiar clicks and latches as doors and windows sealed themselves up again.

"*The question is, what do they want?*" Shell—Shelly—asked from my earbug.

"Shelly? Where are you?"

"*I was home. Now I'm headed for the Institute. The place is one big bunker underground and it's got stuff I need.*"

"Shelly, no—the Institute has to be their target!"

"*Well duh. But it's got backdoors, Director Ali will make sure we don't get mousetrapped.*"

Sheriff Deitz cleared his throat. "Would you mind sharing?"

"Shelly— " I took a breath, recited an access code. Angel did something on her computer, and Shelly's voice came through the main board's speakers.

"*—to get to the Oroboros' files,*" Shelly was saying. "*Best source of current superhuman intel we've got and we need to know our enemy.*"

The lights on the main board blinked out and the emergency lights outside died.

"What just happened?"

Angel started swearing, hitting keys. "You said one might be Phreak, the Wrecker's hacker? Well he just locked down our security systems. We're blind."

"What about the emergency system?"

She hit more keys. "He's denying access, but it looks like he can't use any of the system himself—he can't use our cameras or send out the stand-down. Everybody's still headed for safety."

"*And I'm still here,*" Shelly said. "*So he hasn't gotten to the Institute's secure communications network.*"

"Okay." Sheriff Deitz abandoned the board. "So just what are we up against?"

"Their strongest guy is Gantry—Dozer," I said before Shelly could start. "I think. I'm only guessing about two of them, and even if the maybes are Phreak and Drop then I've got nothing on the last two. And there could be more in the vans."

"So, the ones you're pretty sure of?"

"They're all at least A Class, naturally or because the Ascendant boosted them. Besides Dozer, who's a straight up Ajax-type, you've got Twist. He's a powerful telekinetic who moves things with his mind, but he's got zero range—he has to be touching it; he uses his TK to support his armor so that it works like military-grade powered armor, and he has a spool of heavy carbon-weave cable attached to each arm that he projects up to thirty feet and manipulates like whips. Or super-strong steel tentacles."

"Got it. Next?"

"Balz." I had to think about him. "Also a telekinetic, with a global effect within his range. He's capable of moving and manipulating dozens of objects at once—kind of a telekinetic super-juggler. He wears lighter armor, but he uses his TK to maintain a cloud of flying softball-sized spheres around him. It's anybody's guess what each sphere can do. I've seen them used as flash-bangs, but others have worked as tasers and sensors. They're all high tech, and for all we know some might be Verne-tech."

Angel just smiled, turning back to her closet. "Target practice. Cool."

"My two guesses are Phreak and Drop. You've seen some of what Phreak can do, and I'm surprised Shelly's able to talk to us—his specialty is creating signals dead-zones."

"We have a more 'robust' system than most."

I nodded. "Drop is their driver. He's a teleporter, able to 'port multi-ton payloads, but his targeting range is zero so he has to be on top of whatever he's moving." I chewed my lip. "I have no idea how he's going to get them out of… Oh, *crap*."

"Crap?" Angel lowered the mini-howitzer she was checking and laughed. "Watch your language, missy!"

Sheriff Deitz folded his arms. "What is it?"

"*Hope means that the only way out of here is to cross the boundary and drop out, and since we stopped the Four Horsemen for all they know every gun from the base is going to be waiting for them out there. But if Drop is their driver, to use him for the getaway they have to shut down the extra-reality pocket that is Littleton.*"

"And they'd be insane not to use Drop as their driver," I finished. "A strong enough Atlas-type could fly everyone out, but could he outfly the Navy's jets and missiles and whatever crazy Verne-tech defenses the base has? But Drop can 'port them anywhere with a range of *miles*, so they could have a safe-house in Cuba."

"*More likely offshore, even a local fishing boat would do it. They could have a string of boats ready for them to leap-frog to the Bahamas or Florida. We'd be looking for a needle in a haystack halfway to the horizon.*"

"Either way, unless they've completely neutralized the navy base then they *have* to at least take the ground floor of the Institute and shut down the whatsit rings."

"Borromean rings," Angel supplied. "And the Institute is covered by an Interdiction Field, a Verne-tech defense against teleportation. They're going to have to fight their way in."

"So, they've burned their bridges. No retreat, got it." Sheriff Deitz pulled out his cell, hit a number. "Carl? We've got news for your boys. Yes, this is for real. And it's going to get interesting." He moved the cell away from his face. "Astra, I'm going to need you back in the air. You're the only really mobile pair of eyes we have left."

I pulled up my hood and got going.

I tried not to think about Atifa, or about Shelly heading right for what had to be the point of the Wrecker's attack. Or wonder what had happened to Jacky. Brick and the Three Horsemen had to have been a planned diversion for the base—did that mean the Wreckers had come in without a diversion? But if they had, they'd still have blown the translation system in the Garage behind them to seal the gate; we weren't getting any help from outside.

"Shelly?"

"*Yeah?*"

"What do they *want*? And can they get it?"

She didn't answer for a long minute. "*I still don't know. There's so much going on here, stuff even I don't know about. But the most dangerous stuff is outside, at the base. Phreak isn't getting into our systems, not without taking the ground floor and seizing a terminal. To carry anything out of here they'd still have to get into the Well, and the battleship-plate armor hatches have all closed up. While they're getting through* that*, everything here can be burned, dumped, scrubbed from the computers—that's what everyone here is doing now, prepping to "wreck" whatever the Wreckers could steal.*" I could hear the mounting frustration in her voice; she *hated* not knowing why.

"*They should have come in fast and hard, before we had time to get in and close up! Then they could have gotten something so why—*"

Time to think of something else. I looked down at the town. "Tell me about the Littleton Militia."

"*Um. They're a heavy infantry battalion, two companies divided into eight fire platoons. Lieutenant Colonel Carleton Scott is their commander.*"

"Any supersoldiers?"

"*Nope.*"

"Then they're toast." I should have stayed on the puzzle; now my stomach knotted and I blinked fast to clear my eyes.

"*Probably.*" She didn't sound any happier. "*It's going to be bad.*"

I could see the soldiers by their body heat, spreading out from the armories. It looked like the colonel was assigning a main force to the Institute, but the rest were grouping into coordinated teams that could move to cover the shelters as needed. Some of them helped straggling citizens along, but it looked like nearly everyone was safely in. Looking back up the hill I couldn't see the vans yet.

"They've made one mistake already. They *should* have come straight in after translation, they'd be inside the Institute by now and we'd be fighting our way in to them."

"Maybe they didn't know. Think they'll make more mistakes?"

"More? I hope so. Enough?"

She didn't answer that and I didn't say anything until "There they go."

"What?"

"Our guys just launched drones." An even dozen rose from the grounds and yards around the Institute. Quadracopters, they spread out to cover the nearest streets. "It looks like Phreak isn't getting a total blackout this time—"

The drones started disappearing in bright flashes and Sheriff Deitz cut in. *"Astra, what's going on up there?"*

"I don't know! Something is... I think Drop is sending Balz's exploding spheres up to take the drones! Where..." *Now* I saw the watching spheres, a swarm of dark and cold objects above the trees halfway into town. "Balz and Drop are in town! Halfway between me and the lake!"

"That's around Fillmore and Vine, damn it! How— Drop could have moved one of the vans, couldn't he?"

"Maybe both—he doesn't have to go with them." Below me a couple of platoons peeled away from their positions to head for the streets beneath the swarm. The sphere cloud shrank, most of them sinking below the trees, and then the remaining spheres dropped like they *had* been dropped. Like their puppeteer had abandoned them.

"And I think they just 'ported again," I told Deitz. Looking around the sky I could only see four lonely Littleton drones left.

"Keep watch for the spheres."

"Roger." Would I keep both vans together if I was the Wreckers? Or maybe hopscotch, 'port one forward then 'port up to it when it reported clear? No, I'd...

A downtown business blew up in a red fireball, throwing burning pieces of wall and roof into air the buildings around it.

"Sheriff! Is anybody hurt?"

It took Deitz a moment. *"Nothing on platoon chatter, but it's close to one of the shelters. They're moving."* He didn't say who and I didn't care. I dove hard, looking for the source of the explosion.

I found it. *It* found me—I heard the roar a fraction of a second before the rocket hit me, catching me in the chest, and exploded. The second impact was the ground, a backyard with a hedge and a swing set.

"Hope!" "Astra!" Both my current wingmen chimed in.

"I'm okay! Just stunned." I shook it off, climbing to my feet. Looking down, I groaned. My chameleon-cloth suit was shredded, I was about to engage, and I'd *left Malleus in the Sheriff's Office*. I took off, but swung over the hedge and flew low around the house I prayed was unoccupied—and jinxed barely in time to miss taking the next rocket. It exploded against a young oak that wasn't going to get any older.

"Woah! Astra!" The voice cut into my earbug, open channel.

"That's some piece of camo-gear you had—too bad it didn't hide you from lidar!" An air-ripping swarm of armor-piercing rounds tracked across my chest and kicked me into the wall of the house. A third rocket punched me through it but not before I saw who was hitting me. I knew the Scooby armor, knew the voice, and knew who'd let the Wreckers into the Garage.

"Balini? Why?"

"Because I can! They'll give me power! Do you have any idea how much it blows *to enlist, go through hell in boot camp, get a breakthrough and wind up being barely stronger and tougher than human? To be nothing more than a* freaking *weapon platform?"*

"You don't—" I bounced off the ground dodging his next shots by luck, put my back to an unshredded tree, and saw him. He stood in the middle of the street now, in full Scooby armor, shoulder mounts clicking to track me. "You don't have to do this."

"And you don't have to move, Astra. Look, I've painted you." He had; three red dots made a tight triangle on my battered breastplate. *"You're a nice kid. Sit this out, it'll be over soon. You move, I'll end you."*

He turned his head, the dots not moving. *"And that goes for the rest of you!"* he shouted at—I guessed—Colonel Scott's men. *"I hear a ping, she's gone!"*

"Hope, move!" Shelly screamed in my ear. *"Do something!"*

I heaved a laugh. "Sorry, Shelly. I've got noth—" Not true. My right hand crept in from the tree, along my hip and now I tried not to breath. My armor's pocket sat by the lower catch, and in it...

"Shelly, I need a D."

"How big?"

"Big."

Two heartbeats later a Littleton drone crashed into the street between us as I grabbed the challenge coin in my pocket, flew, and *threw*. The same shape as my old throwing disks, the challenge coin cracked his helmet as his first salvo roared by under me, laser-lock broken by the drone. Before he could do more than stagger back I dropped on him with a full gravity assist.

Armor shrieked and crumpled as I grabbed and smacked him down face-first to get at the weapon mounts. Hooking his helmet, I popped it from the suit's neck ring and found the release-catches that had to be there. The thump of boots on pavement almost launched me until I saw the fire-platoon sprinting my way.

"I've got him!"

"And we'll keep him." A young corporal in blue jeans and armor pulled up beside me and saluted, holding up a set of Blacklock restraints. Another produced a sandman pack. Balini swore incoherently, his bloody face twisted, and I wondered if I'd broken his jaw.

"Okay then." I yielded my prisoner, keeping him pushed against the cracked pavement as they cuffed him.

"You won't win!" He ground out before they hit him with the extra strength sleepy-time pack. "You can't keep them from getting what they want!" And he slumped.

"Well that was clichéd," Shelly commented.

"But not wrong." I stood, looking around. Half the businesses and homes on the street were on fire, and I heard explosions from two directions. It was happening. It was all happening and there was no cavalry riding to the rescue. The Wreckers had brought more in the vans, maybe every Scooby, maybe more wild-cards, and there was *nothing*, no plan…

I looked at my left hand, started laughing.

"What? Hope, are you cracking?"

I fumbled to pull off my glove. "She said not to take it off until I had to!"

"Take what off?"

"This!" I got the glove off. Fingers bare, I stared at the moonmoth silk ring for a breath, then grabbed one of the ends and pulled the bow open, yanking it off my hand. It fluttered to the ground.

"No eyes, here, you're going to have to tell me."

"Ozma's ring," I said weakly. It just lay there on the ground.

"Still not getting it."

"She told me I was traveling, gave me a lace ring. So what—"

The tornado arrived.

Chapter Twenty Six

"I have the best friends!"

From the Journal of Hope Corrigan

Tsuris' tornado paused over the lake, thickening its twisting water spout while spinning off tiny figures and one...dragon?

"*That's not possible!*" Shelly yelled.

"That's *Ozma*! She *came* from an extra-reality world—why can't she get into another one? Especially with Tsuris' tornado to ride! Wait, how are you *seeing* this?"

"My neural link with Shell! The bio-seed in my head didn't have time to fully grow into the link before I moved to Littleton, but we're together now! She's here!"

"You bet your sweet booties I'm here." Shell ghosted into existence beside me. She wore a black athletic shirt that read *Orwell's Little Sister* in white. "Ozma kitted up a poppet powered link to cover the extra-reality leap to you and Shelly, and Vulcan fabricated a quantum-signaling booster to cut through the base's interference field—didn't you wonder how I could talk to you at the base yesterday when before I couldn't reach you unless you were in Guantánamo?"

I mentally face-palmed. How could I have missed the significance of Shell's "shipping" commentary about Jacky and the Master of Ceremonies and Darren and me last night?

"And I'm here flying Galatea, too! So, see you! Have to conserve bandwidth!" She popped like a rainbow soap bubble, showing off. I looked up at the night sky, just on time for the rain to hit.

It hit hard and I could guess how; Tsuris was scattering the funneled lake water into instant water-laden cloud—he'd probably brought a *big* load from Lake Michigan too—and it was like being under a rainshower head. I doubted he could cover more than a few square blocks, but that was all he needed to put out the fires. I couldn't see anyone in the rain, then spotted Megaton's signature flare arrowing down towards me. He roared in, went vertical to kill his descent, cut his blast and dropped to the steaming pavement in a showy three point foot-knee-fist landing.

Megaton had lost all of what he'd called his Geek Weight over the last months of hard training and looked more like a track and field athlete now than a wrestler, but even if he'd still been soft and round with his first-day weight, standing there in red and black leather he was the most beautiful thing I'd ever seen. He pushed his goggles to the top of his helmet and looked me over.

"Hi, boss. Where's your cape?"

I could feel myself grinning like an idiot. "Back at the office with my big metal club. Let's go get it."

Shelly fed Shell/Galatea a grid-map of the town and the others arrived as we did. Crash and Grendel rode Terreflore, sitting behind Kindrake. Tsuris and Galatea flew in above them, Galatea using a shoulder-harnessed quadricopter wing I'd never seen before—two interlocked propeller rings to each side. She ditched the wing attachment on landing, leaning it against the wall and stepped up to stand beside me. Her blue and silver chrome form, slick with rain, shown in the streetlamps.

"Where's Ozma?"

"Sorry boss." Megaton shrugged regretfully. "She couldn't send Tsuris' tornado and ride it at the same time. Said it's like flying a kite—one of you has to stay on the ground."

I nodded. Too bad, but we still—

"Hey Astra, who're your friends?"

I turned and realized we had company. Deitz and Angel stood in the doorway, Angel with her tri-barrel over her shoulder.

"Sheriff Deitz, Deputy Sweet, please meet Galatea, Megaton, Grendel, Crash, Kindrake, and Tsuris. The Young Sentinels. Everybody, Sheriff Deitz and Deputy Sweet, the law in town."

"When we're not at war," the sheriff corrected. "Carl is in charge of the proceedings right now, and my authority only extends to the shelters. Come in out of the rain." Another explosion lit the night from the direction of the Institute. "And all that."

We trooped inside. Shelly's face was already on the big board, and she beamed at us.

"Hey guys, welcome to Littleton! The bang you just heard was one of the two vans, a scouting platoon lit it up but it was empty. The Wreckers—yeah, the Wreckers—are taking their own sweet time."

"Why?" Jamal asked. "Not that we're complaining since we got here in time for the show."

I finished clipping my cape on, complete with deputy badge, and raised my hand for attention. "They think they have all night, guys. They're all boosted by The Ascendant, and they think no help is coming. And with Drop moving them around, Balz scouting for them, and—Sheriff, they may have all of the heavy Cerberus unit, three of them anyway—they think they can handle everyone in here with them."

Sheriff Deitz nodded at my little summation. "And you think you guys can turn it around?"

"We can try. But, Sheriff? I think if the fighting is focused right now, we should begin evacuating everybody who's not shooting."

"Already on it. As soon as Scott's boys nailed down the points of contact we began walking and shuttling from the shelters furthest from the action. With the night and now the rain, the Wreckers may not even know."

"*Or care*," Shelly said from the board. "*They haven't tried attacking civilians or taking hostages—I think they think they're the Good Guys.*"

"And Good Guys have rules." I nodded. That fit with how my fight with Dozer had gone last year, even my stay as The Ascendant's guest.

"*Yeah they do. Guys, they believe breakthroughs are the next step in humanity becoming ascendant beings—so they're mortal gods but in their book that means* benevolent *gods. They'll show mercy when they can, and won't harm anyone normal who isn't fighting them.*"

"When they're not executing norms for killing or trying to kill us 'ascendant beings'," Tsuris added.

The floor shook and the night outside lit up. Shelly looked away from her screen, turned back.

"*So here's the deal, guys. Colonel Scott has half his troops dug in at pre-prepared points in a covering pattern around the Institute. Most of the rest are moving outside the perimeter, looking for contact so they can call in the brilliant-missiles Scott has for artillery. They're not playing around, Hope—their nastiest pieces could kill you. But so far they've got no confirmed kills, and we've…lost a few. So let's end this.*"

And they all looked at me.

"Hey, Hope," Shell ghost-whispered in my ear. "That's your cue."

We can't, can we? I looked around at everyone and my Blackstone-trained internal tactician kicked in, whispering *maybe we can*. For all our training, half of our team was what Rush liked to call new and shiny and Lei Ze called *green*—the Green Man hadn't been a real battle so much as an unnatural disaster—and with the exceptions of Grendel, who'd been "born" in an insane horror of psychotic bystanders and twisted and rampaging breakthroughs, none had seen a *battlefield*. I had no idea how half of them would react to deadly, mortal, man-to-man combat.

But... Grendel was almost unkillable *if* they could stop him at all. Galatea was a *drone* piloted by Shell, she'd brought racks of ordnance, and even getting blown up didn't mean the end of what *she* could do. Tsuris and Megaton...both could work it from standoff-range and support each other. Crash was in some ways the most dangerous of all of us as long as he didn't get stupid, and he was the most careful of us, too. Kindrake... *No idea, keep her safe, let her improvise around us.* So, the Young Sentinels vs. the Wreckers?

Two unknowns to deal with, but we could win. If we can't win we can find that out and work the edges, evacuate Littleton, maybe even keep them from completing their mission. And Shelly was in the Institute and not alone—we couldn't *not* try. I felt the smile growing across my face. We were here to save Littleton.

Crash knew the look, and pumped his fist. I heard a "Yes!" from Tsuris, an almost sub-sonic growl from Grendel.

"Give me a moment, guys." Staring at the board, which Phreak still kept mostly dark, I looked blankly at the overlayed streets while my thoughts raced.

"Three points—we need to find the Wreckers, we need to keep our own side from shooting at us as we move, and we need to identify and counter two unknowns. Once we have a target I can lift Grendel. Crash can speed in. Kindrake, I'm sorry but Terraflore is too big and...he's too big a target. Can you divide him into your flight of drakes? Crash can get you and them around if he's got a bike. You two are a team for the rest of the night. Sheriff? Do you have a handy motorcycle?"

"Take mine," Angel offered. "It's a Yamaha ultra-light—I've driven it around most of Cuba." She fished in her desk for her keys, looked back at us. "What? A girl has to have a hobby."

I blinked away the image of Angel driving from town to town, bar to bar. She probably had drinking songs about her now.

"Okay, we'll coordinate with Colonel Scott first, get the likely contact points. Crash will scout on the bike and tell us where the Wreckers are, we'll go in as I said. Shelly? Can you and Galatea coordinate to act as Dispatch for this? We need threat-recognition as we go, especially for the unknown two or three we're dealing with."

The sheriff started talking to the colonel. Angel took Crash out to show him her bike. Everyone else pretty much relaxed, taking the whole thing like the prep meeting for a hot-range exercise. All except for Kindrake, who looked more than a little lost. Watching her with Grendel, I knew he didn't see it; he was in his zone, his body changing as muscles bulked and adjusted themselves for the coming fight.

He looked up at me. "I want Dozer." A troll staking out his fight. The biggest, of course, *Eric*. Mr. Ludlow.

"You can have him." I crossed my arms, looked away and caught Kindrake's eye where she leaned against Angel's desk. I had no idea why Kindrake was *here*, but I could only be grateful. *And now she's your job too, so suck it up little girl.*

Tilting my head at the coffee machine got a nod from her and she joined me. I wasn't Jacky—*don't think about Jacky*—but the Littleton Sheriff's Office kept a decent cupboard and the pot was fresh; I poured and made mine while she decided what to put in hers, turned to lean against the counter beside me and watch the room. I turned my head so she could see my smile. "Are you okay?"

"Sure." She shrugged. "I just— I'm CAI certified, but that was mostly search-and-rescue, emergency support, stuff like that. *You guys...*"

"Yeah. We mostly do emergency response, too, but the Sentinels are a fighting team. And the Young Sentinels are, too, or we will be once we're all old enough to qualify. Half of us have a few more months."

"How can you fight *here*?"

"I don't think the American Superhero Association is going to hear what happens here, do you? And we're a little out of their jurisdiction." I leaned in closer, bumped her shoulder. The goth-girl was older than me, taller too, just like everyone else, but I felt like the big sister. "Stick with Crash, you'll be alright."

"Thanks." She watched me for a moment while I sipped, then paid attention to her own cup. "That's not—" She blew on her coffee, looked back at me. "*Why* are you fighting here? I mean, it's not your town—from what I get, it's a place that's not even *here*, so nobody will ever know."

I looked at her, and didn't even have the words.

"Astra?" Sheriff Deitz got my attention, stepped over to the board.

"Stick with Crash," I repeated softly. Straightening I gave her shoulder a light squeeze and crossed the room without looking at anybody, feeling like a complete fake.

"Scott thinks they're somewhere here," the sheriff said when I joined him. He pointed to a block of houses with deep backyards close to the Institute. "They keep making and breaking contact in the streets around this block, and he thinks that Drop is sending the Wreckers out, making hard contact, then jumping out and picking them up. Which we think he can do as long as he has relative coordinates to his arrival zone."

"And he's getting that here from Balz's spheres."

"Yup."

"Confirmed threats?"

"Just the ones you've told us about. Dozer, Balz, and Twist, and they're bad enough when they drop right on a platoon. No contact with the two unknowns and no sign of any more of our own Cerberus team."

"Okay." *Please God, let Balini have been the only traitor*. We just couldn't face the Wreckers *and* three more hard-trained Scoobies working together. "Crash, your turn. Do *not* drop out of hypertime anywhere near the area—go through and come back. Remember what Balz did to Rush last year."

"Yes, boss." He pulled on his red racer's helmet and was gone through the open door. And then he was back. We never heard the bike. "The general's right. They're in back of one of the homes, operating out of a big van. I saw three, Balz's spheres all over, but couldn't see in the van. He can move the whole thing if he wants, right?"

I thought of the big steel platform with the "pilot's chair" I'd seen last year. "We think so. Okay people, let's go."

The rain had mostly stopped but now it picked up again, this time covering the whole town. It couldn't *all* be Tsuris, and Shelly guessed that his brief but intense shower had convinced the pocket reality's own weather system that it was time to water the grass. I asked Tsuris if he could bring up some more lake water to thicken the rain as we went in, and he acted like I was asking him if he knew how to walk. Or maybe crawl.

We launched when the water fell in sheets with a light scattering of fish. I could barely see Tsuris' blue and gray form less than thirty feet from me, and behind him Megaton's flare almost disappeared in the curtains of rain. One thing we had absolutely changed from my dreams was the whole town was *not* going up in flames; even the most enthusiastic fires below us were giving up and calling it a night.

Dangling from my grip, Grendel waited patiently for me to drop him and Shell thoughtfully provided a red targeting pip for the van and Dozer; without it even I couldn't have seen them through the rain and the screen of tree branches.

"*You realize that you two look ridiculous,*" Shell commented from her view through Galatea behind us. "*Like a hummingbird airlifting a cat—it's just* wrong."

And like always, she'd forced a laugh out of me when I needed it. "Just because *you* can't. Okay everyone, three, two, one, go!"

I dove and released my one-hand grip on Grendel's wrist. Falling through the rain, he dropped through the aerial perimeter of guardian spheres below us for a perfect driveway-cracking landing between the van and his target. Down the street beyond Balz' perimeter, Crash dropped out of hypertime with Kindrake, and her flight of tiny drakes clinging to them like bats exploded upward to attack the lower spheres. Megaton opened up on the higher ones with precise blasts while Tsuris focused the rain into a reverse-waterspout over the van and yard and Galatea hovered, ready to flush missile racks.

The armor-clad figure Shell had virtual-labeled Dozer charged Grendel according to plan and I dropped to land on the other side of the van as they crashed together. My super-duper vision picked up two glowing human heat sources inside. *Step one: destroy the Wrecker's mobility by taking out Drop*. I punched a hole in the van, dropped my maul, grabbed with both hands and ripped the hole into one I could get through.

Neither occupant was Drop or anyone else I knew, but I'd brought enough sandman packs. "You're under—" The boot to my face landed harder than a normal could have kicked, not hard enough to hurt more than surprise but I still stumbled back. The unarmored guy climbed out through the hole to meet me, laughing.

"Astra, luv! Me and the gents were wondering when you'd show up. I was thinkin' you'd got trapped outside and I'd come all this way for bugger-all."

He stepped down and planted his feet wide, not paying any attention to the roaring and shaking battle on the other side of the van or the rain soaking his cargo pants and leather jacket. A fitted black mask covered his whole head to hide everything but his eyes, which wrinkled over the smile I couldn't see as he opened his arms and gave the universal curling *come and get it* gesture with both hands. I'd never seen him before—or at least heard that voice—but he looked awfully happy to see me.

"So c'mon luv, give us a kiss. Take your best shot."

"*Hope, he thinks he can take you!*"

"Really? 'Cause I wasn't getting that at all!" Shell wasn't telling me anything I didn't know, but there was no *time*. His companion in the van could engage any second, and the longer I took *here* the more likely Dozer and Twist could double-team Grendel or the rest could get away. I swung.

For a horrible second I thought I'd killed him; he flew away from me, the force of my hit lifting and throwing him across the drive and through the tall picket fence into the next yard. I flew after and found him picking himself up, laughing again.

"Is that your *best*? Your stonking great beasty back there could slap me harder! I could be in London right now, good-timing it on the pull and the piss, so c'mon and give it to me, luv!"

I swung again and then again into his unresisting mass, realized Shell was yelling *"Try something else!"* in my ear. Screaming my own frustration as he laughed, I fell back and pulled a sandman pack from my belt. He wiped a drop of blood from his lip, looked at it and at the pack.

"Oh no, luv. Now it's my turn." He charged with the speed of someone who didn't even notice their own body weight. *This* time I braced—a big mistake.

My world lit as I took the full hit he shouldn't have been able to deliver if the kick before had been his limit. It felt like I'd been hit by Boomer again. Braced, I didn't fly far before sliding—fetching up against the van where we'd started. I shook my head, desperate to clear my vision, and *he* lit up as Galatea's flushed missile swarm slammed into him. He walked out of the fireball, still laughing.

"Shell!" I stared, panting. "He's getting bigger!" His cargo pants had hung loose before, and now his clothes—which *hadn't* been blown off—stretched tight over growing muscle. I scrambled to my feet, retrieving Malleus only to hold it uselessly.

"He's adaptive—a force absorber! Get Shelly to ID him!"

"How are you going to stop him?"

"Crash! Get Cr—"

The eye-twisting blur that came in from my left *wasn't* Crash's red and white, it was *black*, and then Crash twisted into sight as *two* speedsters whirled across the yard.

They'd counted on us. Or on the Sentinels.

And surviving spheres were dropping close, pulling in to the center where the fight was.

"Get Crash out! Now! Crash—Kindrake!" I didn't have time to think about the disaster the situation had turned into. Smashing the van's engine block with a back-swing in passing, I ignored the one I'd dubbed The Brit to get to Grendel—tangled with Twist's cables while Dozer pounded him or tried to.

I landed on Dozer with a two-handed downswing into his armored back that hammered him to the ground. "We're *out!*" Not waiting see if Grendel understood, I threw Malleus *hard* and when Twist went down with Malleus in his armored chest I grabbed Grendel and leaped for sky, The Brit still laughing behind me.

Chapter Twenty Seven

"If the fight goes against you, unless you're standing on ground you have to protect or with people you can't leave, you get the hell out. Standing your ground when you can't win and don't have to is for dead heroes."

Atlas

Angel patched the nasty cut high on Crash's neck, while I stood by the big board and called myself every bad name I could think of.

Crash dubbed the new speedster Mack the Knife, and he had the right; hundreds of hours sparring and practicing Bagau katas in Sifu's school had turned the panicked kid I remembered from the night at Puccini's last year into an opponent the other speedster—a nasty knife-fighter according to Crash—hadn't been expecting at all. He'd managed to back the guy off until Galatea had started targeting him with computer-guided auto-bursts. Then he'd gotten himself and Kindrake out of there, and now we were all back in the Sheriff's Office, dripping and dispirited while Sheriff Deitz watched the door and talked to Colonel Scott.

I'd lost track of *missions*, and if Crash had gone down then Mack the Knife could have gotten to Kindrake before she'd known he was coming. And the way that The Brit had been hulking out, the sandman-packs Crash had brought might not have even worked.

"Do you think they're new Wreckers?" Megaton had his helmet off, and he kept rubbing his face and looking over at Angel and Crash.

"No." I sighed. "I think they're more mercenaries. Like the Three Horsemen. They're…hard."

Shell had shown me Crash's helmet-cam replay of his encounter with Mack the Knife, and just watching had shaken me again. The Brit might *talk* like a happily sociopathic brawler, but he wasn't Brick; he'd been controlled, known exactly what he was doing at every step. And Mack the Knife… Crash's fancy martial-arts moves hadn't set him back more than a second and he'd still come horribly close to slicing an artery. Crash thought Mack had avoided his suit since he couldn't tell how armored it was, and the image of blood flying from the sweeping cut below his chin was going to stay with me. Crash had managed a countering disarm then stiff-punched the guy in the solar plexus and bugged out as instructed while Mack was half paralyzed and then running from Galatea.

Megaton finally turned away from Angel and Crash. "Kindrake and I managed to take out most of Balz' spheres," he offered. "I think."

I nodded, giving him credit. "And Shell and I powered up the biggest Bad Guy they're fielding. The Brit can handle Colonel Scott and his militia now, just by himself." Squeezing my eyes shut, I tried to rotate the tension out of my back and shoulders. "And Balz could have another crate of spheres ready to go."

I tried not to think too hard about the fact that the Wreckers might be *one* man down now, maybe permanently. I'd been rushed, and I might have killed Twist.

Grendel flexed, popping joints. He wasn't blaming me any more than the others, and now he shrugged massively. "Ozma should be here."

"Mack the Knife would have…" My brain refused to *think* of what Mack the Knife could have done to her before she knew he was even there. Maybe our resident sorcerous could have come another way, but she wasn't a field cape. Grendel made a sound that told me he'd managed to complete my sentence in his head, probably with visuals.

His voice dropped. "So what do we *do*?" No, no blame in his anthracite-black eyes, but no giving way either.

"We tell Shelly to get herself and everyone else in the Institute out the back door, that we're not keeping the Wreckers out?"

All we could do was evacuate everyone not pinned down, wait for the Wreckers to shut down the rings and drop Littleton back into the world when they were ready to leave. *That* part of my dream was going to happen. If only Jacky and her boys could get *in*. Not to mention everything the navy base could bring—

I stopped breathing, eyes wide, and *knew* what the Wreckers had come for. And I knew how to stop them from getting it.

"Shell. Shelly." I addressed the air. "Their target has to be in Littleton. What are the odds they came straight for the Garage, left the navy base alone?"

Ghost-Shell popped in at my elbow. "Pretty good. If the Four Horsemen were a planned diversion, they did get us to move all but the heavy armor out of the Garage. All they had to do is leave something behind them to blow the translation system and the power plant, and that shuts the Navy out until sometime tomorrow." Shelly nodded her agreement from the big board.

"So the navy base has no portable translation rig?"

"*They do*," Shelly said. "*But they've got to set it up inside the boundary line and then tune it. That takes a while.*"

"Shell? Can *you* send a message?"

"Are you kidding? I'd be calling from Chicago, and they're locked down so tight now that a call from God wouldn't get accepted. I don't know if it's them doing it or Phreak's work."

"Okay." The hair on my neck was standing up and I'd gone light-headed. I tried to breathe slow, focus on keeping my feet on the floor. "So, say you're Jacky and all this has happened. What would you do?"

"I'd get back to the Garage, be ready to go when the gate opened again. But—"

"And I'll bet that Captain Lauer would do the same thing. *Will*, because they won't be waiting till tomorrow."

"Yeah, but the Wreckers won't open the Littleton Pocket until they're ready to teleport over the horizon with whatever they came for! They'll be gone!"

"So we open the pocket *first*. We make my dream come true." I straightened and crossed the room to Crash and Angel. "Crash? I need you to do another job tonight."

"They're moving," Grendel said in my earbug even though I could see that in the virtual-screens Shell was projecting for me. *"Colonel Scott's men just reported contact with The Brit. The platoons in contact are falling back without engaging."*

"Good." I nodded to Tsuris. All of us except Kindrake, who had joined Shelly inside the Institute, were back out in the rain. Tsuris, Megaton, and I waited one street over from the Institute, and Shell had turned the spot into a virtual Dispatch for me, ringing me with multiple virtual screens only I could see but let me see everyone's mask-cam views and even the network feeds the Littletone Militia had been able to cobble together. So while others stood in front, I waited at the corner of Sunnydale and Camelot.

Two worse-omened street names were hard for me to imagine but the Wreckers had given us more time than I'd hoped for, time enough to think about street names and other things. "Tsuris, you've got The Brit. Remember—"

"Don't try and blow him away, just stop him from moving forward till it's our turn."

"Right." Shelly had been unable to identify The Brit, but if what we knew about absorptive adapters was true then pushing against the kind of wind-jet Tsuris could pull down on him would expend his stored energy reserves—so long as Tsuris didn't feed The Brit *more* if he decided to just stand and take it.

Tsuris lifted off in a blast of wind, and Megaton followed on his own blasting column of fire. Kindrake's flight of rainbow drakes followed *him*; she could direct them from inside with Shelly.

"It'll work," virtual-Shell said beside me. She wasn't bothering to match her ghost-self to the environment and now her too-dry shirt read *Come and take it!* I wished that the soldiers deployed between the Wreckers and the Institute with Shell-Galatea, could see it. "Tsuris will slow The Brit down, Megaton and Kindrake's pets will keep Balz's spheres off of Tsuris while he does. But this won't stop them."

"I know. But it will slow them down and save lives. How's Grendel?" Grendel waited with Galatea, the two of them making an obvious target for Dozer and Twist when they arrived—part two of the plan to keep the casualties down.

"He's stoic."

"Really? Tell him I challenge him to Dance Dance Revolution when this is over."

"Now he's laughing and Scott's boys are looking at him funny."

"Hey, I might be a white girl but I have some moves. Tell him!" I hid my own smile. Stoic Grendel was a brooding troll, intimidating even to our own side, but *laughing* he sounded like a cheerful avalanche and was completely human no matter what he looked like. Let them look at him funny; a laughing Grendel was a morale booster.

Balz's sphere-swarm arrived, the explosive ones I remembered too well. In the screens I could see that the primary targets weren't the soldiers or my team but the hard emplacements Colonel Scott had dug for his machine guns—the positions he'd evacuated trusting my plan, which meant the exploding spheres only blew apart military hardware. Still no sign of Mack the Knife, and I prayed that my gambit of keeping anyone knifeable off the ground for him to play with had kept him out of it.

If not, Colonel Scott had a surprise for him.

"And Dozer and Twist have arrived! Switching you over to Shelly—got to focus on Galatea!" Shell faded out from the feet up, paused with just her head. "Oh! And Colonel Scott wants to talk."

"We've laid out the welcome mat, Astra. Are you up for it?" The old soldier didn't sound too worried, but he'd probably been doing cool-under-fire all his life even if it broke some kind of code for him to have clear targets he wasn't shooting at.

"We're all improvising here, sir! Tsuris, you're up!"

I had no time to wonder if I was grateful that I hadn't killed Twist or not. Tsuris dropped his focus on The Brit and brought the rain—intensified it, really, with more fish, and under the sheets of water I felt the air change. Part *three*. And now it was my turn. I picked up my payload and launched.

"*Hope!*" Shelly broke in. "*The bench team is coming but needs more time!*"

"How much more?"

"*Minutes maybe. They're almost in position.*"

"We'll try and give it to them, but I'm not sure who'll be standing when they get here." And then I was over the Institute, looking down on the sodden field of battle. The machine-gun emplacements were gone and the Institute's doors blown open. Below me, Galatea flushed her micro-missiles at Balz's remaining spheres and used her short-range shoulder and boot jets to close with Twist. Grendel had configured his morphic form for maximum toughness, and now he pounded the ground and ignored Dozer to charge The Brit with an air-shaking roar, and that was all the time I had to see details.

Dozer looked up just before I hit him with the truck.

It was an old truck, solid steel body, the kind of ride that got terrible mileage but could roll a few times without coming apart or even crumpling much, and it hammered Dozer into the soaked and spongy Institute lawn. I followed it down to flip its shattered wreck aside and pounded Dozer before he could recover.

His helmet was something new; it didn't break and now I knew how Twist had survived, but my punch still snapped his head back— and *hurt*. I ignored the flash of pain in my fist to grab and throw Dozer against the closest tree with my left. The old oak shivered with the impact, bits of bark and wood flying, and he bounced back to land on hands and knees in the churned-up mud and grass.

I stepped forward. "It's over, Eric! You don't have to do this!"

I couldn't see his face, and his answer was his charge. He hit me like a speeding semi-truck, slamming into me and carrying us both through the wall behind me and into the Institute lobby in an explosion of bricks and mortar. My head rang and the world grayed out. When I tried to push him away he grabbed an arm to hold me in place and hammer me. My head rang again and this time I bit my tongue, then I got in a curl-and-kick to throw him away from me. My flying missile-drive threw us both back out onto the lawn in another explosion of wall. We both tumbled, but I made it to my feet first.

"Eric! Stop!" My fist ached, my right shoulder ached, the side of my head throbbed hotly and my vision wobbled. I spat blood. Beyond us, The Brit grappled with Grendel and Galatea had lost an arm to Twist. Flashes above us and flying pieces of sphere coming down with the rain told me Megaton and Kindrake were keeping Balz's arsenal away from us. Barely.

"*Hold on—still coming!*" Shelly gasped in my ear, sounding like she'd been fighting as hard as me. "*Phreak is into the Institute system—we've lost ground floor access! Ali's evacuating the techs!*"

The world lit up, and not because I'd been punched again—to my left a line of flash-bang mines spiked into the campus lawn lit off in a string, which meant Mack the Knife had finally tried to mix into it. The military wasn't stupid; they'd developed area denial measures set to the hyper-fast movements of speedsters years ago—Balz had used a variant of it on *Rush* last year, and Colonel Scott had unpacked their own supply the moment I'd told him we had a hostile one on the ground.

I forced myself to focus on the fight in front of me; I didn't see an unconscious body which meant Mack had escaped back into hypertime, but he wasn't our problem now.

Dozer charged *again* but this time his feet slipped, digging divots out of the wet lawn, and I met him with an overhead elbow-drive into his back. He spread-eagled into the lawn, rolled, and pushed up to catch me beneath the edge of my armor. I folded around his driving shoulder, and his arms wrapped around my legs, kept me from flipping over off his back. He threw me down and swung, and I barely managed to roll my head out of the direct line of his punch as my head rang *again*. This time I *flew*, taking us both and with no sense of direction other than away. Dozer let go to fall.

I let him, trying to breathe and recover. Eric was soaking up my hits, taking it in return for the chance to work me, going for a knockout over a win-by-decision, and I didn't know how many more hits I could take. I twisted my head to each shoulder, testing my spine and my equilibrium while Dozer climbed back to his feet. He began backing away, toward the Institute. Message clear: *you have to stop me.*

I dove.

"*Spheres!*" Shell yelled. I twisted but my world flashed into light and disappeared. I felt the hit as I crashed.

I didn't—quite—black out, and endless hours of fight-training with Watchman turned my crash into a graceless roll that kept rolling for the crucial distance I needed to recover enough of myself to know what was going on again. No more spheres followed me, but looking up from the ground I blinked and saw Dozer coming on like a runaway train. His fingers brushed my foot as my leap into the air threw me beyond his reach. Breathing to slow my racing heart, I took the crucial moment to get my bearings, feel the battle. Galatea was *down*, in pieces like she'd forced Twist to literally tear her apart to keep her off him once her micro-missile batteries were exhausted. Grendel and The Brit staggered and rolled across the scarred and pitted field, locked in a take-no-prisoners wrestling match as The Brit hammered away with a fist or elbow when he could. He kept trying to escape as Grendel wrapped him in limb-locks.

"Shelly, is Phreak getting through?"

"*He's seizing systems, but Shell and I are gestalting—keeping him out of the core and away from the Interdiction Field controls for now!*"

Okay, maybe Shell had just abandoned Galatea to focus on their fight to shut Phreak out—if he got to those controls then Drop could 'port straight in and they'd be on top of their goal. "Maybe—"

Dozer ignored me now to charge for the destroyed doors of the Institute.

"We're out of time! Wherever the bench-team is—"

They arrived in bounds that brought them through the screen of rain and trees, three big and beautiful armored Scoobies firing as they came, *yes*! Rockets and sabotted tracer rounds reached out to touch Dozer with flaming trails and darts of light, shredding his armor and throwing him across the mud-soaked field. Drones dropped from the sky to light up the scattered clusters of spheres still in the air in a brief aerial massacre.

Then the surviving spheres dropped, pilotless and dead. The Master of Ceremonies condensed from the air, dropping down out of barely-there mist to land on The Brit and bite into him like a monstrous leech. The big guy screamed once, high-pitched and cut short, and went limp. I spun in place, looking for a target, but Twist was raising his hands. Dozer had finally got smart or he'd been knocked out; either way he stayed down.

"Shell? Shelly?"

"*Phreak's down—Jacky's team got him and they're not getting in!*"

And just like that it was over. It was over and we'd won.

We'd won.

Chapter Twenty Eight

"Sometimes winning just means you're the ones left to bury your dead, other times it's more than that, but whatever else winning means, it means you go on."

Astra, *Notes From a Life*.

The rain shut off like someone had turned a faucet, that someone being Tsuris since for the last few minutes the only rain falling had been supplied by the lake. I looked up and realized that the stars over Cuba were different than the stars over the pocket universe that had contained Littleton.

"*They never guessed!*" Shell/Shelly laughed in echo of each other. "Tsuris' lake-storm covered our drop back into the real world—they didn't even notice the hotter air!"

And that had been the biggest gamble; if the Wreckers had noticed *we* cut power to the Borromean rings and collapsed the extra-reality pocket ourselves, they could have hit the Institute sooner or fallen back to Drop and 'ported away before the bench-team arrived. Because of course the "bench team"—Jacky, MC, the Scoobies and the rest—had been waiting for us, especially once Crash had crossed the boundary back into the world and told them our plan.

I laughed, still spinning. "Are you two going to unlink? Because you sound really weird together." I felt something shift in the back of my head, like unfusing the quantum-link gestalt the two of them had made changed a balance I felt through my own link.

Virtual-Shell appeared beside me, back in my head again. "That was weird from the inside, too."

"*No kidding,*" Shelly seconded through my earbug. "*We'll have to think about it separately when we have time, but right now Captain Lauer wants to see you.*"

The captain had to come to me; I headed for Grendel where he stood over the comatose Brit with MC. MC looked wired, the big vampire almost vibrated in place and I had to wonder what kind of kick went with The Brit's blood in his powered up state. *Grendel* just looked half-beaten, his nose smashed, mouth bloody, one long fang snapped off and his scalp torn to pour blood into his eyes.

Through my whole desperate fight with Dozer, he'd just hung onto The Brit and taken it, letting the villain expend power with every hit and clinch; now his injuries had stopped bleeding and his changeable body was already healing. He stood and watched The Brit while Scott's boys applied shackles and sandman packs.

I reached up to touch his swollen jaw. "Sorry."

"It'll heal." He popped the broken fang out, tossed it away. "You?"

Me? My body was one big ache, and with the adrenaline high draining away I didn't want to *think* for at least a day. If I could arrange to stay away from home for a couple of days so my superhuman constitution had time to take care of the deep bruises before my parents saw them, I would be very, very happy.

"It'll heal?"

He smiled, wide and toothy. "Yeah. Good job."

"Astra?" Captain Lauer dismounted from an armored personnel carrier and stepped carefully across the deeply torn and pitted lawn to join us.

"Good evening, sir."

"Is it?" He looked at the holes in the Institute. "How did you figure out their target was the Littleton Pocket itself?"

"It's the only thing that made sense, sir. Shelly said they couldn't get to any of the Institute projects before we could destroy them, and they were just letting all of Littleton's residents evacuate without trying to stop anybody so they couldn't have come here after somebody. Unless they were inside the Institute, but—"

"But if they were, then the slow and methodical approach made even less sense," he finished for me.

"Yes. But the one thing in the Institute we couldn't destroy or evacuate was the thing that generates the extra-reality pocket. And…"

"And?"

"It fit, sir. The Ascendant—the Ascendancy— they think of themselves as superior beings. Shelly called them mortal gods. Well, right now they're hiding and gods don't hide. The Ascendant wants his own Mount Olympus, somewhere safe he can build a temple to himself and gather his followers without interference."

"But you can only get into the pocket from its corresponding location in the real world. Wouldn't that make it easy to find?"

I took a breath, let it out. "Ozma transported my whole team here on a tornado, sir. I think, if you have the right kind of power and a beacon to help you find it, you can get from there to here from anywhere in the world. And they have Drop and Phreak."

"They *had* Phreak. Artemis took Crash and your other vampire and half my light-armored with her; they and their scratch-team caught Phreak with his full rig. The only ones we didn't get were Drop and the speedster you so colorfully named Mack the Knife."

My smile hurt but I couldn't stop. I'd *known* Jacky would know just what to do, better than I did.

"I'm sure he has another name, sir."

"I'm sure he does."

More APCs came down the street, loaded with more soldiers and sailors. Sheriff Deitz and Deputy Sweet arrived in their own jeep, lights flashing, and the sheriff stopped and got out by an officer that had to be Colonel Scott. I'd never met the slight and gray-haired soldier, and he looked more like a professor than a military man, but he walked through the wreck of the field like he'd seen a million of them. He and the sheriff joined us while Angel went to talk to the soldiers handling Twist. He really needed a scar or a cigar or something to go with the black unit beret.

I shook the colonel's hand. "So, what happens to Littleton now?" Beyond the Institute the buildings that showed above the trees didn't show any smoke—Tsuris had drowned every fire—but I wondered how many shops and businesses had to be rebuilt.

He rubbed his face, looking at the closer devastation. "We finish evacuating. And we move all the Institute projects and files to the navy base. Ali says they've already started."

"But it's over. Isn't it?"

"Not until we bring the pocket back," he explained. He waved at the star-speckled sky. "You'll notice we're sitting open to the world right now? But we don't know what will happen when we power up the rings again. It's never been tried."

"Oh. Well—" I straightened, tested my aches and pains. "Sleep is overrated."

"You're not kidding," Shelly agreed. *"I'm setting up an intravenous coffee drip down here, we've got to move the Oroboros' files out of their segregated system and upload the whole thing by secure satellite uplink, and Shell can't help at all with this— FYI, Shell processed the mask-cam footage from Jacky and Crash's roundup of Phreak and his gear. So guess what they found? The high security flash-drive Fisher and the feds are looking for."*

"No!" I almost laughed; it was too good.

"Yes. It's been wiped and Phreak's not talking, but Shell figures it had code that he needed but had wanted to keep completely off the grid—must have really *messed him up when they had to leave Chicago a bit earlier than planned last year. So that's keeping her busy, but if you want to pick up bits of Galatea, Vulcan will be grateful. And then you could help Ali's people load the heavy stuff."*

From Grendel's snort, it sounded like she'd patched him in, too.

I looked at the colonel, captain, and sheriff. "Well gentlemen, it looks like I have my own marching orders. If you'll excuse me?"

I detoured to see Jacky and Crash and get Malleus back first, where I'd left it in retreat. It felt good to have it back in my hand.

We didn't get the last of the Institute loads out until well past dawn, and the day's work also involved setting up shelters for Littleton's displaced citizenry; just because we optimistically hoped to be home by nightfall didn't mean we could be stupid about it. I found Mr. Darvish and Atifa and was able to assure Mrs. H that Shelly and Shell were both fine.

The government of Cuba had to know about the sudden appearance of Littleton, but all we got was Mr. Black dropping by to extend the Tyrant's offer of supplies and transportation if necessary. That, and the caravan of trucks from Guantánamo City laden with meals prepared by every café and restaurant in town and probably a lot of private kitchens, too.

I still wasn't sure about the Tyrant, but that showed class.

On my second trip to the temporary camp to bring more supplies out of Littleton *just in case* I spotted Angel and Naked Man, in pants this time. He stood near the lunch line, his curly black hair standing out above most everyone around him. A circle of Cubans who'd unloaded their meals had gathered and I could hear the back-and-forth of a dialogue, fluent Spanish, or at least is sounded fluent to me. Angel stood nearby, eagle eyes on him and everyone in threat range. I scooted over.

"What's going on?"

"He has a new audience for his message of peace and universal beinghood. It happens."

"I don't understand." And really I didn't, even if everything going on had kept me from thinking about it until just now. "Why is he in Littleton? He seems harmless."

"He is, unless you try and hurt him."

"What happens?"

"We don't know. There've been five attempts but we haven't found the ones who tried yet. He's here because of the three kidnappings."

"*Why*?"

"His message. Him. Take your pick." Angel 's sharp face got a soft look that reminded me of Jacky in Holybrook Rest.

I was wondering what *that* meant when someone tapped me on the shoulder. I turned and didn't recognize the rough-looking Cuban standing in front of me, but Angel eyeballed him and decided he wasn't a threat to her alien preacher while I fumbled for polite Spanish and finally gave up.

"Yes? Can I help you?"

He nodded respectfully and held out a letter, dropping it in my hand before I had time to think. Nodding again, he turned and disappearing into the crowd without a word.

I stared after him, and then turned the letter over. It was a folded piece of parchment-style stationary, stamped with red wax, and I broke the seal and opened it to unfold a page filled with handwriting so fine it was nearly calligraphy.

Dear Hope: I realize this mode of communication is a bit archaic, but I find that I loathe tweeting and texting and emailing and all the other impersonal modern forms. Since I am pressed for time I will skip over the usual pleasantries other than to say that you are looking very well, all things considered. I wanted to assure you that while the Ascendancy's activities enabled my own, I was never a part of their plan and since your own family might have become involved I felt that you should be involved as well. I hope you will forgive my once-again intrusion into your sleep, but time was short and the detour to fly from Washington to Guantánamo by way of Chicago was worth the risk. I will say that the results were most entertaining; certainly you exceeded my expectations.

Until next time.

There was no signature. Turning the letter back over, I looked at the wax seal. I'd seen the stamped fox-face symbol before on a business card.

"Is there a problem?" Angel glanced at the letter to make sure it wasn't dangerous to her responsibility.

"No, at least I don't think so."

I called Shelly.

"*Hmm? Kind of busy here. Ali's disappeared, and they're desperate enough to find out what she took with her that they've enlisted me and Shell to shake the sacred tree that is the Institute Secure System and see what falls out. I've never seen such a thick non-disclosure agreement in my life. What do you need?*"

I popped up a few feet to scan the busy crowds. Around me helicopters landed and took off, trucks unloaded and departed for the base and for Guantánamo, and...

"Never mind. At least we don't have to wonder about Kitsune anymore. How did he escape Veritas' mole-hunt?"

She didn't ask how I knew. "*I think that Kitsune can transform into someone deep enough that he's them. If he believes it, he can answer personal questions 'truthfully'—makes you wonder if he could ever change so completely he forgot who he was. Anyway, he left a note that we'd find the real Ali vacationing in Bermuda with a faked memory of winning a vacation to a very exclusive and isolated spiritual retreat. Got to go.*"

"Go," I laughed. It was all I could do. "See you soon." I hung up and landed. There was still a lot to be done.

The last evacuees of Littleton were the eight militia members killed defending their town from the Wreckers.

All work stopped as the base chaplains and Littleton ministers conducted a very brief service before Naval Intelligence claimed their bodies; NavInt would provide cover stories for their deaths before sending them home to loved ones who would believe they died anywhere but here. I prayed with the Navy chaplains, and then got back to work.

The sky was dark when the Institute carefully repowered the Borromean rings and I and everyone else watched Littleton fade from sight. The crowd cheered, and then all we could do was wait.

Fortunately we didn't wait long; the Garage's translation system hadn't been damaged by the Wreckers on their way through. Balini had gotten Phreak access to the system, which had allowed him to translate them through and then wreck the Garage's computer system and power grid behind them. The Navy had finally let Shell help, at least with that, and with an installed generator and backup system from the base she was able to retune the translation system to the Littleton Pocket in minutes. An hour of testing and exploring later, they concluded the Littleton Pocket was stable as it had ever been and began shuttling us in.

I said goodbye to my Scoobies. Balini had knocked them out at the beginning of the night with aerosolized sandman packs in the Dog House before he opened the Garage to the Wreckers, and Corbin got tight-jawed just asking about my fight with him. When they found out what happened to my challenge coin, Corbin gave me his own. It earned him a surprise hug. He was an Ajax—he could take it.

Jacky and I got back to Holybrook Rest well after midnight. She'd seen off her boys from New Orleans first and the rest of the team stayed at the naval base overnight. Mr. Darvish got back before we did, and had prepared a late dinner-board for his guests to refresh themselves with as they trickled in. We snacked and took turns with the shower before turning in, and I dropped into dreamless sleep.

Dreamless for a while, anyway.

Chapter Twenty Nine

"It's the action, not the fruit of the action, that's important. You have to do the right thing. It may not be in your power, may not be in your time, that there'll be any fruit. But that doesn't mean you stop doing the right thing. You may never know what results come from your action. But if you do nothing, there will be no result."

Mahatma Gandhi

I stood in a crystal gazebo someone had perched on top of an enormous white gasbag. The taut inflated surface sloped out and away beneath the little structure to disappear into the sea of clouds surrounding the great white balloon. Through the gazebo's crystal-clear roof, the stars overhead shone bright where the weirdly blue and white-banded full moon didn't wash them out with its light. The night air wasn't as cold as it should have been for as high as we seemed to be, making me wonder about air-impermeable force fields. Suspended in a shallow oil-filled chalice, a single flame added warm gold to the silver-blue moonlight to illuminate the open chamber.

    I wasn't dreaming, but I wasn't awake either. All the horror movies had it wrong—in dreams you either don't question anything, no matter how weird, or you know that you are dreaming.

I wasn't panicking: no racing heart, no rushing adrenaline to make me hyper-aware and gear me up for fight-or-flight action. But I wasn't where I should have been, with no idea how I got there.

At least I was wearing the indestructables I'd gone to sleep in, a good thing since I wasn't alone.

"Do you like it?" The lady sitting on the throne—if you made thrones out of floating stone blocks covered in mother of pearl—spoke reverently, as if we sat in church.

"Yes." I sighed happily. "It's my favorite place."

"True." Somehow she knew I meant the clouds and stars. "Although you aren't often up here in company, and you certainly haven't visited as a guest in a cloudhome."

"Cloudhome?"

"Well, a virtual recreation, anyway. It was *my* favorite place."

The lady beside me wore a high-necked white bodysuit tight as a second skin. It did nothing to hide her lean form and elegant limbs although it covered her from her toes to her fingertips. Over it she wore a loose white caftan dress so gauzy it almost wasn't there. The exposed skin of her hands and face was a rich, light and unblemished chocolate and her perfect skin and high cheek-bones would make a New York supermodel cry, but her perfection wasn't at all cold; warm brown eyes, framed by a high forehead and thick black hair pulled back tight to fan into a proud mane, reflected merriment.

A perfect eyebrow arched.

"Are you trying to guess where I'm from?"

"I suppose I am."

"Will you be alarmed when I tell you I'm from the year 2152, Common Era?"

"Are you really?"

"My quantum soul certainly is. I was born much earlier, and the Moon wasn't blue then. Do I look like a centenarian?"

"Um, no?" She sat easily, straight and regal as a queen, with fewer lines in her warm skin than a teenager.

"The wonders of future medicine. I am—or I was—the Western Warden of the Confraternal Unity, a political block of the Twenty-

Second Century. To be more precise, I had a turn at it. You may call me…Jenia. Yes, the first name I chose for myself. This was my home, rather modest by future standards except in its location. I am gratified that you like my little shrine, but shall we go inside?"

Going inside meant standing still as the floor of the shrine sank, taking us down through the cloudhome's gasbag.

"So what did you do to the Moon?" I asked as we sank.

"We added air and water, increased its size and mass, widened its orbit, and sped up its rotation."

"How did you do *that*?"

"Carefully."

Right… It finally occurred to me to try and get Shell's attention, but a sub-vocalized call got nothing. Since the quantum-signaling our neural link relied on wasn't being blocked by Guantánamo's security anymore, that probably meant I wasn't signaling at all and strengthened the asleep-but-not-dreaming hypothesis. And yet still not panicking, which was amazing since it meant that yet someone else had access to my head.

Our open-sided elevator finished its descent, dropping us into a wide but low-ceilinged room with curving walls of floor-to-ceiling bay windows. The Spartan white room held no furniture or decorations, although outlines on the floor hinted that stuff should be there, and with everything I wanted to ask the question that came out of my mouth was, "What happened to interior decorating in the future?"

Her smile turned whimsical. "It went virtual. Here is what it sometimes looks like through an accepting neural link."

Between one blink and the next the room turned into a fairyland. The walls and ceiling disappeared so that we stood in a forest glade of wild grass and flowers. One large but sculpted tree, hung with dim lanterns, stood alone in the glade with us. Fireflies danced above the grass.

"Okay, that's just…wow."

"It is much easier to redecorate, and to update your wardrobe, when you have a blank canvas to work with, don't you think?" My hostess's white gown had burst into glowing rainbow colors patterned with jewels in a style I'd never seen before but looked vaguely Celtic. Her "throne" stayed white.

"Ma'am—"

"Call me Jenia. Or Mistress Jenia if you must be formal. Master and mistress returned as polite modes of address around 2070. They denote mastery of a skill or some other achievement."

"Really?" I couldn't help it. "What if you're gender-neutral?"

"Mister, of course." She clapped her hands and laughed at my expression. "This is so much fun! I could boggle you all night, but we really must become serious. I have invaded your sleep to meet you. Well, for you to meet me."

A seat, looking like the same mother-of-pearl but smaller than her throne, rose out of the grass. I tested it, and although it looked hard as stone a field wrapped around it shaped itself to my weight.

"You don't seem too impressed by me," she observed.

"I've sort of gotten used to Ozma?"

She laughed again. "Certainly her throne is more real than mine, now. So let us proceed. The night is old and there are things that you need to know. I, like your neural-linked companion Shelly, am a quantum-ghost. Unlike her I am a ghost from a potential future that now will never be—at least not in quite the same way. The Teatime Anarchist collected me along with his nest of records on his final trip, before the day that he and his darker brother died.

"As you can guess now, I am speaking to you the same way that young Shelly does, only more completely." She paused kindly to let me wrap my head around all that.

"Was it a good future?"

She smiled. "I thought so, although the years arriving to it were certainly a hard road. I *hope* we can make them easier. The first thing I must tell you..." her smile widened, "is the final secret of the Oroboros."

I blinked. "They have *another* one?"

"Yes!" She clapped her hands again. "I really *have* missed you. Now the secret is simple but depends on knowing something about the Teatime Anarchist, a limit to his power—and since he rarely told the truth and never all of it to anybody there is no reason why you should know.

"It is as simple as this; for him time spent in the probable futures or the realized past was the same as time spent in the present. So if he traveled forward and spent a week in New Washington, for example, a week passed in the here and now, in the all-important present moment. Do you understand?"

I nodded, shook my head. "I think so, but why is that a limit?"

"Simply that if he spent weeks in the future studying and acquiring its secrets then his 'evil twin', as you liked to call him, was free to mess about back here without obstruction. Every present action that eventuated while he was in the future was one that he could not come back and undo. He was traveling in the future when the other one triggered the California Quake."

Her smile had gone. "Thus, the Oroboros. I'm sure they represented themselves to you as being initially a research group. And they were, but they didn't do research just for the government. They cataloged events, studied their significance, prepared tools, in order to have a resource waiting in the future, *whatever* future came, so that the Teatime Anarchist could call for it and go home. The Oroboros wrote the Future Files, and I am the last Oroboros of my own probable future timeline."

Her smile came back. "And already as I am now, a quantum soul tending my library, when he brought me back with his last collection. I think he knew it would be his last trip and that meant the Oroboros' mission was going to change."

"*You* brought the other Future Files! The ones that Shelly didn't recognize."

"Yes, and I am its keeper, in the same way that Shelly—Shell now?—keeps yours. I am not what Shell is, the quantum-computer I am installed in is much more limited than hers. But I find myself more a librarian by nature these days and she has wider responsibilities, so I am content to help the Oroboros the way that Shell helps you, if not as fully and actively."

"If I'm not your responsibility, why show me all this now?"

"Because we have finally met! A little earlier than in my original probable history, but this is still something of a milestone. And you are stepping onto a wider stage now, your life is going to become much more interesting than it already is."

Her ageless face grew serious. "You have checked the Ascendant for now, and you are going to find that he and his Ascendancy may be your greatest enemy. And others have noticed you as well, for good and ill. Things will get difficult, and I wanted to show you…" She waved a hand at the glade and it disappeared, reverting to the white room and the passing clouds.

"I wanted to show you that all will be well." The ceiling went invisible to show me the stars again and, sailing beneath them, the strange and impossible blue moon.

"Not certainly, of course, but possibly, and more *probably* now because of what all of you did in Littleton. Aunt Hope."

Epilogue

"Do you really think she's—she grows up to be—the *Western Warden of the Confraternal Unity*?"

I lay stretched out on my stomach, watching Atifa show Grendel and Kindrake where to add another wing to her sandcastle. Kindrake had tried to pass off Her Little Highness' requested construction project, but big tough Grendel had a weakness for small cute things and Atifa had the universal child-sense that told her when she'd found someone who would bow to her wishes.

Shelly—Shell—whoever—raised her sunglasses to better see the builders. "She already knows how to order everyone around." With Galatea in pieces and the government still twitchy about her virtual presence in anything linkable to their systems, she and Shelly had reentered gestalt mode to share the day at Littleton Lake. I was going to start referring to her as The Shellys when she did this.

Mistress Jenia had gently booted me out of her virtual world after calling me 'Aunt Hope', leaving me to have a panicked midnight conversation with Shell—who had only just learned about her before I did. Jenia had needed *access permission* from Shell to link to me, and Shell had given her a one-time pass only on the condition that she could listen in.

The Shellys' thoughts skipped a track. "Do you think that we should offer Deitz and Lauer our help with security for the conference tomorrow?"

"Not our circus, not our monkeys," Jacky yawned from my other side.

"What?"

"Polish proverb. Today it means that when the government calls a top-secret international conference and decides it's okay to hold it in a building where they're still fixing the front door, it can handle its own security."

From our umbrella-shaded beach blankets, we watched the volleyball game going on between Jamal, Mal, Reese and, of all people, Ozma. Last night she'd flown down with Nox and Nix, the mundane way in the Sentinels' reserved jet. Blackstone came too, to keep things official and nice for the certification review board. The US Marshals let them in because she promised to make Littleton tornado-proof, and she was doing a good job keeping the game honest—she'd informed Jamal if he sped and Reese if he blew a *puff* of wind they'd be her new beach hat.

I looked at my friends, and thought about the Bees. I'd gotten a text from Julie, just LIOB –*Love In Our Bond*, the Phi Mu statement of sisterhood. She'd ended it with "Later!" and a smiley face that matched mine, so things would be okay again. But we hadn't been Hope and the Bees for a long time now, really. Not since the fall of our freshman year. And I realized that I was okay with that; circles could grow as well as shrink, and different wasn't wrong.

Kindrake said something that made Atifa laugh loud enough for me to hear over the music and the game, and my smile got wider. Kindrake could wait, too, and the questions that came with her. The lake was just too inviting, Jacky really needed to let more sun touch her Snow White skin, and even the troubles back in Chicago could wait another day. I stretched, feeling fewer aches, and bounced to my feet.

"C'mon girls, it's time to get wet!"

Waiting for Wearing the Cape, Book 5?

Sign up for the Wearing the Cape Newsletter at wearingthecape.com for a quarterly newsletter, updates, and the 2015 pre-release read of the first five chapters of Mr. Harmon's next Astra adventure, *Ronin Games*!

Also, watch for the *Wearing the Cape: the Roleplaying Game* Kickstarter campaign in 2015.

Glossary
(Wearing the Cape through Young Sentinels)

Acacia: aka, Stephanie Dupree. A vampire-wannabe lucky enough to experience a "turning" breakthrough instead of dying, Acacia was victimized by a deranged "Master Vampire" and rescued by Jacky. A mentally fragile young woman, she is under Jacky's protection and watched over by the Master of Ceremonies and his minions when Jacky is not in town.

Aftershock: The first "supervillain," dubbed Aftershock by the media, is a Chicago gang member who gained the power to project brick and steel-shattering sound waves. He and his gang decided to rob a bank, leading to the first superhero vs. supervillain fight between him and Atlas and beginning the media-practice of giving all public breakthroughs codenames if they don't choose one for themselves first.

Ajax: aka Professor Charles Gibbons. One of the founding Sentinels and the naming breakthrough of the Ajax Class, Ajax wore Greek-style armor and carried a huge short-handled battle maul. He was also tenured professor at the University of Chicago (he wrote *The New Heroic Age*, the seminal work on superheroes and the Post-Event Era), and was one of Astra's trainers. He was killed in the Whittier Base Attack by Seif-al-Din, and Astra carries his maul in his honor.

Alex Chandler: Atlas' older brother, Alex Chandler is probably the greatest unsung hero of the New Heroic Age; a partner in a Chicago marketing firm, after the Event he was the one who convinced John to become Atlas, complete with cape and mask. He steered the public-relations campaign that put the public on the side of the Sentinels, and helped the shaken public to see superhumans as potential superheroes rather than dangerous freaks. He still manages the Sentinels' public-relations and marketing alongside The Harlequin, but since Atlas' death he has done it from his Michigan Avenue office rather than from the Dome.

Andrew's Designs: Somebody has to help capes look good and not so much like happy cosplayers. That's Andrew, the premier costume designer for capes who can afford his exclusive services. He designed most of the Sentinels' and Young Sentinels' costumes. Andrew is something of a mystery; he is well-built, very fit, and carries himself like an ex-soldier—not exactly a normal thing in the fashion industry. Meeting him, Astra and others have wondered if he might be a cape himself (*some* keep secret identities, after all).

Anne Marie Corrigan: Anne Marie is the daughter of an old blue-blood Chicago family. She scandalized high-society by marrying John Corrigan, who was a decade older, from a much lower class of family, and not yet successful. When Faith, her oldest daughter, died of a childhood disease, Anne Marie founded the Faith Corrigan Foundation. She throws charitable art and social events where she collects millions of dollars in donations from Chicago's elite towards medical research and children's aid at home and abroad.

Artemis: aka Jacky Bouchard. Jacky was the victim of a deranged breakthrough who was obsessed with her and believed himself to be a true vampire of the Dracula variety. He killed her parents, kidnapped and imprisoned her, and used his vampiric powers to drain her will before he drained all of her blood and turned her. She staked and decapitated him, burned him to ashes, and scattered him on Lake Michigan. Jacky never had any vampire obsessions before, so she did not "inherit" that part of her supernatural breakthrough; she is not repelled by crosses or garlic, does not need permission to enter a home, and now she is the world's only known vampire "daywalker."

The Ascendant: Just three years after the Event, Doctor Simon Pellegrini wrote *The Sleeper Must Awaken*, the manifesto of The Foundation of Awakened Theosophy. An organization dedicated to using meditative imaging and "enlightenment" techniques to trigger breakthroughs in its followers, it was dismissed as one of the more harmless "origin sellers". Unknown to the public, Dr. Pellegrini was also the Ascendant, a supervillain terrorist who claimed credit for several mass-disasters which killed hundreds or thousands while triggering handfuls of breakthroughs. It is believed that the Ascendant was behind the Green Man attacks on Chicago.

The Ascendancy: Discovered to be behind the Wreckers, the Ascendant has disappeared while at the same time declaring the *Ascendancy*. So far the only known members of the Ascendancy are the Ascendant and the Wreckers, plus escapees from the Detroit Supermax breakout (many of them teens) who may have stayed with him. The DSA is closely monitoring all former members of the Foundation of Awakened Theosophy as well. The Ascendancy believes that 1.) breakthroughs are the next step towards racial apotheosis, and 2.) that as transcendent humans, breakthroughs are spiritually awakened and superior and should "guide" unawakened humanity.

Astra: aka Hope Corrigan. The titular heroine of the stories, Astra achieved an A Class Atlas-Type breakthrough when the Dark Anarchist dropped the Ashland Overpass on her in a messy assassination aimed at someone else. In short order she became Atlas' sidekick and then the youngest member of the Sentinels. Family: her parents are John and Anne Marie Corrigan, her brothers are Aaron, Josh, and Toby, and she has an older sister (Faith) who died when Hope was only three.

Atlas: aka John Chandler. Atlas was the first Post-Event superhuman to be caught on film (impressively catching a falling plane), and the first to put on a costume and give himself a superhero codename. Only eighteen at the time and "Just a boy from Texas, ma'am," Atlas dedicated his life to protecting others and advancing the image and position of superheroes. The naming breakthrough of the Atlas-Type, he died at the hands of Seif-al-Din while protecting the President during the Whittier Base Attack. In many ways he is the archetype by which superheroes are measured.

***Barlow's Guide to Superhumans*:** Barlow's Guide is a famous publication, updated annually, listing all known superheroes, their powers, and brief biographies. It's pretty thick, and it established the Power Scale (A Class through D Class) denoting highest to lowest power levels and the Power-Type lists.

The Bees: Julie Brennan, Annabeth Bauman, and Megan Brock. The Bees were that circle of It Girls you hated or idolized in high school: glamorous, from "good" families, and supremely confident. When Shelly died during high school freshman, year Julie led them in "adopting" a broken and lost Hope. Julie is the bossy leader, Megan the group's snarker, Annabeth the nice one who just likes everyone to be happy, but since graduation they have all shown other sides of their character (especially Annabeth). They remain very important to Hope, although she struggles to maintain the connection under the pressures of her superhero career.

Doctor Beth: Doctor Jonathan Beth is the Sentinels' resident physician, and a researcher of "superhumanology." He studies breakthroughs and the manifestations of their powers, and has written many monographs and given lectures around the world. He carries lollypops for good patients and reminds Astra of her family doctor.

Blacklocks: Capitalism means that a service is created for every need. Blacklock Security is a developer and supplier of superhuman restraints, everything from titanium shackles and cells to "sandman" tranquilizer packs, hoods, and more exotic means of restraint. Today most heavy-duty shackles are referred to as *Blacklocks*.

Blackout: The lead drummer for Freakzone (see Freakshow), Blackout is a "supervillain" breakthrough capable of generating and controlling clouds of dark particles. He can concentrate these particles to create insubstantial shapes of pure darkness, or spread them wide to create vast clouds of obscuring mist.

Blackstone: One of the Sentinels' founders and a mentor to Atlas and later to Astra, Blackstone was a retired US Marine turned stage magician. His power is essentially "stage magic"—he can appear and vanish both himself and objects he pulls from his hat or waves away (teleportation), fly (levitation), and spin completely convincing visual illusions. He has always been the team's intelligence analyst, and after the deaths of Atlas and Ajax, the last founding members, he became the team's de-facto leader.

The Block: California's superhuman prison, the Block is famous for being escape-proof (so far). Bryce Walters, the Plasma Projector whose hatred for breakthroughs triggered his own (he took a shot at Astra during the recovery mission in LA), is known to be incarcerated there.

Breakthrough Powers: Breakthrough powers come in all shapes and sizes, although most tend to conform to "types" made popular by media exposure or societal beliefs, and they range from trivial or close to human ability (D Class) to amazing (A Class). Power naming conventions vary; the most common powers are named after the first breakthrough witnessed exhibiting them (Atlas-Type, Ajax-Type, Volt-Type, Verne-Type, Merlin-Type, etc.), or a classic type (Speedster, Kinetic). *(Author's note: one of the best sources for power-types is the TV Tropes wiki, under Stock Superpowers. But beware, TV Tropes is best read with someone who can force you to stop.)*

Brick: Brick, a mid-A Class Ajax Type, began his career as a Sanguinary Boy in Chicago. When the Sentinels took down the team and he was convicted of Manslaughter, the US Military offered him parole in return for military service. He went AWOL in China, reappeared in Cuba where he fought Astra a second time, and is probably now back in military service (with heavy security measures).

The Brotherhood: In the aftermath of the Event, many street gangs found themselves becoming minions to street-level supervillains. Chicago developed two such supervillain/minion gangs: the Brotherhood and the Sanguinary Boys. The two fought constantly for turf rights to various criminal activities (mainly protection rackets, prostitution, and street-distribution for the Chicago Mob).

Burnout: aka Roger Carr. Burnout was one of the super-celebrity creations of the entertainment industry. A talented singer who manifested pyrokinetic powers (immune to heat, able to generate and control flame), he became a huge recording pop-star—which lead him into drugs, groupies, and eventually convictions for multiple counts of statutory rape and drug possession.

Byzantium: The Caliphate War ended with the establishment of the first incorporated organized US Territory in more than a century, when the US claimed and occupied the ten percent of Turkish territory west of the Bosporus, the strait separating Asia Minor from Europe. The US Congress restored the old name of Constantinople to the half of Istanbul west of the Bosporus and made the city the capital of the new US Territory of Byzantium. The territory has become a magnet for the hundreds of thousands of Christian refugees being driven out of the Muslim states of the Middle East and North Africa during and since the Caliphate Period. Coptics, Eastern Orthodox, Nestorians, and others are all immigrating to Constantinople and its territory even as many Muslim Turks are leaving— making it likely that by the time Byzantium holds the promised referendum to determine its final status as America's 51st state or as an independent nation, Muslims will be a minority in the territory.

The Caliphate (Alliance): In post-Event Turkey, Armagan Acar, an army officer and ardent nationalist, found himself possessed with the secret gift of superhuman persuasion; he could turn the loyalties of whole regiments and crowds with his words. Within a few years he had risen to be Turkey's Prime Minister and drawn the principle states of the Arab League into an alliance to counter the new League of Democratic States. Founded on Islamic Nationalism and anti-Semitism, the new league named itself The Caliphate. When the Palestinians of the West Bank and Gaza tried to join the Caliphate, Israel refused to allow it. Tensions and accusations escalated until the PLO launched a Caliphate-backed takeover of the West Bank. Massacres of overwhelmed Jewish communities ensued, and the Caliphate militaries invaded Israel. The League of Democratic States backed Israel. The ensuing war was short and resulted in: 1.) The dismemberment of the Caliphate, 2.) The ejection of all Palestinians from the West Bank and Gaza and their absorption by the ex-Caliphate powers,

3.) The establishment of Eretz Israel (all of Israel and Palestine) and Kurdistan, 4.) The creation of the US Territory of Byzantium (from all of Turkey's territory west of the Bosporus), and 5.) The creation of The Caliphate as a terrorist organization.

The Caliphate (The Undying Caliphate): Armagan Acar died in the nuclear destruction of Ankara (reprisal for the nuking of Tel Aviv), but part of his superhuman inner circle survived and united with superhuman Caliphate jihadists to found the Undying Caliphate, an Islamic-nationalist terrorist organization sworn to driving the hated Crusader Occupiers from Byzantium and Eretz-Israel and reversing the outcome of the Caliphate War. Seif-al-Din is their most infamous member, but they number in the dozens with cells throughout the Middle East and elsewhere.

Capes: There are a few reality television series devoted to superhumans, and *Capes* is one of the better ones. It is entirely action footage shot by camera crews following different CAI capes around on patrols and missions, and interviews with the subjects.

Chakra: The Sentinels' most controversial member, Chakra is an A Class Mentalist who gained her tantra-based breakthrough powers during an episode of epiphany-triggering episode of ritual sex. She describes her powers as Tantric Magic, but while they are charged by tantric rituals they largely conform to classical psionic powers (forms of telepathy, ESP, precognition, psychic healing, and levitation). Although now a full-time Sentinel, she holds a degree in psychology—she studied sexual behavioralism—and was a licensed sex therapist. After becoming a Sentinel she capitalized on her fame to write *The Sacred Gates*, a book on sacred sex.

Charmer: Donald Gerrold was a C Class Mentalist with the ability to *charm*. Anybody hearing his voice and seeing him would like him instantly and trust him explicitly. It would wear off later, which meant that getting his victims to do anything too out of character would be completely obvious, but he did find a use for his power: selling expensive cars to rich people who were already looking to buy.

The Chinese States: Also known as the Secession States, these are the territories which revolted against Beijing in the aftermath of the brutal suppression of minority and politically distrusted breakthroughs following The Event. They are currently struggling to suppress their own would-be warlords and being assisted by Indian and League troops. It is expected that most will confederate with a reformed Beijing to reunite China, but at least four will almost certainly go their own way: Tibet, Xianjang, Manchuria, and Hong Kong.

Citizens for Human Rights: CHR is a political activist group which loudly advocates restrictions on superhumans and superheroes. They have picketed to protest the special legal treatment of superheroes—such as being able to testify while wearing a mask—and to support superhuman registration and the right to know when they are living next to superhumans.

Crash: Jamal Carter's mother died in a pedestrian accident, putting Jamal into Chicago's family services system. Less than a year later, running from a street-gang intent on "tuning him up" triggered his breakthrough. Suddenly an A Class Speedster, he gave his persecutors a brutal beat down before being stopped by Rush. Jamal is now under the guardianship of Sifu (Master Li), who is teaching him how to control himself and his powers, and is a member of the Young Sentinels.

The Crew: Superhero vs. Supervillain fights can cause a lot of damage that has to be cleaned up quickly, and the Crew is a superhuman contracting company which specializes in fast cleanup. It hires Ajax-types, strong telekinetics, and other superhumans with powers that do the job. Crew members often take on codenames like Border, Irons, Brace, and Gantry, and when they aren't cleaning up after superhuman fights they are traveling to disaster areas where reconstruction speed is vitally important.

Crisis Aid and Intervention Teams: The Sentinels' original contract with the City of Chicago set the template for Crisis Aid and Intervention teams, which make contracts with municipalities much like private security companies and emergency-services providers. CAI franchises such as the

Guardians and the Knights are extremely popular with state and local governments because they guarantee uniform standards. They are popular with superheroes because they act collectively to provide legal and insurances services as well as collective bargaining support. CAI teams are certified through their agencies, but still need licenses issued by state governments and are always subject to jurisdiction requirements.

Cryo: Cryo is a Brotherhood supervillain, an A Class Cryokinetic. He tried to "freeze" Astra during the Pullman Tower Fight, and she broke his arm with a thrown rock.

Senator Todd Davis: Senator Davis was a "strong national security" advocate for the regulation and control of superhumans, and the author of the Davis Bill. He died in the Ashland Overpass Bombing, the Dark Anarchist's intended victim.

The Dark Anarchist: (See first The Teatime Anarchist) The Dark Anarchist is the Teatime Anarchist's "evil twin," split off in the breakthrough event which gave them both the power to travel to the past and future. Neither could change the past, but they could visit "probably future" and then come back to the present to change them. Both decided to create a better, or at least safer, future, but they diverged significantly as to means. This led to a time-war which lasted several years, in which he stole his twin's code-name and framed him for a host of crimes and assassinations. Astra named the Dark Anarchist, and outside of a select group who had direct contact with him or very high security clearance and need-to-know, nobody knows about him at all.

Sheriff Paul Deitz: When Astra met Deitz, he was the sheriff of the sleepy community of Grand Beach; as it turns out, he is a US Marshal assigned to watch over Witness Protection subjects and other individuals the government needs to babysit. His current assignment is as the sheriff of Littleton, and he has proven to be very good at it. His partner is Deputy Angel Sweet.

The Department of Superhuman Affairs: The DSA is a department, like the Department of the Interior, rather than an agency, like the FBI. This is important; it means that the Secretary of Superhuman Affairs is a member of the President's cabinet and reports to her directly. Without its own law-enforcement arm, the DSA relies on the US Marshals Service, which has its own chain of command. The DSA also directs a branch of the Secret Service, fielding breakthrough agents whose main responsibility is the protection of the President and the federal government from superhuman threats. Both US Super-Marshals and Secret Service agents are sent, with lawyers and investigators, when it looks like "supervillains" might be compromising local government and law enforcement. Lastly, the DSA works closely with the FBI on counter-terrorism and counter-intelligence operations, and aids the Justice Department in its mission to prosecute civil rights violations and public corruption when breakthroughs are involved. All of this creates something of a mess of competing missions, but it also means that the officials and agents of the DSA work very closely with the other federal departments and the Secretary of Superhuman Affairs (called the Director in-house and by the media) is senior to the directors of the various agencies. There are no DSA "superheroes." DSA superhumans always dress civilian or in DSA uniforms.

The Dome: The Chicago Dome is the Headquarters of the Chicago Sentinels. It is located in Grant Park, across from Michigan Avenue. It sits in open park, a solid and half-buried bunker with wide sight lines and lots of space for evacuating civilians from the area; one story has it that the city planners initially intended to put the Sentinels' headquarters in one of the new Post-Event high-rise business building projects, until Blackstone—a former US Marine—"had words with them."

Dane Dorweiler: aka The Dane. Annabeth picked Dane to be her boyfriend in sophomore year of high school, and the big good-natured goof went along with it. They have been Danabeth ever since, and are now engaged. The only thing Dane cares as much about as Annabeth is soccer, and he has already gone pro; he flies back to Chicago for a full weekend at least every couple of weeks and he and Annabeth are joined at the digital hip. Hope likes him quite a bit and once had a crush on him she will never admit to.

Dozer: aka Gantry, aka Eric Ludlow. Dozer is a member of the Wreckers, the supervillain crew working for The Ascendant. Formerly Gantry, a B Class Ajax-Type war veteran and member of the Crew, Eric was Astra's first superhuman "fight" (she had to restrain him during a drunken tantrum). Now one of the Ascendancy, Eric has exhibited A Class level powers.

The El Paso Guard: The Guard is El Paso's resident CAI team. Unlike most CAI teams, they are heavily involved in traditional police work. They also wear a common uniform, hide their faces under concealing helmets, and have ironclad secret identities. This is because, with the chaos in northern Mexico and the power of the Mexican cartels just across the river, El Paso sits on the most dangerous border in the western hemisphere. They do their job so well that national crime statistics list El Paso as one of the safest cities in the country. They're still scary.

Lieutenant Emerson: Ralph W. Emerson is the senior detective in charge of supernatural matters in *his* quarter of New Orleans, and Detective Negri's superior. He is a cadaverously thin Creole who only needs a top hat to play Baron Samedi.

Euphoria: A C Class Neurokinetic, Euphoria is able to light up the pleasure center in a target's brain to create a euphoric, incapacitating high with none of the nasty aftereffects of drugs. Her ability works instantly if she can touch her target; at a distance it takes a bit longer. She can make someone an addict through repeated exposer to her power, and while a Chicago Guardian she hired herself out as an escort. Secretly working for the Dark Anarchist, she may have been the one who got Rush to unknowingly work for him.

Extreme Solutions: A superhuman mercenary and security agency, Extreme Solutions is careful to keep its operations lawful. It will match superhumans to client needs for a hefty fee, and has many powerful breakthroughs on retainer.

The Deal: An informal agreement between supervillains and superheroes, The Deal says that villains try to avoid killing capes, don't out them if they maintain secret identities, and above all don't go after their families. In return, when capes serving warrants come after villains they try to avoid using lethal force.

Detective Max Fisher: Detective Fisher is the senior detective on the CPD's Superhuman Crimes Detective Division, assigned to all cases involving superhuman powers, and he may not be real. He (and Astra) is aware that he is a character from a short-lived and forgotten series of detective novels written over a decade ago. He doesn't age and can't be killed (although he can be beat up), and has memories that don't match reality. He *hopes* he's the series' author and a delusional breakthrough; he *might* be a persistent thought-form created from the author's obsession before he died.

Doctor Cornelius: Rafael Jones was a college student majoring in metaphysics and seeking drug-assisted enlightenment when the Event changed the world. His hallucinatory and epiphanic breakthrough transformed him into one of the most powerful Merlin-Types known. He is a master of Hermetic Magic (also called Deccanic Magic), and a tormented man who would very much like to give up his "enlightenment." He is a close associate of Orb's.

The Fortress: Described as the superhero's Hard Rock Café, the Fortress is a cape-memorabilia museum, a café, a club, and a Chicago landmark. Astra has seen many CAI capes hanging there, including Caterwall, Bombshell, Jack Frost, Hardlock, Red Robin, Blue Fire, Foxlight, The Cardinal, Wisteria, Flashback, and SaFire. Cosplaying groupies usually far outnumber the actual capes, who often don club-wear versions of their sturdier field costumes to party.

Freakshow: *No we're not your daddy's villins/ we're not chillin' then we're killin'/ we want you, best be willin'.* From *Murder Night*. The entertainment industry made breakthroughs with even a little talent the new pop-stars, while "supervillains" took over the genre of music formerly known as gansta-rap. The result is groups like Freakzone, a hugely popular villain-rap band. Freakshow, their lead guitarist, is able to shapeshift into various animal-human hybrid forms, even mixing them for truly chimeric combinations, and he uses his power in his act.

Galatea: A chrome gynoid (female android) robot creation of Vulcan's, Galatea is variously a low-sentience AI and a drone shell for Shelly to "pilot." Her configuration is subject to change and she has various modular add-ons like micro-missile racks and boot and pack jets, and she has been destroyed several times. The public believes her to be a human-shaped drone, which is more or less true, and fans endlessly debate who her pilot is.

The Godzilla Plague: Somehow, somewhere, some insane Verne-type thought it would be a great idea to create a race of Godzillas that were designed to attack pollution sources (mainly nuclear plants and, well, *cities*). The creatures go through two stages: a stealth-stage where they lurk in the depths, eat lots of fish, and lay eggs, and the monster-stage, where they grow much bigger and seek out contamination. Their primary weapon is a plasma jet that can melt steel and their secondary weapon is the ability to generate local electromagnetic pulses that interfere with electrical systems. Godzilla periodically appear and attack coastal cities and it has proven impossible to find all of their eggs. Predictably, Japan seems to get an unfair share of Godzilla attention.

Father Graff: Wherever there are supernatural breakthroughs in abundance, the Church takes an interest. Father Graff is the representative of the Congregation for the Doctrine of the Faith—the Holy Inquisition—in New Orleans. He considers Jacky one of the *beati mortus* (blessed dead), is warily respectful of Jacky's grandmother, and is as responsible for protecting misunderstood supernaturals from overzealous faithul as he is for maintaining purity of doctrinal practices in the face of the syncretic mysticism that runs through the town.

Mr. Gray: The Department of Superhuman Affairs has a strong interest in New Orleans' supernatural community (especially the vampires). Mr. Gray is the local DSA station agent and, loosely, Jacky's local DSA "minder" when she's in town. He is also a supernatural himself, one of the fey, and that makes him a mystery; most fey hang with the Seelie Court in San Francisco.

Graymalkin: Hope's cat.

The Green Man: Almost nothing is known about the Green Man. "He" appears to have been able to transform himself into a disembodied "spirit" capable of possessing plants and generating amazing waves of growth. He threatened Chicago with successive eruptions of green, but proved vulnerable to extreme heat at the center of his manifestations. There is speculation that he may have been boosted by the Ascendant.

Grendel: Brian Lucas is a transformed A Class Darwin-Type (he "adapts" to his environment and opposition). Grendel lost his family when the Ascendant exposed several thousand victims to a psychotropic gas which triggered hallucinations, rampages, and several psychotic breaks and breakthroughs, and was permanently transformed into a gray and monstrous humanoid form which is the baseline for all his changes. He is potentially stronger than the strongest Ajax-Type. Grendel has joined the Young Sentenels, and has also sworn himself to Ozma's service (he is currently the Royal Army of Oz) in return for her promise to help him gain justice for his murdered family.

The Guardians: The Guardians are one of the largest CAI franchises in the US, with teams in most states. The other seven Crisis Aid and Intervention teams in Chicago are all Guardian teams, named for their districts (South Side Guardians, West Side Guardians, etc.). They, and the Sentinels, are all coordinated through the city's Dispatch Department in The Dome, under the direction of the Sentinels and city coordinators.

The Hammer: When the Russian Mob in Boston killed Silversmith and his family with a car bomb, an unknown vigilante dubbed The Hammer brutally wiped out the organization's senior members; one of the reasons organized crime outfits generally leave capes alone. If they do go after capes, they do it when the cape is in costume and on duty, and they *leave his family alone*. See also: The Deal.

The Harlequin: The Harlequin, called Quin by her friends, was an acrobat and aerialist with Cirque du Soliel in Las Vegas. During a performance her rig snapped and she fell thirty feet to the stage—and *bounced*, her body permanently transformed to a rubber-like substance. Her skin is the texture of latex, her bones the density of hard rubber, and she is almost immune to direct kinetic damage; she will bend and bounce back under an impact, whether from a fall or bullets or a hit from Astra, which would injure or kill a normal person. Her transformation also makes her a lot stronger than the average person of her trim athletic build, and she can run faster by "bouncing" along. She is a trained martial artist and marksman (although she doesn't normally use guns), and is the Sentinel's field medic as well as its publicity and marketing coordinator, which she does with Alex Chandler.

Have No Fear: *No backing down, no giving in./ I pick my fights, but I fight to win./ Though the Reaper draws near me I cry,/Conquer or die!* Have No Fear is an all-breakthrough band of Hillwood Academy alumni. They are also CAI-certified capes, able to drop in with disaster relief and stage a concert afterward. They're *the* most successful music group in history, and rumors of artistic differences are completely exaggerated.

Hecate: Dr. Charlotte Millebrand, antiquarian, folklorist, Merlin-Type wicked witch, and Chicago Outfit assassin, tried to unite the second team of Villains Inc. to take down her bosses and seize control of the Outfit. The mob-war left civilian bodies everywhere, and Artemis put three bullets through her heart during their final fight.

Hero Beat/Power Week: These are both superhero magazines. *Hero Beat* is a breathless fan-mag oriented towards teens, while *Power Week* is a more serious publication, a sort of cross between Time and People Magazine with a focus on superhumans.

Hillwood Academy: There is a lot of trauma in childhood, and teen breakthroughs create their own unique set of problems. Hillwood Academy is a boarding school for teen breakthroughs, many of whom came from bad circumstances or were isolated by their breakthroughs. It has become famous for its more illustrious alumni, and a television action-drama has been (loosely) based on it. Hillwood Academy handles students grades 7-12: younger students go to Whitlow's Academy.

The Hollywood Knights: There is a term, *Hollywood heroes*, applied to superhumans who go to LA to act on television and in the movies. The Hollywood Knights began as a movie cast, but morphed into a team which makes a movie about their "adventures" each year, the rest of the time acting as a disaster-relief CAI team and doing charity events. Its current roster is: Rook (an A Class Atlas-Type and the team leader), Balder (a photokinetic), Starkness (scary), Ceres (a florakinetic), Fire Lily (a pyrokinetic capable of *killing* fires), Maui (a tattooed Maori shapeshifter). Seven was a member when Astra met him, but he has transferred to the Sentinels.

Humanity First: Members of Humanity First believe that breakthroughs are a threat to humanity which must be checked by whatever means necessary. More fanatical members believe—against all evidence—that breakthroughs aren't even human. Their beliefs and activities have been compared to Aryan Nation and other racial supremacist groups.

Iron Jack: aka John Corrigan. Iron Jack is a transforming A Class Ajax-Type. He is a highly successful Chicago architect, and he experienced his breakthrough on the day of the Event. He became a reserve Sentinel, and has been able to maintain a secret identity because of his ability to unrecognizably transformation himself (in Iron Jack form he looks like a statue of iron plates and rivets). He kept the secret even from his children, which gave Astra a *second* shock on the day of her own breakthrough.

Director Kayle: The President of the United States was aboard Air Force One returning from a campaign trip to LA on the day of The Event. Air Force One made a crater and Vice President Kayle was sworn in as President Kayle the same day. President Kayle is the main reason that federal superhuman-restriction laws were not passed in the first weeks after The Event. He created the Department of Superhuman Affairs, built the alliance system that became the new League of Democratic States, and successfully guided the United States through the internal and external chaos that was much of his eight years in office. He hand-picked his successor, Touches Clouds, shepherded her through her successful presidential bid, and in return she made him Director of the DSA. As the Director, he prefers to work quietly and behind the scenes, but make no mistake—he is one of the great power-players in Washington. Many conspiracy theorists believe him to be a secret superhuman; the only way to explain his amazing success.

Kitsune: Kitsune is believed to be Yoshi Miyamoto, an old man who disappeared from an elderly care center in Osaka Prefecture. A true shapeshifter, who apparently also has the magic ability to invade dreams and who may actually *believe* himself to be a spirit-fox, he engineered the war between Villains Inc. and the Outfit to avenge the deaths of his daughter and granddaughter. A thief—or at least someone not adverse to stealing things in pursuit of his goals—Kitsune is wanted in several countries. His current goals and plans are unknown, but he has taken a liking to Astra for no apparent reason. Perhaps she reminds him of his granddaughter.

Legal Eagle: aka Tommy Brannigan, esquire. Just out of law school, Tommy learned how to fly when his weekend skydiving vacation went horribly wrong. Since flight is his sole power, Tommy went into law instead of trying to become a cape. The media dubbed him Legal Eagle, which he doesn't mind at all; he quickly carved out a niche serving

Chicago's capes and superhumans, and is on retainer for the Chicago Sentinels and the city's Guardian teams.

Lei Zi: Her name means Mother of Storms and comes from Chinese mythology. Lei Zi is an A Class Electrokinetic Type, able to fly by electrostatic levitation, suck the power from electrical systems or burn them out with power surges, and draw from the atmosphere's static charge to generate lightning and ball lightning. The daughter of Chinese Nationals who fled China during its collapse into warring states, she served a tour of duty in the US Military. Blackstone recruited her to be the new Field Leader of the Chicago Sentinels after the death of Atlas.

Lunette's: A bar and club in LA, Lunette's mostly caters to a breakthrough crowd. Unlike the Fortress, it is not a high-profile establishment and non-breakthroughs usually get turned away by the bouncer at the door; mostly it is a refuge for breakthroughs, capes or otherwise, a place where they can hang out with others who are like them or who at least understand them.

Marc Léroy: A relative newcomer to New Orleans and reluctant member of the vampire community, Marc Léroy is a bodyguard for hire, fencing master, and owner of the *Salle D'Armes*, a fencing school and his home. He hides a secret or two of his own.

Mrs. Lori: Mrs. Lori is one of Chicago's grande dames, a fearful arbiter of social approval. An intimate friend of Mrs. Corrigan's deceased mother, Hope's grandmother, she both disapproves and approves of just about everything that Anne Marie and Hope do.

Mama Marie: Marie Bouchard, "Mama Marie," is Artemis' (Jacky's) grandmother and one of New Orleans' reigning voodoo queens. She is a powerful force in the local community and Lieutenant Emerson walks carefully around her. Whether Mama Marie's voodoo is backed by real breakthrough power is open to question. Best be careful, anyway.

The Master of Ceremonies: Jacky calls him MC to his face, but it is doubtful anyone else does. Mister Hans Lichter, the self-styled Master of

Ceremonies, is the unofficial but very real Boss of New Orleans' vampires. MC prefers things *peaceful*, and is willing to go to great lengths to make them so. He also owes Jacky a great debt, despite the fact that she burned down his house, and watches over Acacia and does other favors to repay her. He likes having her around because she scares the other vampires at least as much as he does (she can come at them in the *day*).

Megaton: Malcom Scott was just your average high-school student, a bit of an overweight science geek who muscled up, lost a few pounds during sophomore year, and joined the school wrestling team to escape bullying. His breakthrough gave him the power to fly by "blasting" like a rocket and to project powerful destructive blasts in defense—and accidentally killed an innocent bystander. Now a member of the Young Sentinels, Mal seeks redemption as a cape.

Doctor Mendel: Dr. Alice Mendel is the mental-health counterpart to Dr. Beth, retained by the City of Chicago to vet all of its contracted CAI heroes for mental fitness. Understandably, she has taken advantage of the situation to study superhuman psychology close-up and has written many papers and monographs on the subject.

Metrocon: "Capecons" are the biggest events in the cape-watcher's calendar. The biggest annual capecon is Chicago's Metrocon, which combines with the National CAI Conference, the largest training and expo conference in the country; three days of serious training and lectures, three days of inter-team competition and fun. New York and LA hold sister-conventions and each year sees is a much wider second tier of smaller capecons across the country hosting regional training and events. Of course fans flock to the capecons to see the capes, buy merchandise, and cosplay, but the conventions are also job-fairs for breakthroughs seeking to introduce themselves to local teams and pass qualifications, and even professional CAI heroes seeking to move up into bigger and more visible teams.

Michael: An aging mega pop-star who saw his stardom fade in his thirties, Michael experienced a breakthrough the day of the Event which changed him into a human hologram. Now eternally young and able to manipulate his image to change his wardrobe and hairstyle, glow, and even generate visual pyrotechnics, Michael returned to songwriting and the concert-tour circuit with a revitalized career. Unlike Nimbus, although immaterial he can still talk (nobody knows how).

Detective Paul Negri: A Cajun from Church Pointe Acadia and a New Orleans police detective, Paul is also a lycanthrope; a Benandanti—a Good Walker—shaped by his mother's Italian legends rather than the local loup-garou stories. Jacky is his "civilian consultant" and window into New Orleans' vampire community.

Nimbus: Some transformations are so complete that you are no longer human. Nimbus never related the circumstance, but whatever triggered her breakthrough it transformed her into a being of pure intangible energy. To relate to others, she shaped her body of light into a form approximating the one she had before, appearing like a glowing angelic nude with the details smoothed out for purposes of modesty. She could fly at the speed of light, focus her power to project bolts of incredible energy, and was of course intangible and immune to most forms of physical damage. Nimbus' powers made her easily the Sentinels' deadliest member. She died in the Whittier Base attack, killed by an A Class Projector whose "sonic" attacks disrupted atomic structures of any kind.

Father Nolan: The pastor of St. Christopher Parish (St. Chris), Father Nolan is also Hope's spiritual advisor and the senior chaplain for Chicago's CAI teams. He is a round little priest with penchant for unorthodox homilies and a vice for Double Stuff Oreos. (*Author's note: Father Nolan is my homage to Father Blackie Ryan, the beloved priest and detective made famous by the late Andrew M. Greeley.*)

Orb: A top-shelf private investigator who makes LA her home, Orb is blind and deaf. She is also a breakthrough, her power taking the form of a silvery orb she absolutely mentally controls. The orb floats by her shoulder and she somehow uses it to see, hear, and even speak. Its actual form is malleable, and faced with the need for self-defense she has been known to shape it into a needle-pointed dart capable of driving itself through flesh with absolute precision.

Origin Chasers: Origin chasers are people who intentionally pursue breakthroughs. It is a hazardous pursuit; since most breakthroughs occur under stressful or traumatic circumstances, the consequences of not achieving a breakthrough are often damaging if not fatal. Origin chasers have most commonly used physical peril, extreme physical stress or trauma, or psychoactive drugs to attempt their breakthroughs, and every year thousands of would-be breakthroughs wind up in hospital emergency rooms and morgues.

Origin Sellers: A new industry has been born which caters to origin chasers. Origin sellers provide "monitored experiences" for attempting "safe" breakthroughs. The most ethical origins sellers are "breakthrough boot-camps" which provide their clients several weeks of intense physical stress (known to trigger physical breakthroughs) and "breakthrough retreats" (guru-guided meditative retreats known to trigger mental breakthroughs). These services don't increase the odds of any specific stressor triggering a breakthrough, but clients are likely to survive them without damage and may even gain physical or mental benefits. The least ethical (and usually black-market) origin sellers push designer drugs which, if they work, are likely to result in psychotic breaks and weird and twisted breakthroughs.

Ozma: An A Class Merlin-Type, possibly *the* most powerful supernatural breakthrough known, Ozma believes that she is literally *Ozma*, the Empress of Oz as portrayed in Frank L. Baum's famous Oz books. She looks sixteen, acts one hundred, and all of her long-term plans are aimed at reconquering Oz and liberating her people from the Gnome King and the witch Momby. Currently she is a member of the Young Sentinels while she gathers and creates magical resources for her campaign. Her companions are Nox and Nix, two dolls animated by the Powder of Life, and she has recovered many of her magical treasures including her scepter-wand and Magic Belt. One of her favored means of subduing opposition is to turn them into hats.

The Paladins: Founded by Daniel Nathaniel Allred of Vermont, the Paladins are an anti-government survivalist group with chapters across the country. Since the Event, they have focused on breakthroughs and especially on capes, who they believe plot to seize control of the government and rule as a "master race". They mostly spend weekends training and stockpiling for The Day They Come For Us, but they have more militant members who believe in taking the fight to the capes *first*.

Pieman: A teleporter of unknown class, Pieman is a "performance-villain." He picks public figures he believes are in need of pie-ing, sends them a lovingly baked pie by courier delivery, then delivers the second pie up to seven days later; in person, in public, to the face. He is wanted in twelve countries, although most law enforcement agencies are not terribly interested in catching him.

Platoon: aka Tom, New Tom, Willis, the Bobs, etc. Platoon is a Redux-Type breakthrough of unknown magnitude. A band of multiple clones with some sort of telepathic group-memory who provides security and services at the Dome, he is also apparently a highly trained DSA field agent(s), a member of President Touches Clouds' Secret Service detail, the major-domo at Restormel, and so on. Astra wonders if he/they have a Bob vacationing somewhere for the rest of them. Artemis wonders if he/they are political officers for Director Kayle.

Prayer for Heroes: *St. Michael, defender of man, stand with us in the day of battle. St. Jude, giver of hope, be with us in our desperate hour. St. Christopher, bearer of burdens, lift us when we fall.* The author of the Prayer for Heroes is unknown; first circulated on the net, it is now inscribed over many monuments and many more gravestones, the unofficial prayer of Catholic superheroes.

President Touches Clouds: The day of The Event Jennifer Touches Clouds manifested an A Class Aeriokinetic-Type breakthrough, enabling her to generate and control air currents strong enough to allow her to fly and put out fires. She became one of the Sentinels' founding members, and three years later left the team to go into politics, eventually becoming

President Kayle's successor. America's first female President, first Native American President, and first superhuman President, she is hugely popular and has continued most of President Kayle's international and domestic policies unchanged (something which makes conspiracy buffs mutter darkly in their basements).

Protectors: Protectors is a law-enforcement procedural television series, about a fictional CAI team and the local police and court system, low on character drama and high on first-responder work but also superhuman crimes and court cases. It tends to feature "ripped from the headlines" stories.

Psijack: aka, Bradley Clark. An unassuming and very successful contract negotiator, Bradley secretly contracted other serves. An A Class Mentalist, he is capable of controlling the emotions and impulses of whole crowd. His only limit appears to be that it takes him awhile to "psijack" a person's id, and he may require environmental stimuli (a crowd already worked up, for example).

Restormel: The Hollywood Knight's headquarters in Beverly Hills, Restormel is shaped vaguely like a white castle tower with crenellations along the edge of the roof—which includes a "flying entrance" and a roof garden. Yeah, it's a big clubhouse, but it's a serious base too.

The Ring: The Ring is an international alliance of terrorist organizations. While diverse in goals and aims, the membership of the Ring has been known to pool resources for joint operations; the largest operation to-date has been the Whittier Base Attack, which did not go well for them. The biggest Ring players are: the Caliphate, One Land (Chinese nationalist-communists), and Mexico Libre (the rebellion in northern Mexico fronted by the cartels).

Riptide: A former LA street-villain and a Hydrokinetic-Type who can actually transform into water, Riptide joined the Sentinels after he met them during rescue operations following the California Quake and fought beside them during the Whittier Base Attack. His mother and sister died in the quake, and he is now guardian to his young nephew, Carlos.

Rush: A college all-star wide receiver, Rush was known for his trademark phrase "What's the rush?" He was expected to go pro as a first-round NFL draft pick until he triggered his breakthrough in the final game of his senior year, racing to catch the pass for a final and winning touch-down and turning into a blur. Denied fame in professional football, he trained for a year and then "tried out" for the Sentinels. He is an A Class Speedster, able when speeding to accelerate his personal time and live ten times as fast as the clock, and to drop between seconds entirely by jumping into the frozen world of hypertime.

SaFire: A B Class Atlas-Type, SaFire is a member of the West Side Guardians. Her costumes favor purple-and-pink flames, and she is one of the Fortress's more flamboyant (and colorful) event hostesses when not on duty. SaFire is a certified EMT who specializes in getting accident-victims to hospitals fast and alive, and Astra admires her tremendously.

Sakura Wind: Sakura Wind is one of Japan's rising hero-pop bands, comprised entirely of hero idols.

The Sanguinary Boys: The Sanguinary Boys are Chicago's other supervillain gang (see the Brotherhood). Notable Sanguinaries are Brick, Vacuum, an aerokinetic who could suck the air right out of your lungs, Lighter, a standard pyrokinetic who preferred vodka as a starter, and The Surgeon, a slicer with extendable razor-sharp nails and a taste for pain. The bunch of them got taken down by Astra and Artemis in the Great Roundup.

Seif-al-Din: The Sword of The Faith and the most powerful Caliphate superhuman. A ten-foot giant with the shadows of enormous black angel wings rising from his back, skin glowing in undulating spots of bright and dim light, swinging a great burning sword, Seif-al-Din is stronger than an A Class Atlas-Type. He has died twice so far, the second time, at Whittier

Base where—after he killed both Ajax and Atlas—Astra hit him in a kinetic strike using herself as the missile and then killed him with his own sword.

The Sentinels: Atlas, Blackstone, Ajax, and the other founding members of the Chicago Sentinels met during the critical days following the catastrophe of The Event. They founded the Sentinels partly as a public-relations move, but the team became the template for Crisis Aid and Intervention Teams across the country. The Sentinels served abroad, as volunteers with Heroes Without Borders, during the worst of the China War and in the Caliphate War, and Sentinels have died in action (Impact, Minuteman, Nimbus, Ajax, and Atlas). Today the Sentinels are the most famous superhero team in the world, with a huge marketing campaign built on them which includes movies, a television action series, a comic and book series, a roleplaying game, shirts, posters, action figures, and *plushies*.

Seven: A Hollywood hero and celebrity, Seven possesses the power of Luck—in his words, "total, godlike, serendipity." His luck will keep him alive and healthy under any circumstances, and molds his life like a guardian angel with his best interests at heart and a wicked sense of humor. After rising to stardom and joining the Hollywood Knights, Seven met Astra and the Sentinels. When the deaths of three of its members left a void, he transferred to the Sentinels and moved to Chicago.

Shelly: Shelly Boyar-Hardt is Hope's BFF, and she and Hope shared a superhero obsession. When Hope was fifteen Shelly jumped to her death, an origin chaser convinced that the fall would trigger her own breakthrough. But in a way, she got her wish: the Teatime Anarchist used 22nd Century technology to record a quantum-copy of her mind to use as a seed for the Artificial Intelligence CPU of a computer system in which he stored all of the historical files he collected in his trips to the future. He then tricked Hope into accepting a neural-link from the same advanced technology, which Shelly can use to share Hope's physical senses and even shape virtual realities for her, allowing Shelly to appear to Hope as a virtual-ghost. She also remotely pilots robot drones—Galatea—as a Young Sentinel.

Supernaturals: Not all breakthroughs conform to superhero types—in fact, outside of the countries heavily influenced by western media, few of them do. More conform to older stories, folk-tales, legends and myths, and even in the US, individuals who are more into vampires or fairies, or who are deeply into magic, are likely to follow those types. Spellcasters are Merlin-types, but all other "supernatural" breakthroughs are simply typed as Supernaturals. "Divine" breakthroughs are a smaller subset of this group, although few are willing to call one of the cherubim a "supernatural," at least not to his face.

Deputy Angel Sweet: Deputy Sweet is Sheriff Deitz' partner, and they have been together long enough that they function almost telepathically. Where Deitz is the more social and public-relations minded of the pair, she focuses on her arsenal of guns (she believes in bringing the right bang to any fight).

The Teatime Anarchist: Almost nothing is known about the Teatime Anarchist. The public knew him as a superhuman terrorist of unknown powers (teleportation was suspected), who issued a manifesto accusing the US government of plotting to gain control of its superhuman citizens and through them seize a dictatorial power. He apparently issued audio and visual files on the internet claiming credit for a host of bombings which claimed the lives of dozens and issuing threats (the media dubbed him the Teatime Anarchist because of his vaguely English accent). He was killed resisting capture shortly after the California Quake. The truth is more complicated; he was really a time-traveler (see Shelly), and he died by what is arguably the most unique act of suicide ever (see the Dark Anarchist).

Tin Man: Carl Mueller, an A Class Telekinetic, began as a career burglar and became part of Villains Inc. He uses his power to animate and remotely control "puppet" drones of various configurations, from mechanical spiders used for stealthy breaking-and-entering to huge mechanical dragons.

Tsuris: Reese Lasila is an A Class Aerokinetic-Type, and in a world of often unique breakthroughs, he's unique in his own special way: he appears to have inherited his father's breakthrough air-control power (which is impossible). Being compared to Jetstream, dear old Dad, all the time created "issues" leading to Reese' attending Hillwood Academy. He has since been recruited by the Young Sentinels, and is an asset to the team although his attitude still needs adjusting (Ozma is working on it).

Sean Redmond: Superintendent of Police Sean "Big Red" Redmond replaced Superintendent Garfield as the appointed head of the Chicago Police Department after Garfield was implicated in events leading to the second war with Villains Inc. Known as The Fixer, Superintendent Redmond is cleaning up the CPD and changing its relationship with the city's CAI capes for the better.

Terry Reinhold: The writer of *Citywatch*, a weekly newspaper column devoted to the doings of Chicago society, Terry has increasingly found himself covering Chicago's superhuman celebrities. It helps that he is on good terms with The Harlequin and Astra. Terry describes himself as "A male Lois Lane who stays out of trouble."

Mal Shankman: State Representative Mallory Shankman is a political demagogue who has made his career protesting superhumans generally. Popular with a paranoid segment of the population, he can be counted on to be behind every major anti-breakthrough protest (if he doesn't start it he gets out in front of it).

Sifu: Edward (Ted) Li is an A Class Speedster. Not much is known of his past, other than he was born in Philadelphia, but he served during the China War and afterwards he remained in China for a few years before returning and opening a martial arts school to teach Bagau. He is a friend of John Corrigan's, taught Hope self-defense and Chinese tea ceremony, and is now Crash's guardian and teacher; although he puts on the mask for city emergencies, he is not an active cape.

Darren Tomlin: Darren is a lawyer on retainer to New Orleans' vampire community, a good-natured minion. He lives with Marc above at the fencing school, and is quite possibly the most beautiful man in the world.

Variforce: One of the replacement Sentinels recruited after the Whittier Base Attack, Variforce is a former US Marshal and an A Class Energy Projector capable of generating and shaping variable-property force fields. He uses them as shields, flying wings, cutting blades, etc., and has demonstrated the ability to stand off attacks form A Class Atlas and Ajax-Types with them.

Veritas: A mysterious and annoying DSA agent, Veritas can hear lies, any lies in any format (he reads campaign speeches for laughs). This doesn't mean he knows whether any given statement is true or false—only whether or not the statement's giver meant it truthfully. He does have a sense of humor; it's just very strange and very well hidden.

Villains Inc.: Patterned after the old Murder Inc., Villians Inc. was the supervillain arm of the Chicago Outfit. It has been taken down twice by the Chicago Sentinels so far. The Villains Inc. roster has included Undertaker, Knox, Trophy, Stricture, The Message, Hecate, Tin Man, Flash Mob, Warp, and Ginsu.

Volt: An aspiring actor with surfer-boy looks, Volt rode his A Class Electrokinetic breakthrough to movie-star fame in Hollywood before becoming the president of California's superhuman union and going into politics. Astra killed him in the fight in the Dark Anarchist's secret base, an event so clichéd that if it wasn't a state secret it would have its own movie.

Vulcan: Verne-Types are one of the strangest breakthrough types; able to "invent" and build impossible machines and technologies which nobody else can duplicate, they make flying suits of powered armor, ray guns, force field generators, anti-gravity ships, teleportation cubes, etc. Vulcan is the Chicago Sentinels' resident Verne; he uses fabrication devices to mold "polymorphic molecules" into an infinite variety of impossible elements and alloys to make gear for the team. He is Galatea's creator, and made the team's air-car as well as Astra's armor.

Watchman: aka Lieutenant Dahmer. Watchman is an A Class Atlas-Type who manifested his powers during US Army basic training. He served in both the China War and the Caliphate War, and after his final tour (where he met Astra, both as a recruiter and later at Whittier Base) he was recruited by the Sentinels to help fill the holes in their roster and to further train Astra.

The Wreckers: Given their name by the press, the Wreckers are the known action-arm of the Ascendancy, all of them breakthroughs whose powers have been boosted by the Ascendant. Known Wreckers are: Drop (a teleporter capable of moving multi-ton loads), Phreak (a cyberpsi hacker), Twist (an armored telekinetic wielding unbreakable carbon-alloy cables like living whips), Dozer (an armored Ajax-Type), and Balz (another telekinetic controlling a swarm of multi-function spheres). They have been deployed as a hit-team and a breakout crew. One of them, Dozer, has a history with Astra; before becoming Dozer he was Gantry, a member of the Crew and Astra's first "fight."

ABOUT THE AUTHOR

Marion G. Harmon (Marion for his great-grandfather, George for his father), is a former financial advisor and sometime bagpipe player living in Las Vegas. *Wearing the Cape* was his first novel, quickly followed by *Villains Inc.* and *Bite Me: Big Easy Nights*, and *Young Sentinels*. *Small Town Heroes* is his fifth book, fourth in the Wearing the Cape series, and he guarantees that there will be more stories to come set in the Post-Event world. He also promises that he will get to his comic space opera science fiction story, *Worst Contact*. Really.

Printed in Great Britain
by Amazon